HOUSE OF WAR

HOUSE OF WAR

*The Story of Awo's Followers and
Collapse of Nigeria's Second Republic*

Dare Babarinsa

Spectrum Books Limited
Ibadan

and

TELL Communications Ltd
Lagos

Spectrum titles can be purchased on line at
<u>www.spectrumbooksonline.com</u>

Published jointly by
Spectrum Books Limited
Spectrum House
Ring Road
PMB 5612
Ibadan, Nigeria

and

TELL Communications Limited
10, Acme Road,Ogba Industrial Estate
PMB 21749, Ikeja
Lagos, Nigeria

in association with
Safari Books (Export) Limited
1st Floor
17 Bond Street
St. Helier
Jersey JE2 3NP
Channel Islands
United Kingdom

Europe and USA Distributor
African Books Collective Ltd
The Jam Factory
27 Park End Street
Oxford OX1, 1HU, UK

ISBN: 978-029-385-X (Limp)
ISBN: 978-029-420-1 (Cased)

Printed by Polygraphics Venture Limited Ibadan

DEDICATION

To my friend
Cyril Egborge
who died in a motor accident on
Thursday, March 23, 1989.

CONTENTS

DRAMATIS PERSONAE

*Chief Obafemi Awolowo: Elder statesman, veteran opposition leader, patriarch and presidential candidate of the Unity Party of Nigeria, UPN.

*Alhaji Shehu Shagari: Scion of the late Sardauna of Sokoto, Ahmadu Bello, and First Republic minister. He emerged the president of Nigeria under the banner of the National Party of Nigeria, NPN.

*Dr. Nnamdi Azikiwe: First titular president of Nigeria and leader as well as presidential candidate of the Nigerian Peoples Party, NPP.

*Ibrahim Waziri: leader and presidential candidate of the Great Nigerian Peoples Party, GNPP.

*Adekunle Ajasin: UPN governor of Ondo State whose struggle for power with his ambitious deputy triggered off trouble in the UPN.

*Akin Omoboriowo: Ajasin's estranged deputy-governor whose controversial victory in the 1983 governorship contest ignited riot in Ondo State.

*Victor Ovie-Whiskey: The chairman of the Federal Electoral Commission who presided over the 1983 electoral fiasco.

*Bola Ige: UPN governor of old Oyo State whose regime was rocked by internal bickerings and intrigues.

*Lateef Jakande: Veteran journalist and populist UPN governor of Lagos State.

*Olaiya Fagbamigbe: Publisher and strong contender for the leadership of the Akure UPN. He defected to the NPN and was killed during the riot of August 16, 1983.

*Sunday Adewusi: Enthusiastic partisan of President Shehu Shagari. He was the Inspector-General of Police.

*Emeka Ojukwu: Former leader of the defunct secessionist Eastern Nigeria (called Biafra) and chieftain of the NPN. He was Dr. Azikiwe's principal rival in Igboland.

*Busari Adelakun: Barely educated earthy politician from Ibadan. He was a thorn in the flesh of Governor Bola Ige and finally defected to the NPN.

*J.O. Ayo Ariyo: Civil war veteran and retired lieutenant-colonel. He conducted the second round of elections in Ondo state as FEDECO commissioner.

*Umaru Dikko: Powerful Shagari minister. He was the main strategist of NPN controversial landslide victory in 1983.

*Segun Adegoke: Ajasin's commissioner for information. He was one of the most prominent UPN leaders who checkmated Omoboriowo.

*Bode Olowoporoku: Astute grassroots organiser and leading member of the Omoboriowo group. He was later appointed minister in Shagari's cabinet.

ACKNOWLEDGEMENTS

This book is the product of a decade of interviews, research and painstaking toils. I was inspired to write it by an incident that occurred on Wednesday, August 17, 1983. Akure was just recovering from the second day of post-election riots following the declaration of Chief Akin Omoboriowo, the candidate of the National Party of Nigeria, NPN, as the governor-elect of Ondo State. By 4 pm., the city appeared calm and I decided to walk to my office on Oyemekun Road, Akure to file my story to the headquarters of the Concord Group of Newspapers, Ikeja, Lagos. I was accompanied by my cousin, Thompson Akin Fagbohun, who was spending his vacation with me.

We picked our way through the debris, the litters of charred bodies and vehicles. It was an eerie scene straight from hell. There were few people on the streets and no vehicle at all. The police had succeeded in clearing a narrow path along the main Oba Adesida Road. After sending my report, I hurried home but not without a scene. Shortly after we passed Ondo Junction, we became aware of blaring siren. Behind us, a police landrover was coming, headlight on, at full speed. Fully armed anti-riot policemen in the open back of the landrover were shooting sporadically. We suddenly realised the street was empty except us and an old woman on the other side of the street. I wanted us to dodge into the open drainage, but Thompson hesitated and we dashed across the road into the safety of surrounding houses. The few doors that were opened were quickly slammed in our faces and we kept running.

When the siren had faded, we retraced our steps. Many people were killed that day in Akure during the police pacification effort. It was only by the grace of providence that one survived that era. I have written this book to show my gratitude to God. I believe also that I have a duty to chronicle that era for future generations of Nigerians and Africans trying to implant democracy on our treacherous soil.

This task would have been extremely difficult but for the co-operation of Chief Michael Adekunle Ajasin, first civilian governor of Ondo State and his erstwhile deputy, Chief Omoboriowo. Both of them granted me lengthy interviews, not minding the inconvenience. I also spoke to Chief Segun Adegoke, Ajasin's commissioner for information, and Dr. Bode Olowoporoku, estranged Ajasin follower and an Omoboriowo partisan. I am grateful too to Chief Reuben Famuyide Fasoranti and Chief Adebayo Adefarati, both members of Ajasin's government, who also spoke to me.

I am grateful to the following people for throwing more light onto the dark era of the Second Republic in their interviews with the author: Senator Uba Ahmed, Mr. Idowu Odeyemi, Dr. Tunji Oyejola, Chief Ebenezer Babatope, Mr. Bamidele Olumilua (later governor of Ondo State), Chief Olusola Akintayo, Messrs J.A. Ijabiyi, Ayodele Morakinyo, Clement Owolabi, Fola Aboloyinjo, Oluyemi Oni, and Lucas Afeniforo.

My gratitude also goes to Chief Moshood Kashimawo Olawale Abiola, publisher of the Concord Group of Newspapers and the management of the paper who provided the enabling environment that made this project possible. I am especially grateful to the following people: Dr. Doyinsola Abiola, the editor-in-chief, Yakubu Mohammed, then the editor, Duro Onabule, deputy editor who later succeeded Mohammed as the editor, and Dayo Onibile, the unsparing taskmaster who was our news editor.

I am indebted to the founding quartet of *Newswatch:* the late Dele Giwa, Ray Ekpu, Dan Agbese and Yakubu Mohammed. I must not forget to thank other colleagues in *Newswatch* where I worked after I left *Concord* in 1984, especially Olusoji Akinrinade and Nyaknno Osso.

I am appreciative of the following people's assistance and suggestions in the making of this book: late Cyril Egborge, who was my classmate at the University of Lagos and also my flat mate at Akure; Dr. Olajire Olanlokun, Professor Jide Osuntokun, Messrs Taiye Osuntokun, Ayobami Okeniyi, Dejo Akanbi, Thompson Akin Fagbohun, Ebenezer Popoola, Dr. Olatunji Dare, Banji Kuroloja, and my colleagues at the

Concord office in Akure, especially Modupe Osewole, my predecessor as the state correspondent, and Austen Adekanye.

I am deeply indebted to the following who took active part in the research and preparation of this book: Kayode Ajala, Mr. Israel Ibuoye, former principal of Ife Anglican Grammar School, Ile-Ife; my wife; Adekemi Ibipomola my sister Mrs. Ebun Adetunji, and my brother, Captain Samuel Adeyinka Babarinsa.

My colleagues in TELL magazine were also of immense assistance. I am grateful to Nosa Igiebor, Dele Omotunde, Onome Osifo-Whiskey and Kolawole Ilori. Omotunde volunteered to read the manuscript and made very useful suggestions. Ilori made available to me his corpus of knowledge about Ondo State during the Second Republic. I am also indebted to the following, also of TELL: Emmanuel Bodemeh, Chuks Onwudinjo, Folorunso Sanni, Idowu Awoyinfa, Bayo Akinyemi, Gbenga Olagunju, Olusegun Olakitan and Paul Akhalu. I am indebted to Franklin Oyekusibe, the cerebral artist who designed the cover of this book.

I thank the staff of Ghandi Research Library, University of Lagos, and the National Library, Ebute-Metta, Lagos for their cooperation and assistance. There are many more people who have been of assistance in the successful completion of this project, especially Mr. J.B. Abegunde, former head of service in Ondo State, and Professor Samuel Aluko, both of whom provided useful insight into the working of the government.

I cannot exhaust the names of everyone who had been of assistance in the writing and research of this book. Some, it would be impolitic to mention now mostly because they are still holding sensitive positions in government.

I am grateful to my daughter, Oluwanifesimi Abeke, without whose joyful intervention, this book would have been completed many months earlier. All of us are responsible for the merits in this book, but I am the only one culpable for the errors therein.

PREFACE

The manuscript of this book was completed by June 12, 1992. I had looked forward to its public presentation by the time the new elected regime came to power in 1993. I did not know that this manuscript would have a history of its own that is almost as dramatic as the history narrated in *House of War*. It is ten years ago and now, the book is available to the public for the first time.

This book has been a victim of the turbulence and tribulations that have engulfed Nigeria since 1992 and the personal misfortunes of the author. I never wanted to bring this book out during the military era. I had thought that Chief Moshood Abiola, who was my employer in the Concord Group of Newspapers, would preside over its public presentation. Because of my personal relationship with him, I had no doubt that Abiola would be willing to play a prominent role in the book's public presentation. I was optimistic when Abiola became the presidential candidate of the Social Democratic Party, SDP, one of the two parties formed by the military junta. From all indications, he was set to defeat his rival, Bashir Tofa, of the National Republic Convention, NRC. Then the unexpected happened. The dictator, General Ibrahim Babangida, voided Abiola's victory at the June 12, 1993, presidential election. Instead of Nigeria berthing at the port of democracy, it became marooned on an island of instability and dictatorship. Sani Abacha, Babangida's right hand man, seized power and unleased the worst dictatorship that Nigerians had ever seen. I cannot in anyway think of making a public presentation of my book while Abacha lasted in power. Abacha died suddenly on July 8, 1998.

With the new dispensation following his exit and the programme for the return to elected government in full swing, I was optimistic that it was time the book was presented to the public once the elections were completed. But, Adekemi Ibipomola, my wife of 14 years who had been my pillar of support during the darkest period of my life, died suddenly on Friday October 1, 1999. I was too devastated to continue with my plans. I had not recovered from this seismic blow when I fell under a heavier calamity. Oluwanifesimi Abeke, my eleven-year old daughter, died suddenly on Friday September 28, 2000, virtually on the first anniversary of her mother's transition.

Despite these heavy blows, I decided to work on the release of the book to the public. But another blow fell again on December 23, 2001. Chief Bola Ige, the deputy leader of Afenifere and attorney general of the Nigerian federation was killed in his home in Ibadan, capital of Oyo State and old war camp of the Yoruba nation. Chief Ige loved me like his own son. The gun smoke of that assassination still cast a pall on the future of democracy in our country.

Through these experiences, I had learnt that happiness has a delicate body. You cannot always be too sure of its treacherous embrace. I am trusting in God, for, He is the God of New Beginnings. I believe that all these are past and that the future would be sunny and full of fulfilled promises. But I will never forget those who have departed for they are parts of my life and my effort to get this book published. I know I owe it a duty to the memories of these loved ones, and the right of Nigerians to know the truth about their not-so-heroic past, to get this book published. Now I have fulfilled that duty.

Teledalase, Lagos.
June 20, 2002.

PROLOGUE

I resumed in Akure, capital of Ondo State of Nigeria, Monday, June 20, 1983, as the chief correspondent of the Concord Group of Newspapers. The fair weather of the day was interspersed with intermittent rainfall and thunderclaps as we travelled from Lagos, the then federal capital, via Ore and Ondo town to Akure, a journey of 346 kilometres. My companions, in the Peugeot 504 station wagon, were mostly youths from Ondo State and it was not long before discussion shifted to politics. Alex Ekwueme, the vice-president, was then leading a team of the ruling National Party of Nigeria, NPN, on campaign tour in the state. President Shehu Shagari was 'boycotting' the state, argued some of my co-travellers, because he knew he had no chance there. One middle-aged man in the vehicle however cautioned that Shagari might still come and turn the table against the Unity Party of Nigeria, UPN, the party in control of the state government.

I got to Akure at about 2 pm. and held discussions with Modupe Osewole, my predecessor, who was then proceeding on study leave. I was not new to Ondo State, since I am also an indigene. As a kid, I had schooled in Ikere, Akure, Idanre and my home town, Okemesi, accompanying my itinerant father who was a civil contractor. Before proceeding to the Obafemi Awolowo University, OAU, then University of Ife, I was a teacher at Ire and Ikole, both in Ekiti North Division of the state for two years, until 1976. As a student of the University of Lagos, I had led delegations as the president of the National Union of Ondo State Students, NUOSS, to Akure on several occasions. As a student leader, I had met some of the leading actors in Ondo State politics, including Chief Adekunle Ajasin, the governor, and Chief Akin Omoboriowo, the deputy governor. But this time, I knew my bill was no longer the fanciful adventurism of NUOSS, but serious business. Osewole told me that Ondo State was a dangerous and treacherous terrain for a reporter.

In fact, by the time I resumed in Akure, Ondo State had already acquired a reputation as a hot spot of politics. It was one of the five states controlled by the opposition UPN, namely, Oyo, Ogun, Lagos, Bendel and Ondo states. But the ruling NPN had made inroad into the heart of the party. People were then looking forward to seeing how these 'factors,' as the defectors were known, would affect the fortune of the party in the five states. The then forthcoming elections were the first to be conducted under the civilian regime which came to power in 1979 after 13 years of uninterrupted military rule. The last time elections were conducted under any civilian regime was the Western Nigeria election of 1965, during which widespread irregularities roused the people to revolt against the regime of Chief Ladoke Akintola in those *wet e* days.

Because of the memories of the bloody aftermath of the 1965 polls, some of the older generations were apprehensive with the coming of the elections. Many people, however, felt that gone were those days when political opponents were drenched with petrol and set ablaze. Nigeria had changed from a nation of only four unequal regions to a federation of 19 states. Its politicians and soldiers have been tempered by crises and conflicts and a civil war that claimed about one million lives. But the prize of power was at stake and the combatants were ready to put every weapon into battle.

Nigeria's Second Republic was a peculiar story of hope and despair. When the soldiers departed in 1979, the politicians were hesitant, unsure, almost shy. Supreme power had been bestowed on Alhaji Shehu Shagari, an experienced politician who was better known for his paradoxical anonymity and ideological translucence. The electorate, as it were, had preferred the rule of this serene and sedate statesman to that of the better known and more predictable candidates. As the politicians climbed the stage, the soldiers remained in the shadow, and as time passed, the politicians forgot this fact. The politicians have found it too easy to forget and they did not see the danger laying ambush for them.

The collapse of Nigeria's Second Republic was both a Nigerian and an African's tragedy. Covering an area of 923,768 square kilometres, and with a population of 88.6 million people, Nigeria is the most populous black nation in the world. Nigeria is Africa's leading oil producer. Its lush vegetation from the swampy and rain forests in the south to the sparse vegetation at the edge of the Sahara Desert, the land is a food basket. It is potentially one of the richest nations in the world. It is blessed with rare minerals like iron ore, gold, coal, columbite, limestones, tin and petroleum. The nation has therefore been aptly described as African sleeping giant. It is indeed a beggar sleeping on a throne of gold.

Nigeria's inability to manage her wealth is not the cause, but the consequence of her inability to manage her political fortune. Like the Noah's ark, the Nigerian ship of state contained so many strange bedfellows. The nation was a product of European compromise at Berlin in 1885 and the physical presence of British imperialism. When the nation became independent, October 1, 1960, after a century of British rule, it was faced with the centrifugal pulls of three big regions — the West, East and North — with the North bigger than the other two combined. The new state became a melting pot of the more than 200 ethnic groups and nationalities that the British lumped together into this its former colony. The new power elites, preferred to handle the state as if it was the Tower of Babel, instead of a Noah's Ark of shared destiny. Abubakar Tafawa Balewa, the first federal prime minister, and his fellow elites could not handle the dynamics of state thoroughly and the system grounded to a halt, January 15, 1966, when Balewa, Sir Ahmadu Bello, premier of the North and Akintola of the West and some of the leading actors in the republic were assassinated during Nigeria's first coup.

It was the belief of the military and the generality of Nigerians that an interregnum of thirteen years was enough time for the politicians to have learnt their lesson and play the game according to the rules. But apparently this was not the case. It is said that those who refuse to learn from history are condemned to repeat it. It was my lot to be an eye witness to the re-run of the history of the First Republic with its fatal consequences, in the events of 1983, especially in Ondo State.

After Osewole showed me the ropes, I settled down for business. My first despatch to Lagos which appeared on the front page of the *National Concord,* Saturday, June 25, 1983, reads:

A war of words is now raging in Akure, Ondo State capital, between federal government controlled media and those controlled by the state government. The war is between the federal government-owned NTA Channel 11 and the Federal Radio Corporation of Nigeria, FRCN, Akure on the one hand and the state-owned Ondo State Broadcasting Corporation, OSRC and Ondo State Television Service, OSTV on the other. The four media houses are campaigning for the two main political parties in the state - the UPN and NPN.

National Concord learnt that the two federal-owned media stations have been barred from broadcasting or transmitting anything that could be in favour of the UPN or against the NPN. News bulletins on Radio Nigeria, Akure, usually begins with the itinerary of NPN gubernatorial candidate, Chief Akin Omoboriowo, and how he was 'received by mammoth crowds' in every town he went. The same is true of the NTA Akure. The UPN is only mentioned in both media houses when the NPN is reacting to an act or a statement by its opponents.

On the other hand, both the OSBC and OSTV have blacked out the NPN, except when there is bad news to be broadcast in respect of the party. The latest NPN presidential campaign tour, led by Vice President Alex Ekwueme, was not mentioned in the state media, except when the UPN Principal Publicity Officer, Mr. Banji Kuroloja, described the itinerary as a 'fruitless campaign tour.'

The state-owned OSBC now ends its bulletin with the UPN party anthem, while the FRCN Akure continuously remind the people to vote the NPN, 'the winning party' to power in the state.

That was my first taste of the Second Republic's death race as played out in Ondo State. It is for this now that I bear witness.

1

The Tempest

Tuesday, August 16, 1983. The sun rose early in Akure and bathed the city with terrifying brightness. It was the fourth day the people had been expecting the result of the gubernatorial election; and because of this, the city was awash with rumours. The first indication that something momentous was in the offing was from the two radio stations in the city.

Radio Nigeria, Akure started its dawn broadcast with music from Sunny Okosuns, a popular Nigerian musician's latest record:

Baba ti ba wa se
Baba ti ba wa se o
Ohun t'o n ja wa l'aya
Baba ti ba wa se.

Father has done it for us
What we think is impossible
Father has done it for us.

At the end of the music, there was then an announcement asking the listeners to wait for an important broadcast at 7 a.m. Then, another record by Christy Essien-Igbokwe, titled: 'Give Me a Chance.' There was no six o'clock news, no advertisements, just the two songs.

1

That morning was the climax of the battle of the airwaves between the federal government-owned Radio Nigeria and Ondo State Radio. For days on end, Ondo State people had been asked by the state radio to rise and punish anyone who attempted to rob them of their votes. On the morning of August 16, the radio continued its chanting that 'he who betrays the fatherland would be destroyed by the fatherland.' Blaring from Ondo Radio were the evocative songs of the sixties that roused the people to revolt against the Ladoke Akintola regime, principal of which was Hubert Ogunde's 'Yoruba Ronu' (Yoruba should Reflect):

Yoruba so'ra won di boolu
F'araye gba
Bi won gba won s'oke
Won a tun gba won si sale o
Awon ti won ti n joga l'ojo to ti pe
Won pada wa d'eni
A n f'owo bi s'eyin o.

Yorubas have turned themselves into football
For the world to kick around
As they kick them up
So they kick them down
Those who have been leaders from ancient times
Have now become
Those who are pushed to the rear.

At seven, as already promised, Radio Nigeria, Akure did not join the network service. Instead, a strange and unfamiliar voice came on air. It was that of Dapo Alibaloye, the gubernatorial returning officer. In a shaky voice, Alibaloye announced the much awaited result. After making a short speech about the powers conferred on him by the Electoral Act, he declared that Chief Akin Omoboriowo, the National Party of Nigeria governorship candidate, had been elected. According to Alibaloye, Omoboriowo scored 1,288,981 votes to the incumbent's 1,150,383 votes. The governor-elect had scored 54.31 per cent of the popular votes to Governor Ajasin's 42.78 per cent. For the other candidates, the result was as follows: Olufemi Ijasan of the NPP, 18,766 votes or 0.79 per cent; A.K. Omosule of the GNPP, 11,720 votes or 0.49 per cent; Segun Onwuwuke of the PRP, 7,454 or 0.31 per cent; and Dare Omoboye of the NAP, 13,848 or 0.85 per cent.

At the end of Alibaloye's speech, the new governor-elect came on the air. It was the most rambling victory speech imaginable. It was short and uninspiring. Omoboriowo promised a reprieve for the people from 'Ajasin's tyranny'.

From the commencement of the presidential election, the Outside Broadcasting (OB) van of the Ondo State Broadcasting Corporation, OSBC, had been in the Government House. From there a short speech was made by an unidentified speaker who many believed was Chief Segun Adegoke, Ajasin's commissioner for information. 'The result announced by FEDECO is totally unacceptable,' the speaker declared. 'We have been insulted by these criminals in our own fatherland. That verdict will not stand.'

As soon as Alibaloye finished his announcement, Akure exploded. Within ten minutes, there was smoke all across the city. Houses and people were being set ablaze in one moment of communal madness. One of the first to go was the FEDECO headquarters in Erekesan Market. Since many people identified the building as the source of their anger, they converged on the place. It was being guarded by about 24 armed anti-riot policemen. The place was virtually empty except for these guards. But the rioters were not daunted and they swarmed on the building in their hundreds. One of the policemen on guard, seeing the angry mob, fired and he was subsequently lynched. The commander of the police contingent then ordered the rest to hold fire. Amidst the shouts of 'Awoo!' the battle-cry of the rioters, the policemen abandoned battle and retreated on foot to the Ondo State Police Command Headquarters, five kilometres away. About 16 vehicles were burnt with the FEDECO headquarters, including the police landrover.

Chief Olaiya Fagbamigbe, a leader of the NPN in Akure, was one of the few people who had sensed there might be trouble. Fagbamigbe, a former UPN member of the House of Representatives, decided to brave it however. His wife, Ebun, said a few days to the mayhem of August, she had been approached by a stranger who showed her a list she claimed contained those who were slated to be killed.[1] Her husband did not completely believe the story, but he decided to take certain precautions. The Sunday after the gubernatorial election, Ebun said she saw some men surveying the Fagbamigbe's family house. That evening Olaiya Fagbamigbe, after persuasion from a friend, decided to do something. He brought in some tough boys to stay with the household. But by Monday, August 15, nothing happened and the thugs went their ways.

The night of August 15 was a truly happy day in the home of Olaiya Fagbamigbe. All the children were home and the family gathered in a communal rite. The children were discussing their problems, especially that of school fees. Fagbamigbe, a typical Ondo State man who knew the value of education, was all ears. It was only Ebun who felt the sense of foreboding and was uncomfortable. For the children, it was just another holiday time, except for the presence of a lonely police guard whom the authorities had obliged their father. For Fagbamigbe himself, the situation was under control. He had spoken to a senior police officer in the afternoon who assured him that a curfew would be imposed on the state.

Tuesday, August 16, was to be uniquely different. Ebun had risen early, at 2 a.m. When her husband rose too, she persuaded him that it was time to flee, but he derided her, saying she was giving way to a woman's fretting. As the day crept in, Fagbamigbe was aware of the charged atmosphere, but he believed the police would be able to control the situation. He heard Alibaloye's announcement at 7 a.m., and then despatched a congratulatory message to Omoboriowo through his driver. A few minutes after Alibaloye's announcement, Fagbamigbe noticed there was, suddenly, total silence over Akure. Fagbamigbe was again listening to entreaties, now fervent and passionate, from his wife, and he was about making up his mind when one of his elder brothers, James Fagbamigbe, entered. Pa James supported his brother that a man should not flee his own home no matter the danger. Overwhelmed, Ebun was reduced to private agony.

Then Fagbamigbe looked out and saw an angry mob at his gate. He again phoned the police. The officer at the other end advised him to find his way out and seek protection at the police headquarters. By that time, the advice was useless. One of the houses in the sprawling 11, Methodist Church Street, Akure, residence of the Fagbamigbes was already on fire. Luckily, however, the children had escaped. The lonely police guard had escaped through the back door. Only Ebun and the two brothers were to face the wrath of the mob.

The mob gained entrance into the main building and captured the two men and Ebun. The two men were made to do a mock dance of death while neighbours shut their doors or peeped through their windows. After so much beating and torture, the two men were reduced to bloody pulps. A motorcycle was then placed on them, they were doused with petrol and set on fire.

Mrs. Fagbamigbe's punishment was similar but different. She was stripped almost naked, made to do a mock dance like her husband, preparatory to her being burnt. She was made to drink petrol. But miraculously, the match sticks would not light and by a truly divine intervention, Ebun Fagbamigbe was rescued from the mob and she took refuge in a neighbouring Catholic convent.

Tunde Agunbiade, the former majority leader of the state's House of Assembly was in a celebratory mood on the morning of August 16. He was with Chief Omoboriowo at the heavily guarded residence of the new governor-elect at the elite Ijapo Estate in the early hours of the day. There was much rejoicing when Alibaloye's expected broadcast came, proclaiming Omoboriowo victorious. After that, Agunbiade said it was time he went to his own house. 'Why not wait for sometime,' Omoboriowo cautioned him. 'The town is tense. Let's see how events would unfold.' But Agunbiade was already in his Kombi bus. 'I am an Akure man,' he said, 'I can take care of myself.'

Agunbiade reached his home that morning only to realise there was no road for retreat. He was captured by the angry mob that had already set his residence on fire and he was beheaded.

Richard Agbayewa did not belong to the same class of partymen like Fagbamigbe and Agunbiade. Agbayewa, chairman of the NPN in Akure, was a prosperous businessman and well-known philanthropist who was formerly a secondary school proprietor. He was a foundation member of the party before the fiery new converts came and changed its hues. For most of 1983, he was fighting a running battle with these new converts for the control of the party and therefore he was not a favoured person in the new Omoboriowo court. But like most NPN men, he was identified with Omoboriowo's victory by the populace.

A lady had come to him at dawn on August 16 to congratulate him on his party's victory. Suddenly, there was a chilling silence. The big compound, not too far from the palace of the Deji of Akure, seemed suddenly empty. Without his realising it until it was too late, members of his household had escaped and Agbayewa was now alone with his lady guest. He was in ordinary loin cloth. Then he saw strange sinister faces by the window, the doors, everywhere. He was caught by the mob along with his guest, hacked to death, and the one storey building set ablaze. A similar fate befell Chief A.O. Orisalade, also a member of the old NPN and the state secretary of the party.

The flame of fury gutted every part of Akure. Idowu Odeyemi, editor of Omoboriowo's *Premier* newspaper was driving to the old Secretariat junction to buy the day's dailies when he heard Alibaloye's announcement over his car's radio. By the police station overlooking Oba Adesida Road, Odeyemi saw a sea of heads attacking the multi-storey LACO store owned by multimillionaire former chairman of Wema Bank, Lawrence Agunbiade. Sensing imminent danger, he made a U-turn and headed for the safety of Ijapo Estate.

It was not just partymen who were in danger. Senior federal government officials, officials of FEDECO and Radio Nigeria and other men identified with the NPN were also at risk. Petrol stations which had opened early were forced to give free petrol to the rioters. The rioters blocked every street of Akure, erecting barricades of burning vehicles, tyres, wood and assorted matters. As the day progressed, the city was covered by a pall of smoke. It was a dangerous time. Nobody was safe and you only needed to be accused of being a sympathiser of the NPN to earn a death sentence.

The angry mobs sweeping the city were cheered on by Ondo Radio. Apart from the evocative Yoruba songs, revolutionary songs from the West Indies were also aired. One of them was the song of Peter Tosh (*Stand Up, Stand Up, Stand up for your right, Don't give up the fight*). The radio said Omoboriowo was taking refuge at the police command headquarters. Though the information was false, the rioters attempted to take the headquarters by storm. Unfortunately, the headquarters was without surrounding walls. The western slope of the headquarters was hedged in by tall wild grass. It was in this grass that the rioters engaged in battle with the police. Expectedly, they were repulsed. The grass was filled with corpses.

Though the state headquarters of the NPN, adjacent to the police headquarters, was torched, the police successfully defended the office of Radio Nigeria, also not far from the police headquarters. An attempt by the rioters to storm the transmitting station of Radio Nigeria in the Federal Housing Estate along Owo Road was also repulsed with casualties. Another battle zone was Ondo Road on the way to the army barracks. Many houses including an hotel and the office of the Federal Information Service were burnt. However, none of the rioters dared move near the army barracks.

After Alibaloye's announcement of 7 a.m. on Radio Nigeria, the radio went off the airwaves which were now totally dominated by OSBC. It was a gory commentary coming from Ondo Radio which enjoined the rioters to track down the "thieves, and traitors." It reported that Omoboriowo, unsure of his safety at the police headquarters, had now escaped and was on his way to Lagos. It announced that he was taking the Akure-Ilesa Road and that he would pass through Ile-Ife to Lagos. The commentator said the governor-elect was in a grey Peugeot 505 with Akure registration number. Though Ondo Radio did not say it in many words, the inference was clear. You would be doing a public duty if you find and assassinate Omoboriowo and the radio was going to help you locate him.

The inflammatory statement coming from Ondo Radio added fuel to the fire raging all over the state. In Ado-Ekiti, heartland of the Ekiti people, vengeful band of rioters, many of them wielding axes with their faces painted in devilish patterns, roamed the city, burning houses of perceived Omoboriowo supporters. A strange thing happened in Ado that day. Scores of people guarded the homes of Chief Afe Babalola, chairman of the governing council of the Federal Polytechnic, Ado-Ekiti, and that of Chief Samuel Falegan, former managing director of the Federal Mortgage Bank, who were regarded as 'good NPN men.' But properties belonging to many other NPN chieftains, like Chief J. E. Babatola and Major-General Adeyinka Adebayo, who was of immense assistance in the take-off of the Ondo State government-owned Obafemi Awolowo University, OAU, (the name was later changed to Ondo State University) were not spared.

Disturbances in other towns followed similar patterns. At Oye-Ekiti, the home of the local chairman of the NPN was set ablaze following Alibaloye's announcement of Omoboriowo's controversial victory. The house, built of modern cement blocks, did not catch fire despite the continuous use of petrol, and in frustration, the mob destroyed the louvre glasses and other fittings, before descending on other houses owned or occupied by people with the least association with the NPN. Suspected NPN sympathisers who were tenants had their properties gathered outside (where the landlord was not known to be an Omoboriowo man) for the bonfire. Ghanaian teachers, who were away on holiday, had their properties burnt where they were unlucky to be tenants in houses owned by suspected NPN men.

Ire Ekiti, hometown of Alibaloye, was eerily calm on August 16. The two roads leading into the town were barricaded with burning tyres. A day earlier, two lorry loads of anti-riot policemen, in anticipation of trouble from angry neighbours, had moved to Ire to protect the country home of Alibaloye. The policemen discharged their duties that day and nothing was destroyed.

In Ikere-Ekiti, the town was almost evenly divided between the Awoists and the NPN. They, therefore, engaged each other in pitched battles and the town was covered with a pall of smoke lasting two days. At Efon-Alaaye, houses of suspected NPN sympathisers were destroyed and one man was killed. At Okemesi-Ekiti, a car was burnt while several houses and vehicles were destroyed by Awoist rioters. Almost every town and village was affected by what the people quickly dubbed the 'Omoboriowo War'.

The fury of that Tuesday did not spend itself out until very late in Akure. All the streets in the city were barricaded with all sorts of materials — planks, scraps of iron, old vehicles, burning tyres. Hordes of angry mobs paraded the streets shouting 'Awoo!' But if the uprising was a self-righteous reaction to a perceived robbery, it soon became an instrument of vendetta by those who had been looking for ways of dealing with supposed enemies. It also became an opportunity for hooligans to loot, steal and extort money from victims.

Dr. Tunji Oyejola, the man who was the state's returning officer during the presidential election, was almost a victim of these hooligans. By the time Alibaloye's verdict came over the radio, Oyejola was ready for work. As a senior civil servant, he was to resume at 7.30 a.m. While his household was still debating the implications of Omoboriowo's victory, news came to Oyejola's Araromi Quarters residence that there was trouble in the town. He changed into a casual sports wear and looked forward to spending the day in leisure. But the tell-tale of uncertainties was in the distant pall of smoke. Soon there was commotion at the gate of Oyejola's one-storey residence. An angry mob was trying to break in through the gate, shouting for Oyejola's head for being a 'FEDECO man'.

'Where is Dr. Oyejola?' a member of the mob asked as Oyejola went to the gate. He identified himself and told them that he was not involved in the gubernatorial election. He only conducted the presidential election.

'Yes, he is our man! Baba O! He did well for Papa! (that was Chief Awolowo). Better man!' Shouts rang out from the mob and soon, they started singing a new song. Some of them came onto the balcony and Oyejola realised many of them were under the influence of alcohol. To pacify them, he gave them a bottle of spirit which the ring leaders consumed immediately. After that, they left and immediately Oyejola spirited members of his family into a safe house of a relative. But some of the hooligans kept coming back, demanding money and drinks. By the evening of that day, Oyejola, unable to cope anymore, fled into hiding.

Some people were not so lucky. A permanent secretary in the state's civil service who was on the verge of retirement and who took a mortgage loan to build his house had it burnt along with his three cars. Many people who had no connection with Omoboriowo or who were just prosperous were singled out by envious neighbours as NPN men and had their properties destroyed. Junior workers of FEDECO, Radio Nigeria and of the NPN secretariat or personal staff of known NPN chieftains were not spared. Some of them paid with their lives.

The night of August 16, 1983 was a terrible one in Akure. Nobody knew which house would be torched next or whether one would be roused from one's bed by some men bearing short axes. Like agents of the devil, some of the rioters continued their actions throughout the night. By Wednesday August 17, many of the streets in Akure were still blocked. As the dawn broke, the town was in the grip of a terrible rumour that Omoboriowo and Sunday Adewusi, Inspector-General of Police, were coming with a massive force for vengeance.

The rumour was not without foundation. By noon that Wednesday, the city was strangely quiet. Then a long convoy of police vehicles, clearing barricades, roared through the city in a show of force. This time around, the police were prepared to show Akure people their unassailable fire-power. They fired indiscriminately on any moving object though most of the streets were deserted. Along the main Oba Adesida Road, an old woman of about 75 was killed near the National Electric Power Authority, NEPA, transformer close to Ondo Road junction. At Oke-Ijebu, not far from Omoboriowo's headquarters, 10-year-old girl was shot and killed as she went to a nearby medicine store to buy drugs for her mother. In this attempt at pacification, scores of lives were lost.

Omoboriowo's reaction to the riot was one of considerable agitation. Early in the morning of August 16, there had been mutual self-congratulations and back-slapping among Omoboriowo's supporters and preparations were being made for a great victory feast later in the day. But as news got to the Situation Office about those killed, Omoboriowo convened a crisis meeting. It was then decided that the situation was grave enough to warrant that Omoboriowo go to Lagos immediately to seek federal help. The meeting was especially critical of the police's support considering the 'hostility' of Police Commissioner Emmanuel Allagh to Omoboriowo. The meeting then decided that the governor-elect should see President Shehu Shagari and Sunday Adewusi, and impress upon them the necessity to hold Ondo State at all cost.

Omoboriowo left for Lagos with some of his top aides including Rufus Aboloyinjo and Ayodele Morakinyo, two of the old UPN defectors who were fiercely loyal to him. They stopped briefly in Ondo town (they did not take Ilesa-Ife Road as speculated by OSBC), and moved on to Lagos via Ore. On getting to Lagos, they called briefly at the home of a top supporter of Omoboriowo. Unknown to the men from Akure, their host had heard the rumour that Omoboriowo had been killed and he was now convinced that he was beholding a ghost. Believing that he had seen a ghost, the host bolted from his sitting room. It took some persuasion for him to know that he was seeing a living Omoboriowo.

In order to puncture this ugly rumour, Omoboriowo appeared on the Network Service of the Nigerian Television Authority, NTA, alongside Dr. Walter Ofonagoro, historian, and an upstart politician who had recently been appointed director-general of the authority to supplant the former incumbent. With delight, both of them proclaimed that Omoboriowo was still alive in flesh and blood.

Omoboriowo's mission to Lagos was of doubtful success. He held meetings with Chief Adisa Akinloye, the NPN chairman and with Adewusi, both of whom promised to help. But President Shagari, who was said to be of a different opinion about winning Ondo State at all cost, refused to see Omoboriowo. Omoboriowo also held meetings with top officers of FEDECO including Victor Ovie-Whiskey, its chairman. After about a week in Lagos, the most unhappy governor-elect in the land returned to Akure within a battalion of anti-riot policemen.

Happenings at the Ajasin camp were of a slightly different kind. The governor was on his breakfast table when news came that there was fighting in the town because Omoboriowo had been declared governor-elect. Soon, the Governor's Lodge was crowded with top party officials and there was despondency in the air. While Chief Ajasin was holding informal deliberations with his top advisers, the inflammatory broadcast from the OB van in front of the governor's main residence, was going on. The discussions in the lodge were sometimes heated and some of the people there talked of taking up arms to defend democracy. Ajasin cautioned that people should not resort to violence. 'God's judgment is greater than that of man,' he said.

At 10 p.m., Wednesday, August 17, two lorry loads of anti-riot policemen stormed the transmitting station of OSBC, at Oba-Ile near Akure, chased out the workers and knocked out the transmitter. Thus ended the notorious rule of the airwaves by the OSBC. It was time again for Radio Nigeria to resume transmission and it seized its own monopoly too with a sustained message that the people should give Omoboriowo a chance because he had been chosen by God. On the closure of Ondo Radio, Emmanuel Allagh, was to say later: 'It became clear that the station was not helping the cause of peace by broadcasting what amounted to open incitement of its listeners to take laws into their hands.'[2]

Though by Wednesday, much of the violence had died down, sporadic killings and arson were still going on. Worried community leaders, traditional rulers; chiefs and religious leaders were calling on Governor Ajasin to do something about the violence. On Thursday, August 18, a delegation of the Nigerian Police headed by Mohammadu Gambo, which also included Victor Pam, the police director of operations, . Ahmed Sheidu and Commissioner Allagh, called on Governor Ajasin. Gambo, a master of diplomacy, expressed surprise at the austerity of the Governor's Lodge, a mere two-bedroom mansion. He said it was a reflection of Governor Ajasin's modesty. He then pleaded that the old man should appeal to the people of the state to give peace a chance. Ajasin replied that he was ready to make such appeal, but that he would not speak on 'NPN Radio' (Radio Nigeria, Akure). He asked the police to remove the siege on OSBC and allow the station to resume transmission. By this time too, most of the workers of OSBC, fearing reprisals from supporters of Omoboriowo, were in hiding. Gambo promised that the station would be allowed to resume transmission and he was as good as his words.

On Friday, August 19, Ajasin was on Ondo Radio, his voice crisp and clear. It was as much a plea for peace as well as a victory speech of sort. He dealt extensively on the antecedent of the crisis and the current impasse. 'You have amply demonstrated that your will as expressed by your votes and actions should always be respected,' said Ajasin. "My people, I feel very grieved that lives should be lost and properties destroyed in this unfortunate development brought about by the blatant rape of democratic process by some agents of FEDECO.'³ He then disclosed that he had decided to challenge Omoboriowo's purported victory at the election tribunal.

'The Omoboriowo War,' was it a spontaneous reaction or a planned perfidy? Expectedly, Omoboriowo said it was a planned insurrection to destabilise the civilian regime of President Shagari by the implacable Awoists. Omoboriowo returned to Akure, Tuesday, August 23, 1983, where he held a press conference, breathing fire of revenge. 'The present situation in Ondo State, I dare say, has no relevance to the conduct and results of both the presidential and gubernatorial elections,' Omoboriowo declared. 'It is part of a premeditated and systematic plan to liquidate all known NPN leaders in the state. It is common knowledge to our people that most of the thugs who burnt down these houses and properties were sent down to Ondo State from Lagos and Ogun states by UPN leadership in Lagos. Some of these are still lodging in the Government House, Akure.'⁴

Omoboriowo alleged that the UPN plan was hatched in utmost secrecy. 'Throughout the voting, unknown to us, the UPN, the ruling party in Ondo State, employed massive terrorization, kidnapping, brazen tampering with electoral personnel and processes to rig the elections,' said Omoboriowo. 'It is more regrettable when it is discovered that these activities received the co-operation of certain characters within the Nigerian Police and the Nigerian Security Organisation in Ondo State. The federal government is hereby warned to view the present situation in Ondo and Oyo states as a tip of the iceberg in UPN's plans to foment trouble all over the federation. The UPN will ever remain condemned by posterity for giving this to our people as a price for their 32-year steadfast, albeit fruitless, support for Awolowo and his men of darkness.'⁵

Uba Ahmed, the national secretary of the ruling NPN, told the author that 'those who performed operations in Ondo and Oyo states were trained in Ogun State.' Ahmed alleged that Governor Bisi Onabanjo of Ogun State had a security outfit, with the permission of President Shagari, under the leadership of a retired major. He alleged that it was this security outfit, financed by the state, that was used to train the thugs. He said the whole operation was 'pre-planned and premeditated.'

But Adegoke, Ajasin's commissioner for information, countered that there was no way violence of that magnitude could have been planned. 'Since that time, many people have been convicted for taking part in the violence, some of them condemned to death,' said Adegoke. 'Do you think someone would be under the sentence of death and he would still keep his silence? Even soldiers involved in failed coups do confess under sentence of death. It was not possible for anyone to plan that kind of violence. If it was planned, then, many people must have been undergoing training for months to carry out those terrible things that happened. How can anybody anticipate that some people would be mad enough to declare Omoboriowo governor of Ondo State?'

Professor Samuel Aluko, Ajasin's special adviser on economic affairs, too was of the firm belief that the violence was spontaneous. 'Violence was not planned, at least not by the UPN,' the renowned economist said. 'They delayed the result for so long that even women warned that if they declare NPN elected, there would be trouble because everybody knew NPN could not win. Tempers had risen because of the delay.'

Omoboriowo was steadfast in the defence of his controversial victory. He claimed that he never fled Ondo State because of the violent reaction of the people but because of 'urgent party matters'. He claimed further that some UPN leaders had placed a ₦300,000 price on his head and that 'a notorious assassin' in Lagos had already been paid an advance sum for the assignment. Said the governor-elect: 'I think I have credibility in my state. And the fact that so many people voted for Awo does not mean they wanted Ajasin also.'

On the British Broadcasting Service, BBC, African Service on the night of August 23, Omoboriowo continued his familiar line of argument. 'By the time I moved into the NPN with my large followership, it was a mass movement from Awolowo's party to the NPN,' he declared. 'By the grace of God, I managed to win 54.7 per cent. But for the difficulties imposed on us by the UPN and Governor Ajasin, its gubernatorial candidate, we probably would have performed better. I expected 55 per cent lead.'

But the implication of Omoboriowo's victory was clear to many discerning Nigerians. It meant that within one week of presidential election, the UPN lost 35.48 per cent support while the NPN gained by 34.18 per cent. But to members of the Awoist camp, this was political abracadabra. 'Everyone in Nigeria knows that the elections in Oyo, Ondo, Bendel, Borno, Cross River and Anambra states were manipulated by the NPN in their bid and desire to hoist on this country a totalitarian one party state,' said the UPN National Directorate of Organisation in a statement. 'It is unbelievable and rather unfortunate that the NPN that failed woefully in Ondo, Oyo and Anambra states in the presidential elections could within one week come up to announce to the whole world that it had won elections in grand style in these three states.'

Speaking with the BBC, Chief Awolowo waxed philosophical. 'Violence is a kind of effect of a fundamental cause and you don't deal with effect to cure the cause. You deal with the cause in order to cure the effect.' Chief Ajasin on his part declared flatly: 'Nobody can get away with this in Ondo State. This state is 95 per cent UPN.'

Wole Soyinka, Nigeria's celebrated playwright, political activist and human rights campaigner who was later to win a Nobel Prize for Literature, described the 1983 election as a 'selection' process. 'Discredited, condemned and rejected, even loathed by the majority of Nigerians, the National Party of Nigeria, buoyed by the image-building of its leader by the Western press - meek, unassuming, detribalised, the guarantor of peace and stability etc, *ad nauseam* - went confidently ahead to commit the most breathtaking, in sheer scale, electoral fraud of any nation in the whole of Africa,' declared Soyinka. 'At every level, from acts of brutal ejection of the opposition at the polling booth by 'law-enforcement' agencies to the simplest but most daring motion of all, swapping the figures at the very point of announcement, the scale of the robbery is unprecedented, truly mind-boggling. Wherever all other measures failed, the secretaries to the states electoral commissions simply announced the wrong figures, or else, the National Electoral Commission in Lagos announced the forgeries.'

Despite the carnage and the chaos, life had to go on. On the day Omoboriowo became governor-elect, Mrs. Mobolaji Osomo, one of Ajasin's loyal commissioners, was in Lagos. It was she who was asked to contact Chief Godwin Kolawole Ajayi, a Senior Advocate of Nigeria, SAN, and one of the nation's most brilliant and articulate attorneys, for the legal battle ahead. Ajayi, one of the intellectual pillars of the Awoist group, was not a partyman directly, but mainly a faithful falangist who featured prominently in the many legal battles (like the Shugaba case, the case of Governor Mohammed Goni versus FEDECO) involving the party. He started out as a young lawyer in the chambers of Chief Awolowo. It was this lion of the bar who was asked to handle Ajasin's petition.

By constitutional provision, the chief judge of the state was to appoint members of the election petition tribunal. This lot fell on Dr. Olakunle Orojo, author, jurist and scholar-per-excellence. Orojo made himself the chairman of the panel which also had as members Eddy Ojuolape, I. Afuye, S.A. Akintan and Ayoola Ogunleye — all judges of Ondo State High Court. The composition was made known Monday, August 29 in Akure.

The general election earlier suspended, had to go on. Ajasin soon received a letter from the FEDECO boss, Ovie-Whiskey that the Senate election would now be September 19, House of Representatives September 22 and in conclusion, House of Assembly, September 26. Chief O.I.A. Afe, the former state's electoral commissioner who fled during the 'Omoboriowo War', was replaced by Colonel J.O. Ayo-Ariyo. Ariyo was the Ondo State resident electoral commissioner before he was moved to Bendel State to conduct the elections. Now he was back to familiar ground.

As for the members of the NPN, the victory of Omoboriowo was a *fait accompli*. Major-General Adebayo came to Akure a few days after the August 16 and 17 riots, and told a press conference that if the UPN persisted in spreading violence, then the NPN too would meet 'force with force'. Chief Omoboriowo also set up two committees, one headed by Professor Opeyemi Ola, also a defector and the other by General Adebayo to advise him on the structure of the new administration. He let it be known that by October 1, 1983 all political appointees of Ajasin stood summarily dismissed.

Speaking in a nationwide broadcast from Abuja, September 11, President Shagari warned that troublemakers would be visited with the full weight of the law. Said the president: 'Reports received from all parts of the country, including the initial comments by various political party leaders, indicated that the presidential elections were free, fair and largely devoid of violence.'

Earlier in a congratulatory message he sent to Omoboriowo, Shagari said he was convinced the governor-elect was the one preferred by the people of Ondo State. He assured him of total backing. 'Government is determined to maintain peace and order in the few areas (Ilesa-Ife Senatorial Zone in Oyo State and Akure, Ondo, Okitipupa areas of Ondo State) affected and indeed, throughout the country,' Shagari said.

If Shagari was confident that Omoboriowo would ride the storm, the feeling from the opposition camp was equally determined. In the vanguard of the psychological campaign was the *People's News* of Niyi Oniororo. In editorials, cartoons, news items and opinion pieces, the *People's News* waged the war on its every page. In a front page story, 'Omoboriowo Fainted,' carried in its edition of September 1, 1983, the newspaper declared: 'The hot ambition of Chief Akin Omoboriowo to become a governor of Ondo State has now become a terrible absurdity as he was said to have fainted twice within the last five days for lack of sleep. In the last few days, the so-called governor-elect of Ondo State, Chief Omoboriowo, has lost weight and we are told that he is feeling more and more empty in his heart and more and more hopeless in his future. The man's heart has been in turmoil, and his head has been aching violently.'

In Omoboriowo's *Premier* edition of August 30, Idowu Odeyemi, the editor, fired back at the critics: 'Let them swallow this bitter pill. Whether they like him or not, whether they want him or not, Chief Akin Omoboriowo will be sworn-in on October 1, 1983 as the next Ondo State executive governor for four years. There is nothing anybody can do about that. They can go on rioting for the next four years.'

Surprisingly, there were many people who were prepared to do just that if Omoboriowo's victory was upheld.

2

Genesis

Early in the morning of Saturday, June 10, 1978, the delegates started to arrive. By noon, Omolere Nursery School, on Ado-Ekiti Road, Akure, the venue of this important meeting of the Ondo State branch of the National Committee of Friends, NCOF, was parked full. The accredited delegates were only 51, with three representing each of the 17 local government areas. The rest were interested spectators who had thronged the venue of this 'secret gathering' since the ban on political activities, imposed by the military when they seized power in a bloody coup January 15, 1966, was still on. The agenda: election of a candidate to contest for the post of governor whenever the military lifted the ban on party politics. Three candidates were in the race for the party flag: Chief Adekunle Ajasin, veteran party stalwart and retired school principal, Reverend Abiodun Iluyomade, who was at the time the principal of International School, Ibadan, and Ayo Fasanmi, a pharmacist based in Osogbo, Oyo State, (later capital of Osun State).

For the men and women gathered that afternoon in Akure, it was time again to trade in political ambitions after 12 years of watching from the sidelines as the soldiers managed and often mismanaged the shop. It was common knowledge that the Committee of Friends was just the old Action Group, AG, one of the old political parties that the soldiers proscribed on coming to power in 1966. Since then, the AG and its new alliances, like the other major parties, had learnt to put on the garment of disguise and survive in the shadow. It would soon be time to step out of that shadow and join the race for power.

Chief Obafemi Awolowo, leader of the AG and now of the Committee of Friends had nominated three elders of the party: Chief C.A. Tewe, Mr. Phillip Akomolafe and Chief Reuben Fasoranti to preside over the shadow election. The three candidates had worked hard during the past several weeks and it was now time to witness the harvest. The prelude to the gubernatorial contest was the nomination for deputy-governor ticket. Then Mr. Akin Omoboriowo, secretary to the Committee of Friends, Ondo State branch was the only candidate, and he was elected by acclamation. After that, the 51 delegates cast their ballots for the governorship flagbearer. Ajasin carried the day with 32 votes to Fasanmi's 19. Iluyomade, a relatively new comer to the fold of the committee, scored no vote.

As victory was proclaimed Fasanmi and Iluyomade stepped forward to congratulate the victor. Then Ajasin and Omoboriowo, two men who had worked together like father and son for the past two years embraced. At that moment, the 26-year gap between them dissolved in the midst of camaraderie and they were exultant. Ajasin represented age and experience; Omoboriowo, youth and vigour. The marriage seemed made in heaven. At that time, what both men could see before them was victory and more victories and years of glory and power. The assembly broke into celebrations and Omolere Nursery School, where tender minds are trained became the nursery bed of new ambitions and hopes. The Committee of Friends had taken a giant step towards the Second Republic. It seemed such a long yesterday since the military intervened in politics in 1966.

Chief Awolowo, leader of the AG and his party were perhaps the greatest beneficiaries of the January 15, 1966 coup. Before the coup, Awolowo had been engaged for almost a decade, in a titanic struggle for survival when he was pitched against old friends and dedicated and enduring foes. Jeremiah Oyeniyi Obafemi Awolowo, born March 6, 1909 in Ikenne, Ogun State of Nigeria, among the Remo clan of the

Yoruba nation noted for their commerce and thriftiness, was secretary of the Nigerian Motor Transport Union in the 1930s. A virtually self-made man, he trained variously as a teacher, a typist and before proceeding to England to study law in 1944, had earned a degree in commerce through home studies. He was at one time a reporter with the *Daily Times* and also a produce merchant. Before he became first leader of government business in Western Region in 1952, he had one of the most flourishing legal practices in Nigeria.

Throughout his long political career which started in the 1930s, when he was the secretary of the Nigerian Youths Movement, NYM, in Ibadan, it had been Awo's lot to carry both the benefits and the burden of Yoruba nationalism. The Yoruba are the principal national group southwest of the Federal Republic of Nigeria. They are one of the pillars in the Nigerian mainly triangular struggle for political power, vying with the Igbo of the East and the Hausa-Fulani of the North. They constitute the main people of Ondo (including the new Ekiti State), Oyo (including the new Osun State), Ogun and Lagos states and a substantial part of old Kwara State. They are also to be found in the old Bendel State of Nigeria, Togo and Benin Republic and there are pockets of Yoruba settlements in Brazil, Sierra Leone and the West Indies. The Yoruba, though traditionally divided into principalities, nation states and kingdoms, are united basically by a common culture, language and legends. They all claim Oduduwa as the progenitor of the race and Ile-Ife as the National Garden of Eden. Yoruba nationalism, however, was a modern phenomenon whose catalyst was the dynamics of the new Nigerian state. It was the natural reaction to foreign domination, first by the British and later the political hegemony of the Hausa-Fulani and the economic and commercial competitiveness of the Igbo.

Before proceeding on his legal studies in 1944, Awolowo had been involved in the nationalist politics of the NYM which was later rendered impotent by the bitter struggle for leadership by its Yoruba and Igbo elites. It was in the NYM that Awo (as he was popularly called) came into contact and collision with Dr. Nnamdi Azikiwe, an American trained journalist and orator who defected from the NYM to form his more successful National Council of Nigeria and the Cameroon NCNC. While a student in Britain, Awolowo formed the Egbe Omo Oduduwa (Oduduwa Descendants Union), as a counterweight to the rising and fervent nationalism of the Igbo and their Igbo State Union, personified by the towering profile of Dr. Azikiwe. On returning to Nigeria, Awolowo mobilised notable Yoruba sons and traditional rulers for his cause and the *egbe* was formally launched in Ile-Ife in June 1948. Adeyemo Alakija, former president of the NYM, was elected president while Awo became the general secretary.

When the AG was formed in 1951 by Awo, it fulfilled the worst fear of the NCNC. The party was later to win majority of seats in all elections held in the defunct Western Region, except the federal elections of 1956 which was won by the NCNC, before the AG crisis of 1962. The rise of Awolowo was helped by a cultural renaissance sweeping throughout Yorubaland. Writers like Daniel Fagunwa and Joseph Odunjo were extolling the virtue of the Yoruba tongue; Hubert Ogunde, Kola Ogunmola and Duro Ladipo were sweeping the theatre world while Haruna Ishola and Kehinde Dairo were reawakening the Yoruba virtues in music.

Rising contemporaneously with Awolowo in the North was Ahmadu Bello, a great grandson of Uthman Dan Fodio, the 19th Century Fulani cleric and revolutionary who overthrew the Hausa Habe dynasties to establish the Fulani aristocracy and created the new Sokoto Caliphate. Bello, a trained teacher and local administrator, became the leader of the Northern Peoples Congress, NPC in 1951. Analysts and historians have written a lot about the rivalry between Awo and Zik (nickname for Dr. Azikiwe). It was true that in the context of nationalist politics of the late forties and early fifties, the only towering rival for Zik was Awo. But Zik had never really been a serious contender for supreme power in the new Nigerian state. He was contented with the role of catalyst and partial participant. The real rivals for power were Awo and Bello, who held the traditional title of the Sardauna of Sokoto, and their rivalries had dictated the pace of Nigerian politics either during the period of party politics or party politics in disguise (military rule). Both

Awo and Bello believed in their roles in history and their actions were motivated by their deep sense of it. Both men were not modest men. Awo was a man of calculated courage and forthrightness and Bello too could not be accused of the traditional Fulani coyness and cunning. Both men were brilliant and innovative and both regarded politics as war.

The 1959 pre-independence federal election came and Awo was roundly beaten. He approached Zik and his NCNC for a coalition, conceding that the former should be prime minister with Awo serving as minister of finance in a coalition government, but he was rebuffed. The victorious NPC too would have nothing to do with the AG and its leader and Awo retreated to the National Assembly as Leader of Opposition. By October 1, 1960 when Nigeria attained independence the political topography of Nigeria was clear: Awo dominating the West, Zik, the East and Bello, the North.

When Awolowo became Leader of Opposition in Lagos, he left the Western premiership on the lap of Chief Ladoke Akintola, his deputy in the party, a wily lawyer, journalist and politician who was famous for his mastery of the Yoruba language and oratory. Awo was soon to find himself pitched in battle against Akintola. The premier accused Awo of unnecessary interference in the daily governance of Western Region. He was also accused of dictatorship and wanting to impose 'communism'. Awolowo, on his part, accused Akintola of treachery, disobedience and tampering with the AG's laid down principles on agriculture and social services and the party's avowed opposition to the ruling NPC. On May 25, 1962, the schism in the party led to fighting on the floor of the Western House of Assembly, Ibadan, by pro-Awolowo MPs and Akintola's supporters over the motion to remove Akintola as premier. Abubakar Tafawa Balewa, who was holding fort for Bello in Lagos as federal prime minister, declared a state of emergency in the region, appointing Adekoyejo Majekodunmi, a nominated senator, medical doctor and Federal Minister of Health, as Administrator.

On November 2, 1962, **Awolowo** and 27 of his lieutenants were arrested and charged with treason. They were later sentenced to various terms of imprisonment on September 11, 1963. Meanwhile, Akintola, expelled from the AG, formed his own Nigerian National Democratic Party, NNDP, with his faction of the AG in coalition with a break-away faction of the NCNC led by Chief Remi Fani-Kayode, who later became the deputy premier. The AG, denied of its leading role in government, barred from government patronage and the money that filled its coffer from it, pushed into opposition in its own power-base, its leaders in jail and its supporters in disarray, was like a wounded dragon. It waited eagerly for the next election and the verdict of the people.

'The basic disagreement was just that I favoured a national government and co-operation with the Northern Peoples Congress while he (Awolowo) opposed both,' said Akintola.[6] Akintola said the economic, educational and commercial aggressiveness of the Igbo was a greater danger to the Yoruba than the political hegemony of the Hausa-Fulani. He pointed out that most of the top public posts in the federal public service, armed forces and the police, were held by the Igbo, and only an alliance with the Northerners of the NPC could rescue the Yoruba from political annihilation. Awolowo's supporters countered that the West was rich enough to provide for its citizens and become the bastion of alternative government at the federal level instead of struggling with the East for the post of second-fiddle.

Akintola was restored to the premiership of Western Region in January 1963 without any fresh elections, despite the ruling against him by the Privy Council in London. As part of the NPC manoeuvre to deal with the Western crisis, Nigeria severed the last constitutional link with Britain and became a Republic on October 1, 1963 with Zik, who had been governor-general since 1960, becoming figure-head President. The Mid-West too was excised from the West increasing the number of regions to four. Akintola delayed and dithered and finally mustered his brittle NNDP which was in alliance with the NPC into parliamentary election on October 11, 1965. Because of the widespread electoral malpractices and rigging by the NNDP, the election finally put a torch to the tense West. There was total breakdown of law and order and

Akintola's regime was rendered virtually impotent. Tafawa Balewa, Bello and Akintola were making plans for the suppression of the general revolt in the West with military force, when the soldiers struck on January 15, 1966.

The first coup, led by Major Chukwuma Kaduna Nzeogwu, drew a bloody curtain on Nigeria's First Republic, but it did not completely break the political impasse in the Western Region. Akintola was killed just like Ahmadu Bello, his political mentor. Also killed were Abubakar Tafawa Balewa, the prime minister of the federation, and Festus Okotie-Eboh, his finance minister, as well as a number of top military officers. There was a temporary lull in the tempest of violence sweeping the West, as if numbed to silence by the bloodshed unleashed by the young majors.

Chief Awolowo and his men remained behind bars despite the coming to power of the military. The new government of Major-General Thomas Aguiyi-Ironsi, who inherited the rump of the Balewa government after crushing the coup of the majors, proscribed all political parties and threw the army of politicians out of business. Enormous pressure was mounted on the Ironsi regime and especially on Lieutenant-Colonel Adekunle Fajuyi, the first military governor of the West, for the release of Awo from prison. Initially, Ironsi was wary, moreso when there were security reports indicating that Major Nzeogwu and his co-plotters had planned to release Awo from prison and proclaim him the new prime minister of Nigeria armed with the power to rule by decrees. Ironsi was advised at the time that Awo may have known about the coup that swept away his bitterest foes. However, by the time Ironsi knew the contrary was the case and he was prepared to release Awo and his lieutenants from prison, he too became a victim of Nigeria's turbulent politics. Ironsi, Fajuyi and many other army officers, mostly of Eastern Nigeria origin, were killed in the counter-coup of July 29, 1966 which was led by a triumvirate of then Major Murtala Muhammed, Captains Martins Adamu and Theophilus Yakubu Danjuma. The bloodbath of that July and the pogrom that was to follow in the North were the prelude to the bloodier civil war.

Then Lieutenant-Colonel Yakubu Gowon, who was Ironsi's chief of staff, emerged as the new head of government. He granted Awolowo and his men freedom August 3, 1966.

The release of Awo brought hope to the West which had been bitterly divided since the AG crisis of 1962. The pogrom against Easterners, especially the Igbo, in the North and the attendant bloodshed of the July coup had not spared the West. Awo toured the region in an attempt to reunite the people and restore their confidence in the polity. During these tours, the old networks of the AG were explored and kept alive. It was during these uncertain hours in the annals of the nation that the seed of the Committee of Friends and the future Unity Party of Nigeria, UPN, germinated. During this time of crisis, a Western Leaders of Thought meeting took place in Ibadan, the Western Region capital, which included many leaders of the old AG and some leaders of the NNDP and Awo was subsequently proclaimed Asiwaju (leader) of the Yorubas.

The early days of the Gowon era were the flowering time for Awo who soon became the vice-chairman of the Federal Executive Council and federal commissioner (minister) for finance. Chief Anthony Enahoro, who was vice-president of the AG, became the leader of the Mid-West (later Bendel State) Leaders of Thought meetings and later federal commissioner for information and culture. Bola Ige, former federal publicity secretary of the party as well as Bisi Onabanjo another stalwart, became commissioners in the cabinet of Colonel Adeyinka Adebayo, who succeeded Fajuyi as military governor. Awolowo was to maintain contacts and often controlled with the party cells at the grassroots throughout the 13 years of military rule, especially after he resigned from Gowon's cabinet in 1971.

Two events were to test Awolowo's claims to the position of Asiwaju: the civil war and the Agbekoya uprising. Having failed in his bid to negotiate peace with Lieutenant-Colonel Emeka Odumegwu-Ojukwu, the leader of the secessionist Eastern Region, Awo swung his support to the federal side in 1967. His joining forces with Gowon was crucial to the victory of the federal forces, a decision for which the Igbo of the ill-fated Republic of Biafra, never forgave him. Of more immediate impact in the West was the Agbekoya ('Farmers Reject Hardship') uprising. Agbekoya, an association of peasant farmers formed to protest high taxation during the civil war, virtually held the government of Western State (Gowon created 12 states out of the four regions in 1967) to ransom during the gory riots of June and July of 1969. The farmers were only persuaded to lay down their arms when Awolowo toured the state, appealing to the farmers not to open another war front.

The outcome of the Agbekoya riot showed that the West still possessed the incendiary properties that earned it the tag of 'Wild, Wild, West' during the Akintola era. Surprisingly, the targets of the rioters were not just soldiers and government officials, but also traditional rulers. Oba Samuel Akinsanya, the Odemo of Ishara and close friend of Awolowo, was chased out of his palace by rioters who believed he was party to the tax hike. Olateru Olagbegi, a founding father of the AG who defected to Akintola's NNDP, and very much influential as the Olowo of Owo, also had to flee from irate rioters. In the aftermath of the riot, Olagbegi was later deposed as the Olowo. The Oba who suffered the worst fate was Olajide Olayode II, the Soun of Ogbomoso, Akintola's hometown. Oba Olayode was beheaded by the rioters who also killed three of his chiefs. Eight days earlier before he met his tragic death, the Soun had hosted the cream of Nigerian society in Ogbomoso when he installed Colonel Benjamin Adekunle, the legendary commander of the Third Marine Commando Division of the Nigerian Army, as the Ashipa of Ogbomoso.

The decisive manner in which Awolowo intervened in the Agbekoya uprising increased his mystique in the West and Nigeria as a whole. The AG members continued to meet under cover, keeping the leader informed. The leader of the party in the then Ondo Province of the Western State was Chief Ajasin, who, before the coup of 1966, was the president of Egbe Omo Oduduwa. Awolowo moved in to reconcile himself with some of his estranged followers who had parted ways with him during the crisis. But the core of the party remained those who had been steadfast like Ajasin in their loyalty to the leader and the party.

The promise of General Gowon to hand over power to an elected civilian government in 1976 increased the tempo of the work of the party. When Awo resigned from the government in 1971, it gave him more time to devote to the party, and the party organisation became stronger. When Gowon reneged on his promise, the faithful did not lose heart but continued their work. The pivot of the party was the Committee of Friends which made its yearly public appearance during the birthday celebration of Chief Awolowo when it organised debates and lectures as parts of the anniversary celebration.

In the then Ondo Province, party members were meeting regularly in the home of Chief Reuben Famuyide Fasoranti, a very experienced teacher and an old guard of the party. Sometimes in the early days, he would host the party meeting at Iju-Ita-ogbolu Grammar School where he was the principal and sometimes in his wife's Omolere Nursery School compound, directly behind his residence in Akure. Apart from Chief Ajasin, other prominent members of these early meetings included Mr. Phillip Akomolafe from Ilawe, Chief C.A. Tewe from Okitipupa, Chief J.E. Babatola from Ado-Ekiti and Chief P.E. Olukoju from Akoko area.

The meeting gathered strength with the overthrow of General Gowon July 29, 1975. The new regime, led by General Murtala Ramat Muhammed, promised to hand over power in 1979 and looked into the agitation for the creation of more states. When the federal government set up the committee for the creation of states, the Akure meeting became expanded and shifted venue to Saint Peter's College, Akure. Chief Ajasin remained the chairman, but more people from different walks of life and political persuasions were now in attendance. Notable among the new entrants were Chief Gabriel Akin-Deko, who was Awolowo's minister of agriculture in the fifties but later fell out with him during the AG crisis, and Chief G.B. Akinyede, another former NNDP stalwart.

The creation of states issue was a dilemma for Awoists. Chief Awolowo, for many decades, had been a convinced federalist who had advocated for the creation of more states in the country. When Gowon split the four regions into 12 states in 1967 on the eve of the Nigerian civil war, people saw Awo's hand behind Gowon's glove. But Awolowo too had been accused of harbouring feelings for Yoruba irredentism. Therefore, while Awo did not publicly oppose the creation of more states after 1967, he was also not too enthusiastic about it.

This reputation of being lukewarm to the issue of state creation was causing concern within the Awo camp. In fact, both Akin-Deko and Akinyede believed at the time that Awolowo was the man standing between them and the idea of an Ondo State. By 1975, many prominent Ondo State citizens joined their counterparts from the other parts of the former Western State for the splitting up of old Western State. The Ondo State movement was holding its meetings at the Liberty lodge of Chief Akin-Deko in Ibadan. The Ibadan group possibly believed that the Awoist group meeting in Akure may, in fact, be working against the creation of Ondo State. Awo was known to have favoured the creation of states along ethnic boundaries. Therefore, since the Yoruba were one nation, it was correctly deduced that he was opposed to further splitting of the Western State. In fact, parts of his political objectives since 1950 had been that all Yoruba people, both in the North (now Kwara State) and Lagos, should be under the direct control of the regime in Ibadan, the capital of the West.

Late 1975, a delegation of prominent Awoists met with Awolowo at his Oke-Bola residence in Ibadan asking him to declare support for the splitting up of Western State. Chief Awolowo was said to have expressed reservation about further creation of states, arguing that most of the new states would not be economically viable and would further divide the people. Members of the delegation, however, prevailed on Awolowo because they argued that it would be politically inexpedient to want to put a final stop to agitation for more states.

With the green light from Awo, states creation movements in the West received an added boost. The Committee of Friends machinery was thrown into full action, backing the petition for the splitting up of Western State into Oyo, Ondo and Ogun states. General Murtala Muhammed split the 12 states of the federation to 19 on February 3, 1976, constituting the old Ondo Province to Ondo State. It was one of the last official actions of the head of state who was assassinated during the abortive coup of February 13, 1976.

It was time of victory for Ajasin and the state movement, but someone else was attempting to run away with the prize. Akinyede, flamboyant politician and businessman, advertised it for the world to know that his support and hardwork was cardinal for the birth of Ondo State. He convinced a group of Ondo State traditional rulers that he deserved to be honoured for his labour. They, therefore, decided to honour him with the title of Balogun (generalissimo) of Ondo State. This caused consternation in the Awoist camp and they felt that Akinyede was trying to take 'undue' advantage of a joint effort.

The linchpin of the Awoists reaction to Akinyede's ego trip was Akin Omoboriowo, then a senior assistant registrar at the University of Ife (now Obafemi Awolowo University), who was planning for retirement after 10 years of service. Omoboriowo participated actively in the state creation movement, but he was not involved in the earlier meetings of the Awoists before 1975. Omoboriowo obtained his first degree from the University of Ibadan in 1965 and in 1972, he got another degree in law from Unife. He, therefore, set to cut his wisdom teeth in law with the Akinyede case. Since he was still in the employment of the university, he sought the help of another lawyer friend of his who filed a motion in the Akure High Court to stop the installation ceremony. Though the case was still-born, the government was forced to step in and stop the Balogun's hullabaloo altogether.

Omoboriowo retired from Unife later in 1976 at 44. He settled down in Akure, a young man burning with enthusiasm and vigour. He and his family of five children put up in Akure where he set up a relatively well-equipped law chamber. Since his youth, he had been a fanatical supporter of Chief Awolowo and once in 1965 was thrown into jail for this belief on the order of Chief Remi Fani-Kayode, the deputy-premier in Akintola's government. It was natural then for this young man to find a prominent place in the league of Awoists who were already being overtaken with placidity after the victory of the state creation efforts.

With Fasoranti becoming principal of Olivet Baptist High School, Oyo where he was posted to at the end of one session in Iwo in 1973, Omoboriowo became the secretary of the Committee of Friends. The meetings were still being held in Fasoranti's residence, with Ajasin still serving as chairman. Omoboriowo virtually abandoned his fledgling law practice to devote his time for the Awoist cause and his Peugeot 404 saloon car became very familiar with residents of Akure. The meeting became expanded with young people like Dr. Bode Olowoporoku who was brought in by Phillip Akomolafe, his uncle and mentor; Mr. Wumi Adegbomire, a man in the same generation as Omoboriowo who was an Action Grouper right from youth, as well as many other persons. The rumour that the military had already made up its mind to hand over power to a Northern-based political party with Alhaji Inua Wada, an uncle of the late General Mohammed as presidential candidate, did dampen some of the supporters' zeal, but the tempo of enthusiasm was still high.

By 1977 and early 1978, the Akure meeting was liaising with the Unife group which included men like Professors Samuel Aluko, Banji Akintoye, David Oke, and Adeniji Adaralegbe and Dr. Falaye Aina. The two groups, as well as similar groups throughout the country, were meeting with Chief Awolowo regularly at his residences in Ibadan, Apapa and often at Ikenne, his country home in Ogun State.

The meetings with Chief Awolowo often took the form of rigorous intellectual exercise. He would select individuals to present papers on various aspects of Nigerian national life — the funding of universal free education at all levels, funding of free health service, revenue generation and allocation, external trade, full employment and the funding of the party machine.

The meetings were exciting and participants felt they were in the presence of history. Earlier in 1978, after a spirited debate, the Committee of Friends settled for the name Unity Party of Nigeria, UPN, and adopted the party's four cardinal programmes of free education at all levels, free health service, integrated rural development and full employment. The overriding ethos of the moment was confidence and nobody exemplified this more than Awolowo himself who was certain of becoming president come October 1, 1979, when he would 'introduce irreversible changes' in Nigerian's life.

Early in 1978, after the party had settled the issue of name, party symbols and programmes, Chief Awolowo started making consultations about those to lead the party in the coming electoral battles. In the various 19 states, the pattern of party leadership was becoming discernible. In Ondo State, there were two clear groups: the Akure group led by Ajasin and which included Fasoranti, Omoboriowo and Akomolafe; and the University of Ife group comprising Akintoye, Adaralegbe and Oke led by a renowned economist, Professor Samuel Aluko. There was also a Third Force led by Ayo Fasanmi, a member of the Constituent Assembly who belonged to the more radical mould, and had the support of some of the new generation of politicians. All the three groups were interested in fielding candidates for the post of governor.

The candidate of the UNIFE group was Professor Akintoye, a renowned historian and author and one of the intellectual firebrands of the committee. On the face of it, Akintoye had a very good chance. The Unife group after all, was involved in all the national planning of the committee and they constituted the inner council of the Awoist movement. But early in 1978, Chief Awolowo called Aluko and sought his support for the candidacy of Chief Ajasin. After Aluko reported back to the group, Akintoye agreed to defer his ambition — he later became a senator during the Second Republic.

It was apparent to a few others that Awo's favoured candidate for the top job in Ondo State was Chief Ajasin, a loyal and dedicated palladin with whom he weathered the tempest of the turbulent sixties and who remained unbending in his faith in the leader. In the early fifties, during the incubation period of the AG, Ajasin had prepared the policy paper on free education which had become the core programme of Awolowo's social policy and the hallmark of his career. Ajasin had served in the federal parliament and was once the chairman of the Western Nigeria Development Corporation, but he had never held any ministerial job. Awo, therefore, felt it was time to reward him. He was also convinced that the job of governor should be trusted in experienced hands since he believed youths were still opened to temptation of greed and capriciousness. Indeed, Awolowo blamed most of the misrule of the military on the relative youth and inexperience of the military leaders. For similar reasons, he favoured the candidacy of Canon Emmanuel Alayande, a durable follower and an educationist like Chief Ajasin, for the governorship of Oyo State. (Alayande was defeated during the shadow election by Bola Ige, his former student). Awolowo's candidate for Lagos State was Alhaji Lateef Kayode Jakande and for Ogun state, Chief Bisi Onabanjo, both veteran journalists who had remained prominent falangists of the Awo camp for several decades.

When Chief Awolowo summoned Ajasin for the discussion on the nomination issue, the latter too was already thinking along that line. Ajasin was 70, but was still agile and mentally alert and lately served with credit as the chairman of Owo Local Government. Until 1975 when the military took over private secondary schools, he was the principal of Owo High School, an institution he founded in 1963. Moreover, he was the leading survivor of the *ancien regime* and had been leading the emerging party in the state since the military take-over of 1966. Therefore, some of the old party leaders had been pressing him to gird his loins for the next round now that the military was leaving. Awolowo told him that he would support his bid for the governorship provided he (Ajasin) appointed a young person as running mate. He also told Ajasin that when eventually the party came to power, he should surround himself with a blend of young men so that the cabinet would not be a gerontocracy.

Ondo State is a land of dichotomy: the Ekiti and the non-Ekiti. The Ekiti constitute about 54 per cent of the population but it is not a comfortable majority that they could dictate the direction and pace of events. Awolowo told Ajasin that since he was an Owo man, it would be advisable that he picked an Ekiti man for deputy-governorship. When Ajasin asked him whom he would suggest, Awolowo named Omoboriowo. Though Ajasin would have preferred one of the older partymen from Ekiti, preferably those he knew since the days of the old AG, he agreed with Awolowo that Omoboriowo was not a bad choice after all. Ajasin met Omoboriowo for the first time during the period for the agitation for Ondo State in 1975; and since then, the young lawyer had impressed him with his dedication, industry, faithfulness to the party and the leader and his intellectual alertness.

After the agreement with Ajasin, Awolowo met Omoboriowo separately during one of the brainstorming sessions of the Committee of Friends in Awolowo's Ibadan residence. The elder statesman asked Omoboriowo to tell him his favourite candidate for governorship race for Ondo State. Omoboriowo began to reel out some names including that of Ajasin. When he mentioned Ajasin, Awolowo asked him to stop, saying: 'That is the person after my heart.' He said Ajasin had proved, during difficult times, to be totally faithful, dedicated, honest and reliable. Awolowo said further that it was such a prudent and experienced man who should be entrusted with managing a young, poor and struggling state like Ondo. He then briefed Omoboriowo on his earlier discussion with Ajasin pointing out that Ajasin had agreed to pick him as his running mate.

In government circles of Akure in early 1978, members of the Awo group were not popular. The civil servants derided them as day-dreamers who were bent on hoodwinking the populace with the promise of free education at all levels. Moreover, the state government had not been spared by the caustic journalism of the *Nigerian Tribune*, a paper that Chief Awolowo founded in 1949. The ban on politics was on and yet here was a group openly flouting the fiat of the federal military government. Therefore, the state government and its agents were willing to keep Awo and his followers at arm's length.

Early in 1978, Omoboriowo, as the secretary of the Committee of Friends in Ondo State, went to government owned Catering Rest House, (now part of the government guest chalets), Akure, to book accommodation for Chief Awolowo, who was coming to town to address his supporters on the coming shadow election. Though the Rest House had minimal patronage, Omoboriowo was informed that it was already fully booked in advance. After some argument, the manager reluctantly allocated an old chalet that had not been used for ages, if that was acceptable. A beggar has no choice since Akure, at that time, had no comparable hotel. Omoboriowo called one of his friends, another staunch Awoist, and both of them physically laboured for four hours, washing, cleaning and polishing the place to make it habitable for their leader.

That night Awolowo came. He sent for Ajasin in Owo and they had a long discussion on the coming electoral battle. Though Awo suspected that the military might have a preference for another political party, he believed the wishes of the people would overwhelm them. He was in an optimistic mood, and both old men could smell victory at the culmination of their life-long struggle to change the face of their fatherland. They discussed the proposed shadow election, the state of preparedness of the Awo camp and the trend of politics in the country generally.

The following morning Awolowo met some of the other key party leaders, including Omoboriowo and Fasoranti, in his guest chalet. At 11 a.m., they drove in a convoy to Fasoranti's Omolere Nursery School. The place was packed full with supporters, both the Akure group and the Unife group were adequately represented. The veteran politician recognised some of the old men with whom he weathered the dangerous sixties — people like Aluko, Babatola, Akerele, and Olukoju. After exchange of pleasantries, Awolowo went to the business of the day. He told the people to get set for the shadow election, named the date of the contest, and nominated Tewe, Akomolafe and Fasoranti, as people to organise the election. He gave verbal guidelines on the election and concluded that 'we need to put our house in order before the ban on politics is lifted'.

The two strong candidates, Ajasin and Ayo Fasanmi, represented the dichotomy in the new state. Fasanmi, like Omoboriowo, is from the majority Ekiti while Ajasin is from Owo, one of the minority groups. Iluyomade, the dark horse from Ondo town, had no chance at all. Many of the leaders from Ekiti felt it was the turn of their group to produce a governor, arguing that in the former Western State, they were virtually sidelined. In the old West, two Ekiti men, the late Lieutenant-Colonel Fajuyi and his successor, Adeyinka Adebayo, became governors but their impacts, partly because of the shortness of their tenure, had been minimal. Because of this perception, Omoboriowo had difficulty in persuading some of the Ekiti leaders to back Ajasin in preference to Fasanmi. He met with Obas and opinion leaders within the group. 'Why are you backing a non-Ekiti man against an Ekiti man who is contesting?' Omoboriowo was queried repeatedly. He would explain why Ajasin rightly deserved the honour this time around, leaving out the details of his discussion with Chief Awolowo, and concluding that 'our own chance would come'.

But the Ekiti lobby was a strong one that was determined to leave no stone unturned in achieving its ends. Its candidate, Fasanmi, was busy on the national front as a leading member of Awo's team to other parts of the country. Therefore, he did not have sufficient rapport with the grassroots and it was easy for the Ajasin-Omoboriowo team to cut the ground under his feet. His supporters, therefore, felt that what they needed was time to put their house in order. On Friday, June 9, 1978, the Ekiti leaders met at Ido Faboro in an uncompleted church where they resolved to call for the postponement of the date of the nomination contest. Chief Omoboriowo was one of the Ekiti leaders present at that meeting. To underscore Fasanmi's handicap, he had just returned that very day from one of the national assignments given him by Chief Awolowo.

When the delegates met the next day at Omolere Nursery School, it was apparent that the Ajasin camp had already got wind of the Fasanmi group's plan to press for postponement. When it was tabled before the meeting, one speaker after the other railed against it. Segun Adegoke, a 37-year-old well-to-do lawyer who was educated at the University of London, argued that Fasanmi's supporters had no reason to call for postponement since the group had agreed on the June 10 date. It was clear that the Fasanmi group would have their say and not their way. They conceded and the election went on.

Then, the Ajasin group played their trump card. The group

proposed, and it was accepted, that the issue of deputy-governor should be dealt with first while the gubernatorial contest should crown the day. This was peculiar mainly to Ondo State Committee of Friends since it was not repeated in any other state branch. It had been agreed at a previous meeting that the deputy-governorship candidate, too, should be elected by the whole assembly, just like the governor. By the provisions of the proposed constitution then being studied by the military, the deputy-governor is a virtual figure-head and many of the gathered politicians did not recognise the potential of the post. Omoboriowo was the only candidate who vied for the job and he was elected by acclamation. It was clear then that you could not have an Ekitiman as deputy governor and another Ekiti man as governor. It was clear too that Fasanmi's ambition was destined for a cul-de-sac. He scored 19 to Ajasin's 32 votes. Iluyomade scored no vote.

It was evident at that moment that it was time for Ajasin, the faithful frontier man of the party for many years, to claim his due from destiny. When the AG was formed in 1951, he was its first vice president. At the time of the first coup, Ajasin was 58. He was already a politician of repute who was in the fore-front of Yoruba nationalist movement and the Nigerian triangular struggle for power. Though this man had been so long in politics, not many people had heard of him before he assumed the governorship of Ondo State in 1979. He had neither charisma nor cunning like Akintola, and he did not possess the flamboyance and colour of men like Bola Ige, the Cicero of Esa-Oke. His forte was that he was a loyal party man; the dedicated frontier pioneer.

While Ajasin and Omoboriowo were working for the party at different frontiers, they never thought or knew that their destinies would be so joined. Each was pursuing his own ambition, dreaming his own dreams, of familiar objects, or cronies, colleagues and associates, but not his ally whom fate had appointed. Perhaps, without the other, each would not have been more than mere asterisk in Nigeria's history. But fate decreed otherwise. On June 10, 1978, as the two men embraced in self-congratulations, they finally started on the path of their common destiny.

3

Victory And Defeat

On September 21, 1978, after the federal military government had received the reports of the Constituent Assembly, General Olusegun Obasanjo, the head of state, lifted the 12-year-old ban on open political activities. That evening, Chief Awolowo sent invitation to media houses for 'a world press conference' billed to hold at his Park Lane, Apapa, residence in Lagos the following day where his new party, the Unity Party of Nigeria, UPN, would be formally introduced to the world. By being the first to announce his party, Awolowo had lived up to his reputation for thoroughness. The party flag, its anthem, its manifesto were all in place. Said Omoboriowo: 'By the time the ban was lifted, we were battle ready.'

It was clear to the gathered reporters who listened to the statesman that morning that Awo was virtually certain of victory. While the other political movements were taken unaware believing hitherto that the ban would be lifted on the nation's independence anniversary on October 1, the UPN war machine was already revving. Chief Awolowo said his party would pursue four cardinal programmes: free education at all levels, free health service, integrated rural development and full employment. He promised that all these programmes would take off immediately he became president the following year. After the Friday announcement, the UPN held its highly successful first national congress at the Mainland Hotel Ebute-Metta, Lagos, October 2, 1978, where Awo's presidential candidacy was formally adopted. On Monday, October 16, Awo began a nationwide campaign, selling himself to the electorate.

From the onset, it appeared Awo and the UPN had a big advantage over the other four parties that were eventually registered. These were the National Party of Nigeria, NPN; the Nigeria People's Party, NPP; The Great Nigeria's People's Party; GNPP, and The Peoples Redemption Party; PRP. It was strategically better placed, its leader was well-known and his populist appeal was outstanding. Moreover, his reputation as a first-class administrator and performer as borne out by his record in the former Western Region where he became a pacesetter not only for Nigeria, but for Black Africa, was well-known. Not only did he start the first free primary education programme in Black Africa, he provided free health care for children under 18, and created a first-class civil service. He built the first television station in Africa and the first Olympic size stadium, the Liberty Stadium, Ibadan, and created the culture of setting a minimum wage for workers. He had also earned a reputation as an ascetic, a philosopher, an author and constitutionalist and lawyer per-excellence. These were indeed impressive credentials in a country which often fielded its second division in the crucial games of life. All these put him in good stead in the old Western Region where he once held court and the fruits of his old labour, especially free education, were there to bear him witness. Among the Yoruba, his old persecution by the Balewa-Bello-Akintola axis had elevated him to living martyrdom.

In the sphere of strategy too, Awo and the UPN, held a clear advantage. The party had grown and flourished almost throughout the military era. This had created the impression that Awo was jumping the gun in the political race. There was the insinuation then that Obasanjo had given Awo the undue advantage over his opponents. Though the government continuously warned that the ban on political activities had not been lifted, this did not debar

Awo from going on high profile 'refamiliarisation and lecture tours,' of the country in March 1978. It was said that both the police and the Nigerian Security Organisation, NSO, left Awolowo alone on these tours because of an 'order from above'.[7]

In 1976 too, Chief Awolowo had gone to Ghana for the first Kwame Nkrumah Memorial lecture. He used the opportunity to clear advantage of not only publicising himself, but also unveiling the pattern of loyalty of his new party. Among those who were present in Ghana with him were: Mr. Olanihun Ajayi, Segun Adegoke, Ebenezer Babatope, Alao Aka-Basorun, Gani Fawehinmi, Alhaji S.O. Gbadamosi, Professor Chike Obi, Omoboriowo, Godwin Daboh, Chief Bola Ige, Archdeacon Emmanuel Alayande, Alhaji Lateef Jakande, and Alhaji Garuba Dan Shagamu.

By being so visible, Awolowo exposed himself to too many pot-shots from different flanks. It was clear too that by the time the military lifted the ban on political party activities, Awolowo and his group had locked themselves into a cast-iron situation. They had over-defined their friends and they still seemed like a team in search of more enemies. This certainly would not have been the original intention of the strategy, but it became its consequence. Awo had refused to participate in the Constitution Drafting Committee, CDC which was headed by Chief Rotimi Williams, his former attorney-general in the old West on the excuse that he was not a constitutional lawyer, though he was certainly piqued by the manner of appointment on the radio. This was the style of the new General Murtala Muhammed regime which succeeded the Gowon administration, but by refusing to serve, he also threw away the opportunity of being a member of the Constituent Assembly.

The Constituent Assembly, CA, became the hatchery of the Second Republic leading actors. All the other political parties, apart from the UPN, were more or less formed on the floor of the CA in Lagos. By not being a member of the CA, Chief Awolowo not only lost the opportunity to make friends from different parts of Nigeria he also opened himself to unnecessary and unfair criticism by young politicians looking for opportunities to gain headlines. There were the constant accusations that Awolowo was teleguiding the proceedings of the assembly. This became more evident during the protracted and stalemated debate on Sharia law and when the assembly rejected the motion that the Grand Khadi of the Northern States should also have the right to swear in the president, apart from the Chief Justice of the federation. Chief Awolowo was accused of being behind the two stormy debates and the CA became polarised between those in 'Awo's camp' and those who were not. Awolowo was considered such a threat to the ambitions of some members in the assembly that a motion was proposed to set a 70-year age limit for aspirants to the presidency. It failed. Another motion, which sought to bar those found guilty of corruption and abuse of office since independence (the Coker Commission of inquiry set up by the Balewa regime during the AG crisis of 1962 indicted Awolowo), from participating in future politics, was rejected by the military.

But despite these debits from the CDC and the CA, Awo was still the candidate to beat and he had the most formidable political machine. But during the first congress of his party in 1978, it became clear that Awolowo was subjecting himself to an Iron Law from which there would be no retreat and which would be irrevocable. He showed to the congress Chief Phillip Umeadi, a 56-year-old lawyer who was educated at Ilesa Grammar School, Oyo State, and the University of London, as his vice presidential candidate. Umeadi too was an old politician and he was Chike Obi's deputy from 1960 to 1966 in the Dynamic Party. But in the real context of Nigerian politics, Umeadi, an Igbo from Anambra State, was a paper weight. But by putting Umeadi on the ticket, Awolowo was making a dangerous throw-back to the past when the two Southern parties, the AG and the NCNC formed an alliance in the United Progressive Grand Alliance, UPGA, to oppose the NPC led Nigerian National Alliance, NNA, during the 1964 federal election. But time had not stood still and it was both dangerous and unrealistic to think that both the president and the vice president of the republic would not only come from the southern parts of the country but would be Christians. Other political parties took their cues from the UPN mistake and adjusted their strategies accordingly.

It was also clear from the onset that Awo had a breach on the home front. The ease and relative affluence of his followers during the military era had bred rebellion within Awo's camp and this was to seriously cripple his spectacular bid for power. Notably among the estranged lieutenants were Chief Anthony Enahoro and Dr. Joseph Tarka. Both men were Awo's frontier men in the sixties and they were political warlords in their own rights. Both men were ambitious and thought they too could have a shot at the presidency if the North was in a mood for concession after monopolising power in Nigeria for two decades. However, both men had more reasons for parting with Awo, than just the wine of ambition.

Chief Anthony Eromosele Enahoro, born July 22, 1923 in Uromi, now in Bendel State, was the closest comrade of Awo after the mysterious death of the deputy leader of the AG, Chief Bode Thomas, in 1953. A talented journalist and orator, Enahoro was educated at King's College, Lagos and became, at 21, the youngest editor in Nigerian history under the Azikiwe Group of Newspapers. He was one of the radical leaders of the militant Zikist Movement and he was jailed several times for sedition by the colonial authorities. On his return from prison, Enahoro became a foundation member of the AG in 1951 and later was minister of home affairs in the West. As an AG member of the House of Representatives in 1953, he moved the independence motion which was bitterly opposed by Ahmadu Bello and the Northern elites. Awo had favoured him to become premier of the West instead of Akintola in 1959 against the stiff opposition of the party fathers. When eventually Akintola ascended to the premiership, Enahoro followed Awo to the Federal Parliament. He was jailed 15 years for treason during the famous trial of the AG leaders in 1963 and was subsequently released by Gowon in 1966 along with other opposition leaders.

Like Enahoro, Joseph Servuan Tarka represented a phenomenon in the Nigerian politics of the fifties and the sixties. A trained teacher, Tarka, born 1927 in Gboko, Benue State, virtually created the first revolutionary movement in Nigeria, his United Middle-Belt Congress, UMBC, which took up arms to demand for a separate region for the people of the Middle-Belt. He attended constitutional conferences that led to Nigeria's independence by virtue of his position as deputy president of the AG, and representing the largest minority ethnic group in the north, the Tiv, (apart from the Yoruba of Kwara State). A formidable politician, he was in and out of jail several times under the NPC-controlled Northern Region.

With the coming to power of Gowon in August 1966, Awo, Enahoro and Tarka became part of the federal government. When Awo resigned from the federal cabinet in 1971, it was said that he wanted his two heavyweight lieutenants to follow suit, but they did not oblige. When the Gowon regime became smeared with corruption during its twilight days, the two leading nationalists were not spared. Godwin Daboh, a fellow Tiv and Gboko businessman who was one of those who followed Awo on his Ghana trip, forced Tarka to resign from Gowon's cabinet when he accused him of corruption in a sworn affidavit. Enahoro too was indicted by probes on the preparation for the 2nd African Festival of Arts and Culture, FESTAC, by the Muhammed regime. Both men saw Awo's hands in their travails, especially when their former political boss refused to stand by them in their dark hours. When politics came, the two men therefore shifted camp to the NPN. If they had remained in Awo's camp, at least Enahoro and Tarka would have become governors of Bendel and Benue states respectively. Bendel still went to the UPN, but in Benue, the home state of Tarka, his defection had a dramatic effect as the state voted massively for the Hausa-Fulani dominated NPN.

There were other defections from the Awo political family that were equally noticeable, though of less significance. Samuel Gomsu Ikoku, former secretary-general of the AG and a political fair-weather man, drifted first to the NPN then to the PRP and again back to the NPN. There was Chief Akanbi Onitiri, an old Action Grouper who went to prison with Awo in 1963 and was a principal figure in the formation of the Committee of Friends, but defected when it was clear that he was going to lose the Lagos State gubernatorial ticket to Jakande. There was also Chief Akin Olugbade, a former federal legislator who quietly shifted base to the NPN.

If these men were the recognisable faces, the significance of their defection was far-reaching. The defection of Tarka effectively shut the door to Awolowo in Benue State. Awo's non-participation in the proceedings of the CA also cost him the opportunity of cultivating the league of emerging new leaders in the minority states. Therefore, in the minority states of Gongola, Plateau, Cross River and Rivers, which were enthusiastic fertile ground for Awoism in the sixties because of Awolowo championing of the creation of more states, had become unfriendly territories. Most of the AG leadership in those states, which formed the corps of the new UPN leadership, had atrophied and somewhat removed from the grassroots. As it were, the new order in those states belonged to the uppish politicians who felt no allegiance to Chief Awolowo and were looking for alliance with the highest bargaining power.

When the other parties came out of their shells, it became apparent that the UPN was up to a herculean task. Originally, the big challenge was from two fronts: the NPP and the NPN. The NPP represented the Fourth Force in Nigerian politics, a coalition of minorities which had always been the nightmare of the majority power brokers. It was led by late Waziri Ibrahim, former federal minister and multimillionaire from the Kanuri-dominated Borno State. From the time of the coming of Europeans, the Kanuri, who created the oldest and most durable Islamic state in the Chad Basin had been forced to play second fiddle to the newer, but more aggressive Fulani aristocracy. Waziri's emergence was therefore seen as a true challenge to the old order. More than this, NPP had adherents from all states of the federation including the Hausa-Fulani states of Sokoto and Bauchi and the Igbo states of Anambra and Imo.

The other problem was the NPN. Ideologically conservative and strategically superior to the UPN, it was apparent from the onset that Awo was meeting a worthy opponent in the NPN machine. A virtual reincarnation of the old NPC and the old NNA, the party was formed basically on the floor of the CA. Its moving spirit was a common desire among members to stop Awo from becoming president at all cost. It formulated the zoning system with the stated promise that the North was willing to relinquish power on its own terms. Its *laissez-faire* ideology was attractive to all comers, especially the *nouveau-riche* who blossomed under the military. Soon it became known as the party of the rich.

While the NPN was able to maintain its ranks, Waziri's NPP was a dream too good to come true. Soon there were revolts within the ranks of the new party against Waziri. What became apparent was the rebirth of Nigeria's old problem of tripartite struggle for power. The Igbo, waking up from the relative unease of the early post-war years, came to view the NPP as their own party. They wanted to coerce Waziri to give up the leadership of the party for Dr. Azikiwe who was in temporary retirement in Onitsha, Anambra State.

Azikiwe, born November 16, 1904, by Igbo parents in Zungeru, Niger State, was 'a self-confessed Fabian socialist and like the Roman general Maximums Fabius, Zik knew the virtue of retreat. He had built his entire epic career on this virtue and with calculated cunning and strategic seasonal romances, had stayed for half a century at the epicentre of Nigerian politics'.[8]

The venerable Zik has remained an enigma in Nigerian politics. When he became governor-general in 1960, Zik announced his retirement from politics. Since the intervention of the military in 1966, he has turned ambivalence into a creed. When he was removed through the first coup as figurehead president, he was safely abroad 'on health grounds'. He was to resurface in Biafra and acted as godfather of the ill-fated republic. He abandoned the sinking Biafran ship again in 1969 to make a separate peace with Lagos. In several speeches and pronouncements he let it be known that he was now 'the father of the nation' and was no longer interested in political gladiatorial combats.

It was clear that other political aspirants were interested in keeping Zik out of the ring so that the heart of Igboland would be open for poaching. Said Zik, affirming further that he would not join the political wagon for the Second Republic: 'At present I am regarded by some people as the father of the nation, first president of Nigeria. With bias towards none, therefore, my role at this stage is to reconcile the children where conflicts exist'.[9] The pro-NPN *New Nigerian* hailed the decision in an editorial. 'We congratulate him (Zik) for living up not only to his advice to his contemporaries (a veiled reference to Awo) but also for firmly upholding the dignity of the office of the president of Nigeria which he was the first to occupy,' the paper wrote. 'To have been identified with any of the emerging political parties would have been a let-down since when he held office, he always claimed to be speaking for the nation.' [10]

It was clear to discerning observers that Zik's new protestation of disinterestedness was aimed at the direction of Awo. He had said several times that members of the old brigade should step aside for the new generation. In 1976 he had written a poem where he advised his generation that:

> To stay in the arena of public life, And tussle with our children
> would be wrong, Because it would prolong the din and strife.

It was conventional wisdom then that not only would Zik not come out, he *dare not* come out, because the Igbo, bitter about his acrobatics during the civil war would not vote for him. Awo was one of those who believed in this conventional wisdom. Speaking to Bendel Igbo communities April 1978, Awo had said he was seeking the presidency for the good of the common man. 'For your information, I don't intend to marry more wives nor build more houses.'[11] It was a direct shot at Zik who had just married a new wife and was building a new house.

On Monday, October 30, 1978, Awolowo was received by a crowd of about 120,000 in Ugwo field, Enugu. The crowd was

enthusiastic and it took many minutes before policemen could clear
the way for Awo to mount the red-carpeted dais. At that moment,
Awo was convinced that he had made the best choice by extending
the hand of friendship to the Igbo people by making an Igbo man
his running mate. He told the cheering crowd: 'On October 1, 1979
when I am inaugurated into office as president, no one will demand
school fees from any pupil or student in any institution of learning.'[12]

Soon, Zik issued an oblique statement declaring that 'old men
can still kick.'[13] Political associations scrambled to Onitsha, correctly
reading the handwriting on the wall that the legendary Zik was
changing his stand again. Dr. Nwafor Orizu, former president of the
Senate, who as acting president handed over power to General Ironsi
in 1966, issued a statement purportedly from Zik, alleging that the
latter was declaring for the NPN. On November 15, Zik issued a
more direct statement saying: 'I cannot pretend that I am happy in
the circumstances neither can I feel contented to fold my arms and
hope that the drifting ship of state will stabilise by itself without
direction.' On Monday, November 21, Zik finally declared for the
NPP in Onitsha, effectively shutting the Igbo market from the other
political parties. Zik was formally admitted into the party in
December 1978.

Zik's entry into politics effectively destroyed the NPP as the
Fourth Force. An aggrieved Waziri, who had refused to step down
for Zik as party leader and content himself with being its flagbearer
alone, formed the GNPP with his faction of the party. Replying
those criticising his re-entry into politics, Zik said he was in a
fighting spirit. 'Any offensive against me will attract a counter-
offensive,' he said. 'I will reply fire for fire.'[14]

With the coming of Zik to the ring, only two parties remained
in their original forms: the NPN and the UPN. Even the NPN had
suffered defection at that stage. Aminu Kano, leader of the Northern
Elements Progressive Union, NEPU in the sixties, joined the team
during the CA debate on sharia and had hoped he would be adopted
as the party's presidential candidate. When he was made the NPN

publicity secretary, the tempestuous mallam resigned and formed his Peoples Redemption Party, PRP.

The 1979 battle therefore was between the NPN and the UPN, the two most prepared parties. It was like the 1959 election again with Awolowo leading the phalanx from the South and Shagari holding fort for the late Bello from the North. The two parties concentrated on attacking each other on the national plane and they were the only parties which contested every seat in the federation.

Chief Richard Akinjide, legal adviser to the NPN and former minister of education in the Balewa government, dismissed the UPN's claim to national appeal, saying it was nothing but a parochial organisation. 'Now the AG has come with a new clothing and a new name in the form of the UPN,' said Akinjide. 'Chief Awolowo is UPN and UPN is Chief Awolowo.'[15] Omoboriowo also showed his contempt for the NPN. 'Their innumerable heavyweights have become so heavy that they could hardly conceive any idea that might worsen their decidedly overgrown weights,'[16] said Omoboriowo.

Unlike in many other states of the federation, the campaign in Ondo State was proving to be a walk over for the UPN. Chief Ajasin, the UPN gubernatorial candidate was given a red-carpet reception everywhere he went. Reverend R.A. Ogunlade, the NPN governorship candidate virtually threw in the towel. Chief Ajasin while addressing a campaign rally at Erinjiyan-Ekiti, hometown of Ogunlade, alleged that Ogunlade was originally in the UPN, but he crossed over because he lost the chance of contesting into the state's House of Assembly on the party platform.[17] The campaign was a new experience for most of the politicians. The UPN leaders keyed their campaign on the reputation and legacies of Chief Awolowo whose achievements the people perceived as unsurpassed in the field of politics and social engineering.

But elections would not be held only in the old Western Region and by the time The Federal Electoral Commission, FEDECO, blew the whistle for the poll, it was clear that Awo was up to a tough task.

The five candidates who contested the presidential elections were Chief Awolowo, UPN, Dr. Nnamdi Azikiwe NPP, Alhaji Waziri Ibrahim, GNPP, Alhaji Shehu Shagari of the NPN and Mallam Aminu Kano of the PRP. FEDECO announced the timetable for the elections as follows: Senate, July 8; House of Representatives, July 14; State Houses of Assembly, July 21; Governorship, July 28; run-off for gubernatorial election if necessary, August 4; presidential, August 11. All the parties concluded their campaign rallies Friday, July 7, 1979 and then rested their cases in the court of the electorate.

When the results of the senatorial election started coming in, it was clear who would control the destiny of the Second Republic. The NPN led with 36 and other parties trailed behind them with UPN 28, NPP 16, GNPP 8, and PRP 7. In a desperate move to swing the pendulum of the election in his favour, Awolowo announced a unilateral alliance with the other three parties apart from the NPN, asking candidates of the UPN to step down for candidates of these parties in some states of the country apart from Ondo, Oyo, Ogun, Lagos, Bendel and Kwara states. Apart from Kaduna State where the PRP's Balarabe Musa was elected governor allegedly because of this alliance, Awo's tactical move hardly affected the pattern of the election. Predictably, Shagari scored the highest in the presidential ballot with 33.8 per cent of the vote cast. His total score was 5,688,587 votes while Awo with 4,916,651 votes scored 29.2 per cent.

But Chief Awolowo was not going to take his defeat with folded arms. He believed that Shagari had got a helping hand from the military government and FEDECO. He alleged that despite this, Shagari was not duly elected president since he failed to satisfy section 126, 2(a) and (b) of the constitution which stated that:

> A candidate for an election to the office of president shall be deemed to have been duly elected where, there being more than 2 candidates for the election (if) (a) he has the highest number of votes cast at the election; and (b) he has not less than one-quarter of the votes at the election in each of at least two-thirds of all the states of the federation.

While it was clear that Shagari satisfied the first requirement by winning the highest votes, it was disputable if he fulfilled the second condition. He won at least 25 per cent in 12 out of the 19 states but he scored 19.94 per cent of the votes cast in Kano State. This was foot-in-the door for the NPN.

Despite consistent protestation of impartiality by Obasanjo and other top members of the military junta, Chief Awolowo had always been suspicious of the umpire role of the soldiers. Most of them were already far advanced in their career when Awo was vice chairman of the Federal Executive Council. But Awo had not endeared himself to the junta by publicly promising that he would probe the military on his becoming the president. After the first two elections, he and Waziri accused the military of partiality in favour of the NPN. When Awo sent some members of the UPN to help him supervise the election in some of the states in the North, they were promptly rounded up and detained. They were not released until after the elections.

But the real problem of the 1979 presidential election was not whether or not the military manipulated the election, but the interpretation of the two-thirds of nineteen states. Before the August 11 presidential poll, it had been a settled conventional wisdom that the answer was 13 states. Chief Michael Ani, the chairman of FEDECO, had used the figure 13 in all former dealings with the political parties. Both the CDC and the CA had also held the opinion that the two third of 19 was 13. Recalled James Oluleye, a retired major-general and member of Obasanjo's cabinet: 'Although the definition of two-thirds of 19 did not escape the members of the Constitution Drafting Committee, but the matter was dropped when the chairman (Chief Rotimi Williams) assured them that two-third of 19 was 13 and nothing else. It was further argued that in case more states were created in the future, the insertion of the definition would necessitate an amendment to the constitution which will be a laborious exercise.'[18]

The nation waited with bated breath after the August 11 poll. By Tuesday August 14, when all the results from all states in the federation were announced, except that of Kano State, it was becoming clear that no candidate may emerge on the first ballot and the nation may have to settle for an electoral college made up of the newly elected members of the federal parliament and the state assemblies to decide the winner. Chief Ani apparently was not certain what course of action to take after the commission received the result from Kano and Shagari scored 19.9 per cent. That day Chief Akinjide told the nation via Radio Nigeria, Kaduna, that FEDECO should declare Shagari the winner because he had satisfied the provisions of the constitution. Akinjide, defeated NPN governorship candidate for Oyo State, argued that two-third of 19 is not 13 but 12 2/3. He said therefore, Shagari only needed to score one-sixth of the votes in the 13th state which he already did in Kano.

On the afternoon of August 14, Chief Ani hurried to Doddan Barracks, the nation's seat of power for a secret meeting with General Obasanjo. Hitherto, Ani had nurtured the public image that his commission was totally independent of the military government. Present at the secret meeting were also Major-General Shehu Musa Yar'Adua, the chief of staff supreme headquarters, who was Obasanjo's second-in-command, Rear-Admiral Michael Adelanwa, the chief of naval staff, Air-Commodore John Yisa Doko, the chief of air staff; Alhaji Mohammed D.Yusuff, the inspector-general of police; Dr. Augustine Nnamani, attorney-general of the federation; Allison Akene Ayida, the secretary to the federal government and Yaya Abubakar the permanent secretary (political) of the cabinet office, who took the minutes. The meeting eventually agreed that FEDECO could interpret the law as it deemed fit, adding that it was too late to amend the law. [19]

In the afternoon of Thursday, August 16, 1979, after waiting for five days, Nigerians heard the unfamiliar voice of F.O.L. Menkiti, the presidential returning officer, on the radio. Hitherto, Chief Ani had made all formal public pronouncements on behalf of the commission. Menkiti shared Akinjide's interpretation of the electoral law, and he declared: 'The Federal Electoral Commission considers that in the absence of any legal explanation or guidance in the electoral decree, it has no alternative than to give the phrase 'at least two-thirds of all the states in the federation' in section 34a subsection 1(c)(iii) of the electoral decree (the constitution had not come into force, and the election was conducted with identical decree) the ordinary meaning which applies to it. In the circumstances, the candidate who scored at least one-quarter of the votes cast in 12 states and one-quarter of two-thirds, that is at least one sixth of the votes cast in the 13th state satisfies the requirement of the subsection. Accordingly, Alhaji Shehu Shagari is hereby declared president of the Federal Republic of Nigeria.'

Predictably, FEDECO's interpretation angered the other four parties and they were thrown into initial confusion. On Monday, August 20, four days after Menkiti's statement, Dr. Azikiwe, Chief Awolowo and Alhaji Waziri addressed a joint-press conference at Eko Holiday Inn, Lagos, where they denounced the result and called on the federal government to intervene and annul it. Azikiwe, who read a prepared speech on behalf of the three said: 'This declaration is a blatant and deliberate attempt to deprive the people of this country of their right to elect a president of their choice. It is more! It is a brazen act of fraud on the entire nation and an unwarranted assault on democratic principles. The decision of FEDECO that 'two-thirds of 19 states' of the federation means anything less than 13 states is fraudulent, dishonest, and is completely unsupportable by law and common sense. This decision has already exposed our great nation to public ridicule'.

FEDECO's decision was hailed in many quarters too. *West Africa*, the venerable London-based weekly newsmagazine declared in an editorial: 'The resulting declaration of a definite winner has come as a great relief to Nigeria. It means that the man with the greatest popular support and with the most widespread popular support will be the new president; the voice of the people has been heard. Chief Michael Ani and his colleagues deserve congratulations on what was a difficult and brave decision.'[20]

In the flush of victory, the NPN did not lose its head. It recognised that despite the public show of solidarity between Awo, Zik and Waziri, they were really strange bed fellows who were only united by common adversity. The weakest link in the triumvirate was Zik. During the bitter campaign, Awo was believed to have supported FEDECO's attempt to disqualify Zik and Aminu Kano over their tax problems, and Zik's quarrel with Waziri too was common knowledge. Moreover, many people believed that the NPP had no other reason for existence except to have a share in the pork barrel. Claude Ake, a political economist, said of the party: 'A subclass foot-loose in search of opportunity, the NPP is not noted for strong passions or ideological purity, and its loyalty is fitful. The NPP wants a share of federal power somehow because political power is a critical part of the economic base of its leaders. Besides, the NPP fears that it would be quickly dissipated as a political force if it remains out of office.' [21]

A day after Zik addressed the press on the rejection of the result at the Eko Holiday Inn, some members of his party, with his mandate, commenced a meeting with a delegation of the victorious NPN in the same hotel. The three-day meeting presided over by Tarka, who had recently won a seat into the Senate, was the final summation of series of consultation that had been going on for weeks. Others on the NPN side were Chief Toye Coker, Professor G.A. Odenigwe and Mr. Denis Ukume. Leading the NPP delegation was Chief Matthew Mbu, a First Republic minister. Others were Chief R.B.K. Okafor, Mr. Chimezie Ikeazor and Chief Adeniran Ogunsanya. After three days of hankering, the NPP agreed to become the junior partner in government, share ministerial and board appointments, and bargain for a better pension for Zik.

As promised, Chief Awolowo took his case to the Election Petition Tribunal, challenging the declaration of Shagari as president-elect. The tribunal, presided over by Justice B.O. Kazeem, had as members A.I. Aseme and A.B. Wali; all justices of the Federal Court of Appeal. Incidentally, Kazeem, a Yoruba from Lagos, was the leading prosecution counsel of the Balewa government during the trial of Chief Awolowo for treasonable felony in 1962. Awolowo lost his case at the tribunal and duly appealed to the Supreme Court.

It was at this time of fast-moving events that the highest judicial office in the land changed hands. Nigerians suddenly learnt that Sir Danley Arthur Alexander, a West Indian jurist from the Island of Saint Lucia, who started his career in the Western Region as solicitor-general and permanent secretary, ministry of justice, 1960-

63, and had been chief justice of the federation since 1975, was going on retirement. Under the Supreme Court's regulations, he would have been due for retirement in January 1980, but it was said that by the terms of his contract, being a foreigner, he had to leave in 1979. On Tuesday, August 21, a day after Chief Awolowo filed his appeal, Atanda Fatayi-Williams, a judge of the Supreme Court and a Lagosian like Kazeem, was sworn-in as chief justice of the federation to replace Alexander.

Justice Fatayi-Williams was not a new man to election petitions. He was appointed a judge in the former Western Region October 7, 1960 and had risen steadily on the bench until his crowning glory in 1979. During the First Republic, eleven petitioners of the AG challenging the election of Akintola's NNDP candidates during the controversial 1964 federal election, had their petitions dismissed in his court with substantial costs.[22]   After the 1965 regional elections, Fatai-Williams had sent a congratulatory letter to Akintola 'not so much on the results of the regional elections about which I have no doubts whatsoever, but on what is certainly going to be a most crushing and dramatic defeat of the forces of disunity and disintegration.'[23]

All these have been interpreted by Awoists that Fatai-Williams was one of Chief Awolowo's committed opponents hiding under the sober gown of a judge. After his appointment, Chief Awolowo sent Fatai-Williams a congratulatory letter, saying 'I wish you all the best, and pray that God grant you more than ever before the wisdom and courage to meet the demands of your high office.' The new chief justice also received similar congratulatory letters from many eminent Nigerians including Dr. Azikiwe.

The Fatai-Williams Supreme Court dismissed the petition of Awo, affirming that two-thirds of 19 states was twelve two-third states. In a bizarre twist, the Supreme Court then ruled that its judgment in this case shall not serve as precedent in the future.

Chief Awolowo, having lost in the highest court in the land, took his case to the court of public opinion. In an address to the UPN congress in December 1979, Chief Awolowo alleged that Fatai-Williams was chosen to become the chief justice because he was the choice of Shagari out of three candidates presented to him by Obasanjo. The former head of state, now in retirement in Abeokuta, the state capital fired back, asserting that it was the defunct Supreme Military Council, SMC, that appointed Fatai-Williams.

Chief Awolowo returned the fire: 'You and Alhaji Shagari considered three candidates — Chief Rotimi Williams, Dr. Justice Udo Udoma and Mr. Justice Fatai-Williams. The Nigerian public should be told why you left it to Alhaji Shehu Shagari to make a discretionary choice from among these three giants of the Bar and Bench, and then used the SMC as rubber-stamp for Alhaji Shagari's decision.'

Fatai-Williams later contended that he was unaware of any consultation with Shagari over his appointment as chief justice. 'I was not aware nor was I told of any consultation between General Obasanjo and Alhaji Shagari over my appointment,' said Fatai-Williams. 'Until Chief Awolowo actually filed his election petition on August 20, 1979, which was the very last day on which he could have filed it, General Obasanjo could not assume that any of the unsuccessful candidates would petition against the result. It was therefore, natural that he would discuss various matters concerning the handing over of power during those ten days with somebody who, at that time, had emerged as the president-elect. The government of the country could not and should not wait until Chief Awolowo and the other candidates had made up their minds whether they were going to file an election petition or not.' [25]

Apart from Shagari, Obasanjo and Fatai-Williams, another person singled out for attack by the UPN hierarchy was Chief Ani, the FEDECO boss, who curiously maintained his peace with the same eagerness with which he hitherto spoke to the press.

For Awolowo and his supporters, the loss of the presidency was devastating. They had invested everything and were totally convinced that they were on the threshold of triumph. With the 1979 defeat, it was time again to work for the future when the nation would not repeat 'the mistake of 1979'. Said Bode Olowoporoku, one of the leading newbreed in the party: 'Without prejudice and basing our objective conclusions on the facts before this nation, Chief Obafemi Awolowo stands out outstandingly among the contemporary leaders of Nigeria to lead this great nation and indeed he is THE LEADER of the revolutionary Nigeria that promises to emerge anew.'[26]

Yet despite the songs of lamentations and recriminations, the UPN did not do badly in the big league. To NPN's seven governors, the UPN had five, the NPP secured three and both the GNPP and the PRP had two governors each. UPN also won 28 seats to NPN's 36 in the Senate. The NPP had 16, PRP had seven and the GNPP won eight. But losing the presidency for the UPN made all the difference.

Dr. Azikiwe, having secured and sealed the pact between his party and the NPN, sent a congratulatory message to Shagari and urged Nigerians to accept the verdict of the Supreme Court and support the new president. On October 1, 1979, Shagari, in the midst of thousands of Nigerians who had thronged the Tafawa Balewa Square, Lagos, was sworn-in as the first executive president of Nigeria by Chief Justice Fatai-Williams. Obasanjo and his junta had kept their promise. With his 33.8 per cent of the popular votes, Shagari could barely be said to have scored a pass mark, but he was the best in the class. On the eve of his departure from power, Obasanjo amended the constitution, abolished the electoral college and substituting it, with a run-off election to resolve a tie in the presidential contest.

Shagari was magnanimous in victory. Immediately on assuming office, he sent letters to other parties, inviting them to join his 'national government'. On Wednesday, October 3, the UPN Central Working Committee met in Awo's residence at Apapa to discuss Shagari's offer. The UPN accepted the offer in principle because 'no patriotic Nigerian would refuse an offer to take part in rebuilding the country politically, economically and morally'.[27] But UPN's condition for friendship was an impossible one. It asked Shagari to adopt the UPN programmes of free education and others. It proposed that the two sides should meet on these programmes.

'It is not impossible that your party has such a plan,' replied the UPN. 'But where it is desired that political parties with divergent concepts and plans should work together on one and the same building, the first obvious thing to do is to arrange for them to meet and try, if possible to harmonise their building concepts and plans. In other words, the first thing to think about are the minimum programmes, the economic and political objectives or goals which the parties would pursue, if and when they agree to participate.' Rejecting the UPN condition, Adamu Ciroma, the NPN National Secretary, regretted that the UPN was insisting on its own programmes. Both the GNPP and the PRP also refused the offer to participate in the federal government.

From that moment on, both the UPN and NPN, doomed to a common destiny, followed parallel paths to attain it.

4

A Spell Of Fair Weather

The defeat of Awolowo in the presidential race did not terribly affect the heady spirit of the new men in the saddle in Akure, capital of Ondo State. October 1, 1979 was Shagari's day in Lagos; it was Ajasin's day too in Akure. At 71, Ajasin assumed office as the oldest head of government in Nigerian history. His head was covered with a carpet of rich grey hair, he looked frail, about five feet seven inches tall, with deep-set eyes. He was not a formidable man and unlike Awolowo, whose very presence evoked vitality and authority, Ajasin was the picture of a man past his prime. By contrast, Akin Omoboriowo, the new deputy governor, was a vigorous man of 47, alert, spare, and rightly a man of the moment.

But the 1979 campaign had revealed an astounding and unexpected reservoir of energy in the septuagenarian Governor Ajasin. He toured the whole state, went into every town and city; hamlet and settlement and spent two weeks in the riverine areas reaching the electorate by boat. Therefore, Ajasin, during the campaign, had proved the legendary Zik right: old men can still kick. It seemed in those heady days of October that Ajasin and his young deputy had found the perfect chemistry. The litmus test for this mutual faith was the appointment of commissioners, board members and other top government officials. In doing this, Ajasin relied heavily on his young deputy.

Immediately Omoboriowo became the deputy governor- elect,

58

top members of the UPN looking for positions in the in-coming administration, hurried to Ijero Ekiti, hometown of Omoboriowo, because it was clear that he would be very influential within the new dispensation. Ajasin was willing to keep to the spirit of his agreement with Awolowo that the new cabinet should contain more younger men. Therefore many read the handwriting on the wall that the best way to get to the bosom of Ajasin was through Omoboriowo. Out of the 12 commissioners that were eventually appointed, eight were men suggested by the deputy governor. Some of these people got into the cabinet over those favoured initially by the governor. Professor Samuel Akin Agboola, retired professor of geography from Obafemi Awolowo University, OAU, (then University of Ife), from Odo-Owa, who became commissioner for agriculture and rural development, was one of those suggested by Omoboriowo. Others who came in by the grace of the deputy governor were Mr. Ojo Babatunde (employment and establishment), Mr. Olawumi Falodun, (health), Dr. Michael Bode Olowoporoku (economic planning and statistics), Dr. Nathaniel Falaye Aina (education), Chief Segun Adegoke (lands and survey) Mrs. Alice Mobolaji Osomo, (trade, industries and co-operatives) and Mr. Ebun Ogunyimika (youths and sports).

All these men and the lone woman were people who had served the party since the days of the Committee of Friends. They were also competent people with proven ability in their own rights. The horse-trading and wranglings that went into their appointments was a prelude to the bitter strifes of the future. In making these appointments, Ajasin not only satisfied the dichotomy of Ekiti and non-Ekitis in Ondo State, he also took cognizance of the diversity of local governments.

Omoboriowo had met Adegoke, one of the commissioners at a magistrate court in Ondo town early in 1976. He was impressed by the way the young lawyer argued his case that morning, and after the day's sitting, approached Adegoke. It was there and then that their friendship started as Adegoke became a member of the

Committee of Friends and later the same year, was a member of the 25-man entourage that followed Awo to Ghana. Adegoke, born September 29, 1941, at 38 in 1979, was already a prosperous lawyer. Handsome and well-groomed, he was flashy and showy, and did not appeal to the conservative taste of Ajasin who preferred another candidate from another town in the Ondo local government area. But Omoboriowo mobilised Ondo people and persuaded them to support the candidacy of Adegoke.

Agboola, from the same local government as Omoboriowo did not pose much problem and his candidacy sailed through. Leaders of the party in Ado-Ekiti prevailed on Omoboriowo to back the candidacy of Babatunde, their son, though the governor had preferred S.O. Ogunlusi, a medical doctor from the same town. Ogunlusi lost. Similar situation occurred in Akoko area where the party leaders preferred Adefarati, although Ajasin had earlier wanted Kayode Ogunleye, a lawyer. The candidacy of Olawumi Falodun and Ogunyimika did not pose much problem either. Chief Tewe, one of the fathers of the party from Ilaje Eseodo, suggested the name of Osomo to Omoboriowo who successfully sold the suggestion to Chief Ajasin.

The most problematic choice was that of Dr. Olowoporoku from Ilawe who was opposed by his uncle, Phillip Akomolafe. Olowoporoku, had a doctorate degree in economics from the University of Manchester, England. He was introduced to the Committee of Friends by Akomolafe, his uncle, a durable politician and Action Grouper from the sixties. Akomolafe regarded Olowoporoku as his own son and it was he who introduced the latter to Omoboriowo in the early seventies. Then Akomolafe had brought Olowoporoku to OAU seeking employment for him as a graduate assistant. Akomolafe was Omoboriowo's teacher at Saint Peter's Teachers College, Akure, and he had been following the progress of his former student, who was now a senior assistant registrar. Olowoporoku was employed. He later brought the young man into politics. Now that a commissioner was to be taken from Ilawe,

Akomolafe felt he was the right candidate and not his ward. A meeting was later held in Akure to resolve the issue and the elderly man was persuaded that it was the policy of the party not to keep men of Ajasin's generation in the cabinet.

Those who were Ajasin's direct appointees into the cabinet were Chief Fasoranti, (finance), Chief Adebayo Adefarati (local government and chieftaincy affairs), Mr. Olufemi Ilori, (works and transport), and Mr. Joseph Kayode Aderibigbe, a retired chief magistrate who became Attorney-general and commissioner for justice. Omoboriowo himself was to oversee all parastatals and chieftaincy affairs. In addition to the 12 commissioners, Ajasin also appointed four special advisers including the distinguished economist, Professor Aluko, who was made economic adviser.

Omoboriowo was also instrumental to the appointment of Professor Christopher Sunday Ola, a lawyer and chartered accountant, as the secretary to the government. The whole cabinet was virtually assembled during the period when Ajasin was leading a government-in-waiting before October 1, 1979. While swearing-in the new commissioners on October 8, 1979, Ajasin gave a piece of advice to his team whose grave import was only to be felt in future. 'In taking decisions, we would be guided by the overall interest of the people,' he said. 'Sectionalism will be discouraged and objectivity will be the hallmark of our deliberations'. [28]

The new deputy governor was also instrumental in the appointments of many board chairmen and members to government parastatals, including the Odu'a Group of Companies, which was jointly owned by Ogun, Oyo and Ondo states. Lawrence Agunbiade, a wealthy businessman and insurance broker, and one of the new pillars of the party, was made the chairman of Wema Bank, one of the banks of the Odu'a Group, through the influence of Omoboriowo.

Early in the life of the new administration, an incident happened that was to eat into the tremendous influence of Omoboriowo over the governor. One Sunday afternoon, Chief Ajasin sent for his young deputy. It was an unusual call since Ajasin preferred to keep Sunday free from official chores. Omoboriowo suspected that something untoward might be in the offing. He therefore went to the home of Professor Aluko, discussed his suspicion with him and persuaded the special adviser to accompany him to see Governor Ajasin. Aluko obliged.

When the two men got to the sprawling Government House, the old man had an interesting story to tell. Early that morning, a well-known party stalwart from Owo, Ajasin's hometown, had called on the governor. The caller came with elderly members of his family. When the governor asked him his mission, he said he had come with his family to thank the governor for making him the chairman of Nigerian/Romanian Wood Industries, NIROWI, a company jointly owned by the Ondo, Federal and Romanian governments, in Ondo town. The man showed Ajasin his letter of appointment. 'I am surprised,' Ajasin told Omoboriowo and Aluko. 'I know the man very well. He is a strong supporter of our party, but he cannot be chairman of NIROWI because he is an illiterate.'

Omoboriowo, who was in charge of all parastatals, apologised for making the appointment. He said he had thought the man was a university graduate. Ajasin asked them to suggest a replacement. After some names were mentioned, Ajasin then asked: 'What of Ariyo?' Ayo Ariyo, a retired lieutenant-colonel, and civil war hero, was from Ipoti Ekiti in the same local government with Omoboriowo. In 1976, he and Omoboriowo had contested for the chairmanship of the local council and Omoboriowo had defeated him by a wide margin. But the military governor then, Wing-Commander Ita David Ikpeme, who had the final say on the appointment of chairmen, uneasy with the Awoist credentials of Omoboriowo, had passed him over to pick Ariyo as chairman. 'Ariyo ran a very good local government. I think we should give him the job,' Ajasin said. Ariyo was subsequently appointed chairman of NIROWI.

After this incident, Ajasin now guarded his prerogative to appoint chairmen of parastatals, though he still left the appointments of other board members in the hands of his trusted deputy and a special committee headed by Ade Adefarati. Though most of the recommendations of this committee on board membership were upheld by the governor, he would not shift ground on that of the chairmen. One of the most protracted was the appointment of Wumi Adegbonmire, who became chairman of Ondo State Investment Corporation, Akure. Ajasin wanted to make him political adviser, but Adegbonmire, retired managing director of OAU bookshop, Ile-Ife, foundation member of the party and well-known freelance journalist from Akure, wanted a more substantial job. Fasoranti, the leader of the party in Akure local government, also believed that Adegbonmire deserved more. With the support of Omoboriowo, Ajasin yielded ground to the pressures from his lieutenants and made Adegbonmire chairman of the Investment Corporation.

It was becoming apparent now so early in the new administration that other competing centres of influence were emerging, apart from the deputy governor. Under the new American-style Presidential Constitution, the state governor was the state government. Power flows from him and all authorities were used in his name. Unlike the British system which Nigerians inherited at independence where the premier was only first among equals, the presidential system permitted no such niceties. The governor alone in his cabinet was still a majority. While the positions of commissioners and special advisers were clearer, that of the deputy governor was full of ambivalence. While he was elected on the same ticket with the governor, the latter was not obliged to assign him any job and he might well content himself with playing the role of a loyal valet. His main role was to be the governor-in-waiting in case the governor was incapacitated, impeached, or died. Therefore, the position of the deputy governor was one of prestige, without power nor responsibility.

Despite these apparent constitutional limitations, Omoboriowo believed that he deserved more if only because of the role he played during the period of the Committee of Friends. He knew also that the situation was not exactly the same in other UPN- controlled states. In Oyo State, where Chief Bola Ige had emerged as the new UPN governor, Chief Sunday Afolabi, the new deputy governor, was almost on an equal footing with the governor. Afolabi, like Omoboriowo, was in charge of all parastatals, but unlike Omoboriowo, he was truly in charge. His own governor did not change tempo right in the middle of the journey. Afolabi not only nominated all the board members, but also all the chairmen of corporations. In the other UPN states of Bendel, Ogun and Lagos, the governors there did not give any ambiguity about who were in charge and the deputy governors resigned themselves to their subordinate roles.

Omoboriowo decided to do something about the new twist of events. He wrote Ajasin a secret memorandum ten days into the life of the government, October 10, 1979, pleading with him that party leaders were becoming sensitive about the manner the governor was making the new appointments into the statutory boards. He suggested that as a strategy of shielding himself (Ajasin) from the direct pressures of the party members and lobbyists, he should constitute another committee (apart from the Adefarati committee) to deal with board appointments. 'It occurred to me,' Omoboriowo stated in his letter, 'after a long introspection that as a strategy, it would be very helpful that before making impending board appointments into statutory corporations, which are the exclusive preserve of the governor, we constitute a mini-committee of the state's party executive'. Omoboriowo then suggested four other party leaders, apart from himself, who should constitute this special committee. These were the governor, Chief Fasoranti, Mr. Falodun and Mr. Ogunyimika. The governor ignored the advice.

The import of Ajasin's change of style was not lost on Omoboriowo who hitherto was said, with some exaggeration, to be ruling while the old man was reigning. It was clear that Ajasin, now firmly in the saddle, had become open to more pieces of advice than when he was a mere gubernatorial candidate or governor-elect. One of the more potent sources of official advice was Chief Emuleomo, whom Chief Ajasin inherited from the military regime as head of the civil service. Emuleomo, an astute and experienced administrator and career civil servant, was said to have been surprised that Ajasin surrounded himself mostly with men who held their offices to the fortuitous suggestion of his younger deputy. It did not help matters that Emuleomo and Professor Ola, the new secretary to the government did not see eye-to-eye on many matters, and it was becoming increasingly clear that Emuleomo was having the greater influence. The post of secretary was a purely political appointment. Hitherto the head of service had combined the two functions, but the military had favoured a separation of the two jobs. It however, also bred competition and envy. Professor Ola was dropped suddenly in May 1980 and Chief M.A. Popoola, a former permanent secretary, was appointed in his place.

By late 1979, Omoboriowo had started complaining to some members of Ajasin's government that Chief Ajasin was side-stepping him in taking major decisions. He told this group that even when Ajasin agreed to re-engage those permanent secretaries inherited from the military, the governor did not inform him. Under the new constitution, the permanent secretaries held offices at the pleasure of the governor, though they were career civil servants like the head of service who was their leader. Omoboriowo also did not take kindly to the fact that the re-appointment and re-assignment of the permanent secretaries were announced by Chief Emuleomo and not Professor Ola, his friend.

The first meeting of the pro-Omoboriowo commissioners was in Chief Fasoranti's house. At that time, it was just a spontaneous reaction and not an attempt at conspiracy. Those who were present were Olowoporoku, Falodun, Babatunde, Ogunyimika and Aina, apart from the host, Fasoranti. They knew that Fasoranti was highly respected by Ajasin and his words carried a lot of weight. They recited Omoboriowo's complaints to Fasoranti who promised to speak to Ajasin and report back to the group. Falodun was then delegated to get the feedback from Fasoranti. After some few days,

Falodun reported that Fasoranti was avoiding him. There was no feedback from Fasoranti.

The Omoboriowo group, *(Omoboriowo said he was not aware that the Ekiti commissioners were meeting until 1981)* therefore decided to be meeting without Fasoranti. At that time in 1979, Olowoporoku was yet to get his own official quarters as a commissioner. He was therefore staying at Green Spring Chalet, one of the official guest houses of the government. It was completely fenced round and the high walls shielded the compound from inquisitive eyes. Those now attending the meetings were Olowoporoku, Babatunde, Falodun, Agboola, Aina, Ilori and Ogunyimika. All of them were from Ekiti, except Ogunyimika who was from Idanre. Explained Olowoporoku: 'The meeting then was to make sure how we advise Ajasin to make use of his deputy.' The tactics of the group was to meet whenever Ogunyimika or Falodun brought a complaint from Omoboriowo. These two men were the contacts between the deputy governor and the group.

The choice of the two men was deliberate, since both were men of considerable weight in the party apart from just being commissioners. Olawumi Falodun, born September 24, 1927 at Araromi Ekiti, was a member of the AG's federal executive from 1964-66. An old principal like Chief Ajasin and a graduate of the University of Legon, Ghana, he was also familiar and friendly with Chief Awolowo. A deeply religious man, much given to introspection, Falodun was also the UPN Ondo State secretary. Ebun Ogunyimika, like Falodun, was an old politician and he was AG member of the House of Representatives from 1964-66. A man of limited education, with only secondary school training, Ogunyimika was typical of the UPN barons: self-made, ebullient, and a man that cannot be ignored. Wealthy and generous, he was the founder and proprietor of Ebun Ogunyimika Comprehensive High School, Atosin-Idanre. Like Falodun too, Ogunyimika was also a member of the state's executive committee of the party, being the UPN treasurer.

When Omoboriowo complained to these two men, they would bring the report to the group. After deliberations, the group would then decide what advice to offer the governor or other line of action to be taken to favour the deputy governor. Falodun would then table the group's decision before Ajasin, as if it was his own personal advice to the governor. When Olowoporoku was given his own quarters, the members started rotating the meeting among the participating commissioners in their residences.

It was not long before the group suffered setbacks. Firstly, Aina, who was also a lecturer at OAU where Omoboriowo was an administrator for 10 years, dropped out. Also people started noticing the unusual congregation of these commissioners, especially their colleagues who were left out: Fasoranti, Osomo, Adegoke, Aderibigbe and Adefarati. Curiously too, all the commissioners brought into the cabinet by Omoboriowo, except Adegoke, Aina, and Osomo were now involved, and apart from Ogunyimika, they were all Ekitimen. Sinister motives were read into these conclaves and it was not long before the governor got wind of it. As if to confirm the worst, the participants would toe identical lines at cabinet meetings while Chief Omoboriowo would often sit throughout heated debates, with a blank face, uttering very few words.

By January 1980, while this clandestine politicking was going on, all was still well from all appearances. Chief Omoboriowo and all the other young men in the government still addressed Chief Ajasin as papa, the affectionate honorific title that the governor shared with Chief Awolowo among party faithfuls. Omoboriowo was still Ajasin's closest comrade-in-arms, from all indications; but underneath, a fierce battle was brewing. The governor was now reading motives into every action of his deputy. Soon after he was given charge of all parastatals, Omoboriowo had made very visible tours of the dam projects being constructed by the state government under the glare of klieg lights and media blitz. With the unmasking of the Ekiti commissioners' meeting, this was now interpreted as an attempt to portray Omoboriowo as a man of action to the public, vis-a-vis, the governor.

Whether Omoboriowo understood the likely consequences of these little games or not, it was not clear. Early in 1980, Adegbonmire, the chairman of the Investment Corporation, wrote to the deputy governor asking him to come and commission the Crumb Rubber Factory, at Araromi, on a certain date. Omoboriowo minuted on the file to the governor: 'Your Excellency. Above is for your information.' That was the last he saw of the file, though the factory directly belonged to his schedule, he being in charge of all parastatals. The next time he heard about the crumb factory was an announcement on Ondo State Broadcasting Corporation, OSBC, that the governor was going to commission the factory. Of course, he was not invited to the ceremony.

The Second Republic spell of fair weather in Ondo State thus lasted for only three months.

5

Clash Of Wills

Six months into the life of the civilian administration, it was apparent to discerning observers that a schism was developing within the new Ondo State government. The cause of this was the manifestation of Omoboriowo's ambition so early in the tenure of the new government, according to Ajasin's loyalists, while Omoboriowo's group accused the governor of intolerance, and dislike for the majority Ekiti people. Whatever was the reason, it was clear that the growing rift harboured the promise of a battle royal. By the time Ajasin woke up to the perceived threat of his deputy-governor, Omoboriowo had built a formidable network of power and influence not only within Ajasin's cabinet but also in the Ondo State House of Assembly, the civil service and other sectors. Therefore, if the governor was intent on taking on his deputy governor, then he was in for a long and protracted struggle.

Because of his advanced age, there was an understanding that Ajasin would spend only one term in office, though there was no agreement to this effect between the governor and his deputy. It was the belief that while Ajasin would step out in honour, he would be given a generous pension. There was no doubt in anybody's mind that the person to succeed Ajasin as governor of Ondo State, had to come from Ekitiland. While the gubernatorial ambition would have been a long shot for Omoboriowo in the pre-1979 days, since Fasanmi and Akintoye were more formidable Ekiti candidates, with his wearing the deputy-governor's toga, he was now in a vantage position. But Ajasin was determined to leave power only on his own terms and certainly not in disgrace. Omoboriowo said in perceiving him a threat, the governor was misjudging him since he never originally planned to be deputy-governor or governor. Said he: 'My original ambition was to be a member of the Federal House of Representatives and practise law side by side, but God decided otherwise'.

In the battle of wits and wills, it was Ajasin that made the first false and almost disastrous move. Early in 1980, during a cabinet session, Ajasin made a remark that members should allow flexibility in discussing issues concerning the inherent dichotomy of the Ekiti and non-Ekiti. He said he did not believe that the 1963 national census, on which the Ekiti based their numerical superiority over the rest was correct and it should not be referred to, in economic and social matters, like a holy writ. 'How can anybody believe that Ilawe-Ekiti is more populous than Ondo town?', asked the governor. Ilawe, by the 1963 census, had 80,833 people while Ondo had 74,343. By 1980, there had been a tremendous demographic shift which benefited principally four towns in the state: Akure, Ondo, Owo, and Ado-Ekiti. By this time, Ondo town was now at least three times as populous as Ilawe Ekiti. Olowoporoku, who is from Ilawe then replied the governor: 'We cannot now question the veracity of that census since it was on the basis of the same census by which you were elected to office, Your Excellency. Even on the national level there would be confusion if you pursue your theory further. Everybody knows that Kano State cannot even contain half the population of Oyo State, yet until another census is done, Kano cannot be denied its right. By the same token, Ilawe cannot be denied its right until another census, acceptable to us, is done'.

There were hot exchanges in the council and the meeting ended on a less than cordial note. Though Executive Council meetings were supposed to be confidential, that night several of Omoboriowo's supporters were in the official quarters of the Ondo State House of Assembly, ODHA, at Alagbaka Estate, about half a kilometre from the Government House, to discuss the issue of the day. Their verdict was that they were now sure that Ajasin hated the Ekiti. The suspicion had been there all along when Ajasin had said that the four big towns, Ondo, Akure, Owo and Ado-Ekiti would be the focus of industrial development. Among these towns, only Ado is Ekiti. This tendency was regarded as a fall back to the old Western Region where Chief Awolowo concentrated government industrial projects in Ibadan, the regional capital and Lagos and Ikeja. While this could be defensible on economic terms, it was hardly politically expedient. Awolowo, coming from the small town of Ikenne, could propound economic logic to back his choice of Lagos and Ibadan, since both cities were even not always politically friendly to him, but Ajasin, even with identical economic arguments would elicit cynicism since his hometown of Owo was conspicuously in the big league.

When the arguments on the distribution of population became public knowledge, it created a big furore. Ajasin was on the defensive and he sent Chief Adegoke, who was also the UPN Publicity Secretary, to plead his case to the people. It was indeed a case poorly pleaded as the babel of voices from the state's assembly, joined the cacophony. When Chief Awolowo met with the governor later, he rebuked Chief Ajasin for his impolitic remark, but this did not banish the ghost of this singular *faux pas* which continue to haunt Ajasin to the end of the Second Republic. The population and parity issue between the sides of the Ondo State's divide was to colour all debates and became the constant predicate of all public pronouncements.

What created more tension in 1980 was the attempt to create more local government councils. The UPN during the campaign, had promised to create more local governments councils and now it was time to redeem that promise. Chief Ajasin set up a committee (to vet the deluge of requests for new local government areas,) which was headed by Chief Adefarati, the commissioner for local government and chieftaincy matters. The six-man committee's report was never made public, but many of the Ekiti members of the ODHA perceived even the act of setting up the committee which had only two Ekiti members as an anti-Ekiti move. Chief Ajasin himself received delegations from many towns and villages demanding for local governments of their own. He was almost exclusively occupied with these demands for about four weeks in his office. Ajasin made it known that the creation of new local governments would be based on the wishes of the people as the sole determinant.

At the end of the day, some of the requests were downright ridiculous. Ita-Ogbolu, a town that can hardly be distinguished from Iju, its very close neighbour, proposed to be a separate local government. Owo town came with a proposal to have it split into four while Ilawe wanted two local governments. Adefarati compiled all these requests which were presented to the governor and were to be tabled before the state's executive council. Several of the Ekiti commissioners suspected that Ajasin, with the local government instrument, might destroy the parity between Ekiti and non-Ekiti side of the state. Hitherto, Ekiti controlled eight of the seventeen local government areas in the state. On the whole, there were more than 100 requests for new local governments.

A day before the Adefarati report was presented to cabinet, Chief Omoboriowo presented a paper to the governor, arguing that the creation of new local governments would create more problems. He therefore suggested that the 17 local government structure be maintained for the time being. Chief Ajasin was impressed. Ajasin begged him not to distribute copies to the other commissioners and Omoboriowo agreed, though by this time, his supporters in government already had copies of the paper. Despite this brief rapport, the issue of creation of local governments continued to generate controversy. The rivalries between the governor and his deputy also continued.

Ajasin continued to cut the wings of his deputy and he remained, only in name, the overseer of parastatals and chieftaincy matters. In April 1980, Chief Okeya, the Special Adviser on chieftaincy matters, minuted to Omoboriowo, as the man overseeing chieftaincy matters, asking him to come and present the instrument of office to the newly selected Alare of Are-Ekiti in Ekiti Central local government. When Omoboriowo passed the file to Ajasin, informing him that he would be going on a certain date, the governor simply ignored him and ordered Adefarati, to go and present the instrument of office to the new oba.

Embarrassed by the governor's action, Chief Okeya spoke to Ajasin after Omoboriowo had complained. It was then that the governor retreated and said Omoboriowo could proceed to Are-Ekiti. But Omoboriowo in turn, refused to carry out the new order and Olawumi Falodun the Commissioner for Health finally presented the instrument of office to the Alare in June 1980.

This testy relationship continued throughout the life of the government. Ajasin also moved against those he believed were supporters of Omoboriowo in government. Professor Ola, the Secretary to the State Government, one of the key people who came to the administration on the ticket of Omoboriowo, was unceremoniously removed in May 1980 and Chief M.A. Popoola, a former permanent secretary, was appointed in his place. Another person who was removed early was Dr. Olowoporoku, the youngest man in the cabinet who was commissioner for Economic Planning. Olowoporoku was a fanatical supporter of Chief Omoboriowo and one of the principal initiators of the Ekiti commissioners' meetings. He crossed the governor's way on every issue and he could barely conceal his contempt for Ajasin whom he accused of being 'too old and parochial' to govern Ondo State. Olowoporoku was accused of taking sides openly against the government in a chieftaincy dispute.

Olowoporoku's exit from government was not without its dramas. Sometime in 1980, he went to convey his wife from Obafemi Awolowo University (then University of Ife), and while they were travelling between Ondo and Akure, they heard the siren of the governor's motorcade and Olowoporoku's driver hurriedly left the highway so that the governor and his entourage could pass. But in the swerving of cars, there was a terrible crash and all the three cars in the governor's entourage were damaged. Ajasin, though shocked, was apparently not wounded and Olowoporoku volunteered his car for the governor to continue his journey to Akure. As they were about to move, Ajasin, who in the confusion did not see Olowoporoku, asked: 'Whose car is this?' When he was told that it was Olowoporoku's car, he refused to ride in it, and one of the cars in his entourage which was not greatly damaged took him to Akure. That day, the rumour spread through Akure that the Ekitis, after waiting vainly for the old governor to die, had finally set Olowoporoku to kill him. Olowoporoku's driver, who was accused of having caused the accident, was arrested by the police and later released. Olowoporoku, in the company of his wife and with the help of Chief Omoboriowo and other Ekiti leaders later appealed to Ajasin that there was no plot to kill him and that certainly what happened on Ondo road was merely an accident.

In January 1981, Ajasin decided to remove Olowoporoku whom he accused of disloyalty and anti-party activities. He called Omoboriowo and informed him of his decision and that the following day the dismissal would be announced. That night Chief Omoboriowo went round the party leaders in the state, asking them to come and prevail on Ajasin not to sack Olowoporoku. Among those who spoke to Ajasin the following morning on the issue were Chief Akerele, Chief Babatola and Chief Tewe. Ajasin was prevailed upon then but Olowoporoku knew his days were numbered in government. By August 1981 when Ajasin finally removed him from the cabinet, Olowoporoku was prepared.

In December 1980, Ajasin proceeded on leave. There were rumours that he was critically ill. At 72, many people were ready to speculate that the rigour of the governorship job was now taking its toll on Ajasin. Before he left, Omoboriowo insisted that he should be sworn-in as acting governor, but Ajasin refused. Ajasin said since he had been sworn-in as deputy-governor on October 1, 1979, it was not necessary for him to be sworn-in again as acting governor. Omoboriowo's argument was that when Chief Bisi Onabanjo, the governor of Ogun State was going on leave in April, 1980, Chief Sesan Soluade, his deputy was sworn-in as acting-governor. Ajasin maintained his ground. It should be mentioned that the Ogun State example was not repeated either in Ogun State again or in any other state of the federation throughout the Second Republic.

Omoboriowo was bitter that he was not sworn-in as acting governor and when he paid his only visit to Chief Ajasin on his hospital bed at the Lagos University Teaching Hospital, LUTH, he was sulky. He later wrote a letter, full of bile, accusing the governor of undermining his regime as acting-governor of Ondo State. What irked him was that Ajasin was still being briefed on goings on in government especially on financial matters by people like Chief Reuben Fasoranti and Mrs. Osomo who were visiting Ajasin virtually everyday at LUTH.

In its February 21 edition of 1981, the *Daily Times* carried a front page story on Ajasin, headlined: Ajasin Critically Ill. The paper reported: 'Governor Michael Ajasin of Ondo State is very ill and a team of medical experts is now battling to save his life'.

Immediately the *Daily Times* story hit Akure, it caused panic. Many people now regarded it as a confirmation of the persistent rumour that Ajasin was dead. It was not unusual in Yorubaland for the announcement of the passing of an important public figure to be delayed for several days or even weeks. For the supporters of Ajasin, the only trump card they had was to keep Ajasin in the saddle, for despite everything, the advantage of incumbency was tremendous in the intra-party battle. Now if Ajasin's death should be confirmed, then everything was lost. Many legislators and other top notchers of the party, on hearing the rumour of Ajasin's passing away simply went to Omoboriowo's residence to congratulate him as the new governor. An embarrassed Omoboriowo had to tell them that there was no substance to the rumour. He said though it was true that Ajasin was in LUTH on admission, he was actually recovering. He later issued a statement on Ondo State radio, assuring the people that Ajasin was still alive.

Ajasin returned to Akure, Friday, February 27, 1981, to a tumultuous welcome. He did not spare Omoboriowo the length of his tongue, accusing him of wishing him dead, for having written him 'that wicked letter' on his sick bed. He said though it was true that he had an operation for haemorrhage, he was not close to death's door. Therefore, if Omoboriowo was waiting for his sudden death, he had a 'long time to wait'. It was becoming clear now that the gap between the old man and his erstwhile political son was becoming unbridgeable and neither side was willing to shift ground.

The division within the government was manifesting itself in every sphere of activity and it was causing confusion and division within the party. Immediately he came to power, Ajasin had promised in his maiden broadcast to establish a state university. When this became known, the lobbyists swung into action, everyone wanting the university in his own area. The greatest campaigners for this were the people of Ondo town and Ado-Ekiti. The Ondo felt the university rightly belonged to their town because it had all the facilities to play host to a new higher institution. It is the second largest city in the state, with modern houses comparable to the best in contemporary architecture. More than this, Ondo had the first secondary school in the state and the first higher institution, the Adeyemi College of Education, a college affiliated to the OAU. The Adeyemi College had more facilities than many of the new Nigerian universities and the Ondo were lobbying that this was a ready made piece for the state government to turn into the nucleus of its new university at minimal cost.

But Ado-Ekiti, too, had compelling arguments for wanting the university sited in Ekiti. The Ekiti, with Ado-Ekiti as their principal town, are known to have the largest number of home-grown professors in Nigeria. Before the introduction of free primary education in the former Western Region in 1955, the whole area had only one secondary school, — Christ School, Ado Ekiti, founded by the Anglican mission. Since then, however, their eagerness for education had changed the Nigerian landscape and there was no village or town without its cluster of primary schools and secondary schools. The Ekiti people also proffered the argument that their area had no comparable higher institution and that this time around, they rightly deserved the university.

As it was to be expected, the two sides carried their arguments to Chief Awolowo who later met with Chief Ajasin and had no trouble in persuading the latter on the desirability of siting the new university in Ekiti. Chief Awolowo argued that Ondo State people would be the losers if, in creating a new university, an old institution like Adeyemi College of Education was destroyed. He argued that the state could have both its own new university and still keep the Adeyemi College, a federal institution which in future could also become a full-fledge university of its own. To placate the other contenders, however, the new Ondo State University would operate a multi-campus system with the administrative headquarters in Ado-Ekiti. A committee to work out the modalities for this was set up under Professor Oladipo Akinkugbe, a highly respected consultant physician and teacher.

When the 16-man Akinkugbe committee's report was presented to the executive committee of the UPN in Akure, in July 1981, the meeting, presided over by Ajasin, ended in a deadlock since many of the members were dissatisfied with the distribution of the campuses. According to the Akinkugbe panel, the main campus would be in Ado-Ekiti, three colleges of education in Ikere-Ekiti, Ikare and Okitipupa, while the other colleges would be distributed in the following order: Law, Owo; Agriculture, Ikole-Ekiti; Medicine, Akure; Engineering, Ondo; and Science, Ijero-Ekiti. But the Akinkugbe panel placed the campuses at Akure, Ondo, Owo and Ado-Ekiti on phase one for the construction of the proposed university and this was greeted with resentment by those who wanted the campuses in their towns also placed on phase one. This was virtually impossible because of the anaemic state of the Ondo State economy.

Why was it so easy for the UPN to become divided so early in Ondo State and Ajasin to be losing grip before he barely settled down in the saddle? The UPN party constitution placed the governor in a formidable position. As the automatic chairman of the party from the time he emerged as its gubernatorial candidate, he was armed with executive powers and could steer the party to any berth of his choice. But Ajasin's position had been considerably weakened during the early days of his infatuation with Omoboriowo. He was regarded as a man without further ambitions, age was not on his side and many party stalwarts quietly recognised his presence as transient, while Omoboriowo was seen as representing the future. It was virtually a foregone conclusion by 1980 that the next governor had to come from Ekiti and many were putting their bets on Omoboriowo. This was seen as a worthy political investment. Therefore both the governor and his deputy were confronting each other at every forum and Ajasin had to fight for every inch of lost ground from his doughty deputy. That was how the university issue became a big political topic within the party. It was clear that a multi-campus system was hardly suitable for a poor state like Ondo, but Ajasin, fighting on the defensive, had to seek for more friends. The Akinkugbe report was finally adopted at a subsequent meeting after an intervention by Chief Awolowo. Chief Omoboriowo proposed that the new university be named after Chief Awolowo and it was adopted by acclamation.

6

House Of Strife

The real theatre of the struggle between the two gladiators was to be on the floor of the Ondo State House of Assembly. It was virtually a one-party house with only one NPN member out of the 66 seats, and the NPN man won his seat with a majority of less than 50 votes. Yet it was a motley crowd made up of strange bedfellows. Many of the lawmakers joined the UPN because that was the only vehicle that could guarantee them election into the assembly. They knew that anyone who ran with the flag of Awolowo in Ondo State in 1979 had virtually won the victory prize. Therefore, what united them was not loyalty to the party, its programmes or even its legendary leader, but raw ambition and the desire to be on the winning bandwagon by all means. The state assembly was therefore, mostly made up of an impossible crowd of careerists, fair-weather men and carpetbaggers.

In fairness to the lawmakers, many of them came with a rather simplistic idea of government and they were quickly intimidated and dazed by its complexity. Many of them were teachers who had spent their career shuttling between classrooms and staff common rooms and with a seat in the assembly, quickly developed an overblown sense of their own importance. They would not accept that their own constituency was only one out of 66. They interpreted their mandates not to make laws but to help get the roads in their constituencies tarred, to get jobs for their kinsmen and get the ears of the governor. When all these became difficult, many of them were eager to believe that it was because the governor or some of his top aides hated them. Therefore, right from its nascent days, the assembly became a fertile ground for intrigues, conspiracies, rumour-mongering and sheer devilry.

The assembly started off on an inauspicious note. Before he could take his seat in the assembly, Chief Samuel Adebayo Oloketuyi from Igbemo Ekiti, Ekiti Central local government, died mysteriously. There was a serious riot in the town during which the traditional ruler was forced to flee and many houses were burnt. Eleven people were later convicted of arson and related crimes over the Igbemo riot and they were eventually pardoned by Governor Ajasin in February 1981. By April 1980, two other members were dead: Mr. Taiwo Olarewaju Abe and Mr. Theophilus Akin Olaniyan. Death was to pay more violent visits to the floor of the assembly as events unfolded.

By the time they took their seats, many of the legislators came with personal grudges against the new governor. Some of them had lobbied to be commissioners and were passed over for more favoured candidates. While others who had wanted to be House officials had been vetoed by the party. But the real clash was to happen when Governor Ajasin wanted to prune their prerogatives and appurtenances of power. The governor agreed that the assemblymen should be given car loan of N12,000 naira each. However, when they made more requests, especially for loan from the Ondo State Housing Corporation, Ajasin refused. He said if they wanted loan from the corporation, they should apply like any other member of the public and they should be ready to supply collaterals. Ajasin said since they were elected to only a four-year term, it would be wrong for the government to force the Housing Corporation to give them loan of 50,000 naira or more which might take them more than 15 years to pay back with interests. Many of the lawmakers were clearly angry especially when they were given ill-fitted blocks of flats as their official quarters where they were living in a dormitory environment. Many of them resented this since the commissioners and advisers (many of whom never contested elections), were living in better furnished and bigger duplexes and bungalows.

The assemblymen were also influenced by stories emanating from other assemblies all over the country. There were stories that President Shagari was paying some federal legislators with cash from the security votes to get his bills passed. This was also said to be the practice in some other states of the federation especially, Bendel, Kano, Kwara and Benue states. Whether these stories were true or not, the Ondo State assemblymen also wanted Ajasin to have security votes from which this extra expenses could be freely taken. Ajasin refused. Throughout his four years in power, Ajasin refused to include security votes in his budget proposals and the 150,000 naira he spent for security during his tenure was actually diverted from other votes. Therefore, the problem that Ajasin had with the assembly was already latent before the schism in government brought it into the open.

It was becoming clear to discerning observers that Ajasin was having problems with the assembly men from the way they were debating the 1980 budget. None of Ajasin's fundamental proposals, like the building of industries, dams, the Owena Bank and new Ondo State Television Service and the university, passed through without acidic criticism from the members. Contributing to the debate on the budget Friday May 9, 1980, P.O. Olowofela (Ekiti South West 111), criticised the governor for making a budget that benefited mostly the 'metropolitan axis' of Akure, Ado Ekiti, Owo and Ondo. He argued that some of these giant industrial projects proposed by Ajasin would invite untold inflation to the state. He said the building of the 65 million naira glass factory proposed for Igbokoda (it is now in operation) was unwise. He said such a colossal amount should not have been voted for only one industrial project, but should have been split into 13 places of 5 million naira each to build small industries in 13 locations in the state.

In June, 1980, nine months into the administration twenty-three of the 26 legislators representing Ekiti in the state assembly addressed a nine-page petition to Governor Ajasin, accusing him of subverting the state's executive of the UPN, anti-Ekiti bias and of dictatorship. They were angry at the unceremonious removal of Professor Ola and the appointment of Mr. Popoola as secretary to the state government. They alleged that the six-man Adefarati committee on local government creation was done behind the party's back. They also said that the governor interfered with the governing board of the Owo Polytechnic in the appointment of a new rector for the institution. Among those who signed the petition, which was also copied to Chief Awolowo, were Mr. Akomolafe, Ayodele Morakinyo, Owolabi Afuye, J.O. Adebo, P.O. Olowofela, Bode Babatola, S.K. Babalola, A. Jeje, A.B. Ajobiewe, J. Olaoye, and Bode Kumapayi.

The governor, of course, was not short of supporters. In a 19-page rejoinder to the Ekiti legislators' petition, 33 non-Ekiti assemblymen criticised the Ekitimen for their 'violent and intemperate language'. They pointed out that the Ekiti were enjoying 'more than their fair share' of amenities and were occupying more posts than the other half of the state. They alleged that out of the five permanent secretaries appointed by Ajasin, four were from Ekiti. They also stated that there were six Ekiti commissioners out of a cabinet of 12 and they had three of the five Special Advisers. The Speaker, the Chief Whip, as well as the Clerk of the House of Assembly were all from Ekiti, they pointed out. They said these other posts were occupied by Ekitis: they had nine of the chairmen of the 15 legislative committees and commissions, 11 of the 18 secretaries to local government councils, and 85 of the 155 appointments to boards, corporations and commissions. In conclusion, they said the governor had the constitutional right to appoint and fire the secretary to government. Besides, they said that the new secretary, like the old one, was from Ekiti.

The controversy sparked off a press war between the two groups. One Adedara Adeosun, writing in the *National Concord* of September 4, 1980, pointed out that the Ekitis had been having a raw deal since the creation of the state in 1976. Adeosun said of all the nine federal and state educational institutions, only one, the College of Education, Ikere, was sited in Ekiti. The other institutions were the Federal Polytechnic, Akure, (now in Ado Ekiti), the Federal School of Arts and Science, Ondo, the two federal secondary schools at Akure and Ido Ani, Adeyemi College of Education, Ondo, School of Agriculture, Akure,

School of Health Technology, Akure and the Ondo State College of Arts and Science, Ikare. He concluded that this had been the Ekiti's lot because of the 'sheer conspiracy of Ekiti detractors'. The cold war between the assembly and the governor worsened with each passing day and it was only through the efforts of Mr. Bola Akingbade, the speaker, and some other officials of the House that trouble was kept temporarily at bay.

Early in March 1981, Akingbade led a delegation of the House to the United States. In his absence, Richard Jolowo, (Ilaje-Eseodo 111) a lawyer, was elected acting speaker. A few days after Akingbade had safely landed in the US, a general revolt took place in the state's House of Assembly.

On Tuesday, March 19, 1981, Bode Babatola (Ekiti West 111), moved a motion which was seconded by Chief Michael Omoyajowo (Akoko North 111), asking for the removal of all the House officials and the suspension of the speaker and his deputy. The motion was supported by Patrick Akinyomi (Ikale IV) and Yemi Aladejebi (Ekiti South 11). Opposing the motion, Olarenwaju Alley-Obalokun (Owo II) cautioned that such a serious move should have been referred to the parliamentary caucus, a committee of House officials, and top partymen which was presided over by the governor. After a rancorous debate, the acting speaker called for a division among the 42 members present and the motion was carried by 28 votes to 14.

Those who were removed were Alex Adedipe (Akure 1) as majority leader, Festus Olafunmiloye (Ifesowapo 111), deputy majority leader, Samuel Babalola (Ijero 11), the Chief Whip, Olu Ogidan (Akoko North 1), and Mrs. Janet Adeotoye (Ondo East 11, the only female member of the House), both of them whips. The removed officials were accused of hobnobbing with the executive, misusing assembly funds, compromising the legislators' interests and indiscipline.

Ajasin struggled throughout that week and the weekend to contain the damage and appease the aggrieved lawmakers, but to no avail. The parliamentary caucus met on Monday, March 23, and it was resolved that the sacking should be suspended, but the following day the assemblymen went right ahead to fill the vacant positions. Two men re-emerged again from the old team to join the new: Ogidan who became assistant majority leader and Olafunmiloye who became a whip. Other leaders elected were Tunde Agunbiade (Akure 11), majority leader, Joel Fapohunda, (Ekiti East 111), Chief whip, and Taiwo Akinwande (Ondo IV), whip. The House then set up a parliamentary committee to probe the deposed officers.

Ajasin sent further emissaries to the rebellious House and after some days with the calming of tempers, he thought that the lawmakers, now that they had had their way, would be appeased. He therefore sent a new proposal to the House, asking it to approve the nomination of two new commissioners, Professor Oluwole Agbede and Mr. Abiola Lebi. But the House was still in a fighting mood and it threw back the proposal at the governor. Michael Jeje, (Ijero 111) described the governor's request as frivolous. Ajasin then tried a little bit of arm-twisting by reaching the legislators at their constituencies and getting their home base party committee to censor their representatives and call them to order. The Akure UPN, as a result of these moves, expelled Agunbiade, the new majority leader, from its ranks. A statement signed by Chief Fasoranti and Olu Adegboro on behalf of the Akure UPN Constituency 11, alleged that Agunbiade was unanimously expelled for disobeying the 'lawful' directive of the party executive. The dividing line was now taking shape.

Akingbade (Ekiti West IV), returned from his overseas trip to find a letter dated April 1, 1981, asking him to go on compulsory leave until the Olowofela committee, set up by the rebellious lawmakers, finished its investigations. Akingbade, a lawyer from Erinjiyan Ekiti, was an Action Grouper during the First Republic and was also one of the founding members of the UPN in Ondo State. He had won his seat as speaker of the new House at the state's party caucus and he was not ready to give in without a fight. Chief Awolowo too had got wind of the rebellion in the state assembly and many top UPN leaders had urged him to intervene.

On Thursday April 2, 1981, Awo rushed to Akure where he held a meeting with the rebellious lawmakers with the governor in attendance. Both sides stated their cases. Agunbiade for the rebels said majority of members had lost confidence in the leadership of Akingbade. The embattled speaker defended himself, saying that it was against natural justice that he should be tried and found guilty in absentia. He said the Olowofela committee was an evidence of unfairness because it was set up after the officers had already been pronounced guilty. At the end of the meeting, Chief Awolowo directed that the House should suspend all actions. He also announced that he was setting up his own private investigation to be headed by Michael Odesanya, a retired judge of the Lagos High Court. He directed further that no more action should be taken on the matter until he had made his views known on the Odesanya committee report.

Friday, April 3, a day after Awo left Akure, a mild drama occurred on the floor of the assembly. Akingbade had interpreted Awolowo's directives to mean that he would continue as speaker while the rebels thought differently. The sergeant-at-arms had led him to the house, but there on the speaker's throne, was Jolowo, the man who had acted as speaker while Akingbade was away. Jolowo would not vacate the seat, saying that by the resolution of the House, Akingbade should proceed on compulsory leave. Not to enact an ugly scene before the public, Agunbiade, the new majority leader, ordered that the press and public gallery of the House be cleared by security men. After this was done, the lawmakers held a closed door session for two hours and the deadlock was resolved by 21 to 15 votes that Akingbade should proceed on compulsory leave. It was also resolved that the House should adjourn immediately instead of the following week. When the House resumed after the closed door session, the man behind the sergeant-at-arms was Richard Jolowo.

Justice Odesanya carried out his assignment with despatch and handed over his reports and recommendations to Chief Awolowo. He said if the members of the Ondo State House of Assembly should pass a vote of no confidence on the officers, then they should resign. A copy of the Odesanya report also got into the hands of the rebel lawmaker and they decided to act on it and confront the UPN leader with a *fait accompli*.

The argument then was that Chief Ajasin had a great influence on his old friend and through the governor's influence, Chief Awolowo might put his feet down that the House officials be restored in their posts.

On Monday June 8, Agunbiade, the majority leader moved a motion for a vote of no confidence on Akingbade and asked him to resign as speaker. Said Agunbiade: 'There is abundant evidence of diversion and conversion of essential commodities meant for all members of the House by the Speaker for his own personal use, to wit, for sale, and to the detriment of members. Honourable Bola Akingbade has failed to discharge and perform the functions of his office honestly and faithfully to the best of his ability which is contrary to his oath of office.'[29]   The motion was carried by 36 votes to 11 and Akingbade and his deputy were given 24 hours to resign or they would be summarily removed. On Friday June 12, after they refused to quit, both Akingbade and Atiroko were removed as speaker and deputy speaker respectively. Jolowo was confirmed as the new speaker while Olu Adesina (Ekiti North IV), became deputy speaker.

Chief Awolowo was displeased with the decision of the assembly to sack Akingbade and Atiroko. He was baffled also that the lawmakers illegally acquired the Odesanya report and decided to unilaterally act on it without the party leader's views on it. But the old man kept his peace in public, concluding that if the Ondo State lawmakers decided to wash their dirty linens in public, that was their own business. Professor Aluko and Wumi Adegbonmire, the chairman of Investments Corporation, who were both members of the National Executive Committee of the UPN, issued a joint statement accusing the lawmakers of indiscipline and anti-party activities. They posited that the assemblymen were under 'extraneous forces' in taking their decisions to sack all the House officials installed by the party. The triumphant lawmakers were indignant. They warned both Aluko and Adegbonmire to stop 'putting their noses in other peoples frying pots'.

With such a clear defeat at the House, Chief Ajasin was not done yet with trouble. The Ondo State Broadcasting Corporation usually broadcast live, the proceedings of the House. But when the lawmakers started the proceedings for the removal of Akingbade and co, Chief Ajasin sent for his old friend, Chief S.A. Akerele, the executive chairman of the OSBC and requested that the station should black out the assembly from its airwaves. When the lawmakers realised that they were blacked out, they summoned Akerele who quickly confessed that he was obeying the governor's order. The governor was unhappy about this believing that Akerele had exposed him to ridicule. He knew too that Akerele now belonged to the Omoboriowo group. This caused a cold war between the much-influential Akerele and the governor.

Tuesday, August 11, 1981, the day after Olowoporoku lost his job as a commissioner, he appeared in a local one-hour interview programme on the federal government owned Nigerian Television Authority, NTA, Akure. During the 60 minutes before the klieg light, Olowoporoku vented his anger and frustration about Chief Ajasin's government. He said the old man had 'reduced his deputy governor to a clerk simply in his bid to run for a second term'. He accused the governor of morbid anti-Ekiti bias in sacking him and Professor Ola. The attack was vicious and violent and the sacked commissioner held nothing back. It was the bitterest public attack on Ajasin, more acidic than any the opposition NPN ever launched on the governor.

On Monday, October 19, Governor Ajasin again attempted to rally the party to his side at the meeting of its executive committee held in Akure. Presented to the meeting was a new proposal for the creation of more local government which was made by the Ministry of Local Government. The new proposal asked for 53 local governments in the state, 23 for Ekiti and 30 for the rest. The proposal was shot at from different angles by the Ekiti delegates and others whose demands for local government in their areas were not met. The meeting was inconclusive and Ajasin had to adjourn so that delegates could study the report in order to present coherent objections at the next executive meeting scheduled for November 12. By this time, the Omoboriowo group, realising that despite the enormous powers conferred on the governor by both the party and the Nigerian constitution, Ajasin was in a weak position tactically, was now fully in the open and stepped up its attack. The manoeuvring from this time on was byzantine in its complexity and ruthlessness.

On Saturday, November 1, 1981, a meeting of the Omoboriowo group from all over Ekiti was held at Chief Babatola's residence in Ado-Ekiti. It was well attended by delegates from all over Ekitiland including Olowoporoku, some commissioners, state legislators, students and people from the streets. Curiously in attendance too was Dr. Aina, the state's commissioner for education and one of the known supporters of Chief Ajasin. The Lagos people, men like Fasanmi and Akintoye, were conspicuously absent. The meeting, presided over by Chief Akerele, was like a political rally and one speaker after another denounced the regime of Ajasin for its alleged anti-Ekiti bias, its love for Owo, the governor's hometown, and its controversial attempt to create new local government areas. They also pooh-poohed the governor's record in carrying out the party's programmes, especially free education. The meeting passed a vote of no confidence on Ajasin and endorsed Omoboriowo's candidature for 1983.

On Tuesday, November 10, Ajasin made a move against the rebels by sacking Chief Akerele as executive chairman of OSBC. During his earlier clash with the governor over the assembly affair, Ajasin had wanted to transfer Akerele to a less crucial parastatal, but this was resisted by many top members of the party since Akerele too was a founding member of the old AG and a personal friend of Chief Awolowo. On Saturday, November 14, the Omoboriowo group again met in Ado-Ekiti in a show of defiance. They again passed a vote of no confidence on Ajasin and endorsed the candidature of Omoboriowo for governorship on 1983. The second meeting was presided over by Chief Babatola who was chairman of the Ondo State Housing Corporation. The following week, Ajasin again summarily dismissed Babatola from his Housing Corporation job. It was clear now that the governor was ready to deal with the rebel group with the Law of Moses: an eye for an eye and a tooth for a tooth.

Before the removal of Chief Akerele, members of the Ajasin generation serving on boards of government parastatals and other appointments were regarded as virtually untouchable. It was one humiliation Akerele found very difficult to accommodate in his stride. He wrote a 14-page petition to Chief Awolowo, dated February 13, 1982, complaining bitterly about his removal and explaining his role in the unfolding Omoboriowo saga. 'What would highly recommend our UPN chairman in Ondo State, Chief M.A. Ajasin, to a casual observer would be his apparently cool, calm, collected and level headed personality with very soft spoken voice akin to that of a monarch,' wrote Chief Akerele. 'But within our Governor's angelic appearance is a spirit with an iron will that hardly takes anything or incident into very serious consideration except those that go to serve its personal interests - callously vindictive - Machiavellian in his tactics - he encourages secretive and vile gossips and whispering campaigns throughout the state, to such an extent that drivers and secretaries are set as spies on their masters.'

Akerele also accused the governor of nepotism especially in favour of Owo indigenes. Said he: 'There were instances where an Owo man was appointed a Permanent Secretary over and above 15 other officers - another with the Housing Corporation was promoted from grade level 12 to 14; and yet another on grade level 9 at the Ministry of Economic Planning and Statistics was promoted to the grade level 13. This is only to mention but a few amidst his numerous instances of nepotism. Not Owo people alone, his sycophants from other parts of the state are equally favoured, e.g. Messrs. Adeniyi and Afuye from the same constituency at Ikere Ekiti are now serving as full time chairmen of two corporations - Owena Motels and the OSBC - practical illustrations of Chief M.A. Ajasin's double standards.'

According to Akerele, Ajasin 'is addict(ed) to quarrelsomeness and is most buoyant whenever he is on the warpath and would surely ally with the Darkness to fight the Light if that is opportune to his victory. He wins his supporters by means, not by conviction; it is either by cowing them into submission or getting them committed to him or to his course. By suppression and oppression, the Governor rendered the UPN State Executive and his Government Executive utterly impotent but failed woefully to gain utter mastery over the Legislature because the preponderance of the virile youngmen there have their consciences full functioning under the Divine Guidance and Guardianship. These youngmen remain indomitable despite all forms of intimidation and persecution... Chief Ajasin is very rigid, highly inflexible, ruthlessly uncompromising and stubbornly unyielding... It will be much against the interests of our party (UPN) in Ondo State as well as against the interests of the majority of the people of the state themselves if Chief Ajasin should be given, by any chance or ill luck, another chance of ruling this state after 1983...

'I was relieved of my post without prior query accusing me of any wrong doing,' complained Akerele. 'He did not even accuse me of any offence, not to talk of allowing me to make any defence whatsoever. He said that he was relieving me of my post because of the news published in one of the dailies that Mr. Akin Omoboriowo was unanimously adopted as the only gubernatorial candidate for 1983 by the Ekitis. Might be the Governor would have ordered that I be remanded in prison custody if it was my candidature that was so adopted.'

Chief Akerele's lengthy letter depicted the turbulent mood of that time. The following week after the second Ado Ekiti meeting of the Omoboriowo group, Professor Aluko met with the deputy governor. They had been friends since their days at Ife and Omoboriowo respected the elderly economist for his frankness. 'Akin,' Aluko said to the deputy governor. 'You have to denounce these people meeting in Ado Ekiti. They are enemies of our party. Issue a public statement and dissociate yourself from their meetings. Tell them that if you are going to become governor, you are not going to be governor of Ekiti State, but of Ondo State.' Omoboriowo promised to follow Aluko's advice. A few days later, when they met, Omoboriowo said he could not issue the statement because it would be impolitic. Up to that time Omoboriowo had not publicly associated himself with either the rebellion in the House or the meetings of the Ekiti people in government. He was also not present at the two Ado-Ekiti meetings.

Meanwhile, flushed with victory, Ondo State parliamentarians were in a bellicose mood. On Friday, August 8, 1981, the House passed the Statutory Offices (emoluments) law and made it retroactive to January 1, 1981. With this new law, they increased the annual salary of the speaker from 15,000 naira to 17,000 naira. They also upped his allowance from 4,000 naira to 6,000 naira. The deputy speaker would now earn 14,000 naira now instead of 12,000 naira and also had a new allowance of 4,000 naira. The chief whip and the minority leader were now to earn 13,000 naira each with a new allowance of 3,000 naira per annum. The salaries of other members were increased from 12,000 naira to 12,500 naira and also a new addition of 3,000 naira tax-free allowance. A new housing allowance for members was fixed at 2,400 naira instead of the old 1,200 naira for those without official accommodation. The new law also provided that 'a member of the House shall be reimbursed for the cost of hiring two legislative aides on grade level 08 and 05 as well as setting up and maintaining an office in his constituency.' To prove that they were not thinking of themselves alone, they increased the governor's and the deputy governor's consolidated allowances to 10,000 naira (formerly 6,000 naira) and 6,000 naira (from 4,000 naira) respectively. The bill was rail-roaded through the first, second and third readings the same day.

Governor Ajasin protested that the legislators had no right to unilaterally increase their own salaries when this was not provided for in the budget. He also decried their back-dating of the law, arguing that it was wrong for a civilian regime to be backdating its own laws like a military government. In protest, he vetoed the bill and the lawmakers lifted the veto with a resounding majority. Ajasin however did not collect either the old allowance nor the new throughout his tenure as governor, taking only his 20,000 naira annual salary earlier fixed by the military and endorsed by the National Executive Committee of the UPN.

Professor Aluko believed that by confronting the governor openly the legislators were guilty of anti-party activities. He took his allegation to Chief Awolowo and alleged too that some of the legislators were on the pay roll of the rival NPN and that they were now working actively for the opposition. But Awolowo would not believe such stories. Recalled Aluko: 'Chief Awolowo said those spreading such stories were only trying to discredit the Ondo State assemblymen and break up the party. He believed they were very loyal and that it was I who was too critical. These people would go back to Chief Awolowo and deceive him and prostrate before him, and by doing that, Awo believed they loved him.'

The issue was again raised at the party's NEC meeting, but Awolowo dismissed it with a wave of the hand. Apart from Ajasin and Omoboriowo, other members of NEC from Ondo State were Aluko, Adegbonmire and Professor Akintoye. Since the NEC took the position that the rebellion in Ondo State House of Assembly was only a quarrel among brothers and nothing to worry about, the revolt found time to spread and take root.

7

Troubleshooting

The internecine war within the Ondo State government soon became public knowledge and this caused worries not only among the members of the UPN but also other citizens of the State. Nothing was spared and not even the person of the party patriarch, Chief Awolowo was above suspicion. The Ajasin faction suspected that Omoboriowo could not be watering his ambition so openly without the covert support of his political mentor. Omoboriowo was a frequent caller at Awo's Ikenne country home. Other members of his family too, especially Ebun, his wife, were also intimate with the Awolowo family. The Ajasin faction then reasoned that Awolowo must have prevailed initially on Ajasin to make Omoboriowo the deputy-governor with the long term aim of finally installing his protege as chief executive having given him a head start over more favoured candidates, especially the mercurial Ayo Fasanmi and the suave Banji Akintoye.

But Omoboriowo believed he justly earned the honour of being close to the old man's heart. Said he: 'I didn't see a more loyal person than myself to Chief Awolowo in Ondo State. Chief Ajasin could be because of age and because they started earlier together, but in terms of active loyalty, I don't think I was second to anybody.'

It was this perceived partiality of Awolowo that made his attempt at patching the crack so difficult. December 18, 1981, Chief Awolowo came to Akure to attend the launching of two collections of his speeches edited by Chief Olaiya Fagbamigbe, a UPN member of the House of Representatives for Akure. Fagbamigbe, a well-known publisher and author, was one of the best loved members of the party in Ondo State. He was involved in the leadership squabble for the control of the party grassroots at Akure with the more entrenched Fasoranti. Since Fasoranti was a right-hand man of Ajasin, Fagbamigbe gravitated to the Omoboriowo camp. When Awo came for the launching therefore, it was seen as Omoboriowo's show. Omoboriowo too was in no hurry to prove the contrary.

Awo was met at the Owena border between Ondo and Oyo states by a delegation of top partymen led by Chief Omoboriowo. As expected, it was only the members of his faction that were present. They then drove in a convoy to the venue of the launching, Saint Peter's College, Akure.

Unlike his practice in the past, Awo did not call on the governor first. Awo was at Saint Peter's for six hours. During the ceremony, Chief Ajasin breezed in briefly, then left. Fasoranti, Osomo, Adegoke and other members of the Ajasin faction were conspicuously absent. Awo stayed the night in Akure and he held meetings with the two factions separately, urging them to bury the hatchet, but his plea was like water poured into a basket.

After Awo's departure, the battle shifted to the state assembly over the protracted struggle to create more local governments. Ajasin had sent a bill to the House asking for the division of the state into 76 local governments. He met a rebuff and instead, the lawmakers' passed their own bill creating 50 local governments. The governor responded by vetoing the bill, but the defiant assembly men overturned the veto with a two-third majority vote of those present. Ajasin supporters argued that the absent members were not informed in the order paper that the bill was coming up for mentioning, saying that the sitting of the House overturning the veto was illegal. Ajasin stuck to his gun that he still recognised only the 17 local governments created by the military. Olu Mafo, secretary of the UPN Parliamentary Council and Agunbiade, the majority leader, replied Ajasin that his action was illegal. 'It would be a most unfortunate thing that people expected to know and uphold the law of the land should denigrate it for whatever reason known to them,' they said in a letter written to Ajasin in January 1982. 'Until any amendment is carried out or it is repealed, the local government law (amendment) of Ondo State of Nigeria remains what was passed by the State House of Assembly on December 18, 1981.'

Ajasin treated the letter with contempt. The Omoboriowo faction then plotted their next move. The state conference of the party was scheduled for Saturday January 30, 1982. They decided that a vote of no confidence would be passed on the governor who was to preside over the conference as the state's UPN chairman. Even if they did not succeed they would have disrupted the proceeding and certainly succeeded in embarrassing the governor. Sensing the tension in the air, Awo gave an order stopping the conference.

Traditional rulers and religious leaders also waded into the crisis. On Saturday February 13, 1982, these leaders met with the two factions at the Government House, Akure. Present were the governor and his enstranged deputy, parliamentary leaders of the party, some commissioners and other leaders of the UPN. The peace meeting was presided over by Itiade Adekolurejo, the Osemawe of Ondo, who was then the chairman of the state's Council of Obas. Others who were present included Adelegan Adesida, the Deji of Akure, Adetula Adeleye, the Elekole of Ikole-Ekiti, Adebayo Adegboye, the Ogoga of Ikere·Ekiti, Bishop S.O. Aderin of the Anglican Church and Bishop Francis Alonge of the Catholic Church.

The meeting lasted for ten hours. It was resolved at the end of the long drawn arguments that Ajasin should pay the new salary scales which the legislators had given themselves. Other agreements included that the governor should implement the 50 local governments law passed by the assembly and persuade his supporters to withdraw all the eight cases pending in the court against the assembly and its functionaries. In return, the Omoboriowo faction pledged to support the governor in the governance of the state and that the assembly would rescind its 'vote of no confidence' passed on Adegoke and Aderibigbe, two commissioners in Ajasin's cabinet.

Five days after the obas' peace move, Awolowo again came to Akure. He had sent to his men in advance that the two sides should prepare their cases and that it was time to settle their differences once and for all. The meeting lasted for two days. The state assembly venue was jam-packed with leaders of the party both from the National Assembly and the local level. Ajasin presented his case against his deputy. He alleged that the crisis within the party was caused by Omoboriowo's 'overriding ambition' to become governor of Ondo State whatever the cost come 1983. He accused his deputy of putting his plans into action immediately the party came to power in 1979, when he allegedly engineered the commissioners' meeting. Ajasin concluded that Omoboriowo had been disloyal to the party, by plotting against the party's leadership and subverting its programme both at the state assembly and the local level, just to create room for himself come 1983.

Presenting his own case, Omoboriowo said the issue of his ambition was secondary to the crisis. He accused Ajasin of dictatorship and sidelining the party executive in running the government. He alleged that Ajasin's excuse for this was that he did not want people 'to run the government for me from the outside.' He said the governor was very obstinate about his own idea on how many new local governments were to be created. He said Ajasin had been hitting at his (Omoboriowo's) supporters within the party just to short-change him in the race for 1983. Among the instances he cited were the removal of Professor Ola as secretary to the government, the sacking of Olowoporoku, Akerele and Babatola. He also said the governor failed to consult him in taking the following decisions: the appointments and deployment of permanent secretaries, appointment of a new rector for Owo Polytechnic, the composition of the state's council of obas, appointment of the council of the then Obafemi Awolowo University (now known as Ondo State University), Ado-Ekiti, the removal of Mr. J. J. Omoniyi, a chartered accountant and Omoboriowo's town's man from the new state-owned Owena Bank board of directors, removal of Professor Adeniji Adaralegbe, another Omoboriowo's town's man from the board of the Investment Corporation, and the appointment of another partyman, A. Babalola,

also from Ijero local government as a full-time member of the Education
Task Force 'so as to spite and destabilise my base'.

He said Ajasin had been doing other things that can discredit the
party in the state. He accused the governor of financial recklessness for
voting 500 naira to each of the 17 local governments to use for
organising reception during his (Ajasin's) tour of the local governments.
He said the governor even encouraged civil servants to be rude to him,
citing the example of Mr. J. K. Kolawole, permanent secretary, works,
whom he alleged was rude to him in November, 1979, in the presence
of the governor. He said that Ajasin unilaterally appointed Idowu
Odeyemi a journalist from Sketch newspaper as the UPN chief publicity
officer and that he had prevented new election of party officials in Ilawe
and Ikale. He accused the governor of masterminding the peace move
spearheaded by the obas a week earlier. 'I felt ashamed to have been
forced to appear before obas to settle party quarrels,' he lamented.

Both sides were not short of weapons. The Ajasin side alleged that
Omoboriowo gave a speech three months into the life of the new
administration at Ise Ekiti, where he said he would help the town when
he become governor come '83. It was then inferred that either
Omoboriowo was wishing the incumbent dead or he was harbouring
a masterplan to topple the government. The supposed cassette of the Ise
speech was then played for Chief Awolowo who pronounced curtly:
'that is not Akin's voice'. Chief Fasoranti then alleged that Omoboriowo
and his faction in the assembly were working in league with the
opposition NPN and that some of them were already on the party's pay
roll. At this juncture Awolowo rose to the defence of his party members,
saying that he could vouch for their faith in the UPN and its leadership.

Omoboriowo then told the gathering a bizarre story that illustrated
the sour relationship between him and the governor. Sometime in 1981,
the governor had summoned the editor and managing director of the
Sketch Press, Ibadan, jointly owned by Oyo, Ogun and Ondo State
governments. While the Sketch people were there, he also summoned
Omoboriowo to the Government House and in the presence of the
deputy governor, Ajasin accused the Sketch team of giving undue

publicity to his deputy. He cited instances where stories about Ondo state government were illustrated with the photograph of Omoboriowo instead of that of the governor. Omoboriowo said he was visibly embarrassed by the action of the governor especially when he confirmed that the governor had summoned the Sketch team all the way from Ibadan to make his complaints. Another instance was the publication of *The Projector*, a weekly news bulletins of the State government edited by Adegbamigbe Akilaya, a top notcher of the party. He alleged that the governor ordered an entire edition of 10,000 copies burnt simply because it carried the picture of the deputy governor on the front page. Subsequently, the governor ordered the stoppage of *The Projector* altogether.

Omoboriowo's bitterest complaint was against Niyi Onioraro, the publisher of the weekly *Peoples News*. Scurrilous, sensational and scathing, the *Peoples News* (now defunct), was a classic example of what a newspaper should not be. It violated all the known canons of journalism, flirting openly with libel and rightly earned the sobriquet of a scandal sheet. As befits a man of Onioraro's reputation, his intervention in the struggle in Ondo State was shrouded in controversies. During the earlier days of the *Peoples News*, the paper carried ceaseless attacks on Ajasin and his supporters, especially the functionaries of the House like Akingbade and Adedipe as well as commissioners like Adegoke. But midstream, after the removal of Akingbade and his colleagues as officials of the House, Onioraro changed course and turned his canons on Omoboriowo and his phalanx. In acidic essays, scandalous exposes and biting cartoons, the *People's News* portrayed Omoboriowo as a reckless philander leading a gang of buccaneering carpet baggers.

Omoboriowo therefore complained to the gathering that Ajasin had sent Onioraro to haunt him and his supporters. He said the government not only patronised the paper with adverts, top functionaries of the government, including the attorney general, 'even encouraged' Onioraro in his reckless path of seditious libel. He concluded that Onioraro was Ajasin's 'instrument of blackmail and oppression' and urged Chief Awolowo 'to kill the so-called *People's News*'. He urged Awo to prevail on Ajasin to 'consult me more as he did before we were sworn-in and to delegate more powers as a deliberate policy because I think I have a lot to offer'.

The two-day meeting adjourned Friday, February 19 only to reconvene again February 26. The litany of accusations and counter-accusations continued. On Saturday, February 27, 1982, an unexpected twist was introduced into the deliberations when a member of Awo's entourage, Chief Ebenezer Babatope, also tabled his own complaint before the gathering. Babatope, a radical author, essayist and former university administrator was one of the closest of the younger generations to Chief Awolowo. As the National Director of Organisation, he ran the UPN machine along with Chief M.C.K. Ajuluchuku, a veteran journalist who was the National Director of Research and Publicity. In many circles therefore, Babatope was rightly seen as Awo's alter ego, a man who had as much influence on the old man as some of Chief Awolowo's elderly associates. This vantage position had exposed Babatope to pot-shots especially from fellow partymen who would want to shoot at Awo's shadow. They were such shots now that Babatope was complaining about.

Babatope narrated a story to the gathering about Godwin Daboh, a businessman in Gboko, Benue State, who had acquired a national reputation as an anti-corruption crusader. Babatope alleged that Daboh came to Akure early in 1982 where he met three leaders of the Omoboriowo group, Olowoporoku, Tunde Agunbiade and Ayodele Morakinyo, a member of the state assembly (Ekiti South III). Babatope alleged that the trio told Daboh that the five UPN governors had been assured of re-nomination by Babatope who was accused of having collected a 250,000 naira bribe from each of the governors. The three men were present and Babatope therefore challenged them to prove their accusation. When Chief Awolowo called on Morakinyo, Agunbiade and Olowoporoku to explain their discussion with Daboh, the three of them denied ever having any discussion with the well-known anti-corruption crusader. Two months after the Akure gathering, Daboh sent Chief Awolowo a cassette which he alleged was the recording of his said discussion with Olowoporoku, Morakinyo and Agunbiade. He claimed he had secretly taped the discussion without the knowledge of the three men.

When the meeting finally ended that Saturday February 27, 1982, Awolowo had succeeded in forging a 'Treaty of Peace.' The five-page document was endorsed by Chief Awolowo, Ajasin, Omoboriowo, Jolowo, Agunbiade and Senator Ayo Fasanmi, who was the chairman of the Ondo State Group of the National Parliamentary Council. One of the strange recommendations of the treaty was the setting up of the party's consultative council made up of 'all (1) Ondo State UPN members in the National Assembly, (2) UPN members in the Ondo State House of Assembly, (3) all members of the Party's State Executive Council, (SEC) and (4) all members of the Ondo State Government Executive Council'. It declared: 'The Consultative Council shall meet at least once a month. No matter of major importance shall be considered in the State House of Assembly or in the State Cabinet without the prior clearance of the Consultative Council. For this purpose, matters of major importance shall include all matters that affect the interest of the people or that are likely to involve public comment at all.'

On relationship within the party, the treaty stated: 'The chairman of the Ondo State Branch of the Party and the SEC shall recognise all democratically-elected chairmen of the Party at the sub-state levels of organisation recognised by the Party's constitution and shall co-operate and deal with them in the organisational work of the Party at those levels. If the democratically-elected chairman of a local government, state constituency, or ward executive committee had been removed from office by order of the chairman or the state secretariat prior to this treaty, the affected chairman shall stand immediately reinstated, but without prejudice to the right of members of any branch to remove its officers in accordance with the constitution of the Party.'

On the new local government proposals, the treaty stated: 'In the specific matter of the Local Government (Amendment) Law of 1981, the Law shall stand as passed by the State House of Assembly on

December 18, 1981; but the Party's Consultative Council shall meet within a month of the acceptance of the terms of this treaty to consider and recommend necessary amendments.' It was also resolved that 'all members of the party shall hereafter refrain from making public statements critical of the party, its leadership, or its programmes,' and that 'all public media that tend to discredit the party, its leadership, or its programmes shall be shunned and avoided by the organs of the party.'

On the relationship between Ajasin and Omoboriowo the treaty stated: 'The Governor of the State shall with due dispatch, delegate specific responsibilities to the Deputy Governor and give him a free hand to discharge such responsibilities. The Governor shall therefore, inform the Party's SEC as well as the Consultative Council of responsibilities he has delegated to the Deputy Governor. No responsibilities so delegated to the Deputy Governor shall be withdrawn unless the intended withdrawal has been first cleared with the Party's SEC as well as the Consultative Council. The Deputy Governor shall in turn report from time to time to the Governor of the State on how he is discharging his responsibilities. The Deputy Governor shall sit in a brief conference with the Governor at the beginning of each working day, whenever both of them are in Akure'.

As could be seen above, the treaty is virtually a new code of conduct for the governor. Ajasin and his supporters were unhappy about the treaty which in effect had made the Consultative Council superior to the governor and his entire cabinet. Chief Awolowo was to monitor compliance with the treaty and prescribe punishment for its breaches. The five signatories shook hands, flashed the victory sign of the UPN and beamed plastic smiles for the cameras. The only person who believed the final antidote to trouble in the state had been found was Chief Awolowo. After the trouble shooter left for his countryhome in Ikenne, the war went on.

While Ajasin retained his grip on his government, Omoboriowo too continued his scheme for 1983. He had the support of the majority in the state assembly and a substantial number of the National

Assembly men from the state.

From outward indications, situation was returning to normal. Omoboriowo followed Ajasin on his tours of local government areas and he became a fixture of the governor's entourage during Ajasin's official public functions like the opening of new workshops or exhibitions. But the war continued fervently and there were no more pretences. Omoboriowo, despite all protestations to the contrary, was now working feverishly towards the nomination battle for 1983.

The decisive factor in Ajasin's favour was his incumbency. Being the governor, he was automatically the party chairman and the UPN constitution virtually replicated the powers of the governor in the party chairmanship. In this case he was the effective chief executive. One of his strategies was to consolidate his hold on the party machinery. In the old days of his romance with Omoboriowo, the deputy governor had gotten many of his supporters to fill influential positions within the party. What Ajasin now did was to neutralize those party officials he could not remove who were in the camp of Omoboriowo.

Falodun, an Omoboriowo supporter and old Action Grouper remained the secretary of the party, but his functions were virtually taken over by other functionaries of the party especially Adegoke, now made the commissioner for information and local government, who emerged the leading praetorian of the Ajasin camp. Rufus Aboloyinjo, Omoboriowo's town's man and party's organising secretary was rendered impotent by Miller Aganyemi an Ajasin partisan. To strengthen his hold, Ajasin also hired Odeyemi, a University of Lagos graduate in journalism who hitherto was the political editor of the *Sketch,* as chief publicity officer. Ajasin complemented the use of these men (Odeyemi later decamped to the Omoboriowo group) with officials of the government who, being members of the UPN, felt they had as much stake and right in the running of the party.

With his control of the party machinery at the centre, the Ajasin camp then engaged in a struggle for the control of the party cells. Virtually in every ward and local government branch of the party, the dichotomy at the centre was replicated. With his offensive at the grassroots, Ajasin checkmated the rebellious assembly men. As the struggle shifted to the grassroots, Ajasin drafted his commissioners, advisers and other top government appointees into the foray. Every weekend, they would troop to their local government areas, selling the candidacy of Ajasin for a second term and portraying Omoboriowo as a disciple of Akintola, treading the paths of betrayal and doom.

But the Omoboriowo group too was not without its own weapons at this stage. It formed a parallel party organisation termed the Youth Wing of the UPN. It gave good account of itself in virtually every local government and party cells. In Ilawe, for example, not only were the UPN officials shunted aside, they were rendered impotent. The Omoboriowo group was composed of younger elements within the party who related more with Omoboriowo's vigorous pace than Ajasin's patriachal stride. They were vocal, vociferous and capable men, but of shallow ideological roots nor did they have the primeval loyalties that bonded the old Action Groupers. The group decided to take its ambition seriously and that of its leader, Chief Omoboriowo. They formed the Committee for Democracy, Justice and Progress in Ondo State. The basic aim of the committee was to ensure the success of Omoboriowo in the party nomination contest and also the victories of its members for state and national assembly tickets.

Party leaders and members nationwide continued to be worried about the political cannibalism going on in Ondo State. Chief Awolowo continued informal talk with leaders of the party, but despite promises made, neither Omoboriowo nor Ajasin was ready to shelve his ambition. Alfred Rewane, former political secretary of Chief Awolowo and a top notcher as well as financier of the party, led a peace team to Akure composed of other top partymen. But the Rewane committee was scuttled at its infancy because the Omoboriowo group accused Rewane of being too friendly with Governor Ajasin and that his mission really was to pave way for the re-nomination of the governor.

Another peace mission headed by Rafiu Jafojo, the Lagos State deputy governor arrived in Akure July 5, 1982. Jafojo's credentials were clear. He was a deputy governor and therefore could empathise with

Omoboriowo. He was also a loyal deputy whose fidelity to Governor Jakande at that time was without question. Therefore, he was entrusted by both sides with their own grievances. But like all other peace missions before it, it was rewarded with failure. On Tuesday July 6, the Jafojo team met with Chief Omoboriowo at the deputy governor's residence. Present were leading members of the Omoboriowo group including the parliamentary leaders. The leaders accused Ajasin of destabilising some of the legislators' constituencies in retaliation for their refusal to support his bid for a second term. They later presented Jafojo with a memorandum titled: 'Additional Complaints and Violations of the Treaty of Peace.' It was signed by Mafo on behalf of the parliamental faction of the Omoboriowo group. While Jafojo came back with bagful of complaints, he could not find solution to the internecine conflict.

By the middle of 1982, there was no more pretence that a war was going on in Akure. Omoboriowo had dropped the veil of the persecuted deputy governor, and now girded himself for the gubernatorial battle. Since he was now virtually jobless, he spent his time to nurture his ambition and planned the strategy for the future. His greatest weapon was promise and he used this to maximum advantage. Unlike Ajasin who could be judged with his current performances, the land of promises is a land of dreams where everything is possible. Therefore, Omoboriowo promised scores of his followers that they would be appointed commissioners, advisers, board members and so on. He promised at least three persons the post of deputy governor: Funsho Akinyosoye, a wealthy lawyer from Ondo who was in the Federal House of Representatives, Prince Olu Mafo and Ebun Ogunyimika. Each of the three, like the scores of others, worked hard for Omoboriowo's success, each believing fervently that he was the closest to the leader's heart.

Ajasin too was moving his pawns with the zest of an accomplished chess player. He dissolved the local councils in all the 17 local governments and appointed caretaker committees, filled with his loyalists, to take charge. When this was done, the Omoboriowo group in the state assembly cried havoc, and quickly passed a resolution declaring Ajasin's masterstroke 'illegal, null and void,' only to be reminded that the power of interpreting laws is vested in the courts. Many observers believe that this tactical move of Ajasin, if not anticipated, should at least be understood by the Omoboriowo camp. Innocent Oparadike, a journalist with the Concord Newspaper wrote: 'It is naive to expect the governor to supinely allow his deputy to use the privileges of his office to unseat the incumbent. These privileges which have become live ammunition in the hands of a proclaimed opponent have to be withdrawn.'[30]

When Chief Awolowo informed party members that a special Congress of the UPN would be held in Lagos, October 25 to 27, 1982, everyone knew it had to do with the contending ambitions of partymen for 1983. Though Awo did not state the reason for it, partymen soon correctly surmised the reason for the congress and they started planning towards it. Each faction of the party wanted to have an advantage over the other during the congress. Five thousand delegates were expected for this special conference made up of elected parliamentarians, party officials at both national and state levels as well as officials and leaders at the grassroots.

Ajasin was the first to make a move to get tactical advantage. The new local government bosses understood their mandates: to sell Ajasin to partymen for a second term. The state-owned Ondo State Broadcasting Corporation, OSBC and the Television Service, OSTV, were commandeered for the governor's propaganda purpose. Though this was subtle, it was nonetheless effective. September 30, 1982, some few weeks to the special conference and the eve of Nigeria's 22nd independence anniversary, Ajasin made a broadcast to the people of the state, enumerating the 'great achievements' of his administration for the past three years. He renewed his pledge, vowing to serve Ondo State better with total devotion. The old man did not sound like a runner at the end of his tether, but like an experienced long distance runner who had just begun his race.

The next day, at the Akure sports stadium, there were screaming banners proclaiming: 'Ajasin, Pride of the UPN'. It was more or less a political rally for Ajasin and Omoboriowo sat stoically throughout the ceremony. The deputy governor knew better than to join the chorus of those singing: 'Three years of Achievements'. Throughout the day, there were congratulatory messages on the State's radio from the local leaders to the governor and in the evening a modest feast at the Government House.

But the Omoboriowo group were not to be intimidated by such show of power. It put out pamphlets and handbills stating the other sides of the 'Three years of Achievements'. Femi Orebe, one of the members of the group wrote in one of the hand circulated write ups: "Whoever inflicted those banners christening the Ajasin Administration as 'Three years of Achievements' and a 'Pride of the Party' on the good and long-suffering people of Ondo State did neither the old man nor the party he so ineffectually leads in Ondo State any good. Whatever good was intended for such a Public Relations job was at best unearned and verily undeserved. It would have been enough especially as the Ondo State branch of the Nigerian Union of Teachers is about going on an industrial action, to stop the wastage which those hundreds of banners must have cost. Or were the contractors unpaid too?' "

The Ondo State branch of the UPN received a letter dated October 6, 1982, asking the branch to send the list of members who would attend the special conference of the party starting October 25. In response, Ajasin sent a list comprising mostly his supporters and only a token representation from the Omoboriowo group. When Ajasin could not be persuaded to change, Omoboriowo petitioned the national secretariat. In a letter to Babatope, dated October 14, 1982, he complained that Ajasin was seeking undue advantage by loading the delegation to the conference with his (Ajasin's) supporters. Said Omoboriowo: 'I wish to appeal to you strongly to ensure that the directives of the National President, Papa Obafemi Awolowo, on this matter which your circular-letter of 6th October, declares, is implemented strictly. We have only one party-the UPN- and only one leader - Papa Awo. We from Ondo State, of course, will ensure that on the 25th

October this directive by your letter under reference is honoured by all concerned without ANY FORM OF DEVIATION.'

Two days to the conference, Saturday, October 23, leaders of the Omoboriowo group came to the national secretariat of the UPN to follow up their petition. In the delegation were Falodun, Oladosu Okeya, a member of the state assembly (Ekiti South 5), Olowoporoku, and Olu Adesina. They were armed with another list of delegates which they pressed should be substituted for the list earlier sent by the Ajasin group. Chief Awolowo later gave the directive that the two delegations be admitted into the special conference. The Omoboriowo group felt victorious.

On the eve of the conference, the shadow boxing continued relentlessly. October 14, 1982, a group of Omoboriowo supporters, led by Bode Kumapayi, a member of the state assembly (Ekiti-North 1), wrote a letter to the deputy governor urging him to resign. The letter was signed by 15 legislators and 31 other party members. The letter, which was copied to Chief Awolowo, was full of bile and bitterness. It reads:

> We have watched with dismay and regret the various anti-socio-political tactics which the Chief Executive of this State, Chief Ajasin, has employed for the past three years to devalue the office of the Deputy Governor (and) also to dehumanise you as a person. Such tactics included keeping you in the cooler and therefore making sure that you, as the Deputy Governor of this state, did not know what was going on in the government of which you are a part. Such major governmental decisions in which you have been prevented from taking part are too numerous to mention; there is no doubt that the ordinary citizens in this state know well that you, as the Deputy Governor of Ondo State, have been pushed out of all governmental decisions and this trend has been intensified in recent days owing to the ruthless struggle of the Chief Executive for re-nomination which, of course, is obvious that he cannot get.
>
> More importantly, we, as your supporters all over the state, have been excluded from all material and non-material benefits arising from all governmental activities. Perhaps, you may not have been aware that all contracts and jobs in such areas as Owena Bank, Ondo State Confidence

Insurance Company, the OSTV and all the newly established industries, including loan to small scale industrialists have all been given out with specific instructions that all the people supporting Chief Omoboriowo should not benefit from such government activities.

With all these, we have wondered what else you are doing in the government of Chief Ajasin that made you not to have tendered your resignation. Our stand on this is strengthened by the recent incontrovertible revelation and exposition that after all, Chief Ajasin was the sponsor of Oniororo's *Peoples News* which carried obscene cartoons and wrote defamatory and highly seditious publications against you and your notable followers in such a reckless manner as to make the whole public treat you and your followers as outcasts if not for the sympathy and political awareness of the masses who quickly discovered that Chief Ajasin was behind it all.

The situation has become worse that when Chief Ajasin tried unsuccessfully to influence the judge against your private criminal litigation against Oniororo, he went to court through his Attorney-General to stop the case by issuing '*nolle prosequi*'. As soon as this episode occurred on 4/10/82, all your followers, who are more than 80 per cent of the UPN members of Ondo State, have met in various caucuses and have concluded that your continued stay in the cabinet of Chief Ajasin is an embarrassment to us especially because, having removed your numerous supporters from both governmental and party posts, Chief Ajasin continues to announce daily the removal of the rest who are still in post.

It is certain that the masses of the people of Ondo State who are already fed up and tired of Chief Ajasin's administration, which is more vindictive than Akintola's, are waiting eagerly to vote for you overwhelmingly in the forthcoming shadow election. We, the undersigned on behalf of the millions of your supporters throughout Ondo State call on you to resign from Chief Ajasin's administration with immediate effect as no role is left in his administration for Your Excellency and your supporters to play.

Omoboriowo did not resign, but led his team to Lagos to fight so that the rules for nomination could favour his side as much as possible. Before departing Ondo State, some eminent traditional rulers, led by Oba Daniel Aladesanmi, the Ewi of Ado-Ekiti, had called a meeting between Omoboriowo and the governor. They said they wanted peace to reign and advised Omoboriowo to shelve his ambition until 1987 and allow Ajasin to run for a second term. Omoboriowo refused. He said the gathering was not the proper forum to discuss party matters. He was prepared to press his luck for the gubernatorial gamble of 1983.

8

The Gathering Storm

By the time 7,000 delegates gathered for the UPN special conference at the National Arts Theatre, Lagos, in October 1982, it was clear that the very soul of the party was in distress. Conflicting currents of ambitions were taking their toll on a party that prided itself in discipline and *esprit de corps*. This had been the fate of UPN's precursor, the AG, when the Akintola camp pitched its tent against supporters of Awolowo over the issue of joining the Tafawa Balewa-led federal government. Akintola wanted an alliance, while Awolowo said no. But this second time around in the UPN, there was no such high principle at stake, no ideological divide, no great variance in the sloganeering of the men of ambition. What was at stake was the spoil of office and raw power.

The struggle was protracted and bitter. The contest generated much heat especially in the five states controlled by the UPN. This was so because party members, thinking that the UPN was in an unshakable position, believed that the surest way to office was to win the party's nomination. Once the nomination was won, it was easy ride to office since the electorate was fully behind the party and Awolowo, its legendary leader. The second driving force of the men of ambition was their second-fiddle mentality. Many of them believed that the party would not be able to defeat the incumbent NPN federal government and therefore decided to concentrate all their resources in fighting for positions at the state levels.

While nomination contest for the 1979 elections was a relatively simple affair since the party then was a mere shadow of its leader, by 1982, the UPN had become a gargantuan monster, hardly understood and barely controllable by Chief Awolowo. Men and women of ambition were trying to emerge from Awo's shadow, building their own separate political fiefdoms. It was clear then that the new complex political reality would change the rule for nomination for the 1983 general elections. During the National Executive Council meeting of the party in Benin City, April 1981, the party accepted a proposal from Chief Babatope, its director of organisation, and set up a nine-man committee on party elections. The committee, headed by Chief Jonathan Odebiyi, a highly respected senator and minister in the defunct Western Region, also included among others, Professor Aluko, Chief Demas Akpore, then deputy-governor of Bendel State and Mr. Ayo Adebanjo, the secretary of the party's legal defence committee. Mr. Nati Iwuagwu of the party's national secretariat served as secretary.

From then on, party members traded their ambitions openly and on the pages of newspapers. What worsened things was a declaration by Chief Awolowo in 1979 that party members who were not members of the NEC of the party could attend its meetings as observers. He also ruled that other party meetings should be thrown open to all members. This encouraged a lot of rowdiness at party meetings and nothing secret or substantial could be discussed beyond the heckler's ear shot. The result was that ambitious party men were always bringing their supporters to NEC meetings. During the December 1981 congress of the party in Lagos, aspiring contestants even brought drummers and bards to sing their praises and turned the venue into a Tower of Babel. Some of the delegates at the Eko Holiday Inn venue of the congress even raised an alarm over the alleged presence of herbalists and traditional medicine men said to have been invited to the venue by some delegates from Oyo State.

Some believed that Chief Awolowo encouraged this atmosphere of indiscipline, or at least, condoned it. He never failed to criticise the governors at party meetings, voicing his disagreements with some of the governors' flamboyant lifestyles, his distaste for their going about with long convoys of cars and howling sirens. ('Anytime you leave your state, you paralyse the government,' he was reported to have chided one of the governors). At the Lagos meeting of December 1981, he advised the governors to listen to constructive criticisms from fellow partymen 'for the purpose of improving the policies of your administration'. He said further: 'It is in this way we can produce an abundance and sufficiency of all good things of life which will benefit every one of the people.'[31]

It was also well known in party circles that Awolowo had had personal disagreements with at least two of the governors: Professor Ambrose Alli of Bendel and Chief Bola Ige of Oyo. The mercurial Alli, a professor of morbid anatomy, though an old Action Grouper, was a dark horse when he emerged as UPN gubernatorial candidate for Bendel in 1979. He beat better known faces like Chief Olu Akpata, L.T. Garry, Mr. Obahiagban, Mr. Air Iyare and Dr. I.M. Okonjo. As governor, he was the personification of executive power and he left no one in doubt about who won the election. In the early days of the regime, he was able to carry the state assembly along with him, even in some of his controversial decisions like the siting of the state university in his home town of Ekpoma. The state assembly also endorsed his decision to give his father a state burial for which a sum of N400,000 was spent. Awo felt this was unfair since the death of a governor's father was not exactly a state affair, and therefore asked Alli to refund the money. He even offered to contribute some money for the refund, arguing that what Alli did offended public morality. Alli ignored the advice. 'I did not drink the drinks,' Alli had defended himself. 'I didn't eat the food. The public ate the food, and drank the drinks. The state burial accorded my father was not immoral. It would have been immoral if I had pinched government money without authorisation'.[32]

Awolowo's disagreement with Ige came early in 1979. As earlier stated, Awo had favoured Archdeacon Alayande, an old stalwart, for the Oyo State gubernatorial seat. But the old teacher had been out-manoeuvred by the intrepid Bola Ige. To gain the upper hand, Ige received a helping hand from Alhaji Busari Adelakun, Alayande's kinsman from Ibadan, a self-taught, barely literate, but astute and populist politician. To compensate him for his crucial role, Ige decided to appoint Adelakun a commissioner when he became governor in October 1979. Chief Awolowo had advised Ige against this, suggesting that Adelakun be given a less sensitive appointment. But Ige not only went ahead to appoint Adelakun a commissioner, but also informed the latter about Awolowo's objection to his appointment.

By 1982, however, Adelakun had become a stubborn thorn in Ige's flesh. He had become one of the principal actors in the struggle to get Ige out of the Government House, Ibadan. Those involved this time around were Chief Sunday Afolabi, an accountant who was Ige's deputy governor; Chief Michael Omisade, lawyer, old Action Grouper, and high-profile chairman of the National Bank; and Alayande. Both Afolabi and Omisade were interested in the governorship which Ige was determined to keep for another four years. But Adelakun and Alayande were involved more in settling old scores. The Alayande faction, while willing to concede four more years to Ige, had never forgiven Adelakun for being instrumental in the defeat of a fellow Ibadan man in 1979. Adelakun, though not a gubernatorial material, eventually was chosen as running mate to Omisade during the stormy shadow election of 1982. Adelakun's ambition was however clear: to stop Ige from getting a second term.

Their disagreement was dramatised during the stormy NEC meeting of the party in Yola, capital of Gongola State, September 8-10, 1982. Prior to this meeting, Ige had removed Adelakun, who served creditably as commissioner for local government and later health, from the cabinet, and suspended him from the state's executive committee of the party. Adelakun was the party treasurer for Oyo State. In Yola therefore, Adelakun presented a petition to Chief Awolowo protesting his suspension and accusing both Ige and his deputy governor of anti-party activities.

Adelakun accused Ige and Afolabi of holding a nocturnal meeting with General Obasanjo at the latter's residence on Osuntokun Avenue, Bodija Estate, Ibadan on June 27, 1982. Adelakun said the secret meeting was at the instance of Obasanjo, who was Afolabi's school mate at Baptist Boys High School, Abeokuta and a friend of Ige. The former head of state had sought to persuade Afolabi to allow Ige a second term. After six hours of discussion, the meeting, which was also attended by M.D. Yusufu, Obasanjo's inspector-general of police, and General Muhammed Inuwa Wushishi, ended in an impasse as Afolabi maintained he would contest the governorship against Ige. No issue about the presidency or the ambition of Chief Awolowo was discussed. Adelakun, who spoke through an interpreter, said Afolabi narrated the story to him.

Both Ige and Afolabi were kept standing for several hours, defending themselves. Ige was later to refer to the Yola meeting as the Day of the Long Knives. What the two men did was akin to heresy since Obasanjo was regarded as an 'arch-enemy' by partymen who placed the blame for the UPN loss of the 1979 presidential election on the retired general. Some of those who spoke had even recommended that the two men be expelled but Chief Awolowo had prevailed, saying that he vouched for the loyalty of the two top stalwarts. A resolution was passed at the Yola meeting condemning the Obasanjo initiative as 'a dangerous, an unwarranted and intolerable intervention in the internal affairs of the UPN.'[33] It also concluded that 'the conduct of the two leaders was most reprehensible. In particular, the council considered that the chairman of the party in Oyo State (Ige)[34] was more to blame for the ill-motivated meeting.' The two leaders were censured, but were allowed to go. It was the last time Ige and Afolabi would stand on the same side of the fence. It was at the Yola meeting, too, that the decision was taken to hold the October special conference.

Trouble was also brewing in Ogun State, where the popular Onabanjo was governor. The onslaught in Ogun was led by Chief Olusoji Odunjo, son of the late Chief Joseph Odunjo, Yoruba pioneering poet, playwright and novelist who was one of the intellectual and cultural giants of the old Action Group. Olusoji Odunjo's deep-seated grudge against Onabanjo was his having lost the gubernatorial nomination battle to the veteran journalist by a narrow margin in 1979.

During the first ballot for the party ticket, Odunjo had tied with Onabanjo and both of them won 20 votes. Those who also contested for the party ticket along with Onabanjo and Odunjo were Chief Odebiyi and Dr. Tunji Otegbeye. Odebiyi had scored six votes while Otegbeye had only four. During the second ballot, both Otegbeye and Odebiyi turned over their support for Onabanjo who emerged the winner with 30 votes to Odunjo's 20. Now, Odunjo was gearing up for a re-match.

On Sunday October 24, 1982, a secret meeting took place in Ibadan by members of the underground Joint Action Committee, JAC, a clandestine club of ambitious men bent on stopping the governors from running for a second term. Its membership covered the belt of ambition stretching from Ogun, Oyo, Ondo and Bendel states. It also had some members from the NPN-controlled Kwara State. Leading members of JAC were said to be Omoboriowo, Afolabi, Chief Demas Akpore, the deputy governor of Bendel State, Dr. Okonjo, Chief Olu Akinyosoye, Mr. Lam Adesina, Mr. Ayodele Morakinyo, Odunjo, Senator Fasanmi, Chief Omisade, Dr. Oluwadamilare Awe, Mrs. Titi Ajanaku, Adelakun, Kunle Agunbiade and Adegbamigbe Akilaya. The secret meeting of JAC in Ibadan resolved to fight against the automatic re-nomination of governors which they suspected would be proposed at the special conference. A few days earlier, JAC had also taken an office at the National Theatre, venue of the conference from where to operate effectively.

Few days before the meeting, a group suspected to be JAC had sent an anonymous letter to Chief Awolowo on behalf of the "representatives of the masses of the UPN of Ogun, Oyo, Ondo and Bendel states," warning that automatic re-nomination of governors would not be acceptable. Except to those who were members, JAC had succeeded in operating totally under cover and it was virtually unknown to the party leadership. Therefore, while Chief Awolowo and his governors were prepared for an intellectual encounter, a new kind of battle awaited them at the main hall of the National Theatre complex.

When Chief Awolowo, accompanied by Hannah Idowu Dideolu, his wife, entered the hall at 10 a.m. on Monday, October 26, for the special conference, he was least prepared for the kind of picketing he met. The hall was filled with protesters, drummers, and singers, all clamouring that there should be no automatic re-nomination for governors. Some of the placards being carried read: 'No automatic re-nomination for UPN governors; Shadow election a Must; Party Constitution is Supreme; Automatic re-nomination of governors will destroy the party; Give democracy a chance.' Earlier when Oyo State deputy governor, Afolabi, made a noisy entrance, he was followed by supporters with placards reading: 'Bola (Ige) is not our 1983 governorship favourite; Bola is finished; Bola not suitable; Remove Bola Ige.' There was no more pretence now — the masquerade has removed its mask in the market place.

Chief Awolowo and his paladins formed a formidable phalanx on the high table. The party band struck the note of its evocative anthem and, in one moment of emotional camaraderie, party members stood up in unison as hoary voices filled the auditorium. The song was written by Awolowo and set into music by Chief Hubert Ogunde, pioneer Yoruba playwright, dramatist, poet and musician.

1.   It's a duty that we owe
     To our great dear motherland:
     To enhance her
     And to boost her
     In the eyes of all the world

2.   Egalitarianism
     Is our national watchword:
     Equality
     Of good fortune
     Must be to each sure reward

3.   Liberty and Brotherhood
     Are the goals for which we'll strive:
     Plus progress
     Plus plenty
     And all the good things of life.

4. Up! Up! Nigeria!
    And take thy rightful place;
    It's thy birthright
    And thy destiny
    Africa's leading light to be.

Despite the intimidating atmosphere, Chief Awolowo was not one
to abandon a battle simply because the odds appeared great. Unlike the
custom, copies of his speech were not distributed on the floor. It was an
emotional appeal for iron discipline within the party. Before launching
on the main track of his speech, he dwelt on the pervading atmosphere
of intimidation, saying that while the majority may have its way, the
minority must be allowed to have its say. He said party members should
not give room for 'tyranny in democracy or autocracy in democracy.' He
explained that tyranny occurs in a democracy when the minority fail to
listen to the opinions of the majority. He said when the majority also
refuse to listen to the opinion of the minority, then democracy would
give way to autocracy. He therefore advised those who had been
carrying placards and distributing leaflets to use the opportunity of the
conference to explain and defend their position with reasons and
arguments. He appealed to members to listen to contrary arguments
and allow reason to prevail.

Chief Awolowo said he had information about a meeting (the JAC
meeting) held earlier by a group of party members where it was decided
that proceedings of the special conference would be disturbed if
discussion did not favour them. He then appealed to such members to
press their case with better arguments instead of threat of force. Going
into the issue of nomination, he said he supported that the five governors
be re-nominated. His arguments were threefold. The governors had
performed well in carrying out the party's programme of free education
and free health services despite financial problems and that there was no
better way to show appreciation than to give them the maximum two
terms allowed by the constitution. The internecine fight for nomination
would sap the party of its energy and vitality and it might weaken it in
the greater battle ahead for the presidential contest. Thirdly, Chief

Awolowo said none of those who had been accusing the governors had been able to substantiate any of those allegations, and he urged party members to deal in facts and not in fictions.

Chief Awolowo also took a swipe at the deputy governors who were now eyeing their bosses' jobs. He condemned the manner in which they were going about their ambition, accusing them of deliberately undermining the regimes of their governors and washing the party's dirty linens in public. 'Is it morally right for the deputy governors to contest against their governors?', he asked. He concluded that party members should then close rank for the battle ahead against the ruling NPN and not waste energy and resources in intra-party squabble. He concluded: 'I have served you all my life with vigour and dedication. I call on you at this hour to join me in saving Nigeria.' [35]

In calling for automatic re-nomination for the governors, Chief Awolowo also extended it more than was expected. He asked that the deputy governors too be returned, and that all parliamentarians, who so wished, should also be returned. This blanket endorsement was unexpected by most members, even those who would have supported the return of the governors. Chief Awolowo, however, wanted peace in the house so that he could have his army intact for the next round of battle.

Events at the time also indicated that both his friends and foes were not leaving anything to chance. That October, the NPP, one of the parties in the Progressive Parties Alliance, PPA, with the UPN, had given its governors in Imo and Anambra states automatic re-nomination. President Shagari too had been given a renewed mandate to contest by the NPN, and when Chief Moshood Abiola, multimillionaire newbreed politician, attempted to challenge the nomination, he was reminded by Alhaji Umaru Dikko, Shagari's powerful minister of transport, that 'the presidency is not for sale'. Abiola was not allowed to even collect nomination papers. Moreover, Chief Awolowo harboured the fervent hope of emerging the presidential flagbearer of the Progressive Peoples Alliance (PPA) and might have felt that the governors should be allowed a second throw to strengthen his hands within the alliance.

The meeting went on recess and reconvened in the afternoon to discuss and debate Chief Awolowo's presidential address. Chief Awolowo informed members that 93 people had signified their intention to comment on his address. The discussion was lively and orderly, but by the trend of debate, it seemed the governors were going to carry the day. The deputy governors came in for tongue- lashing and were accused of undermining the party and sacrificing its interest on the altars of their ambitions. Six persons contributed to that afternoon debate. These include Colonel (rtd) Joe Achuzia from Bendel, Chief Amber Bassey from Cross River State, Mr. J.A. Ijabiyi from Ondo State, and Dr. J.D. Adeniyi from Oyo State. There was indication of trouble however when Chief Mokolade Gbolagunte, the speaker of the Oyo State House of Assembly, made his own presentation. His every sentence was interrupted by hecklers who were shouting 'no! no!!' Not even an appeal from Chief Awolowo would deter them. Gbolagunte was forced to sit down.

At 2.45 p.m., there was a loud explosion and pandemonium broke out. The impression then was that someone had planted a bomb in the hall. In the ensuing melee, people trampled on each other as they rushed for the exits. Six persons, including a woman, were seriously injured while scores of others sustained minor injuries. Amidst the confusion, Chief Awolowo, his wife and some few top partymen sat unmoved on the dais until the hall was cleared. Shoes, handbags, caps, jeweleries and other personal items littered the hall. It was later revealed that Dr. Oluwadamilare Awe, a member of JAC from Ilesha and supporter of Adelakun who was lately removed as chairman of Trans Nigeria Motels Limited by Governor Ige, moved behind Chief Awolowo and took off the lid of a fire extinguisher. Recalled an eye witness: 'The security men quickly took away the governors but Chief Awolowo sat tight; with him were senior officials of the National Secretariat. Those of us from the National Secretariat stayed because we found it difficult to abandon him. If he had run, we would have run faster.' [36]

The meeting could not reconvene again that Monday and was adjourned till Tuesday, October 26. Though Chief Awolowo told the delegates that 190 members had indicated their desire to contribute to the debate, only Governor Jakande actually made a presentation. It was a passionate speech delivered in the staid monotone of Jakande. He delved into the history of the party, highlighting the personal sacrifices of Chief Awolowo, and concluded that while many people had benefited from the career of the party leader, the nation was yet to reap the full benefit of Awolowo's service. He urged members to make every sacrifice possible to ensure that Chief Awolowo emerged as president in 1983. He urged delegates to remember that 'it was Chief Awolowo that won the 1979 elections for us and not the UPN'. In a calculated retraction of Awo's earlier position which many believed was done without the full consent of the party patriarch, Alhaji Jakande suggested that governors should face nomination contest. The hall exploded into thunderous applause. Jakande's proposal was seconded by Senator Olu Akpata and it was unanimously adopted. The meeting resolved, predictably, to present Chief Awolowo as the party's presidential candidate for 1983, and also back his candidature should the PPA decide to field a common list of candidates. The special conference closed at 12:55 p.m.

To prepare and ratify the rules for the forthcoming contest, the NEC of the party held an emergency meeting at the National Theatre the following day, October 27, 1982. Chief Awolowo told NEC members that he was aware of the existence of JAC and accused its members of trying to build a party within the party. Governor Jakande confirmed that members of JAC had sent Dr. Awe and Mrs. Titilayo Ajanaku from Ogun State to persuade him (Jakande) to back them. Awolowo caused five libellous releases from JAC to be read to NEC members. He then turned to JAC members present, among whom were Omoboriowo, Afolabi and Akpore, and asked them to defend the allegations contained in their releases. All of them denied knowledge of the write-ups. Chief Awolowo then ordered that JAC be dissolved, adding: 'People who always want to have their ways at all cost and never provide better arguments but rather want to force their petty ideas on others are anarchists and pocket despots who will ultimately fail.'[37] The meeting then resolved that deputy governors and other government officials wishing to vie for governorship should resign their appointments. It was also decided that an elected electoral college should elect the party's governorship candidate in Lagos, Oyo, Ondo, Bendel, Cross River, Rivers, Kwara, Benue and Sokoto by November 11, 1982.

The hour of reckoning was at hand and candidates worked feverishly to gain advantage and appeal to the electorate. For the UPN aspirants, it was like facing a general election as the party threw the verdict open to the general electorate. Though the rule said only party members could vote at primaries, anybody who so desired could present himself as one. Unlike in some other countries, party membership in Nigeria was an elastic one. Apart from contractors doing government jobs or those holding official appointments as part of party patronage, there were very few people contributing dues to party coffers. There were also many, too, claiming to be members of the party without having membership cards. Their only positive identification with the party was their own conviction that they were members of the party.

The UPN national secretariat issued the following four directives to the candidates and supervisors of constituency meetings:

1. *Supervisor is expected to do the following: (a) Ask one supporter of each candidate for governorship to nominate the number of candidates that such constituency is expected to send to the electoral college. For example, where there are three candidates for governorship race and the constituency is expected to return 20 delegates to the electoral college proper, the supervisor will ask a supporter to nominate 20 names. After each supporter has nominated his own 20 names, there will be a total of 60 names for all to select from. Voting will then be done by a show of hand for each of those sixty names nominated by all the members of the constituency who have voting rights. The 20 delegates will be those who scored the highest 20 marks. (b) The same procedure will operate for all other electoral colleges viz: Senatorial and House of Representatives.*

2. *Supervisors will ensure that only card-carrying members of the party will be allowed to go into the venue of the constituency meeting. Anyone who arrives at the venue without a party card*

> *shall be free to purchase one from the supervisor at the entrance*
> *to the venue of the meeting.*
>
> 3. *A supervisor shall inform the meeting that no school children,*
>   *beating of drums and singing will be allowed at the constituency*
>   *and electoral college meetings.*
>
> 4. *A supervisor shall inform those present that, for the purpose of*
>   *this special meeting, every participant is equal in all respects*
>   *and will be so treated'.* [38]

Events in Ondo State were to indicate the kind of problems that would attend this novel party democracy. As could be seen, it was American-type primaries, where those who wanted can vote once they identify themselves with the party. But unlike in America, party loyalty in Nigeria was something more fervent and visible and people were not aversed to being 'persuaded'. Therefore, the UPN party primaries became a contest of 'persuading' people to come and identify themselves with the UPN and the candidate doing the persuasion.

The NEC had directed that state secretariat of the UPN should purchase cards at one naira per copy and resell same to party members. Those members who could not obtain cards from the UPN secretariat could purchase their own copies from the supervisors at election venues. But the Omoboriowo group suspected that it might find itself at a disadvantage if its supporters could not purchase party cards. Believing that they might not be allowed to vote without party cards, they might decide to stay at home. The group, therefore, protested to Chief Awolowo, saying that Governor Ajasin and his group in the Ondo State UPN secretariat were denying its members the right to buy party membership cards. It also alleged that Ajasin and his group had bought up all the cards sent to Ondo State and were distributing them to their supporters. Chief Awolowo responded to this by changing the rules since the time factor would not allow for adequate investigations and redress if necessary. He directed that the Omoboriowo Group be allowed to buy party cards directly from the national secretariat and that this facility should be open to all other groups. The Omoboriowo group was also allowed to buy at half the price and it quickly purchased

50,000 copies for N25,000. Chief Awolowo also directed that all party members should be allowed to vote at constituency meetings whether they had party cards or not. This, he explained, was to ensure that the most popular candidate was not disadvantaged simply because he was not rich enough to buy membership cards for his supporters.

On November 4, five days to the constituency meetings, a drama was played out in Akure. A group of Omoboriowo supporters caused two members of Ajasin group, Mr. Alex Adedipe and Mr. Olorunnimbe Farunkanmi, both members of the state assembly, to be arrested for allegedly being the brain behind the illegal printing of party cards. The members of the Omoboriowo group who were involved in this drama were Mr. Ogunyimika, Mr. Rufus Aboloyinjo, and Agunbiade, the majority leader in the state assembly. Aboloyinjo said he traced Adedipe to the printing workshop where the latter had allegedly gone to supervise the illegal printing of party cards. Dramatically, too, photographers were present, recording the arrest of Adedipe by the police who had followed the tip of Aboloyinjo to effect the arrest. Senator David Oke made a formal report of this to Awolowo and the latter ordered an immediate investigation, promising that candidates involved would be punished. Mr. J.F. Oresegun, assistant national administrative manager of the party, was sent to Akure to investigate the matter. Oresegun's findings and conclusions were even as dramatic as the event itself:

> From all information at my disposal and provided, Honourable Farukanmi and Adedipe knew nothing about the printing of the cards, as depicted by their statements. It would appear the Omoboriowo faction of the UPN in Ondo State, comprising Messrs Falodun, Ogunyimika, Aboloyinjo, Agunbiade and Olowoporoku, arranged the printing of the cards.
> "Thinking that Ajasin's faction had uncovered their plans as a result of Adedipe's unexpected presence at the premises of Allied Printers, Omoboriowo's faction, through the help of a top police officer, who is a friend of Mr. Ogunyimika, schemed yet another plan aimed at blackmailing and embarrassing Governor Ajasin, Farukanmi, Adedipe and others in Ajasin's group.

Meanwhile, like the other two deputy governors gunning for the governorship job in the UPN, Afolabi of Oyo and Akpore of Bendel, Omoboriowo resigned his job Friday October 29, 1982, following party directives. 'The next few months perhaps weeks, will be momentous in the political and constitutional life of our great party and, therefore, of this virile state,' he told a press conference while announcing his resignation in Akure. 'The journey ahead will be a very rugged one. Sacrifices will be required of all of us so that our great party will, in association with other progressive parties, have the opportunity of managing the affairs of this great nation which have been neglected to the utter detriment of our 80 million people. You and I will be called upon conscientiously to work for our great leader, Chief Obafemi Awolowo, our great party and our great nation'.

By this time, the UPN had approved nomination committees for each of the states involved in the party elections. In charge of Oyo State were Mrs. Oyibo Odinamadu, Ogun; Archdeacon Alayande, Ondo; Chief S.J. Umoren, Bendel; Dr. Tai Solarin, Lagos; Mr. S. Ekeanyanwu, Kwara; Chief Bola Adewunmi; Cross River, Mr. S.A. Ricketts; Rivers, Alhaji Raufu Williams; Benue, Mr. Adenuga Adesina; and Sokoto, Alhaji Ganiyu Dawodu. There were also secretaries and other members. They were expected to appoint supervisors for the various constituency meetings from outside the state. For Ondo State, supervisors were brought from the universities in Ibadan and Ife and The Polytechnic, Ibadan. But Chief Umoren also had to recruit more people from the state, especially teachers, to help with the exercise.

For the purpose of the gubernatorial contest, constituency meetings were to be held November 9, 1982. Those elected at these constituency meetings would then meet at the state capitals in an electoral college to elect the party's flag-bearer.

When the Ondo State party electorate met Monday November 9, they were confronted with three candidates, each wanting to be governor. These were the governor, his estranged deputy and Senator Banji Akintoye. All the three had clear credentials for the job. Ajasin had the advantage of incumbency, though this was also a burden since many of the promises he made in 1979 could not be redeemed because of lack of funds. Akintoye, who had been made to shelve his gubernatorial ambition in 1979, was the candidate of the influential Ife group. He believed that, if Ekiti was to present a gubernatorial candidate, he was the right person for the job. An articulate intellectual, Akintoye was professor of history at Ife before becoming a senator in 1979. His principal supporter was Professor Aluko.

Though many of Omoboriowo's supporters painted him as an Ekiti champion whose destiny was to rescue the Ekiti people from irascible philistines as Fabunmi, the intrepid Oke-Mesi Ekiti general, did in the 19th century when he expelled Ibadan envoys from Ekitiland, he had also built his reputation as an ideologue of the party. He was the author of *Awoism: Select Themes on the Complex Ideology of Chief Obafemi Awolowo,* (published by Evans Brothers Limited, Ibadan 1982), a not too brilliant attempt at foisting the thoughts of Awolowo into the prism of Marxism-Leninism. 'Writing a book on Awoism is by no means an easy task at all, because analysing and treating the political thoughts of one of Africa's most controversial philosopher-statesmen is indeed a difficult assignment,' Omoboriowo had written in Awoism. 'His thoughts are many-sided. His ideology - his science of ideas – is complex and beyond me. Sometimes you think you know it, at other times you think you do not'.

He continued: 'Awoism is a national and supra-national political theory which aims at the orderly and rapid transformation of Nigeria and of Africa – mentally, socially and economically – so that Nigeria, first and foremost, and Africa as a whole will assume their positions among the developed nations of the world within a record time. It implies, by definition, a mental revolution from the current paralysis of social decadence, a revolution in our thoughts, our utterances, in our daily work, in our attitude towards labour and in our inter-personal relationships. In short, it requires a total mental emancipation and a cultural re-assessment. In this regard, Awoism must not, under any circumstances, concern itself with either participating or sharing power with the other unprogressive, reactionary political parties. This position pleases us because we must be seen to be different in colour and character from the others. This, in effect, means that we must not compromise our position because of temporary suffering in the struggle. After all, we have the advantage that our opponents are intellectually indolent and they awkwardly present their policies, which are ludicrous by reason of their grim impotence expressed more and more in slogans of the feudal capitalist oligarchs'.

The three-cornered contest raised tension. Chief Awolowo had held a meeting with the three contestants, August 18, 1982. On his arrival from London where he had gone for his usual medical check-ups, Chief Awolowo had invited warring factions of his party in Oyo, Ogun, Bendel and Ondo states for a one day meeting at his country home in Ikenne. For the Ondo State members, each of the three leaders, Ajasin — Omoboriowo and Akintoye — were to bring 20 supporters each for the meeting. But the meeting could not hold because Awolowo was down with an attack of bronchitis. Awolowo later held a meeting with the three leaders in his bedroom, appealing for peace. But by November 9, on the day of the constituency meetings, all these were apparently forgotten and the atmosphere was charged like a prelude to war.

Electoral college delegates were allocated to each constituency on the basis of its voting strength for the UPN during the 1979 elections. One person was to represent 1000 voters. That was the job at each constituency on Monday, November 9. In many of the constituency centres in Ondo State, it was a carnival-like atmosphere. All the big-wigs in politics were back from Akure and Lagos to the local roots of their power. In many places, schools and offices closed early and all those who cared or could be 'persuaded' found their ways to the voting centres. Voting was orderly in most centres, but there was trouble in some, especially in places where the influence of Omoboriowo and Ajasin was almost equally joined. Akintoye's most visible presence was in Ado Ekiti, his home base, but the contest in most other constituencies was dominated by the duo of Ajasin and Omoboriowo.

What was curious was the interpretation of the electoral guidelines by the supervisors. The rule was that of winner-take-all, that is, whoever had the highest number of votes in a constituency automatically should nominate all the electoral college delegates for that constituency. That was the American system that the UPN was emulating. But the supervisors, except in some few places, decided that the election of delegates should be on pro-rata basis. Some of those who participated in the election said the supervisors decided on this since most members of the UPN electorate did not see why the person who had the majority had to take all. In any case, most communities, not sure where the wind might blow, did not want to put all their eggs in one basket and, therefore, decided to put their feet on both sides of the bridge. Both Ajasin and Omoboriowo protested against this local interpretation of the rule to Chief Umoren who only mollified them with sweet words.

By the night of Monday, November 9, all the constituency elections had been decided and the results were brought to Akure. At the Government House, there was excitement as the results being brought in indicated that Ajasin had secured majority delegates for the Wednesday, November 11 electoral college that was to take place at the State House of Assembly. An elated Bola Aragbaiye, press secretary to Governor Ajasin, the following day, informed the public, that Ajasin had already secured the winning number of candidates for the electoral college. Stated Aragbaiye: 'Governor Adekunle Ajasin of Ondo State was yesterday leading the other two contestants in the UPN gubernatorial primary elections according to unofficial figures of returns so far known. Out of the 610 results already out, Governor Ajasin has polled 494 with Chief Akin Omoboriowo running second with 111 votes and Senator Banji Akintoye in the third position with five votes'.

At the Ijapo Estate headquarters of the Omoboriowo group, there was consternation and confusion in the air. Many leaders of the group had been coming with unsavoury reports about happenings in their constituency centres, ranging from the alleged partiality of supervisors to the fact that some of the supervisors too were of Ondo State origin. In the evening, it was decided to write a petition to Chief Umoren protesting against the conduct of the election and asking him to nullify the results in some constituencies. The petition was submitted the following morning at 7 a.m.

At the Akintoye camp too, the mood was that of despondency. Aluko, one of the leaders of the group, was invited by Ajasin later in the night of November 10. The governor asked him whether it was true that the Akintoye group was negotiating with the Omoboriowo group on the modalities of Akintoye turning over his electoral delegates to Omoboriowo. Aluko denied it and further pledged that whoever emerged as the winner would be supported by his candidate.

The following day, November 11, 1982, when the electoral college was to meet in Akure, was to be the climax of the intra-party struggle between Ajasin, the penitent patriarch, and Omoboriowo, his rebellious Turk. From then on, the equation would be different.

9

Prayers And Protests

On Wednesday, November 11, 1982, thousands of people thronged the Ondo State House of Assembly, Akure, venue of the final lap of the UPN primary election for governorship. It was as if the whole of Akure had descended on the place. Fierce-looking policemen were at hand to prevent trouble, but tension was palpable in the air. Though the election was to commence at 10.00 a.m, the venue was already like a market place by 8.00 a.m. Chief Sebastian Umoren and his men, however, did not arrive at the venue until 11.30 a.m, one and half-hours behind schedule. The nomination committee, with Mr. Felix Okafor as secretary, had a meeting that morning to consider a petition submitted by Chief Omoboriowo, praying that results from Ekiti-Central Constituency Five, be cancelled because of alleged irregularities in favour of Governor Ajasin.

Apart from the petition from Omoboriowo on Ekiti-Central Constituency Five, other petitions, mostly from Omoboriowo's supporters, had also been received by the Umoren nomination committee. These petitions were from Akure, Akoko North Constituency 111, and Ifesowapo, among others. There was also a protest against Olawumi Falodun, the UPN state secretary and a known Omoboriowo partisan, who was accused of obstructing election process in Akure the previous Monday. It was clear that, unless the petitions were answered favourably, Omoboriowo was at the losing end.

The official delegates who were to participate in the electoral college were 1,418 partymen and women. The voting was to be by a single ballot and delegates were to indicate their choice in a voting form distributed at the venue. But the candidates knew that the voting was a mere formality as their fates had been sealed the previous Monday, when the delegates were elected by the various constituencies. Because he was trailing closely behind Ajasin, according to the returns from the constituencies, Omoboriowo's main hope now rested in Umoren acceding to his prayers to cancel the results coming from certain constituencies.

By the time Umoren and his men showed up, the politicians were in a fever of expectations. While the voting was going on amidst so much rowdiness, Omoboriowo left hurriedly to Ilorin, capital of Kwara State, to consult with Mr. Oluwasaanu Olabayo, a charismatic spiritualist and the Rasputin of modern Nigerian politics. Olabayo, self-styled apostle of Christ, was the founder and leader of Evangelical Church of Yahweh, a neo-Judaist African Christian sect that placed much emphasis on predictions and divine interventions. The success of Olabayo in his endeavour was indicated in the calibre of his clientele which once included Chief Awolowo and General Yakubu Gowon. Omoboriowo, born Catholic, came under the influence of this strange but successful spiritualist, who lured him from his earlier equally fervent indulgence in African fetish practices and beliefs. As was his practice, Olabayo had revealed his predictions for 1982 in January of that year in a booklet, claiming that it was a revelation from God directly to him. He had predicted that Governors Alli of Bendel, Onabanjo of Ogun, Adamu Atta of Kwara and Adekunle Ajasin of Ondo State would not be re-elected. He said they would either lose the nominations of their parties or the general elections of 1983. (Both Alli and Attah lost the general elections).[39] It was to this man that Omoboriowo carried his petition at the thick of battle.

With Omoboriowo gone, the fort was left to Fasanmi, who was his chief agent and his other partisans like Jolowo, Olowoporoku and Morakinyo. Despite protests from the Omoboriowo group, Umoren rejected their petitions and duly declared Ajasin the winner. He had polled 707 votes to Omoboriowo's 531 and Akintoye's 44. Senator Fasanmi, despite his protest, gave a brief speech congratulating Chief Umoren and Governor Ajasin. Said Fasanmi: 'On behalf of Chief Akin Omoboriowo, I thank you and your team immensely for a very wonderful job you have done today. The job you have done is like a very brilliant lawyer arguing a very bad case. In any case, you have done it very creditably. I want to assure you that, as far as Chief Akin Omoboriowo is concerned, we will forget the past and we can assure you also that politics of bitterness that had characterised our body politic here will come to an end.'[40] Similar speech was made by Mr. Akin Omojola, the agent for Professor Akintoye. Dr. Falaye Aina, Ajasin's agent reciprocated this gesture. Said Aina: 'I want to assure the two aspirants that it is their participation in this game that has made it a wonderful experience for us all, and that Chief Adekunle Ajasin will from now henceforth forget that there had been a battle in the field.'

At the end of the exercise, however, both Fasanmi and Omojola wrote a joint petition to Chief Umoren, condemning the verdict. Said the letter:[41]

> We the undersigned, on behalf of our respective candidates, namely Chief Akin Omoboriowo and Professor Banji Akintoye, will like to place on record series of electoral malpractices which include the following:
>   1. Areas where no elections were held and certificates of voting eligibility were issued are:
>
>   1. Akoko South Constituency 11
>   2. Owo Constituency 111
>   3. Owo Constituency 1V
>   4. Ilaje/Ese Odo Constituency 111
>   5. Ifesowapo Constituency 11
>   6. Ondo Constituency 111
>
> In the above constituencies, in spite of the fact that no elections were held, certificate of voting were issued.
>   2. In some places, secret elections were conducted without the knowledge of opposing parties.

3.   There were allegations of collision between supervisors and Governor Ajasin's agents to the detriment of our candidates.

4.   In addition to the above, there was massive importation of party cards which were distributed to people from other constituencies.

5.   There were several petitions published by aggrieved and interested aspirants and their agents; and in view of the above, we wish to say that the results of the elections do not represent the true position of things. It is unfortunate that our party; which is respected for its democratic character; can descend to a level where elections are brazenly rigged; and in view of the above, the election results are discredited and therefore unreliable. We hereby reject any results so declared.[42]

As could be seen, the protest was an instance of calculated outrage, but not strong enough to be considered a unilateral declaration of war. If Umoren should concede to Fasanmi and Omojola's request and cancel results from the six constituencies above, it would only reduce Ajasin's margin of victory, not reverse it. There were a total of 137 votes from the six constituencies made up of the following: Akoko South II (8 votes), Owo III, (11 votes), Owo IV (21 votes) Ilaje-Ese-Odo III (38 votes), Ifesowapo II, (30 votes) and Ondo III (29 votes). If these had been deducted from Ajasin's figure, his votes would have shrunk to 570 from 707. It would still have been a winning figure against Omoboriowo's 531 votes. If this scenario had emerged, the beautiful bride then would have been Senator Akintoye with his bargaining chip of 94 votes. But the Ajasin group argued too that but, for the inexplicable rejection of the winner-take-all formula, its candidate would have won a landslide of 928 votes to Omoboriowo's 371 and Akintoye's 63.

While the Ajasin camp was celebrating victory, the Omoboriowo group knew the battle was not over yet. The following day, Thursday, November 12, having returned from Ilorin, Omoboriowo took his case to the court of public opinion. Addressing a press conference in Akure, Chief Omoboriowo alleged that Ajasin won his majority delegates through sheer intimidation of party members, bribery and the use of non-partymen during the election of delegates Monday, November 9. He alleged further that Ajasin openly used government machineries, like the OSBC, vehicles and the involvement of teachers and civil servants in the exercise to give him undue advantage. Accusing the Umoren committee of collusion, he alleged that when his supporters protested about the presence of non-partymen, 'including aliens and beggars,' and those carrying forged party cards, the supervisors usually ignored them.

He said further that there were areas where voting did not take place on the 9th because of violence or the supervisor failing to show up, but the Umoren committee later gave the delegates certificate from such areas to Chief Ajasin on the 11th November. 'Perhaps it was the incident in Ekiti Central V that clearly exposed the Umoren Election Committee as a committee that came to openly manipulate Chief Ajasin for a second term,' said Omoboriowo. 'The constituency is made up of eight towns namely - Are, Afao, Iworoko, Awo, Esure, Eyio, Iropora and Igbemo. Apart from dramatically shifting the election centre from Iworoko (the counting centre for the 1979 election) without letting the Omoboriowo group know, the election was purportedly held in Igbemo at 9 p.m. without the other towns present and all the thirty-three delegates later awarded to Chief Ajasin.'[43]

He also mentioned the incident of violence at Ilaje-Ese-Odo Constituency III. He alleged that 'the pro-Ajasin group violently disrupted the elections by attacking the Omoboriowo group leaving 15 of them seriously injured. They are now receiving treatment at the Igbokoda General Hospital. The speaker of the Ondo State House of Assembly (Jolowo), who represented the constituency, was violently attacked and thrown into Oluwa River. He was lucky to be rescued by Chief Olusola Omonira (a member of the House of Representatives). After the fracas, the election supervisor disappeared dramatically and no election was held. Yet, all the thirty-eight votes in the constituency were later awarded to Chief Ajasin by the Umoren Election Committee.'

In conclusion, Chief Omoboriowo submitted: 'In all, nine constituencies, namely: Ifesowapo II and III (60 votes); Ilaje/Ese Odo III, (38); Owo II and III (34); Idanre/Ifedore III and IV (40); Ikale I (27) and Ondo III (29) were cancelled. But all the votes were later awarded to Chief Ajasin. The votes from the cancelled areas amounted to a total of 238 votes. It is therefore obvious that if these 238 votes had been deducted from 707 awarded to Chief Ajasin, he would have lost to Chief Omoboriowo by 469 to 531.' This would have given Omoboriowo a majority of 62 votes.

At the end of the press conference, Omoboriowo declared: 'We want to make it categorically clear that the result of the elections are totally unacceptable to us in view of the massive rigging and gross irregularities itemised above. We are therefore withdrawing further participation from the shadow elections until the issues involved are disposed of. All we demand is that we should be allowed to democratically elect our own leader. Anything else is unacceptable to us.'

As could be seen, the substance of Omoboriowo's press conference was different from the petition of Fasanmi and Omojola. Akoko South II and Owo IV, mentioned in Fasanmi's petition, were now dropped in the Omoboriowo paper. Instead, we now have five new constituencies added, viz: Ifesowapo III, Owo II, Idanre/Ifedore III and IV, and Ikale I. Now the number of constituencies involved had increased from six to nine and the delegates' votes from 137 to 215.

On the same day of the press conference, Chief Omoboriowo despatched a petition to Chief Awolowo titled:

> *Actual Strife of Truth with Falsehood: Restoration of my Election Victory.*[44]
>
> I wish to state that I actually won the shadow election for the governorship of Ondo for the 1983 elections on November 11, 1982.
>
> However, for reasons best known to Chief Umoren, he manipulated the figures so as to 'rig in' Chief Ajasin! It is the most fraudulent show I have ever seen. When Chief Umoren and Chief Ajasin knew late on November 10, 1982 that I had won the election by the figures coming from different areas of support, they then went into a secret meeting at the UPN secretariat and drove out Mr. Ebun Ogunyimika, the State Treasurer.
>
> Voting at the electoral college scheduled for 10 a.m. on November 11, 1982, was held up until 1.30 p.m. owing to another round of secret meeting at the UPN secretariat between Chief Umoren and Chief Ajasin. At the completion of polling, it became clear that I had won the elections.

The figures recorded were as follows:

Omoboriowo   Ajasin   Akintoye

532 votes   479 votes   94 votes

He then started to assemble the figures which he had earlier on in the day declared publicly cancelled from various constituencies where voting never took place and areas where there were massive irregularities and which had similarly been declared 'cancelled'. It would interest you to know that it was at this point in time that certificates were issued to the supporters of Chief Ajasin in such constituencies. The constituencies are: Ilaje/Ese Odo 111 (38 votes), Ikale 1 (27 votes), Idanre/Ifedore 111 and IV (40 votes), Ifesowapo 11 and 111 (60 votes), Owo 111 and IV (34 votes), Ondo 111 (29 votes), and Ekiti Central 1 and 111 (30 votes), and Ekiti Central V (35 votes).

At the end of all these, Chief Ajasin was awarded 707 votes!! That was how I was robbed of my victory. By the night of November 10, 1982, when the situation was clear that Chief Umoren and Chief Ajasin were out to rig the election, a petition (in my name) was written and handed over to Chief Umoren and Okafor at about 7.30 a.m. on November 11, 1982 to point out these irregularities and the areas where elections did not hold or were cancelled. We insisted that such areas should be announced first before proceeding with the final exercise of November 11, 1982. Chief Umoren disregarded all these and proceeded amidst protests during which policemen battoned and manhandled my supporters very ruthlessly for protesting. The speaker of the State House of Assembly, Chief Richard Jolowo was ruthlessly battoned as well for protesting that election was not held in his constituency, Ilaje/Ese-Odo 111.

Papa, I know that your sense of justice and fair play would revolt against this monstrous 'robbery'. I therefore appeal that I am declared the winner, because I actually won. Chief Umoren cannot deny those manipulations. Anything contrary to this proposition would amount to naked injustice.

In any case, Chief Umoren met Chief Ajasin and Mr. Miller Aganyemi in secret session for two hours on the morning of November 11, 1982. I strongly suspect that that was where the rigging conspiracy was perfected.

Papa, once more, I am the winner of the shadow election and I hereby appeal to you in the name of God, as the Chief Electoral Officer to pronounce on this today, Sir. I look eagerly on to Papa for justice, not any favour at all.

Yours very sincerely,

Akin Omoboriowo
(Candidate with the highest poll).

As could be seen, the substance of Omoboriowo's letter was again different from the facts adduced in the press conference of the same day. Some constituencies not mentioned in the press conference were now listed in the letter to Chief Awolowo. These were Ikale 1, Owo IV, Ekiti Central 1, 111 and V. These untidy contradictions in his prayers could be a result of the intense pressures mounting on Chief Omoboriowo as a result of his narrow loss. It is noteworthy also that he was praying Chief Awolowo and the party to nullify the returns from these constituencies because of what he alleged were election malpractices on the part of Ajasin's supporters resulting in Omoboriowo's loss by default. But he did not ask for the re-run of elections in these constituencies to ascertain the relative strength of the three gubernatorial aspirants at the grassroots. What seemed to have shocked Omoboriowo the most was the massive deployment of government and party resources by Governor Ajasin to press his drive for a second term. That Omoboriowo did not anticipate this was surprising. Nonetheless, he regarded such use of privileged position as not only immoral but reprehensible.

Omoboriowo said the untidiness in the presentation of the petitions of the group was because of the pressure of those tense hours. He told the author: 'The original petition by Fasanmi and Omojola was written on the spur of the moment on the back of a car. At that time, we did not have all the details of what happened at the constituencies. Fasanmi was not a member of the election committee and he could only go by the facts made available to him at that time. But when I returned from Ilorin, I set up a committee to put our petition in a detailed form. I also wrote one petition on my own. Our position was documented by Akilaya; and

I believed in the course of his compiling his report, it was not unlikely that there were serious omissions.'

In not insisting on a re-run of elections in the disputed constituencies, Omoboriowo may also be adhering to a more legalistic interpretation of the UPN election guidelines. The party had ruled after the Yola National Executive Committee meeting that no candidate must employ government machineries for the campaign. But in the ensuing battle, all the governors deployed their supporters in official cars, mustering local government chairmen and other party officials for the battle. Another very pressing issue was even more immediate. In 1978, it had been simple to run for office in the nascent UPN. Now the language of discourse was money. Omoboriowo had rented a campaign office, nick-named The Situation Office, in the highbrow Ijapo Estate of Akure and now had band of personal staff, including publicity officers, and political advisers. These dedicated youths, highly idealistic and impressionable, did not even contemplate their leader kissing the dust on the battle field. Therefore, Omoboriowo had invested his fortune and the fortunes of his co-travellers in his daring adventure for power. One of such men, Funsho Akinyosoye, one of the three whom Omoboriowo promised the deputy-governorship, was said to have invested more than N100,000 in the struggle.

When Omoboriowo and his men saw defeat therefore, most of them were understandably shattered. To compound their predicament, they resolved to boycott the subsequent nominations into the Senate, House of Representatives and the House of Assembly. This gave a free ride to Ajasin's supporters even in Omoboriowo's strongholds like Ijero and Ekiti South. These Ajasin supporters, basking in the glow of victory, interpreted the turn of events as the intervention of God who had finally allowed David to triumph above an ambitious Absalom.

Events in Ondo State were replicated in the remaining four UPN controlled states and also Kwara. In Bendel State, 12 partymen, including the former deputy governor, were in the race for the governorship with Professor Alli. Governor Alli triumphed with 789 votes out of a total of 1,002 to win the party nomination. The closest to him was Rowland Owie, a member of the House of Representatives, who polled 64 votes. Akpore, the former deputy-governor had only 16 votes while Benson Alegbe, the Speaker of the Bendel State House of Assembly, scored 20 votes only. Dr. Isaac Okonjo, a member of JAC and also of the UPN/NEC, who was among the failed gubernatorial aspirants, alleged that the election was rigged in favour of Governor Alli. He gave Chief Awolowo a 14-day ultimatum to cancel the result of the election or see the consequence. 'If they want us to sink the UPN in Bendel State, we shall cooperate beautifully,' he threatened.[45]

In Ogun State, three candidates were attempting to get Governor Bisi Onabanjo's job. Two of these candidates, Dr. Tunji Otegbeye and Chief Odunjo, were faces from the old struggle of the 1978 nomination while a dark horse, Mr. Oladele Onafowope from Ijebu, was also in the race. Onabanjo emerged the winner with 646 votes against Odunjo's 288 votes, Otegbeye's 107 and Onafowope's four votes. The three candidates who lost later protested to Chief Awolowo, but the party NEC upheld the election of Onabanjo.

The least controversial of the elections was that of the immensely popular 'Action Governor' Lateef Jakande of Lagos State. His lone challenger, one H.A. Hakeem-Habeeb, an obscure politician, scored three votes to Jakande's 1,181 votes.

In Kwara State, the old yielded place to the new. The young Turks, led by the urbane Senator Cornelius Olatunji Adebayo, succeeded in deposing the *ancien regime* of the earthy and boisterous Chief Josiah Sunday Olawoyin. Olawoyin, extremely courageous and steadfast, was Awo's point man in the late 50s and turbulent 60s in the defunct Ilorin-Kabba province, which now makes up the present Kwara State. Born February 5, 1925, in Offa, Kwara State, he attended Offa Grammar School and later Ibadan City Academy where he graduated in 1947. From 1956 until 1961, he was a member of the Northern House of Assembly. During the AG crisis of the 60s, he cast his lot with Awo and thus entered a period of political wilderness until the military came to power in 1966. The creation of Kwara State (then called West Central State) by Gowon, catapulted Olawoyin from the role of an underdog to one of the powerful arbiters of public opinion during the military era. He was a director of the Northern government-owned New Nigerian Newspapers Limited, until he resigned in 1979 to enter politics.

Olawoyin was the UPN flagbearer during the 1979 election, but he was worsted by the newbreed muscle of Dr. Olusola Saraki, a flamboyant phenomenon in Kwara who came with the mandate to re-assert the pre-eminence of Ilorin in the state's politics. With the triumph of Adamu Atta, Saraki's protege in the governorship contest, Olawoyin resumed his old role of being the underdog. Having fought so hard for the creation of the state during the regime of Ahmadu Bello, Olawoyin felt history was denying him his just reward. But defeat still presented Olawoyin with even more problems. With his loss, Chief Awolowo gave instructions that the defeated gubernatorial aspirant and his close supporters should be given, inter alia, board appointments in the LOBOO (Lagos, Ogun, Bendel, Oyo and Ondo) states. Many of the newbreed politicians felt that Olawoyin was spreading the largess only to himself and his old cronies of the AG. Despite his generosity of spirit, his amiability and wit, many of them felt Olawoyin was set in his ways, permanently anchored on the shores of nostalgia, and involved in too many local battles to properly respond to the dynamics of the new era. They were not often impressed by Olawoyin's racy tales of his heroic exploits during the fifties and the sixties. To many of them, it was ancient history. These uppish followers were beholding to no one, except Chief Awolowo himself.

The leader of the challengers was Adebayo, teacher, and administrator. Adebayo was born at Oke-Onigbin, Kwara State, February 24, 1941. He graduated from Ahmadu Bello University, Zaria, in 1967 and took a graduate diploma in education from the University of Ghana in 1969. He was a lecturer at the Obafemi Awolowo University, OAU, Ile-Ife, from 1969 until 1973 when he moved to the Kwara State College of Technology. From 1975 until 1978, he was a commissioner in Kwara State, and he worked briefly again at the Kwara State College of Technology before going into full time politics with his election as a senator on the platform of the UPN in 1979.

These were the two men who confronted each other on the Kwara battle field. While Olawoyin was a roughhewed rabble rouser like a general of a guerrilla army, Adebayo was suave like a corporate raider. Both men were determined fighters and both were fiercely loyal to the party patriarch, Chief Awolowo. What was also in the game in Kwara was not just the ambition of these two paladins, but the very future of the UPN. It was an open secret that Jakande was backing the ambition of his old friend, Olawoyin, while Governors Onabanjo and Ige were known to be sympathetic to Adebayo. It was the belief in top party circles that Chief Awolowo was encouraging the ambition of Jakande to be regarded as heir-apparent to the patriarch himself. It was therefore interpreted that an Olawoyin victory would increase the bargaining chips of Jakande in a future contest for supremacy in the party.

Apart from Olawoyin and Adebayo, there were five others who were interested in the governorship ticket. On November 11, 1982 when the delegates met in Ilorin, it was a rowdy affair. There were serious protests and the nomination committee had to shift ground by preventing 168 delegates from voting. These delegates were from Omupo (55), Omu-Aran (45), Ajase, (55) and Ilorin North-West, (13), and the protesters argued that they were not properly elected. Adebayo carried the day with 389 votes to Olawoyin's 235. Chief Awolowo however nullified the election on the recommendation of the nomination committee. He ordered that a new nomination exercise be conducted and that all the 168 delegates prevented from voting during the last balloting should be allowed. Final ballot was held November 27, 1982 and Adebayo retained his crown by beating Olawoyin with 75 votes. He scored 595 to Olawoyin's 520.

However, the real drama was to be enacted in Oyo State where ambitious partymen fought the nomination as if the very fate of the Nigerian Republic was at stake. In Ibadan, the 19th century war camp of the Yoruba and now the largest black indigenous city in the world, politics met war in the valley of confusion, deceit and naked ambition. Ironically, the forces that were arrayed against Governor Bola Ige in Ibadan were the same forces that helped him wrestle the party leadership from the septuagenarian Alayande in 1978. Now on the opposite side were his former deputy-governor, Chief Sunday Afolabi, Chief Michael Omisade, the Maiyegun of Ife, and also the mercurial Adelakun who engineered the Yola trial of both Ige and Afolabi.

Ige was a victim of his own success. By being too beholding to Afolabi and Adelakun who were instrumental to his winning the ticket in 1978, Governor Ige gave the impression that he was only a surrogate governor. Adelakun, as commissioner for local government, was one of the most powerful members of the cabinet, holding himself like a super-commissioner. To underscore his importance in the party, when he was given a chieftaincy title by the Olubadan, the entire UPN leadership, including Chief Awolowo, was in attendance. Adelakun built a network of personal loyalties across the local councils and secured for himself an appreciable pedestal. Possibly because of Adelakun's limited education, Ige must have been tempted to underrate him. Moreover, Adelakun surprised many of the skeptics, including Chief Awolowo, by performing his jobs with appreciable credit in the two ministries he served.

If Adelakun was hindered by his limited education, Afolabi was properly armed. An accountant, born June 22, 1934, Afolabi is from Iree, Osun division, the largest area of the then Oyo State. He was educated at both Offa Grammar School, Kwara State, and Baptist Boys High School, Abeokuta, which he left in 1953. A self-made man, he started as an accounts clerk with the United Africa Company, UAC, in 1954 and by the time he retired in 1978, he was chief accountant of the University of Ibadan. Like Adelakun, Afolabi was one of the many AG youth activists in the sixties who were severely persecuted by the unpopular Akintola regime.

Both Adelakun and Afolabi knew that Ige was a formidable opponent. Despite his intellectual arrogance, his incendiary temper, caustic tongue and his brilliant ability to make enemies, Ige has a way with people that makes them believe him. Fiercely independent and also fiercely loyal to the party, Ige is paradoxically a Yoruba nationalist as well as an avowed Nigerian patriot and Pan-Africanist. He was regarded as a leading ideologue of the party, a man moulded by its peculiar clay, fired in the furnace of its turbulent history, and schooled in its mores. It was not just because of the poetry of his language that Bola Ige was called the Cicero of Esa-Oke - the small Ijesa town precariously perched on the hill where Ige, born September 13, 1930, has his roots, but because he has the poet's disdain for danger. At the age of 32, he came to prominence when he was elected federal publicity secretary of the AG in 1962. Since then, Ige has worshipped in the innermost shrine of the party and was regarded as the leading contender for Awo's mantle with Jakande. Ige first read Classics at the University of Ibadan, 1949-1955, before proceeding to the University of London where he read law and was called to the bar in 1961. He served in the Western State cabinet of General Adeyinka Adebayo as Commissioner for Agriculture and Natural Resources and also Lands and Housing until 1970 when he went into private legal practice. He was one of the leading Nigerians in the anti-apartheid struggle since the sixties when this was merely a rhetorics of succeeding Nigerian governments, and from 1971 to 1975 was the chairman, World Council of Churches Programme to Combat Racism.

By 1982 however, Ige, who was the darling of the party youths, was now fighting for his political life. What gave him a clear advantage was that his opponents were divided and many of them were not sure of why they were in the race. Those in the running were Ige, Afolabi, Omisade, and five other politicians.

Trouble started Monday, November 9, 1982, as the nomination committee conducted elections at the constituency levels. The nomination chairman, Mrs. Oyinbo Odinamadu, national vice-president of the UPN, was bombarded with reports of irregularities and intimidation at the voting centres as thugs and other loafers were employed by some of the candidates to intimidate their opponents' supporters. Elections could not be held in many centres. The following day, Mrs. Odinamadu got a taste of the Oyo style of democracy when a group of thugs forcibly ejected her and members of her committee from the UPN state secretariat which the nomination committee was using as office. Thousands of party supporters also stormed the secretariat protesting against the conduct of the constituency elections the previous day. Odinamadu was wondering whether she was presiding over a nascent civil war or a mere party nomination exercise.

On Wednesday, November 11, elected party delegates, about 1,500, were expected to meet at the Premier Hotel, Ibadan, to elect the party's flagbearer for the 1983 election. Early that morning, the management of the hotel, fearing that violence might erupt, decided to shut the hotel door to the delegates and succeeded in persuading Odinamadu to agree. An announcement was then made on the state radio, Radio O-Y-O, shifting the venue to the State's House of Assembly. But the announcement was only a detour to shield the Premier Hotel from trouble. The main door of the state assembly was locked and angry UPN members stood outside. Then, about 10.00 a.m, Adelakun, the deputy-governorship candidate to Chief Omisade, led his supporters to the venue and forced the door open. His unsmiling supporters, numbering some few hundreds, occupied every seat in the hall. Mrs. Odinamadu and her team were nowhere in sight. Instead, two lorry loads of anti-riot policemen came and asked Adelakun and his men as well as other UPN members who were outside the building to vacate the place. By this time, too, Omisade and Adelakun were present. That evening, Odinamadu held a meeting with the contending partymen. She later announced that the nomination exercise was suspended 'because of circumstances beyond our control in the discharge of our duties.'

The Oyo poll indeed held the promise of violence and bloodshed because of the passions involved. The enstranged friends of Bola Ige who were now fighting on the other side were serious in their beliefs that Ige could not get the party's nomination without their support. Now, not just the battle for power was involved, but the struggle to save face and prove one's indispensability to the UPN and the regime of Ige. On Sunday, November 21, Chief Awolowo called the warring partymen for a peace meeting at Ikenne. Present were Governor Ige, Chief Afolabi, Adelakun, Archdeacon Alayande, Busari Raji and Omisade. Also present were Chief Babatope, Rotimi Abe, Awolowo's private secretary, and Mrs. Dideolu Awolowo. It was at this Ikenne meeting that an unexpected solution was found to the Oyo problem. Omisade and Afolabi agreed to withdraw from the race and allow Ige a free run. The other present, especially Adelakun and Alayande, pledged their support; and Awolowo appealed to Ige to reciprocate the brotherly gesture. At the end of the meeting, a communique was issued, signed by all the Oyo delegates and Chief Awolowo, copies of which were despatched to media houses that night.

The camaraderie lasted as far as the gate of Awo's house. The aftermath of the Ikenne accord was that it gave rise to a new development whereby party members were now criticising Awo in public, an unthinkable heresy in the past. Addressing his supporters in Ibadan, Adelakun said the decision to return Ige unopposed was masterminded by Chief Awolowo. 'What happened at the meeting held in Ikenne was the handiwork of Chief Obafemi Awolowo and not that of the masses who are supposed to be the deciding factor in the exercise.'[46] Omisade, too, was unsparing. 'The decision to return Chief Bola Ige as the UPN gubernatorial candidate without the party's primary election was essentially wrong and cannot be defended on the principle of democracy,'[47] he said.

Awolowo responded to this spate of criticism by beating a retreat. He nullified the Ikenne accord because it was 'now becoming a calculated blackmail case,' and ordered a rerun of the Oyo State nomination exercise Monday, December 6. When the constituencies eventually met again December 13, the turn-out was heavy and police presence was evident at every centre. Still, there were disturbances in some areas, especially in Ibadan. The seven other candidates opposing Ige stayed away two days later when the elected delegates met at the Liberty Stadium to cast their votes.

Chief Sylvanus Ekeanyanwu, who was now presiding over the exercise since Mrs. Odinamadu had stepped aside, said he did not receive any letter from the other contestants indicating they were withdrawing from the race. To help Ekeanyanwu were 600 armed policemen who conducted thorough bodily searches cn all those who gained entrance into the stadium. At the end of the day, they had assorted kinds of charms and dangerous weapons as exhibits. One of the delegates was even found with a small live tortoise crawling on his chest which he claimed was a charm for personal protection. The election, billed to start at noon, finally began at 2.35 p.m. Delegates from 12 constituencies out of the 126 in Oyo State were not allowed to vote because of irregularities and disturbance in their various centres. Chief Ige carried the day with 1,114 votes while Chief Omisade scored 11 votes. None of the other contestants scored up to ten votes. None of them too congratulated the winner. Afolabi, the former DG, scored only six votes.

Many of those who lost the nomination battle placed the blame on Chief Awolowo. Their main complaint was that Chief Awolowo turned his eyes away while the governors were taking advantage of their dual powerful position as state executives and party chairmen. This, they said, was against the NEC decision in Yola. Many of them were unhappy about the verdict of Awo over the exercise when he arrived from London on a brief visit. 'The results of the primaries, so far, are satisfactory to me because all the party officers involved in the exercise have performed well,'[48] he told reporters at the Murtala Muhammed International Airport, Ikeja, Sunday, November 14, 1982. He defended his party despite the rumbles from Oyo, Ondo and Kwara states. 'It is not unusual to witness such occurrences in crucial elections, and it did not portray the party in bad image.' He denied that he was the party's chief electoral officer, saying that he was only well briefed about the results and conduct of the elections. It was after this pronouncement that Awo ordered re-election in Kwara and Oyo states.

Aggrieved partymen came in droves to Chief Awolowo's house in Ikenne with similar prayers seeking the setting aside of results. Petitions came from all the UPN controlled states. A petition from the Omoboriowo Group was also submitted to Awolowo, signed by Omoboriowo himself and nine of his supporters, including Jolowo, Agunbiade and Fagbamigbe, seeking that the victory of Ajasin be set aside. Omoboriowo also visited Awolowo several times, asking that his petition be upheld. By this time too, the group was observing its decision to boycott the nomination exercise and all party activities.

Early in December, the National Executive Committee of the party met in Lagos to deliberate on the reports of the various nomination committees and the petitions that arose from the exercise. Omoboriowo and his leading supporters were absent. Only Fasanmi was in attendance. Chief Awolowo reminded members that the possession of party card was not an issue of the just concluded exercise since all the candidates had unrestricted access to party cards. He advised party members to be sportsmen and abide by the decision of their fellow partymen. He asked Fasanmi, the only member of the Omoboriowo group present, to defend the petitions submitted by and on behalf of Omoboriowo. Fasanmi then remarked that he had since accepted that Ajasin was properly elected. Some members also pointed out the contradictions in the petitions and urged the meeting to reject them. Chief Awolowo expressed disappointment that Omoboriowo should submit petitions without being ready to defend them before the NEC. Professor Aluko then moved a motion that the petitions be rejected 'because they lacked merit' and it was accepted. The party congress on December 8 upheld the decision and also approved the nomination results from Kwara, Bendel, Ogun and Lagos states. A reconciliation panel was, however, set up to persuade the embittered losers back into the fold. It was headed by Alayande.

10

Burning The Bridge

The violent turn of the campaign for the 1982 party nomination had taught Omoboriowo to sleep with only one eye closed. Few days before the special conference in Lagos, two gunshots were fired into the bedroom of Olu Adesina, the deputy speaker of the Ondo State House of Assembly and one of the staunchest of Omoboriowo supporters. Though no one was hurt, Adesina was understandably scared. A few weeks later, Fagbamigbe, Omoboriowo's leading lieutenant in Akure, was attacked while on a visit to a female friend. Fagbamigbe and two other stalwarts with him received gunshot wounds. Because of this uncertain atmosphere, Omoboriowo decided to place his own fate in his hands, after all, the Yoruba say that Ogun, the god of war, favours the fastest man. He was now permanently armed with his loaded revolver. The lone police escort the police obliged him since he resigned as deputy governor was probably as frightened as a frog in this heavy fog of suspicion. This loss of trust made reconciliation very difficult.

After he resigned as deputy-governor, Omoboriowo had told the press in Akure that he would go back to his legal practice if he should lose the nomination contest. The reality of defeat now left him mainly with the JAC game plan. Many members of JAC had vowed to leave the UPN if they should lose the nomination contest.

By the end of February 1983, most of these erstwhile members of JAC were in the embrace of their former arch foes, the NPN. The logic seemed to be if you cannot trust your friends, try your enemies. Odunjo declared for the NPN, Monday November 29, 1982. Speaking at the declaration ceremony in Abeokuta, he told reporters that 'I quit the UPN today because I am a true son of my father.' With him was Titilayo Ajanaku, a woman party activist and many of his supporters. Okonjo of Bendel, Adelakun and Afolabi of Oyo were later to follow suit.

Chief Awolowo was worried by this avoidable dissipation of the party's energy on internal bickerings and he made efforts to get the aggrieved partymen back into the fold. He told the UPN congress in Lagos, December 8, 1982, that Odunjo would not have left the UPN if his (Odunjo's) father was alive. 'One of my sons has gone to the NPN. Well, I hope before long he will join us here so that we will not say of him that he is a prodigal son,' Awo told the congress.[49] Earlier on, he had warned aggrieved members not to go to the NPN. 'I want any aggrieved member of the UPN to note that going to the NPN is a retrogressive action.'[50]

He said the aggrieved partymen should not now abandon the battle when victory was around the corner. 'I call upon Akin Omoboriowo and Banji Akintoye, J.S. Olawoyin, Wenike Briggs and Owen Feibel; Tunji Otegbeye and Okunwa, Hakeem-Habib, Olu Akpata, Idigbe, Akpore and others. - I call upon all those men and their supporters as well as on all the others who contested nominations for elective offices and failed, to rally round the illustrious banner of the UPN which they once loved and I believe still love,' he said. He appealed to them to come back into the fold and 'join wholeheartedly in the historic battle which is now about to be waged in order to dislodge the NPN from power and terminate, once and for all, the evil of feudalism and ethnic hegemony which it represents and which has kept our dear country in chains since the past 25 years.'[51]

After the congress, Chief Awolowo held private discussions with party leaders from different states to assess the fortunes of the party. He was informed that, contrary to his directive, JAC was still alive and its members were now negotiating with the NPN. He asked some of the leaders to act as peacemakers in the states. Awo believed that the talk about the NPN was 'sheer blackmail because many of these people are UPN to the core who would never betray the party'. He urged members to continue having faith in the estranged partymen and not succumb to 'rumour'.

The Alayande reconciliation committee began its work in earnest, meeting party members in the different states. It finally succeeded in achieving almost 100 per cent success in Kwara State, but in other states, especially Oyo and Ondo, it was a herculean and thankless task. The Omoboriowo group said its condition for reconciliation with Ajasin was that Omoboriowo be declared the winner of the shadow election. They also wanted nomination contest to be re-conducted for other elective offices that were done while the group was boycotting the election. The group was, however, told that Ajasin's victory was now irreversible since Chief Omoboriowo and his supporters failed to turn up to defend their petitions at the party's NEC meeting on December 6, 1982. Omoboriowo, indeed, had been in favour of the group attending the NEC, but many of his more militant supporters were violently against it. At a meeting held in Fagbamigbe's house in Akure, Omoboriowo had argued that the group should not continue boycotting party functions. But he was accused of chickening out and was virtually shouted down.

The Omoboriowo group later submitted a memorandum to the Alayande panel asking that a new nomination contest should begin afresh, including that for governor, if the party would not accede to its first prayer that Omoboriowo be declared the UPN gubernatorial candidate. In its submission to the Alayande panel dated December 21, it stated:

> We wish to thank you for coming here to make a try at reconciliation.
> We will like to submit that the exercise of today has been overtaken
> by events for the following reasons:-

(a)   The bone of contention, which is the gubernatorial contest and on which a strongly-worded petition sent through a high-powered delegation to Chief Obafemi Awolowo, in addition to series of personal petitions by Chief Akin Omoboriowo himself, did not receive the attention of the National President. Rather, the National Executive of the party ratified the election of Chief M.A. Ajasin and the Congress confirmed this election without Omoboriowo's side being heard at all.

(b)   After the decision of NEC and Congress and after this Panel had been set up, the National President invited Chief Akin Omoboriowo, with some of his supporters to Lagos. All issues as contained in the petitions were considered. The outcome of the meeting has rendered the meeting of today unnecessary.

If there is to be any reconciliation at this stage, the status quo as at the NEC and National Congress of 6th November 1982 to 10th November 1982, should be restored.

In conclusion, we would like to state that we have responded to today's meeting out of respect we have for the eminent members of the panel.

The submission was signed by Olawunmi Falodun, R.A. Olagunju, Ebun Ogunyimika, J.O. Owoseni and Gbolaga Akintunde, on behalf of the Omoboriowo group.

In the meeting he held with leaders of the Omoboriowo Group shortly after the nomination exercise of November 11, Chief Awolowo appealed to them to keep their quarrel a family one and not drag the UPN into public disgrace. Chief Omoboriowo himself was not present but the group then presented a petition on his behalf which was read by Olu Mafo. Those present at the meeting held in Awo's Park Lane, Apapa residence included Fagbamigbe, Akinyosoye and Professor Opeyemi Ola. As part of the outcome of this meeting, Fagbamigbe later addressed a letter to:

My Dear Leader,
(Chief Awolowo)
Dated November 18, 1982.

Your yesterday's fatherly assignment to me and my colleagues inspires me to write you this personal letter.

I will carry your message of reconciliation to my constituency and I will do my best to spread it to other parts of Ondo State. But I wish to re-emphasise that it is you alone who can revive the spirit of party yeomanry which Chief M.A. Ajasin, our Governor, and his aides have destroyed in the rank and file of UPN members in the state. If anyone says that he can do it without the aid of your wise and courageous decision on the petition which we presented to you, such a person would be misrepresenting the realities of the situation to you.

Papa, the injuries inflicted on our sense of intra-party political sportsmanship by Governor Ajasin's open intimidation, forgery of 166,000 party membership cards, harassments, bribery, abuse of party and governmental privileges, juggling of figures and manipulation of results as well as the undisguised lust to kill are festering fast. It is only a deterrent disciplinary action appropriate to the gravity of the malpractices committed that will heal the wounds and restore the pride of the people in our great party and make them come forth to take up your banner, with buoyant spirit, to the battle for 1983.

Sir, I was shocked to observe that, until yesterday, you never heard that I and two other party leaders in Akure were shot on the night of Tuesday, 2nd November, 1982 on account of the intra party struggle within our party. The event was widely reported in the newspapers, namely: *The Tribune, The Times, The Punch* and *The Concord.* My legislative aide, Mr Akin Akomolafe, in apparent despair rushed to Lagos the following day, 3rd November 1982 and reported it to Mr. Ebenezer Babatope. It was good that I had the opportunity of showing you the wound which I received from the gunshot. Papa, I thank God, for if I had died, you would not have heard and, therefore, no message of condolence would have come from you to my family.

By the end of November, the divide between the two camps had become a chasm. On November 14, 1982, the Omoboriowo group held a meeting at Ijero in which it was decided that the group should team up with another party if the UPN refused to uphold its petitions. Chief Omoboriowo, too, was intent on leaving the UPN at this stage if his prayers were not answered, but his mind was not made up on which direction to go. He toyed with the idea of joining the Nigerian Advanced Party, NAP, of Tunji Braithwaite. The leaders of NAP even met him on a number of occasions but negotiation was fruitless. Then, he shifted his focus to the NPP and after series of meetings with the party's emissaries, he finally met with Chief Adeniran Ogunsanya, NPP national chairman. At a meeting with Ogunsanya in his Surulere, Lagos, residence, the NPP leader cautioned Omoboriowo from joining the NPN, promising him that the NPP would give him an 'honourable place'.

But when Omoboriowo reported his romance with the NPP to his supporters at the now regular meeting in Ijero, they would not accept it. He told the author: 'When I told my supporters that I was joining NPP, they said no, that that would be political suicide. They said NPP is in the same camp with the UPN, the PPA alliance. I said I haven't deviated much in principle (of the UPN). But they said, don't go because Chief Ajasin as governor would use the physical instrument of coercion he has to beat us into submission: that is the police and even the courts. If we join the NPN, not only would we have the security behind us, some of our people who are not being paid can be put in federal parastatals.'

The Omoboriowo group then set up a committee under the leadership of Chief Babatola to negotiate with the NPN. Chief Omoboriowo also met with many NPN leaders, including Senator Uba Ahmed, the party secretary and later President Shagari who assured Omoboriowo that the group would have no problem with the NPN. The Babatola committee concluded negotiation with the NPN on Thursday, December 16, 1982. In attendance were leading members of the NPN. The same day leaders of the Omoboriowo group then moved over to Awolowo's Park Lane residence to honour an earlier invitation. The delegation, led by Omoboriowo himself, also included Chief Babatola, Professor S.A. Agboola, Chief Jolowo, Prince Olu Mafo, Akinlaya and Dr. S.A. Ogunlusi.

The meeting was not a happy one. Chief Awolowo had continued to have disturbing reports about Omoboriowo's flirtation with the

NPN and the group's threat to impeach Governor Ajasin. 'Akin, I heard that you are negotiating with the NPN,' he told Omoboriowo. 'I am surprised that you could go to this extent simply because you lost a nomination contest. What of millions of party supporters who have never gained anything from the party and yet continued to be loyal?' Omoboriowo denied that he was planning to leave the party and pledged his continued fealty to the leader. Awo then confronted Jolowo and asked him about the impeachment rumour. Jolowo denied it, but quickly added that if the need arose, 'no Jupiter can stop us.'

'Does that include me?' Awo asked in bewilderment.

'No Jupiter can stop us,' Jolowo asserted.

Chief Babatola then tabled the group's terms of reconciliation. He asked that Omoboriowo be given back his job as deputy-governor and that Ajasin be compelled to reinstate all sacked commissioners and board members who lost their jobs because of their sympathy for Chief Omoboriowo. He also requested that these men be given arrears of salaries they would have collected. They also wanted Ajasin to drop some of his commissioners, including Adegoke, Osomo and Aina. Ogunlusi also added that Awo should order new nomination exercise if these conditions were not acceptable. Awo remarked that anybody getting his job back would only be at the discretion of Governor Ajasin. He said the group should first settle for peace and then those who lost the nomination can be rehabilitated. He said for them to insist that certain people must get their jobs back was 'humiliating'. He promised however to hold further discussion with the Ajasin group.

As the group was about to leave, Awo called aside Chief Babatola, then 73, foundation member of the defunct AG and a minister in Awo's government in the defunct Western Region. He appealed to Babatola to help pacify the younger members of the group and give peace a chance. Babatola pledged that he would do his best. Awo then remarked to Omoboriowo? 'If you join NPN, then you would have to write another book to counter what you have written in *Awoism.*'

Three days later, Sunday, December 19, 1982, Chief Babatola reported the findings of his committee to an enthusiastic gathering of the Omoboriowo group at Ijero. He told the group that they had reached an agreement with the NPN which only needed to be signed as soon as the general group approved it. Though the group spent about N1.5 million for the nomination bid, the NPN had pledged to fund their coming campaign entirely from the party purse with an initial pledge of N6.1 million. The federal government would also establish a station of the Federal Radio Corporation of Nigeria, FRCN, in Akure for the group's exclusive use. Chief Omoboriowo would be adopted as the NPN gubernatorial candidate while preference would be given to members of the group for other elective offices. To ensure this, NPN candidates already nominated for these posts would be asked to step down for candidates from the Omoboriowo group. Moreover, the police and the National Security Organisation, NSO, would be re-organised and made more responsive to the group's need.

The Ajasin group, besides monitoring the movements in Omoboriowo's camp, brought more reports to Chief Awolowo. Ajasin took counter measures against the group still in government; and on December 21, followed this up by sacking the remaining four commissioners in his cabinet who had joined the Omoboriowo camp. These were Falodun, the commissioner for employment, establishment and training, Babatunde (health), Ilori, (education) and Professor Agboola, (lands and housing).

When it was clear that Chief Omoboriowo was bound for the NPN, many leading members of the group started retracing their steps. Among these were Senator Fasanmi, Senator David Oke and Mr. S.K. Babalola. These people now formed the vanguard of people informing Awo that Omoboriowo had gone far and was now beyond "redemption." On Wednesday December 29, a refurbished UPN had its conference in Akure. Conspicuously absent were members of the Omoboriowo group, except those who had decided to part ways with the former deputy-governor. At the end of the conference, a new set of officers was elected which included Ajasin as chairman, Dr. Aina as deputy chairman and S.K. Babalola as secretary. It was Babalola who told reporters that the state UPN conference had decided to expel six leaders of the Omoboriowo group from the party. Those expelled were Chief Omoboriowo, Falodun, Ogunyimika, Babatunde, all former commissioners, Chief Akerele, Chief Babatola and Chief M.I. Owoeye.

The expulsion brought into the open the fact that the reconciliation efforts were not yielding fruits. Chief Awolowo had earlier invited Omoboriowo to a meeting in his Ikenne home slated for Friday, December 31. Omoboriowo, perhaps piqued by the expulsion, stayed away, but Akinyosoye, who later refused to follow Omoboriowo to the NPN, turned up. Alayande who had also been invited to attend was present. Chief Awolowo then sent an urgent message to Omoboriowo that the latter should meet him at Akure, Tuesday, January 4, where he was to give evidence for Omoboriowo in a libel suit he instituted against Oniororo and his newspaper, *The People's News*. Omoboriowo was, however, absent in court and a medical report was presented to Justice Dele Tosun that the former deputy-governor was indisposed. However, the same day, Omoboriowo appeared in Lagos where he held discussion with President Shagari.

In his testimony before Justice Tosun, Chief Awolowo described Omoboriowo as one of his leading and faithful lieutenants. Chief Awolowo however had harsh words for Oniororo. 'I believe in freedom of the press and the legitimate interest of others,' he told the court. 'But sometime ago, I began to have my doubts as to your (Oniororo's) journalistic intelligence. I believe you wished me well in my political career, but your actions in publishing your newspaper in Ondo State suggested otherwise. Your vicious attacks on the former deputy governor of Ondo State was not the right thing for UPN.' Chief Omoboriowo was represented by Chief Afe Babalola, one of the lions of the Nigerian bar and a Senior Advocate of Nigeria, SAN.

Omoboriowo's absence in court finally convinced Awo that he had lost one of his lieutenants to the enemy camp. He held a meeting with leading members of the UPN still loyal to his banner and implored them to hold the fort. Ajasin assured him that there would be no problem. Many leading members of the party were now trooping to Akure and Ijero to persuade Omoboriowo to remain within the fold. Among these were G.B. Sadiku, a federal legislator from Lagos State who was Omoboriowo's mate at the University of Ibadan, and Mr. Ayo Adebanjo, lawyer, old Action Grouper and member of UPN's NEC who even spent a night at Ijero before he could see Omoboriowo. Governor Jakande also wrote him a passionate letter imploring Omoboriowo to stay within the fold and help Awo's bid for the presidency as Awo had helped them to become governors and deputy-governors. He said it would be tragic if Omoboriowo should abandon the battle at a time when his political mentor needed him most.

Chief Omoboriowo had responded to Jakande's letter on Wednesday January 5, 1983. 'Thank you indeed for your letter and concern,' he wrote. 'I am a man of honour. I know what is right. But a prudent politician has to carry the people with him. I have not declared for any party. There is likely to be an agreement to join a party. This is the corporate decision of the group in the face of Chief Ajasin's war of annihilation on us. Ajasin has prepared the grand design for the massive annihilation of the UPN here in Ondo State. God knows that He has so far used me to stop, if uneasily, this dreadful process.

"My victory was stolen; my stalwarts are sacked from the cabinet and about 40 boardmen and women loyal to me have been silently removed. Yet we have to 'exist' in the world - politically. Where am I? I have deliberately slowed down the pace of my men despite the daily accusation of war sabotage, all in the interest of the party. The party ought to move much faster. Yet you can help at this exigency, sir. I am an Awoist for ever. Let us cast aside lip service (I don't accuse you of one) and assist immortal Awo. Don't be deceived by media news though certain things are happening."[52]

As expected, Jakande sent Omoboriowo's letter to Awolowo for his comment. In a reply the same day, Awo wrote Jakande: 'I have no objection at all to your move. My affection for Akin is undiminished. That is why I am anxious that he should be helped to redeem himself before he makes the final plunge... My concern for Akin is that he has worked himself up into an illusion of grandeur: he now suffers from a kind of psychosis. He thinks and claims that he has majority following in Ondo State. He has nothing of the sort. It pains me much that Akin could be involved in this kind of mess'.[53]

A day after his letter to Jakande, January 6, 1983, Chief Omoboriowo led his team to a meeting with the NPN at Cooper Road, Ikoyi, Lagos. The group formally entered into an agreement with the NPN and agreed to dissolve itself and fuse with the NPN. 'The parties to this communique recognise the historic nature of this political development, and will work collectively and faithfully for the rapid social and economic development of Ondo State through an NPN government which, among other programme, will sustain and maintain qualitative, free education and free health service,' said the agreement. It was signed by Babatola, Ogunyimika, Falodun and Chief Soji Aiyenuro, on behalf of the Omoboriowo group, while Uba Ahmed, Prince Leke Awoyinfa, National vice-chairman of the NPN and Chief Adebisi Ogedengbe, minister in the Shagari government, signed for the NPN. Though Omoboriowo was present, he did not initial the agreement. Chief Fagbamigbe was also present. At the end of the ceremony, one of the chieftains of the NPN presented Omoboriowo with a suitcase containing 150,000 naira in cash, but Omoboriowo refused the gift. He said he was not in the NPN for money.

To Omoboriowo, the decision to join the NPN was inevitable. 'Seeing the suffering, the deprivation and the dehumanising treatment Ajasin had given me over three years, no average Ekiti man can contain the kind of things I withstood' he told the author. 'It is on record that I never reported Ajasin to Chief Awolowo. But it was necessary for all men of goodwill to rise and fight against Ajasin to prevent him from a second term. He is a tyrant and a sadist.'

Predictably, Omoboriowo's opponent thought otherwise. 'The only certificate he had was that he was an Ekiti man and an Awolowo disciple,' said Chief Segun Adegoke. 'Nothing else qualifies him for the governorship of Ondo State. The case of Omoboriowo is clear. It is either the position of governor or nothing. If he had been handed over a gun and told to shoot Chief Awolowo in order to become governor, I have no doubt, Omoboriowo would have done it. Awolowo treated him like a son. If the love he had for Awolowo was genuine, to give up the governorship would have been the greatest evidence. Knowing what he said he believed, knowing what he said he had suffered for the UPN and for the Action Group, knowing the way he deified Awo and worshipped at his altar, for losing a nomination contest for governorship and for him to switch from one extreme to another; it is clear to anyone that this Omoboriowo is a political villain. All that Omoboriowo claimed were his grievances were all afterthoughts to justify his treachery.'

Ajasin was equally unsparing: 'The problem of Omoboriowo was impatience. Because of my age, he thought, in a short time, I would die and he would just step in. So when I refused to die, he started his trouble.'

'He is a person I like very much and I set a great stock by him,' said Chief Awolowo about Omoboriowo. 'I thought he was an honest and sincere politician. I trusted him completely and he knows it. He wanted to contest governorship, very well. When he failed, I thought he would take it like a man. It was later I discovered I had misunderstood him completely. The side he showed to me was not what he really is.'[54]

Professor Akintoye also commented: 'Intellectually, politically and in every sense of the word, Omoboriowo is a small person. He became the Ondo State deputy governor because no one imagined the eventual power potential of that office. Omoboriowo was a victim of morbid and senseless ambition and there was no one who could have had him as running mate in 1979 without running into serious problem.'[55]

But Professor Ade Adegbite of the Department of Chemistry, University of Lagos, believed those vilifying Omoboriowo were only being hypocritical. Adegbite, one of the intellectual pillars of the Omoboriowo camp, had expressed the opinion that Chief Omoboriowo and his supporters would have no option than to leave the UPN if the party refused to overturn the victory of Ajasin at the shadow election. 'If by any error of omission or commission, the party leadership shows apparent lethargy in positively clamping down on the perpetrators of these fascist electoral techniques, it will confirm the general feeling of collusion between the state chairman and party leadership and our general belief that we, in this area of the country, can be taken for granted,' he declared in a letter to Chief Awolowo. 'There is no irreversible path in politics. There are no permanent friends or foes in politics but permanent interests... If the UPN insists on making the beneficiaries of the fraudulent electoral process their (its) candidates in the next elections, people in the state will have no choice but to look for other avenue of ensuring popular representation in the state and National Assemblies.' [56]

Some people were even worried that Omoboriowo and the other decampees may even be short-changing their own political fortunes in the long run. Noted Olusoji Akinrinade, a *Punch* columnist: 'Whatever their contributions to the NPN, the decampees will not be trusted by many hard-core NPN members who will wonder whether their marriage of convenience can really work. In the final analysis, the decampees will not be quite accepted into the NPN fold but will be totally ostracised from the UPN. They may find themselves in some sort of limbo that may be inimical to their careers.' [57]

The Omoboriowo group knew it had to fully explain its decision to the public and it therefore issued a pamphlet on the subject. Its premise was that Omoboriowo was robbed of his right to become governor of Ondo State under the banner of the UPN. Why should he be denied the same chance now that he wanted to offer his service to the people on the platform of the NPN? 'Chief Omoboriowo was dismissed from the party alongside about twelve top party leaders loyal to our group without notice or any charge whatsoever,' the pamphlet stated. 'Yet, people do not consider that we should exist politically. Haven't we a right to political existence in this world? What else could we do? To fold our arms and get destroyed politically for ever? No! Those who know Chief Akin Omoboriowo when he was in the UPN, including Chief Awolowo, can testify to his steadfastness, loyalty, perseverance, dedication, and his open hatred of selfishness, greed and corruption. All that was now being done by the Ajasin radio, OSTV, the *Nigerian Tribune* and the *Sketch* is no more than blackmail. The type that is expected from a selfish, callous and godless husband that is divorced by a dedicated, loyal and trustworthy wife... Ours is therefore a glorious battle for survival, survival of Ondo State as a strong and economically viable state within the Federation of Nigeria. The battle has already begun and by God's grace, we shall win.'[58]

The pattern this battle for survival was taking was one which was causing many members of the UPN grave concern. The decamping of such highly placed persons like Omoboriowo would not only affect party members psychologically, it would also dent the image of the party as a disciplined phalanx. After the signing of the Cooper Road agreement, Awo virtually wrote off Omoboriowo and his supporters, but some members of the UPN still held tenaciously to the belief that Omoboriowo would not change side in the thick of battle. As the day of his public declaration ceremony drew near, Omoboriowo too seemed to be vacillating. After all, a known devil is better than an unknown angel.

On Tuesday, January 11, 1983, he wrote a final letter to Chief Awolowo that betrayed the agitation in the depth of his soul. 'If I act against the wish of the masses, I can be lynched — unless there is an escape valve,' he wrote in his letter to 'Papa'. 'I have been dodging you. Your statement before Friday can save my face. But if I will have to go, I will not leave you for ever.' It was signed 'Yours affectionately, Akin Omoboriowo,' But Awo and his estranged protégé were never to meet face to face again.

Omoboriowo's letter rekindled the hope in the minds of some leading members of the UPN that Omoboriowo may not consummate his nuptial tie with the NPN. As if to confirm this optimism, Omoboriowo had not initialled any agreement with the NPN and the Cooper Road agreement was signed on his behalf. But enthusiasm was dampened when advertisements appeared in the national newspapers, signed by Prince J.A. Ojomo, Ondo State chairman of the NPN and Chief J.E. Babatola for the Omoboriowo group, intimating the public that Omoboriowo would formally declare for NPN in Akure, Friday, January 14, 1983. The advert read: 'The former deputy-governor of Ondo State and UPN strongman, Chief Akin Omoboriowo, will today formally declare for the NPN at a mammoth rally scheduled to hold in Akure. His followers include former commissioners, board and corporation chairmen, former UPN top leaders and party functionaries. Additionally, this group controls 13 local government areas out of the 17 in Ondo State. Chief Akin Omoboriowo and his group's declaration for the NPN is a major breakthrough for our party in that part of the country.'[59]

Despite this advert, the UPN leaders still clung to a thin thread of hope. On the morning of January 14, therefore, Omoboriowo received two familiar visitors from Lagos at his Aramoko Road residence in Ijero-Ekiti — the same compound where his group had taken the decision to decamp. The two were Mrs. Adeyinka Osuji and Mr. G.B. Sadiku, a Lagos parliamentarian. They had come on a last minute mission to dissuade Omoboriowo from going to Akure to declare publicly for the NPN. It was a sour encounter.

They tried to invoke his old love for the party and to remind him that the UPN had honoured him by allowing him to be deputy-governor among many men and women of competence. Omoboriowo was dressed in the familiar pattern of Awo faithfuls — the *buba* and *sokoto* complete with the fez cap — but that was the closest he was now to his old mentor. He had decided it was time to worship at another temple. He told his visitors that it was now too late in the day for him to change his mind. 'I said they should have told the leader to write me acknowledging my victory at the nomination exercise though he would not overturn that of Ajasin,' Omoboriowo said later, 'I would have published that for my supporters to see. I would have told them that in the interest of party solidarity, I want us to accept.'

It was the visitors' second fruitless journey to Omoboriowo's residence. They left for Lagos while Omoboriowo headed for Akure. The NPN rally was at Erekesan market, close to the Central Mosque, Akure. Omoboriowo arrived late, when many of those gathered had thought he had changed his mind. There was a stir in the crowd when he arrived with his wife, Ebun. It was a day Omoboriowo would never forget. 'I don't know whether my wife was excited or reluctant. For me

I did it (the declaration) most reluctantly,' he told the author. 'It was a last resort. It was a painful decision, but I had to take it in the interest of my teeming supporters.'

It was as if he was going to miss his steps as he climbed the stage. He looked uncomfortable, and to the shouts of 'One Nation! One Destiny! One God!' of the NPN, he only responded with a vacant smile. He was raising up the UPN victory salute before he was reminded that, henceforth, he would only need his index finger. Present at the rally were many top members of the NPN including Joseph Wayas, the president of the Senate; Alhaji Sikiru Shitta-Bey, a former UPN senator who had defected to the NPN; Chief Odunjo; Chief Yomi Akintola, a federal minister and son of the late Western Premier; Chief Akinjide, the federal attorney-general; Dr. Umaru Dikko, the powerful minister of transport; and Alhaji Uba Ahmed.

It was a melancholy gathering despite the feeling of celebration of victory. Omoboriowo told the gathering that he controlled 80 per cent following among the people of Ondo State. Still dressed in his Awoist outfit, he restated that his former mentor was a great man, but that he left UPN because of its lack of democratic practice. He denied that he had joined the NPN because of monetary consideration, praying God to forgive those peddling such 'falsehood' for they 'know not or pretend not to know the sufferings, persecution, oppression and intimidation of the masses of the state in the last three years under Governor Adekunle Ajasin.'[60]

Omoboriowo professed his continued belief in Awoism. 'Let me assure one and all that the basic ingredients of the Awoist philosophy will live with me,' he told the crowd. 'All that is happening now is that the salutary aspect of this philosophy is being carried willy-nilly to another political party which, in my considered opinion, is well equipped and ready to propagate it without double standard.'[61]

Now the die was cast. Omoboriowo had crossed the Rubicon and burnt the bridge behind him. There was no turning back. He was off on a special adventure for which there were no guiding maps and no reassuring precedence. He was now fighting against the rhetorics of a lifetime.

11

The Dream Merchants

The defection of Omoboriowo from the UPN to the NPN was only the most dramatic of changing of alliances that preceded the 1983 general elections. These series of defections were to affect two parties most: the GNPP and the PRP. The NPP, UPN and NPN, though all suffered defections, were able to make gains from other parties. In fact, it could be said that both the NPN and the UPN scored net gains from these defections. By the middle of 1983, it was clear that Nigeria would have a choice of only two candidates — President Shagari and Chief Awolowo — though six would be running. The other four candidates had two options: to ally with either of the two powerful candidates or to run independently.

The ruling NPN had gains in Kaduna, Borno, Bendel, Gongola, Oyo, Ondo, Ogun and Anambra States while the opposition UPN had gains in Kwara, Kaduna, Sokoto, Benue, Bauchi, Gongola, Borno, Cross River and Rivers states. On every front, the two parties were confronting each other. Both parties were rich, though the NPN was by far the richer, but the UPN compensated for this by its thoroughness and the high-pitched aggressiveness of its organisation. Both Awo and Shagari had succeeded in being nominated unanimously by their parties for the presidency. When Chief Abiola insisted on contesting the nomination with Shagari, the NPN fathers simply did not allow him to get nomination papers. Therefore, the man to beat in 1983 was Shagari and the challenger was Awo and the beautiful bride remained the legendary Zik.

Shagari was generally perceived as a weak man who left the running of the court to four of his strong subordinates. These four virtually held him prisoner and it was through their actions and utterances that the dynamics of the Shagari's presidency can be understood. Akinloye, the party chairman, controlled the party's massive machinery. Alhaji Shehu Musa, veteran civil servant and secretary to the government, controlled the day-to-day running of the regime. Sunday Adewusi, the inspector-general of police, who was fuelled by a rabid fanaticism for the NPN, controlled the muscle of the NPN regime and manipulated its gargantuan coercive powers. The most powerful of the lot was Umaru Dikko, minister of transport, chairman of the Presidential Task Force on the Importation of Rice; and chairman, Presidential Campaign Committee, who controlled the presidency.

The emergence of Dikko as the prime-mover of power in the Shagari regime was a phenomenon. An industrious and self-assured man, Dikko came into the cabinet with initial disadvantage. He lost in his bid for the senate in his home state of Kaduna which was also controlled by an opposition PRP governor. But his credential was almost impeccable. He was the secretary of the caucus headed by the venerable Isa Kaita that preceded the birth of the NPN. He was also the secretary and later president of the Barewa College Old Boys Association. Among the old boys of this college were all Nigerian former heads of government except Ironsi and Obasanjo. This extraordinary politician, recognising the weakness of Shagari who hated the boring chores of governance, virtually became the de-facto president of Nigeria. Shagari would pass files to him and by the following morning, Dikko would return such files with his comments to the president. His comments invariably became the decision of the president. Soon, fellow ministers, top partymen and contractors who needed something from Shagari knew on whose door to knock.

Though Shagari patented the image of a weak man whose chief

attribute was effacement, it was also the role expected of him by the powerful men who controlled the party. These were men who needed federal might to settle local scores and pursue private ambitions. This was both the weakness and the strength of the NPN. Though it was the Hausa-Fulani caucus that controlled the soul of the party, its basic strength nonetheless was in the national spread of its differing loyalties. More than any other party, it could rightly claim to represent the family of the nation. Apart from the Hausa-Fulani states of Sokoto and Bauchi, the NPN controlled the governments of minority states of Niger, Benue, Kwara, Rivers and Cross River. The UPN, before the 1983 elections, could not claim this kind of national spread.

This apparent strength of the party was also its main weakness. This assemblage of men and women with no uniting passion except the lust for power presupposed that only a strong person could wield it together to achieve some results. Since Shagari lacked this strength of character, the regime blundered from one crisis to another.

The first of such crises was the unexpected deportation of Alhaji Abdurrahman Shugaba, the GNPP majority leader in the Borno State House of Assembly. On the night of January 24, 1980, Shugaba was taken from his family house in Maiduguri and driven across the border to Chad. He later returned in triumph and won a court case against the federal government. The Shugaba affair cemented the growing friendship between the UPN and the GNPP. Another attempt to deport Dr. Patrick Wilmot, a Jamaican lecturer of the Department of Sociology, ABU, Zaria, failed. Wilmot had offered to supply the federal government with the list of names of Nigerian companies and businessmen having dealings with racist South Africa despite Shagari's anti-apartheid rhetorics. Most of those involved were NPN big-wigs who regarded Wilmot's proposal with hostility. Wilmot was finally deported by the regime of General Ibrahim Babangida. Another problem in social control that Shagari had was Adewusi, the inspector-general, who was ready to use his men to suppress forces of dissent. The most devastating was the killing of many peasants in Bakolori village in the president's home state of Sokoto in 1980. The peasants were protesting against the acquisition of their land without compensation for the building of a dam. The area was a stronghold of the GNPP.

Shagari, as a politician, demonstrated a benign lack of social sensitivity. On January 23, 1983, the 27-storey Nigeria External Telecommunication, NET, building was gutted. It was the climax of series of arson on public buildings which had included the 12-storey Republic Building in Lagos and the Audit Department of the Federal Capital Development Authority, Abuja. The NET building cost N31.9 million to build and was the tallest building in Nigeria. This majestic architectural masterpiece was humbled by those suspected to be criminals trying to bury the evidence of colossal fraud in the inferno. Shagari visited the building briefly, then proceeded on a scheduled tour of India. With a morbid sense of humour, Adewusi ordered the arrest of Ray Ekpu, the chairman of the Concord Group of Newspapers editorial board. Ekpu had written, with prophetic insight, that the rate of arson perpetrated under the NPN might even reach the towering NET building. He was then charged with murder since two people died in the inferno.

'Shehu Shagari's tenure is a classic instance of the encounter of the unprepared with the unforeseen,' wrote Olatunji Dare, journalism guru and chairman of the *Guardian* newspapers editorial board.[62] This might be considered an unfair view in 1979 considering the long years of Shagari's tutelage in the corridors of power. Shagari was a politician of modest education and even more modest ambition. Trained as a primary school teacher at the Teachers' Training College, Zaria and Sokoto Middle School, Shagari, born May 1925, in Shagari village, Sokoto State, gravitated into politics under the wings of Ahmadu Bello. He was a member of the House of Representatives on the ticket of the defunct NPC from 1954 to 1966 during which time he served in the cabinet of Balewa for eight years. During the military regime, he was a commissioner in the then North-Western State and later succeeded Awolowo in Gowon's cabinet as the federal commissioner for finance in 1971.

Despite his three-decade long tutelage in the penumbra of power,

Shagari had never championed any cause and had never been known to make any memorable speech. He was a man with neither charisma nor definable identity. His was a face that would get lost in the crowd. But Shagari was a product of the peculiar dynamics of Nigerian politics. He rose so high not only because of his natural ability as a politician of means, but also because he was born in the 'right' corner of Nigeria. At the time he was elected president in 1979, there were many members of the Nigerian elite who believed that the leadership of the country should reside with the Hausa-Fulani oligarchy. But Shagari needed more than the mere accident of birth to win the number one spot. He was a seasoned political strategist who overawed his opponents by guided simplicity and measured eloquence of silence. He was a clever fox who survived in the gathering of impatient lions.

This very ambitious politician claimed his ambition was to be a senator, but that he was persuaded to run for the presidency, yet he fought tenaciously for the job, and employed every known trick in and outside the book to keep it. Nothing illustrated his gift for survival more than the way he dealt with his opponents within the ruling NPN. By 1982 when he was seeking a second term, those who opposed him in 1979 were no longer strong enough to challenge him. Professor Iya Abubakar was in political limbo, Senator Olusola Saraki was fighting for his political fort in Kwara State, while Alhaji Maitama Sule was in 'exile' as Nigeria's ambassador to the United Nations. Abiola, who attempted to challenge him, was sent into political wilderness. All the four most powerful members of his government — Akinloye, Adewusi, Musa and Dikko — were men without constituencies and whose very survival depended almost entirely on the survival of Shehu Shagari. By patenting the image of a man who could be controlled and trusted to cause the least trouble, Shagari ensured that he was invested with supreme power by the rough riders of the NPN.

This patented image was one the opposition viewed with skepticism. 'People say that Shagari is fair-minded, a simple man of God and so on. I don't think it is that type of person *per se* we need for present-day Nigeria,' said Omoboriowo.[63]

But Shagari embarked on his ill-fated journey with exuberant optimism. 'Nigerians have given me the mandate to build a new Nigeria in which there will be peace, stability, prosperity and good government; to build a truly united country which will be the pride of every Nigerian, every African and all peace-loving men all over the world,' he told a press conference in Lagos shortly after he was declared president-elect in 1979.[64] Soon, Shagari was to forget the warning of Obasanjo, given on the eve of October 1, 1979 as he prepared to step into the centre-stage. Said Obasanjo: 'Within the party systems are people on the wings who are only out to maximise their advantage from your personal frustration, anguish and anxious moments in the presidential lodge. Your success will depend on your ability to separate self-seeking associates from genuine friends and advisers.'[65]

On assuming power, Shagari gave himself three primary programmes: housing for all, the building of Abuja and green revolution. But as he became set in his ways, he lost control of events to the rapacious NPN crowd, cocooned as it were, in the glaze and glitter of power, taking consolation in his Benson and Hedges, his favourite brand of cigarette. All these three programmes became avenue for monumental corruption. Shagari houses, as the people nicknamed government houses built by his regime, became an index of how government houses should not be built. Abuja became the Mecca of those looking for easy ways to wealth, once they were armed with the NPN party cards; and the green revolution was only as green as the American dollar that enriched those in charge of the programme. Instead of encouraging Nigerian farmers to grow rice and maize and other products, Shagari set up a special task force under Dikko to import American long grain rice. It was common for Shagari ministers, who were just like the person next door before they got their jobs, to now be boasting of millions in their accounts with a private jet to the bargain.

Perhaps, things would not have gotten as bad as they went, despite his apparent incompetence, if Shagari had cared a bit about the verdict of history. But he was more concerned with being regarded as a good man; he had no ambition for greatness. As his ministers and top party men moved about with suitcases filled with crisp naira notes, Shagari busied himself with sartorial matters; always impeccably turned out in flowing, artistically and tastefully embroidered, street sweeping *babanriga*, with sky-scraping cap. He was always well turned out with designers shoes, solid gold wrist-watches and gold-tipped walking stick. Like Gowon, in his twilight years in power, Shagari enjoyed the trappings of foreign travels, which allowed him to rub shoulders with world leaders, giving him the opportunity to savour the pomp and pageantry associated with his office. He was a dwarf forced by the peculiar dynamics of Nigerian politics to wear the elephantine toga of the presidency.

By the time he was shown the red card in December, 1983, Shagari had succeeded in turning a buoyant regional economic power into a beggar nation. His government's revenue from oil alone for four years was ₦43.6 billion, about 55.3 per cent of the total oil earnings since Nigeria became an oil exporter in 1958. Yet, by the time he left, he had not only rifled through ₦90 billion, he also left a foreign debt of more than ₦20 billion. The ₦90 billion was made up of ₦43.6 million from oil, ₦20 billion from external debt, N10 billion from internal loan, ₦15 billion from internally generated revenue from other sources and an external reserve of ₦3.5 billion left by Obasanjo. By the end of 1983, many Nigerians, mostly politicians, soldiers, favoured businessmen, contractors and civil servants, had stashed away an estimated £16 billion in foreign banks. Most of these thefts took place when Shagari was president.[66]

A story is told of how Shagari excused himself from NPN caucus meeting discussing the pay-off of ₦21.8 million to the party and top partymen. It was a rake off from a ₦329.1 million contract awarded to Fougerolle Nigeria Limited in March 1981 for a part of the Ajaokuta Steel Complex. Shagari left to pray, and by the time he returned, the matter was concluded. Nero fiddles while Rome burns. When one of his associates, worried about the monumental corruption within the government, asked Shagari to do something about it, the president replied helplessly: 'I have been telling them to stop stealing but they would not listen. They are still stealing.'[67]

Shagari's opponents, especially Chief Awolowo, were relentless in their attacks on the regime's handling of the economy. In 1981, Awolowo wrote Shagari a letter dated March 1, warning him about the precarious state of the economy. 'There is frightful danger ahead,' he wrote, 'visible for those who care and are patriotic enough to look beyond their narrow self-interests. Our ship of state is fast approaching a huge rock, and unless you, as the chief helmsman, quickly rise to the occasion and courageously steer the ship away from its present course, it shall hit the rock; and the inescapable consequence will be an unspeakable disaster such as is rare in the annals of man. You will, I am sure, agree with me that the attenuated links - attenuated because of the persistent damage done to them over the years by Nigerian rulers - which bind Nigeria's ethnic groups or, nationalities together, are not likely to survive such a disaster. However, close to the rock as we are, we can still avoid the impending doom. The key to this avoidance is firmly in your hands, and you do not require any special skill to employ it."[68] Awo signed his letter, 'with kind regards, Yours very sincerely.'

Shagari replied immediately with gloating self-satisfaction. 'By the grace of God, I have been the president of our dear country since 1979,' he wrote. 'It is not true that Nigeria is seriously ill or that its economy ails critically. In spite of the oil glut in the world, our reserves are still much higher than in 1979 when I took office. We relaxed imports and have increased our productive capacity. Industrial and commercial companies have all shown increased activities, turn-over and profit. We are successfully pursuing our green revolution programmes and our housing programmes have produced houses just about to be occupied by owner-occupiers. We are vigorously pushing ahead with iron and steel, industrial expansion and other social services programmes. You are, therefore, not serious when you refer to our economy as depressed. Ours is acknowledged world-wide, as one of the fastest growing economies in the world - thanks to our economic policy... I am sure that the country knows the difference between politics and statesmanship.'[69] He signed it, 'Yours sincerely, Alhaji Shehu Shagari, President of the Federal Republic of Nigeria.'

Both Awo's letter and Shagari's reply were made public and NPN chieftains scrambled to fire salvos at Awo on behalf of their leader. Professor Emmanuel Chukuma Edozien, highly respected, University of Ibadan and University of Michigan trained economist, and Shagari's special adviser on economic affairs, joined the fray. He accused Awo of raising false alarm, saying that things had never been rosier than under the Shagari presidency. According to Edozien, external reserve was up by N37.39 billion during the first five months of 1981, gross domestic product increased from N33.4 billion in 1979 to N36.1 billion in 1980, and inflation declined from an annual rate of 16.8 per cent in 1978 to 10.2 per cent in 1980.

Chief Akinloye, the NPN chairman also flew to London, August 1981, to refute the assertion of Awolowo before a London press conference. Akinloye told the British press that Awo's was only a wolf cry. Said he: 'A corrosive campaign of calumny and denigration, against the Federal Government of Nigeria, has just been overtly carried across the international frontier by the leader of one of Nigeria's political parties, Chief Obafemi Awolowo. Chief Awolowo is the chief priest of the Unity Party of Nigeria, UPN. History has, unavoidably but with purposeful accuracy, turned over to the everlasting archives for the state of invaluable memory the political suicide brazenly committed by Chief Awolowo and his party, the UPN, in the 1979 presidential elections in Nigeria. So marooned and obliterated were Chief Awolowo and his negligible sycophantic worshippers that, since the conclusively expected victory of the president of the Federal Republic of Nigeria, Alhaji Shehu Shagari, and the National Party of Nigeria, NPN, the popular party on whose tickets he recorded the landslide victory in the 1979 elections, Chief Awolowo and his clique have wantonly sought to destabilise Nigeria. Chief Awolowo's attempt to paint the country as economically and politically unstable is not only unpatriotic, but the height of falsehood.'

The looting continued while Shagari looked on with benign aloofness. Some of his ministers took up suites at the Federal Palace Hotel at public expenses while, at the same time, maintaining furnished official quarters.

To demonstrate their new status, some party and government officials maintained private homes in London complete with Roll Royces and mistresses. Shagari himself abandoned the low profile of the Obasanjo era, and the prim Peugeot 504 cars gave way to Mercedes Benz cars; with the gargantuan Mercedes 500 SEL, appropriately nicknamed Shagari Benz. By the end of 1982, Shagari was forced by the depletion of the federal purse to seek for special powers from the National Assembly to deal with the looming economic disaster.

He was granted wide powers to deal with the problem and this gave him opportunity to introduce 'austerity measures'. But he was not one to understand how to use such powers since this would involve disciplining the NPN crowd. 'The behemoth, that is the presidency, which the constitution created overwhelmed him,' wrote Ray Ekpu, 'He did not have the intellectual flexibility or the vision of a charismatic leader or the strength of character of a committed visionary to see him through. A man who, according to close aides, didn't like the labour of wading through long memos but preferred one or two-page summaries soon found out that the duties of the job are no snap. They are tedious and gruelling. He did not like the grind; he preferred the grandeur of office. He took the path of least resistance, and moulded the presidency in his own image. Since he couldn't rise to meet its height, he cut it down to meet his size, the size of a fish bowl. Power-hungry men such as Dikko and Adewusi filled the gap.'[70]

Despite his failure as an economic manager, Shagari was a gifted politician and tactician who could not be taken for granted. In 1979, the NPN had entered into an alliance with the NPP which softened the path for the NPN in the National Assembly. NPP members were rewarded for the friendship with ministerial and other appointments. No sooner was the accord signed than the NPN started wooing the members of the NPP into its fold. Moreover, the NPP was treated as a junior partner in government and its ministers regarded as less than equal with the rest. Important decisions of government were taken by the NPN caucus, comprising Shagari, Akinloye, Dr. Alex Ekwueme, the vice-president; Shettima Ali Monguno, the NPN first vice-chairman;

Lulu Briggs, the second vice-chairman; Suleiman Takuma, the party's general secretary (later replaced by Uba Ahmed); Joseph Wayas, the president of the Senate; Adamu Ciroma, a minister; Dikko; Dr. Olusola Saraki, the Senate leader; Idris Ibrahim, the deputy speaker of the House of Representatives; and Olusola Afolabi, the leader of the House. The weekly meeting of the caucus, held in State House, Ribadu Road, (the new name politicians gave Dodan Barracks), was presided over by Akinloye, the party chairman. The cabinet would only rubber-stamp decisions already taken by the caucus and the NPP was unhappy about this. Scared of being swallowed up by the NPN, the NPP finally broke its accord with the party in 1981, giving a three-month notice. The NPN, however, accepted the termination with immediate effect, asserting that 'this is truly the path of honour'. When the NPP ordered its members in government to resign as a result of the break-down of the accord, many of them refused, crossing to the NPN instead.

12

Old Foes, New Friends

At the time the NPP obtained a divorce from the NPN, the opposition parties too were having a roaring romance. Alhaji Ibrahim Waziri and his GNPP had entered into a relationship with the UPN shortly after the controversial 1979 elections. The five UPN governors and the two GNPP governors, Alhaji Mohammed Goni of Borno and Alhaji Abubakar Barde of Gongola State, started meeting regularly and the alliance was quickly dubbed The Progressives. Soon, another door of opportunity opened when the NPN majority in the Kaduna State House of Assembly refused to cooperate with the PRP radical Governor Balarabe Musa. The progressives supported Musa and soon the two PRP governors moved to the progressive camp. The seven governors meeting became a meeting of nine governors, including PRP Governor Abubakar Rimi of Kano State.

Aminu Kano, the leader of the PRP, did not like his governors' flirtation with an alliance dominated by the UPN. Mallam Aminu Kano was a foundation member of the NPC before he formed his radical Northern Elements Progressive Union, NEPU, which was in alliance with the NCNC in the sixties. Aminu was one of the leaders of the Sharia lobby at the Constituent Assembly which he believed Awolowo used his influence to frustrate. He was also a foundation member of the NPN and when he felt humiliated by the party, he decided to go it alone and form the PRP. He believed by befriending the PRP, Awolowo was trying to destroy the party, woo away the two governors and render him irrelevant. Encouraged by Grace Ikoku, an estranged Awoist and secretary-general of the PRP, Aminu attempted to prevent his governors from joining the progressive meetings, and when they would not agree, he expelled them from the party. These centrifugal forces were to employ the time and energy of Aminu Kano until he died in 1983.

The PRP governors wanted the NPP to join the progressives after the break-down of the NPN-NPP accord. They were uncomfortable with the domination of the alliance by the UPN and the apparent friendship between the UPN leader and Waziri. Considering his experience with Zik in 1979, Waziri was understandably lukewarm about any political relationship with Zik. He blamed Zik for the split in the original NPP and felt the party deserved to be left in the cold considering the NPP's double-dealing after the 1979 presidential elections.

The UPN too was wary, considering the chequered rivalry between Zik and Awo throughout their careers. Their first show-down was in 1941 when both of them had supported rival candidates for the colonial Legislative Council. Both Zik and Awo, like the two contestants, Ernest Ikoli, from the present Bendel State and Samuel Akinsanya, an Ijebu man like Awolowo, were members of the Nigerian Youth Movement, NYM. Awo supported Ikoli while Zik cast his lot with Akinsanya. Why either could be accused of tribalism in this contest was strange, but it was a show of influence within the NYM between the Yoruba elite which supported Ikoli and the Igbo elite which supported Akinsanya. Ikoli, a famous journalist, won. An embittered Zik left the NYM and joined forces with Herbert Macaulay, to form the National Council of Nigeria and the Cameroon, NCNC, and Zik became its secretary-general.

A more controversial encounter took place in 1951 during the first election into the Western Nigeria parliament newly created by the constitution introduced by the British colonial masters. The election had been on non-party basis and it was through electoral colleges from the ward level, to the council level and the provincial level which finally elected the 80 members in the House of Assembly. At the time, the AG was a new party while the NCNC was not a party in the traditional sense of the word, but an amalgam of unions and organisations. Each group claimed that it controlled the majority among the delegates elected by the final electoral college and even the AG challenged the NCNC by publishing the names of its own candidates in the September 24, 1951 edition of the *Daily Times, Daily Service* and *Nigerian Tribune.* The assembly finally met January 7, 1952 with a majority of 49 on the AG side making Zik to kiss the dust of defeat. Three members who originally sat on the NCNC side of the house crossed over to the AG, but one of them crossed back. All the three were from the Benin and Delta Provinces, now Edo and Delta states respectively. Zik charged that Awo was able to muster majority support because he appealed to the primordial sentiment of Yoruba nationalism. The drama of the carpet crossers was also exaggerated as if they added anything extra to the certainty of Zik's defeat. Zik later left the Western House and moved to the East where he became the premier in succession to Chief Eyo Ita, an Efik.

There was a brief rapprochement between the two shortly after Enahoro moved the motion for independence in 1953 but by the time of the 1956 elections, again, both the NCNC and the AG were on the opposing ends. After the 1959 federal elections, Awolowo offered to serve under Zik as deputy prime-minister. NCNC strategists cautioned against the alliance because it was believed that Awo and the AG might gain more from it. Instead, Zik became a titular head of state and the NCNC a junior partner in a government dominated by the NPC. Their last alliance during the sixties ended on a sour note. Both the AG and the NCNC (now known as the National Council of Nigerian Citizens), formed the United Progressive Grand Alliance, UPGA, to oppose the NPC-NNDP alliance, the Nigerian National Alliance, NNA, during the 1964 federal elections. The UPGA was defeated and Zik left the alliance again to team up with the NPC in a 'national government', leaving the AG in the cold. The 1979 acrobatics, when Zik called himself the beautiful bride, was too recent to be forgotten. It was therefore with reluctance that the UPN welcomed the NPP into the PPA alliance.

No sooner did the NPP join than a struggle ensued between the UPN and the NPP for the control of the alliance. The NPP controlled the governorship of three states, the two Igbo states of Anambra and Imo and the Middle-Belt state of Plateau. It reckoned that if it could ally with the PRP (controlling two states) and the GNPP (governing two states also), it would be able to negotiate favourably with the UPN. Of course, the UPN had entered into this alliance, which it initiated in the first place, to improve the chance of the party and its leader during the 1983 presidential elections. Any other consideration for the UPN was irrelevant.

This struggle for control soon became public knowledge when the UPN boycotted the PPA summit hosted by NPP Governor Solomon Lar of Plateau State in Jos. This elicited public comments. Lewis Obi, a Nigerian journalist, stated: 'If the speculation is right that the Jos meeting was designed to forge a united NPP, GNPP and PRP axis which would later settle down to negotiate with the UPN, then the UPN must be said to have been out-flanked and double crossed again.'[71] Clement Gomwalk, UPN National Secretary, waded into the simmering controversy by declaring that Chief Awolowo must be fielded as the alliance presidential candidate for 1983 because he was more popular than Dr. Azikiwe. Alexander Fom, the NPP national secretary, countered that Zik was as qualified for the presidency as Awo.

Dr. Azikiwe was the chairman of the alliance, therefore, Chief Awolowo felt that Zik should support him for the presidency in 1983. Moreover, the UPN was stronger, richer and better organised than the NPP, and Awo felt the party had earned the right to lead the PPA. He was not a man who could be comfortable with ambiguities. He, therefore, addressed a personal letter to Zik, dated February 8, 1982, offering him a deal. He wrote: 'Fortunately for us, we could both claim to know from private hints, all over the place, that the burning, indeed, the all-consuming united desire of the vast majority of our people is that you and I should go into a partnership in which you will be the NATION'S GUIDE, PHILOSOPHER AND FRIEND and I its CHIEF SERVANT (capitals by Awo). The details can be satisfactorily worked out and effectively implemented under our constitution. All of us know the honours which you richly deserve, and those will be assured by appropriate legislations'.[72] What Awo was offering Zik was a more generous pension in exchange for supporting his ambition to be president.

The NPP responded to this overture by attempting to build a new party from its friendship with factions of the GNPP and the PRP. Dr. Edwin Ogbu, a former Nigerian ambassador to the United Nations and member of the NPP, announced that the party had agreed to merge with the Eagle PRP (as the PPA faction of the PRP was called) and the GNPP to form a new party, the Progressive People Party, PPP. Chief Adeniran Ogunsanya, chairman of the NPP, denied knowledge of this new party, but there was no doubt that the NPP was involved. FEDECO eventually failed to register the PPP, and by 1983, Abubakar Rimi of Kano State and Abubakar Barde of Gongola State contested on the platform of the NPP.

Hopes were raised that the issue of presidential candidate of the alliance would be resolved but succeeding summits of the PPA failed to reach an agreement on the issue. In fact, Zik and the NPP were ambivalent on the issue. 'I took part in six elections and won five gold medals and in the last elections, I won a silver medal,' Zik told journalists at Enugu airport December 1982. 'I feel the time has come to lay a foundation for a younger or elderly man with wisdom and ability to battle his opponents in the political arena.' Sitting by the side of Dr. Azikiwe at the press conference was Chief Jim Nwobodo, the glamorous governor of Anambra State. Nwobodo said when Zik indicated that he might not run in 1983, party members started weeping imploring the great Zik not to abandon the battle. Said Nwobodo: 'We are not going to play a second fiddle this time; the Owelle (Zik's traditional title) is leading a formidable party to success.'[73] Zik concurred saying, being a democrat, he could not disobey his party.

On Saturday, December 18, the NPP held its fourth national convention at the Civic Centre, Port Harcourt, Rivers State, where the party ratified the nomination of Dr. Azikiwe for the 1983 race. In his acceptance speech, Dr. Azikiwe said he had reached an agreement with Awo that the PPA should have only one presidential candidate. He said if the alliance picked Awo, he was ready to step down, but if it was him that was picked, 'Awo had agreed also to step down'.[74] Awo reacted immediately by issuing a public statement in Lagos:

> I do not want to tell any tale out of court. But I owe the public, particularly my millions of supporters, a personal explanation.
>
> When it became clear that the issue of presidential candidacy among the parties in the PPA was narrowed down to Zik and myself, I met Zik twice at my own initiative. I made it clear on each occasion as I had already done in one of the PPA meetings that because of my age, I could not step down for him in the race for the presidency.
>
> If I were ten years younger, there would have been no problem at all as between him and me. We reached understanding on each occasion. But legitimate forces within the NPP appear to have frustrated these understandings. And Zik, like a democrat, had to bow to those forces.
>
> As I said in my last presidential address to the eighth yearly congress of the UPN, a multiple list of candidates is permissible in an alliance. Besides, a democrat myself, I too, am bound to adhere strictly to the injunction of my party that I should take part in the great historic race for the 1983 presidency.[95]

Many UPN leaders had been warning Chief Awolowo about his alliance with Zik. Omoboriowo wrote Awo a paper in the early days of the PPA alliance warning Chief Awolowo about his association with Zik. But Awo responded: 'Akin, Zik has changed. If you hear the good things he said about me in Benin (at a PPA meeting) you will be surprised.' Recalled Omoboriowo: 'Awo was too trusting. I think it was the obsession he had for the presidency that made him look so naive in the hands of people like Zik. I am convinced that the reason why Zik stayed so long in politics was to make sure Awo did not emerge as president.'

But Zik indeed had legitimate interest to protect. With a stroke of the pen, President Shagari had changed the dynamics of Igboland politics. In 1982, he granted pardon to Colonel Emeka Ojukwu, former rebel leader who had been in exile in Cote D'Ivoire since the ill-fated state of Biafra collapsed in 1970. He also pardoned General Yakubu Gowon, former Nigerian head of state who had been in voluntary exile since 1975 when he was overthrown by General Mohammed whose assassination he was accused of being involved in by General Obasanjo's government. Both Ojukwu and Gowon were paying the price of leadership and it was conventional wisdom that any regime that succeeded the military could not ignore them. Since the campaign days of 1979, the UPN, and later the NPN, and the GNPP were in contact with the two men. Though Gowon ruled Nigeria for nine years, he was not the kind of man to arouse the same passion like the charismatic Ojukwu whose 13 years of exile had built him up into the status of a living martyr. When Ojukwu returned home from exile into a red carpet welcome financed by the federal government, the NPN was convinced it had finally found the scourge to exorcise the Zikist hold on the Igbo psyche.

But a king is not buried alive. Ojukwu knew it would not be an easy task, but the NPN was ready to offer him all assistance. Since he became governor of Eastern Region during the Ironsi regime, Ojukwu had had an uneasy relationship with Zik who was a friend of his (Ojukwu's) father. The criticism that Ojukwu faced for making his father the chairman of one of the government-owned corporations, he believed emanated from Zik's supporters who were disillusioned for being thrown out of business. When Ojukwu declared the former Eastern Region the Independent Republic of Biafra, he exploited Zik's mystique and reputation to promote the health of the new state. One of Dr. Azikiwe's poems was adapted into the Biafran national anthem and he led the regime's early diplomatic offensive which made it to have diplomatic recognition from four countries and support in Europe. But things went sour early enough and when Azikiwe defected to the federal side in 1969, it was as devastating to Biafran psyche as the fall of Enugu, the capital. Now it was time for Ojukwu to prove that he still controlled the loyalty of the Igbo. In setting himself this task by declaring for the NPN January 14, 1983, Ojukwu was throwing down the gauntlet before the wary dean of Nigerian politics.

Ojukwu went about this in two ways: discrediting Zik and his friends in the PPA, and painting the Eldorado before the Igbo if only they would follow Shehu Shagari to the Promised Land. He painted Zik as a faithless politician who abandoned the Igbo at the direst hour during the civil war. He said the same Zik was now flirting with Awo, the 'Yoruba irredentist', who disgraced the same Zik in 1952 in Ibadan, 'tricked' the Igbo into war by saying 'If the East is allowed to go, by any act of commission or omission, the West would follow', and who as Gowon's commissioner for finance, engineered the economic blockade of Biafra, squeezing its jugular veins, starving its soldiers, women and children to surrender and, at the end of the war, humiliated them by not allowing them to convert their Biafran notes to equivalent Nigerian money. It was an emotional campaign for which Ojukwu, Oxford trained-historian, was a master.

Both Zik and Awo were at pains to ward off Ojukwu's spirited attack. Zik dismissed him as a demagogue who led his people to ruins and disaster and, at the end of the day, when a single act of heroism was expected of him, fled. Awo said Ojukwu was a brilliant rascal who equated leadership with showmanship. Said he: 'I was one of those who rebuilt this country, not Ojukwu who betrayed his fatherland and now wants to come back as a senator in a country he wanted to destroy.' He defended his statement during the crisis that 'starvation is a legitimate weapon of war', saying that it was directed against Biafran troops. 'While the Biafran troops were thus growing fatter and healthier, the innocent civilians were dying every minute of disease and hunger.'[76] Not many Igbo were willing to give him a hearing. The two NPP governors in Imo and Anambra states felt, therefore, that they needed Zik in the race to shield them from Ojukwu's direct onslaught. Zik also needed the election to prove that he was still the leader of the Igbo despite the challenge of the bumptious Ojukwu. There were also challenges from others in the NPN camp who were quite influential in their own rights: Ekwueme, the vice-president; Michael Okpara, the former premier; Kingsley Mbadiwe, a former minister; and a rebel flank of the NPP which called itself 'the authentic NPP' led by Senator Nathaniel Anah.

Apart from trouble from Zik's backyard, things were not well within the PPA family. If the NPP had not joined, an Awo-Waziri ticket was a possibility for 1983, but with the coming of the NPP, Waziri suddenly found himself sidelined. He discovered that Awo was making contact with Zik without the GNPP's knowledge. Waziri, therefore, left the alliance, but not with his two governors who disagreed with his decision.

The NPN campaign machine would also not leave the PPA in peace. President Shagari had dismissed the alliance between Awo, Zik and Waziri as an alliance of 'three blind men', who were doomed to stumble. But Shagari reserved his more scathing comments for Zik. Zik told a rally of the NPP in Minna, the Niger State capital, that he had not ruled out the possibility of an alliance with the NPN after the election. When Shagari met the Igbo people in Enugu a few days later, June 4, 1983, he spurned Zik's offer of friendship. Ray Ekpu recorded the encounter in Enugu graphically: 'Shagari said that there is an 80-year-old, a beautiful bride in Nigerian politics (Zik was 79 November 16, 1983), who has been the subject of funny cartoons in the country's newspapers. He asked: 'Have you ever seen a beautiful bride at the age of 80?' As the NPN supporters laughed and cheered, Shagari said that this beautiful bride has a long record of broken marriages — 'the bride had flirted several times since she was married at a young age.' He then listed the bride's ex-husbands: NPC, AG, Biafra, National Youth Movement, NPN. He said, on each occasion, the marriage was dissolved. 'Now, the same bride has gone to marry the UPN and the PPA. I think that, from today, nobody should talk of any bride. She should be called a prostitute.'[77]

Both the NPN and the UPN now centred their strategies on winning the presidential election on the first ballot without a helping hand from the unstable NPP. Dikko said the NPN would not only win the election by landslide, it would also win the 1987 elections 'by moonslide'. Dikko said at a rally in Ibadan that the party had devised a strategy, code-named 'Operation Socket Seven', to win all the UPN states.[78] At another occasion, Dikko said in Akure: 'The NPN is the party that is national; that is the party that can fulfil its promises to you; that is the party that is going to rule Ondo State'.[79] At the launching of the NPN campaign in Akure, Saturday, March 19, 1983, Shagari was in his best element on the soap box. 'For 30 years, people of Ondo State have never been in the centre. Do you want to continue being in opposition?' To which the crowd responded: 'No! No!' Speaking at the same rally, Ojukwu said NPN would not only be the 'superpower' of Nigerian politics, it would gun for 'total power'. With a sense of drama, Ojukwu turned to Shagari: 'We are going to work hand in hand behind your guidance and we are going to make sure that the next Nigerian government that will emerge will be one of all Nigerians.'[80]

Apart from barn-storming, the NPN propaganda machine was effective and the UPN too responded in equal measure. While the chief propagandists of the UPN were Babatope and Ajuluchukwu, those of the NPN were Uba Ahmed and a legion of other free-lancers, notable among whom were Godwin Daboh and Ebenezer Williams, (pen name: Abiodun Aloba) a veteran journalist. 'Chief Awolowo's propensity (as a heretic) for preaching schism and profanity; his penchant for uttering political and social obscenities; his craze for peddling economic junk and jargon, belong to the superlative,' opined Williams. [81]   In his own case, Daboh, who was the chairman of the Benue State Committee for the re-election of the NPN, enjoined Nigerians to vote for the party 'for continued peace, political stability, continued economic growth, abundant shelter, abundant food by 1984 and good government'. He warned that a vote for Awo would mean a vote for 'institutionalisation of rigging, senseless confrontation, corruption, dubious free education, the introduction of detention camps for political prisoners, political hypocrisy and nepotism'.[82]

It was not just in the realm of political rhetorics that the NPN was maintaining a heated contest. The party also had a keen sense of historical symbolism. Its motto of 'One Nation, One Destiny, One God,' was reminiscent of the motto of the NPC, 'One North, One Destiny.' Shagari also presented the NPN flag to the party's 19 gubernatorial candidates, a symbolism brilliantly evocative of the 19th century Sokoto Jihad when Usman Dan Fodio presented the Sokoto flag as a symbol of acceptance to provincial jihadist leaders. In a society that believed so much in shadow boxing, this was portent symbolism.

Shagari also made profitable use of his position as executive president. As early as 1980, he rail-roaded the appointment of Presidential Liason Officers, PLO, through the National Assembly, despite the objection of the NPP. The PLOs, one in each of the 19 states, were to facilitate federal-states relationship ostensibly. But in fact, they became another avenue for rewarding good boys and they acted in most states, especially those controlled by opposing parties, as alternate-governors. The most potent appointment that Shagari made, however, was that of Justice Victor Erereko Ovie-Whiskey, the 56-year-old chief judge of Bendel State, as the chairman of FEDECO in succession to the highly experienced technocrat, Michael Ani, in 1980.

On the face of it, hardly could any nation deserve a better umpire than Ovie-Whiskey. A self-made man, he was called to the bar in 1952 and after two decades in the public service, he retired as chief judge with unimpeachable integrity. Ovie-Whiskey later became a tool in the hands of faceless civil servants and administrators who controlled FEDECO. The Electoral Act made the executive secretary (or administrative secretary for the states) the chief executive and Ovie-Whiskey increasingly found that he was merely a titular head. As events were later to reveal, Shagari showed more than cursory interest in the appointments of these secretaries who controlled the soul of FEDECO.

The new FEDECO was revealed to Nigerians partially during the revision of voters register. When the revised register was revealed, it showed that the Nigerian electorate had almost doubled between 1979 and 1983. Some prominent names were missing altogether and Governor

Ige was registered as a woman. Most of the increases in the voters registers occurred in NPN strongholds. Sokoto now had 5.12 million, a 38.38 per cent increase from the 1979 figure of 3.70 million. Other astounding increases included Kano, 49.02 per cent; Kaduna, 98.24 per cent; Rivers 115 per cent; and Benue, 128.57 per cent. But the population in the opposition states were not so lucky to have increased in such geometric proportion. Registered voters had increased by only 23.89 per cent in Lagos State; Ogun, 15.63 per cent; and Plateau by 3.75 per cent. The opposition parties, led by the UPN, openly condemned this FEDECO magic, but the NPN hailed it, praising Ovie-Whiskey for his competence. When the final list came out, FEDECO announced that it was for sale at N1.6 million for each party.

It was also public knowledge that the number of registered voters was more than the number of voter's cards supplied by FEDECO. This was intriguing since no person would register without collecting his voter's card. Wale Oladepo of the *National Concord* commented: 'One of such states where more voters were registered than the cards supplied was Sokoto which is not one of the high-population pull-centres in the country. Sokoto State was given 4.2 million cards, it registered 5.12 million voters. This represents an increase of about 1.4 million over its 3.8 million voters recorded in 1978. Where did the excess one million cards come from? Simple common sense would prove the figure a fake.'[83]

What really threw confusion to the PPA camp was FEDECO's decision to re-order the election sequence. In 1979, the presidential election had come last, but now the commission announced that it would come first, August 6. Though the PPA was a shaky alliance, the members were united in their fear of NPN hegemony. Since neither Zik nor Awo would step down for each other, the PPA had placed its hope that the House of Assembly election would come first and presidential election last as it was in 1979. With this, it was reasoned, whichever party was leading, the other candidate would withdraw to give the leading person a fair chance of unseating Shagari who became president in 1979 with only 33.8 per cent of the 16,846,633 votes cast. With the change in the electoral calendar, this strategy became an anachronism.

It was like an Exocet missile fired at the PPA camp.

Awo, convinced now more than ever before that Shagari was working for a first round win, intensified his campaign. He too wanted to win on the first ballot, and if possible bye-passing the PPA. The decimation of the PRP and GNPP had swelled the ranks of the UPN faithful. Other dynamics had also been introduced into the presidential race. Tarka died in 1980, dooming any chance of reconciliation between Awo and his old protégé, but opening a new chink in the NPN phalanx in Benue State. The death of Aminu Kano during the 1983 campaign had the opposite effect in Kano as it hardened feelings against his opponents and his estranged political son, Rimi, among the teeming Kano *talakawa*. FEDECO had also registered Nigerian Advanced Party, NAP, led by Olatunji Braithwaite, a radical and rich Lagos barrister.

To better his electoral fortune, Awo did not only try to reach into the hearts of the common people, but also attempted to cultivate the friendship of the elite. He broke the Northern logjam by getting into an alliance with the 'Committee of Concerned Citizens'. These were a group of influential Northern leaders, mostly bureaucrats and businessmen who were convinced that if Shagari was given a second chance, he would turn Nigeria's economic disaster into a calamity. Many people believed the committee was the intellectual vanguard of the shadowy Kaduna Mafia. Winning the friendship of this committee was considered a great breakthrough by Awo, and the leaders of the NPN were alarmed. When Awo made a visible presence at the installation of the new Emir of Bauchi early in 1983, the ceremony was boycotted by many leaders of the NPN.

But the price to be paid for this friendship was steep. On Wednesday, August 3, 1983, Dr. Ibrahim Datti Ahmed, the spokesman for the group told a press conference in Kaduna that the committee had entered into an agreement to help Awo for the presidency in exchange for good governance. He outlined the details of the agreement with the UPN which showed that the group was ready to participate fully in government. In exchange, Chief Awolowo promised to bridge the educational gap between the North and the South, promote Islamic religious and moral education, and remove all restrictions on Muslims in the performance of the holy pilgrimage to Saudi Arabia. An Awolowo federal government would also promote agriculture with the river basin development authorities as its core. It would not automatically renew ties with Israel and would ensure the movement of the seat of the federal government to Abuja in record time. In addition, Awo 'shall appoint people from the North into key positions and ministries so that the participation of the Northern part of the country would be seen in the North as obvious and important. The president shall consult the Committee of Concerned Citizens in respect of such offices that should be occupied by northern states appointees'.[84]

The committee was the first group in Nigeria, apart from political parties, to enter into such an alliance with a major party. Ahmed explained that his men took this line of action 'to put a stop to the shameful and ostentatious corruption being perpetrated against the country and its citizens by the few privileged, but unpatriotic, greedy and inhumane men who have found themselves in positions of trust and authority and have betrayed the trust and perverted the authority for their own narrow selfish ends'.[85] Apart from Dr. Ahmed, a prosperous Kano private medical practitioner and former pro-chancellor of the University of Ife, the group also paraded other distinguished men including Dr. Mohammed Tukur, a former vice-chancellor, Bayero University, Kano, who later became a minister in the regime of Major-General Muhammadu Buhari; Dr. Suleiman Kurmo, former pro-chancellor, Federal University of Technology, Minna; and Alhaji Yaya Abubakar, a retired federal permanent secretary. One of the backers of the group was Major-General (rtd) Shehu Musa Yar'Adua, Obasanjo's chief of staff, supreme headquarters.

The group, a disaffected faction of the NPN, was scandalised by the recklessness, corruption and indiscipline of the Shagari regime. They were also unhappy with the powerful, but unhealthy influence of Dikko in government. Alhaji Mohammadu Kura, a former GNPP stalwart from Bauchi State and NPC parliamentarian during the First Republic who became Awo's running mate for 1983, was a member of the committee. The negotiation took place in Ahmed's Kano residence and the UPN delegation was led by Governor Jakande. The committee, apart from putting down the candidacy of Kura, also fielded candidates for many other posts on the platform of the UPN.

As the date of the presidential election drew near, hopes were raised that the PPA might come up with a formula for the election. On Tuesday, August 2, 1983, the NPP called a hurried press conference and speculation was rife that Zik was going to announce that he was stepping down for Awo to ensure a PPA victory. Dr. Azikiwe, however, told the gathered reporters in Lagos that he had decided to contest the Saturday election. He said the PPA arrangement would come into play during the run-off if none of the candidates won an outright victory. The feelings of the NPP was that if it would be necessary for the party to play its accustomed role as the beautiful bride, then it would be in a better bargaining position in a run-off arrangement.

13

Riding The Tiger

A yo Iluku, 45, financial secretary of UPN Ekiti Central Constituency of Ondo State, was in his patent medicine store at about 6.50 p.m. on Wednesday, May 25, 1983. Iluku, head of a large family which included his aged mother, his wife and a brood of seven children, was one of the pillars of the party in Ado Ekiti. In appreciation of his role, he was made a member of the board of directors of the Great Nigeria Insurance Company, owned by the Odu'a Group. But on this Wednesday, there was no great party matter to attend, and Iluku, with his wife and two of his children, was busy attending to customers in his small store. Two young men came in asking for some prescription drugs. As soon as they identified Iluku, one of them drew out a revolver and shot him twice. As they escaped in an unmarked car, Iluku was dying in his wife's arms.

Ali Iginla belonged to a different breed of politicians. At 67, he was an old breed and tested war horse of the UPN. Like Iluku, he was also head of a large family, which included his aged mother, his wife and seven children and many grand-children. On the same Wednesday May 25, 1983, at about 7 p.m., Iginla was relaxing in the midst of his children and family members in his house on 28, Kajola Street, Ado Ekiti. He was the chairman of UPN Ekiti Central Constituency III. He was discussing with Mr. Joseph Fatoba, secretary of Ward J in Ekiti Central Constituency III, who was on a visit. It was at this time that two young men came in and, in the full view of his family, shot Iginla. He died immediately while Fatoba, who was wounded, died ten days later.

The killings at Ado Ekiti were indications of the violence that attended the campaign for the 1983 presidential elections. Right from 1980, when politicians geared up for the next round, violence had become a recurring decimal. There were three kinds of violence: physical violence, violence against the letters and spirit of the constitution, and verbal violence or threat of violence. The killings at Ado Ekiti indicated that Ondo State occupied a conspicuous place in this gory theatre. Those responsible for the Ado Ekiti assassinations were never apprehended, but UPN leaders put the blame on the NPN.

Ado Ekiti had been a theatre for the test of strength between the two parties. On May 22, three days before the assassinations, there was a violent clash between supporters of the UPN and NPN during which many vehicles were burnt. Earlier, on May 3, 73-year-old Chief Babatola, patron of the NPN, and before the Omoboriowo crisis, the undisputed political leader of Ado Ekiti, was attacked, beaten to a state of coma and was only revived in the hospital. The killings at Ado Ekiti were, therefore, seen as a retaliation for the humiliation of Babatola. The police moved in, arrested all known leaders of the NPN in the city, but the clue to the killings was never found. It was the first time since the crisis began that people would be killed for indisputably political motives.

The tone of the violence had been set shortly after Omoboriowo decamped to the NPN. In January 1983, two giant sawmills, one at Atosin-Idanre, owned by Ebun Ogunyimika, and the other at Ise-Ekiti, belonging to Lawrence Agunbiade were burnt by unknown arsonists who the two men, both top Omoboriowo supporters, said were UPN thugs. The same January, eight houses belonging to Chief R.A. Agbayewa, chairman of the NPN in Akure Local Government (not a member of the Omoboriowo group) were burnt. When Mrs Janet Adeotoye, the only woman member of the Ondo Assembly died in a motor accident with her husband May 8, on Abuja-Kaduna road, the NPN claimed the accident was faked (the police confirmed it was indeed an accident) and blamed it on the UPN.

The violent tone of the campaign in Ondo State was only a part of the dangerous trend that was going on throughout the country. There were killings and clashes in Borno, Kano, Sokoto, Niger, Plateau, Anambra, Bendel, Ogun and Oyo States. Most of the clashes were between the NPN and UPN and in Plateau, Imo, Anambra and Niger, NPN and NPP. While other parties' gubernatorial candidates were given one police escort each, the NPN flagbearers, like Omoboriowo, were provided with a contigent of between six and twelve police escorts on a permanent round the clock basis. Even not all gubernatorial and presidential candidates were given police escorts. Alhaji Waziri Ibrahim and Dr. Tunji Braithwaite, the presidential candidates of the GNPP and NAP respectively, were denied police escorts unti. they protested and were granted one each. Even ordinary NPN 'strongmen' like Adebayo Ogundare, alias 'Bayo Success', the leader of the NPN Drivers' Union, had police escorts. Ogundare was one of the most successful of NPN musclemen as he cruised about the city in a 'Shagari Benz' and other luxury saloons.

The NPN used the police to intimidate those it perceived as its opponents. In Lagos, Adewusi ordered the arrest of Dele Giwa, then editor of *Sunday Concord,* whose paper was daring enough to expose the power struggle between the inspector-general and Akinjide, the attorney-general. In Oyo State, police sealed up the premises of both the *Nigerian Tribune* and the *Daily Sketch*, and their top editors arrested, August 1981. Bishop Eyitene, the commissioner of police in Anambra, simply ignored court orders he did not like. In Oyo State, Alhaji Umaru Omolowo, the police commissioner, withdrew the mandatory police orderly from two judges — T.A. Ayorinde and A.A. Sijuade — for allegedly delivering judgments unfavourable to the police. In 1983, Dr. Azikiwe was prevented physically from campaigning freely in Maiduguri, Borno State, when the police commissioner forbade him from going to any other part of the city apart from the approved campaign venue. Zik had wanted to visit the governor and the Shehu of Borno.

One of the most visible of these partisan police officers was

Omolowo, the Oyo State police boss. On Tuesday, April 26, 1983, Omolowo held a meeting with leaders of five of the six political parties (it was boycotted by the UPN), where he accused Chief Awolowo of fomenting trouble and vowed that the police was ready for him. 'Contrary to the conditions under which various licences were granted, the party leader (Awo) had gone to everywhere to preach the politics of hatred, acrimony, an-eye-for-an-eye, and vandalism.'[86] Babatope of the UPN countered that Omolowo was a partial peace-keeper and asked for the statement he made 'when NPN hired thugs killed innocent Nigerians on the occasion of the declaration of Alhaji Busari Adelakun and Chief Sunday Afolabi for the NPN'.[87]

Omolowo's duty was full of tension. The police had to prevail on Chief Awolowo not to campaign in Ogbomoso, home town of the late Chief Akintola, because of an alleged plot to assassinate him there. In July 1983, one of the most gruesome violent accidents also took place in Oyo State. An advance team of Governor Bola Ige's campaign party had gone to Modakeke, an Oyo settlement on the outlying western arm of the ancient city of Ile Ife. The team was attacked by Modakeke people, a new and passionate group of converts to the NPN, during which seven persons, including Mr. Wale Odelola, a member of the Oyo State Assembly and an indigene of Modakeke, were burnt to death. Three years earlier in 1981, violence had broken out between Modakeke and the Ife people during which 26 persons were killed.

The Modakeke tragedy was a lingering legacy from the bitter Yoruba civil war of the 19th century. That old feud, between the Ife, and the Modakeke people, was now finding re-enactment in the terrain of modern politics. To aggravate the matter, the tussle between Oba Okunade Sijuade, the Ooni of Ife, and Oba Lamidi Adeyemi, the Alafin of Oyo, became part of the pot-pouri in the imbroglio. After Old Oyo Empire was destroyed by Fulani jihadists and their Ilorin collaborators in the 19th century, some Oyo people found refuge in the ancient city of Oduduwa, the progenitor of Yoruba race and settled in the place now called Modakeke. The Ife people treated them as allies and later as cheap source of labour, igniting the Modakeke people into rebellion. Twice in the 19th century, Ile-Ife was sacked by Modakeke warriors who were only restrained by the fear of retaliation from other Yoruba states for Ife territory was regarded as inviolate. Despite being defeated on the battlefield, therefore, the Ife people had been able to maintain their political hegemony over the Modakeke. When Modakeke was not separated from the Ife dominated Oranmiyan Local Government by the Bola Ige regime, they regarded it as another evidence of Ife perennial political domination.

While this was the predicate, another scenario was developing. The Alaafin of Oyo from time immemorial had always resented the prestige of the Ooni. During the days of the empire, his overriding powers had compensated for this, but by the 19th century, with the rise of Ibadan republicans, Oyo had faced steady decline. Being the prince on the throne of Oduduwa, the Ooni has always regarded himself as first among equals among Yoruba Obas. In fact, the co-eval status of the others derives from the fact that they all derived their right to the throne by being descendants of Ife princes. This theory, the Alaafin resented and sought, if he could not convince secular powers of his superiority to the Ooni, to at least bring the latter to his own level. When Governor Ige announced that newly installed Ooni Sijuade would continue as the chairman of the Oyo State Council of Obas like the late Ooni Adesoji Aderemi, the Alaafin considered it a personal humiliation. The Modakeke people too, being of Oyo stock, considered the Alaafin's battle part of their own. Modakeke was to remain a flashing point throughout the Second Republic.

The UPN blamed the Modakeke killings on its arch-rival, the NPN. Babatope, in a statement in Lagos, warned that the people were being forced into a situation where 'they have to defend their precious lives on account of various acts of provocation being daily mounted by the NPN in the state against them'. He said, with the killings, the number of UPN members killed since 1980 had increased to 20: three in Borno, with earlier eight in Oyo and the recent Modakeke six. Governor Ige, too, in a radio and television broadcast said: 'The people will not fold their arms for too long when subjected to this unrestrained physical assault and barbaric onslaught in the face of police indifference.'[88]

Another trouble-spot was Kano where the charismatic Governor Rimi was leading a rebellion against Malam Aminu Kano, the political emperor of Kano's *talakawa*. Rimi had sought to undermine the influence of Alhaji Ado Bayero, the Emir of Kano. He promoted some minor district heads to emirship and made them first class traditional rulers. In July 1981, Rimi issued a query to the emir, asking him to explain why he had to travel abroad without the governor's permission. When this became public knowledge, it sparked a violent riot in Kano City after the Friday Jummat prayer, July 10, 1981. Many houses, vehicles and other properties were destroyed. Four PRP supporters, including Dr. Bala Mohammed, the ideologue of the Eagle-PRP and political adviser of Rimi, were killed by the mob.

The religious riots that swept parts of the North were to pose a greater security problem. On October 30, 1982, some members of the Muslim Students Society, MSS, in Kano City started a demonstration against the siting of a new Anglican Church in the city. The foundation stone of the church had been laid earlier in April that year when Archbishop Robert Runcie of Canterbury, England, the leading Anglican prelate, visited Kano. Now the demonstrators wanted to uproot the church. The police who were already alerted defended the church successfully, but the demonstrators were able to damage three other churches, some hotels and many private vehicles. The demonstrations also spread to Kaduna. By the time the riot was contained, 44 people, including two policemen, had been killed.

The Maitasine sect, an unorthodox, fanatical Islamic sect that deified its leader as the successor of the Holy Prophet Mohammed also caused serious upheavals in the North, especially in Kano and Maiduguri. In the Maitasine riot in Maiduguri, October 1982, more that 400 people were killed including 30 policemen. The government had to call in troops to put down the uprising.

There was also serious violence on the spirit and letter of the constitution. The hallmark of this was intolerance, and the first to pay the price was Alhaji Balarabe Musa, the radical governor of Kaduna State. Musa's problem was compounded by his rebellion against the venerable Aminu Kano. The NPN opposition, who were in majority in the state's assembly, made it impossible for Musa to govern effectively by refusing to approve his list of commissioners and other appointees and by putting every obstacle in his way. Using its two-thirds majority in the house, the assembly finally impeached the governor in 1981. Balarabe Musa refused to defend himself of the charges of the assembly. He was succeeded by his deputy, Alhaji Musa Abba Rimi.

In Ondo State, the members of the assembly who had decamped to the NPN refused to vacate their seats as prescribed by the constitution. Decamping parliamentarians, except those in the Senate, all over the country simply ignored this provision. Another example was Cross River State where majority of assembly members who crossed over to the UPN refused to vacate their seats in the assembly. Governor Clement Isong lost out in the nomination battle to Donald Etiebet, a protégé of Senate President Joseph Wayas.

In Ondo State, the battle lines became sharper. When Governor Ajasin presented four names for appointment into his cabinet, the assembly rejected the list by 31 votes to 23. Those on the list were Dr Falaye Aina, for deputy-governor, and three others for commissioners — Kolawole Babalola, Owolabi Afuye and Benjamin Akintayo.

The NPN leaders also decided to impeach Governor Ajasin. Though they did not control the needed two-thirds majority in the house, it was the belief then that they should continue wooing more members of the UPN, especially those who lost re-nomination. A paper on the impeachment of Balarabe Musa was circulated to NPN members of the house, apprising them of the procedure for impeachment. One of the accusations against Ajasin was that of 'financial recklessness' because he voted N500 to each of the 17 local government councils during his state wide tours. The NPN plan was to impeach Ajasin around June, 1983, and since there was no deputy-governor, the NPN speaker, (who was still officially UPN), Chief Jolowo, would act as governor during the period of the general elections. The plan was still-born because the UPN did not suffer further desertions before the elections and the NPN was not able to get the required two-thirds majority necessary for successful impeachment.

What was responsible for the looming atmosphere of violence was the suspicion by the opposing parties that the NPN would manipulate the forthcoming elections, using its control of the police and its leverage over FEDECO to ensure victory at all cost. The atmosphere of war was complemented by the sabre-rattling of the police and its truculent boss, Adewusi. A special anti-riot squad of 6,500 men was trained for the elections and everyone feared that a portentous event was in the offing. What heightened tension was the cacophony coming from FEDECO. The commission had ordered for 150,000 ballot boxes, but suddenly the federal government ordered for an additional 50,000 ballot boxes on FEDECO's behalf. When the UPN accused the Shagari regime of planning to rig with the additional ballot boxes, Alhaji Shehu Musa, the secretary to the federal government, explained that the government ballot boxes were meant for run-off elections and that FEDECO did not make provisions for this earlier. Governor Jakande of Lagos also alerted the nation that official FEDECO forms were already in circulation in Lagos, more than three months before the elections. Lateef Aremu, the resident electoral commissioner for Oyo State, also said there were one million forged voters' cards in Oyo State.

The UPN, which regarded itself as the government-in-waiting, was the most virulent in its attack on FEDECO's preparation for the elections. When Chief Awolowo returned from an overseas trip, April 8, 1983, he accused FEDECO and the NPN of planning to rig through the electronics media. 'If that happens,' he said, 'we shall destroy any radio station that reports such false figures. We shall take the law into our hands and do what is right.'[89] On Friday, May 13, 1983, Awolowo led a UPN delegation to President Shagari over the elections. He warned that rigging would result to violence, but Shagari countered that he too was interested in peace. Speaking to the press later, Awolowo said despite the assurances of Shagari, the NPN was forging ahead with plans to rig the elections. He alleged that when Governor Jakande of Lagos accused Chief Akinloye of keeping 70 ballot boxes in his house, the NPN chairman did not deny it. He said further: 'If elections are rigged this time, I will just go back home (to Ikenne). I won't even go near the court. That does not mean that the masses might not revolt on their own volition.' [90]

Other party leaders were in bellicose mood and their pronouncements were more like those of generals of warring armies than of democratic parties preparing for elections. Arthur Nzeribe, maverick multi-millionaire senatorial candidate of the NPP said: 'I have been warning since August 1982 that I will meet NPN fire for fire, blow for blow, rigging for rigging, rice for rice, salt for salt and naira for naira.' [91] Governor Ige of Oyo State also said: 'Be battle ready. Be prepared to deal with anyone who might attempt to steal your votes during the forthcoming elections. Be prepared to do what you did in 1965 if the NPN steal your votes.' [92] Ige said on another occasion: 'For anyone who attempts to rig election in Oyo State this year, only his orphans and widows will hear the results.' [93] Chuba Okadigbo, Shagari's special adviser on political affairs reached for an aphorism: 'They (the opposition threatening violence) should not forget the dictum that he who rides on a tiger's back will sooner or later find himself inside the tiger's stomach.' [94]

The politicians were putting their money where their mouths were. All parties hired tough boys and musclemen and often relied on the more predictable eloquence of violence. Some of these musclemen were organised around political warlords. In Anambra State, the muscle men in support of Ojukwu, who was contesting for the Senate, called themselves the Ikemba Front, IF, made up mostly of veterans of the civil war who fought on the Biafran side. There were also the Imo Youths Organisation, IYO and the Okpara Solidarity Group, OSG, named after the former premier of the defunct Eastern Region, Dr. Micheal Okpara, who was now a chieftain of the NPN. The Ogun State government also set up a 'security organisation', and duly informed the federal government, but some NPN top notchers believed it was made up of mostly musclemen paid directly from the state coffers. Uba Ahmed, the NPN scribe, even alleged that the Ogun State government was using the cover of the state security organisation to train guerrillas who would forcibly overthrow Shagari in the event of Awolowo losing the elections. He said Ogun State government, by setting up the organisation, was abusing the benevolence of President Shagari. 'Would any state government have dared it if Awo was the president?' asked Uba Ahmed.

Campaigns were not polite encounters. When Awolowo came to Ibadan, UPN supporters came with mock coffins of Adelakun, Afolabi and others who defected from UPN to the NPN. 'They are not dead yet,' Chief Awolowo told the enthusiastic crowd of one million on Mapo Hill. 'Wait until August when they would be dead politically and we shall bury them'. There were few elevating thoughts on the campaign trail. Ojukwu, too, was doing everything to win the Igbos to the NPN. Said he: 'Political power is in the North; economic and bureaucratic powers in the West; Igbo too will like to share in political, economic and bureaucratic powers'. Even Ibrahim Waziri, who in 1979 caught the imagination of the nation with his 'politics without bitterness,' was now lost in the cacophony.

Yet there were occasions for cheers. At the independence anniversary held in Abuja, October 1, 1982, all the political party leaders were present. The only absentee was Mallam Aminu Kano who was represented by a top aide. Chief Awolowo and Dr. Azikiwe were cheered into the celebration ground and the NPN leaders were polite and solicitous. It was there that Shagari announced the award of the highest honour, the Grand Commander of the Federal Republic, GCFR, to Chief Awolowo and the second highest national award, Grand Commander of the Order of the Niger, GCON, to Mallam Aminu Kano. Even after the Abuja encounter, Shagari informed Ajuluchukwu, during a private discussion at State House, Ribadu Road, that he was ready to meet Chief Awolowo privately and partake of the elder statesman's in-depth insight about the nation's precarious economy. Shagari offered to come to Awo's private residence at Park Lane, Apapa. When he was informed, Chief Awolowo refused to permit Shagari to come to his house. He said whatever advice he would offer would be made publicly. There would be no meeting ground.

14

The Drum Of Chaos

The sabre-rattling at the national level was being reflected at the state levels. In Ondo State, there was no seeing eye-to-eye between the NPN and the UPN stalwarts. The battles were fought both on the streets and on the airwaves. The NPN fulfilled its promise and installed a radio station, the Federal Radio Corporation, FRCN, in Akure, almost exclusively for the use of the NPN and hired one of the brightest media administrators in the country, Oluremi Oyinsan, to run it. There was also the Nigerian Television Authority, NTA, to complete the federal media presence. There was also the *Premier* weekly newspaper, owned by Chief Omoboriowo and edited by Idowu Odeyemi, an accomplished journalist, suave and sedate, who seemed however, a total misfit among the political rough-riders of the NPN. Countering the NPN arsenals were the state-owned radio and television stations complemented ably by Oniororo's *People News,* the privately owned *Nigerian Tribune* and the state owned *Sketch.*

Despite the formidable machinery of the federal government, the NPN people were having a rough time. The massive re-alignment that was expected in Ekiti with the decamping of Omoboriowo did not materialise. The situation worsened with the assassinations in Ado Ekiti. Therefore, there were only two NPN strongholds in Ekiti — Ijero and Ilawe — though it had substantial presence in Iyin (hometown of General Adebayo), Ise, and Ikere-Ekiti.

The attitude of the national NPN leadership did not help matters. Shagari simply refused to tour Ondo state and shore up the fortunes and morale of his men against the gargantuan electoral machine of the UPN and the towering reputation of Chief Awolowo. August 3, 1983, President Shagari was being expected in Ado-Ekiti where he was to lay the foundation stone of the proposed Federal Health Centre (it never took off), and officially open the Federal Polytechnic in the town. Chief Omoboriowo and other top NPN leaders, including Chief Afe Babalola, who was then the chairman of the Federal Polytechnic, were in attendance. There were wailings of sirens and fleets of 'Shagari Benzes'. The rain came at noon, and the crowd, having lost hope that Shagari would turn up, dispersed. Shagari did not show up.

The Ondo NPN was also riven by bitter internal rivalries between the old NPN members and the defectors who apparently had seized the initiatives. They were peeved that Omoboriowo got the gubernatorial ticket from Jacob Familoni, a situation that did not arise in Oyo State, where the NPN flagbearer was an old timer, Dr. Victor Omololu Olunloyo, a mathematician of solid reputation. Some members of the old NPN went to court to challenge Omoboriowo's candidacy, but were pressured to withdraw the suit. As if to perpetuate the dichotomy, the old NPN operated from the NPN secretariat on Oba Adesida Road, Akure, while the UPN defectors had their own 'Situation Office', the gubernatorial campaign headquarters, where Omoboriowo held court.

Some faction of the NPN, led by the state chairman, Prince John Ojomo, said they were not even consulted before Omoboriowo and his group were admitted into the party. The rivalry was at every level and it was intense. Said Omoboriowo of the old NPN: 'A good number of them did not want us to win. They were embarrassed by our coming into the NPN. They did not consider it serious business that we should have an NPN government in Ondo State. They wanted us to be limited to winning 25 percent of the votes so that they can continue to get federal patronage'. When Chief Afe Babalola was offered the chairmanship of the NPN campaign committee, he declined. Babalola was an old NPN.

The old NPN ace card was money. When Omoboriowo decamped to the NPN, some of the decampers were promised 70,000 naira each to compensate them for their loss of employment in Ajasin's government including those decampers in the State Assembly who had their salaries stopped. These were made up of 30 state legislators, 10 national assembly members and four commissioners. But by June 1983, the NPN said it could not pay the sum, and reduced it unilaterally to 25,000 naira each. In the end the decampers were only paid 15,000 each.

The NPN too did not live up to its promises on other fronts. Contrary to its reputation as a party of limitless resources, it was miserly in its funding of the Ondo State NPN. The staff of the 'Situation Office' were having problems with their salaries and it took some persuasion before Omoboriowo got an official 'Peugeot' car for his campaign tours. By June 1983, the Ondo State NPN had run up a debt of almost one million naira. The party, therefore, sent an urgent call to its headquarters in Lagos, demanding ₦4.4 million to fight the election. The expenses included ₦330,000 for the mobilisation of the 66 state constituencies, ₦300,000 'to soften up' FEDECO officials, police, *obas* and selected leaders. Provisions of ₦13,200 were also made for paying electoral officers (at ₦200 each). Presiding and polling officers (at ₦100 per polling booth of which there were 6,600 in Ondo State) were to be given a total of ₦660,000 and party agents of NPN opponents, (at ₦10 each) ₦660,000.

It was a herculean task to get the NPN to pay up. Moreover, funds meant for the state were in the safe-keeping of the old NPN who were signatories to the party accounts. Despite several fence-mending meetings, the relationship between Chief Omoboriowo and Prince Ojomo, the party chairman, was never warm. In May 1983, Omoboriowo suggested that the party funds should be managed by a committee selected by both camps. In a letter dated May 2, 1983, he stated: 'The chairman must never give the impression that he is just to dictate to us on how we would disburse scarce funds at this hour of critical need. I also invite your attention to my position in this matter as the principal character in the arena in a year of election'. This, however, did not completely thaw the ice.

Omoboriowo also got caught in the maelstrom of party intrigues. Chief Akinloye, the NPN national chairman, wanted a shot at the presidential ticket come 1987. By the NPN zoning formula, it would be the turn of another zone to present the party flagbearer at the expiration of Shagari's second term. Akinloye knew that his struggle would be in two stages: to defeat the Eastern zone where Vice-President Ekwueme was a hot contender and having won that battle, presumably, to defeat contenders in the Western zone. Part of the catalysts that would enhance Akinloye's candidacy would be if his home state of Oyo was 'delivered' to the NPN. The only rival of stature, after the exit of the ambitious Abiola, in the NPN against Akinloye would be General Adebayo, the former governor of Western State. Since Adebayo is from Ondo State, it would be better if the state was not delivered so that he would not be on the same advantageous pedestal as Akinloye. This was the reasoning of the Omoboriowo group on why the NPN leadership was not too enthusiastic about its needs.

Omoboriowo, indeed, suffered special disadvantages. Apart from being treated as an outsider by the state's old NPN, the national secretariat of the party was not forthcoming. To compound the problem, Ondo State had no representation on the party caucus, the shadowy group that steered the party leadership, unlike his hey days in the UPN where he was a priest in its *sanctum sanctorum*. Now he had to wait like a supplicant and book appointments with Akinloye, Shagari or the leading party apparatchik like Uba Ahmed. Close to the elections, Chief Omoboriowo finally had an audience with the party caucus during which General Adebayo was also invited. The meeting was in Ekwueme's office. After listening to Omoboriowo's complaints, the party fathers decided to do something about it. Shagari gave him a personal donation of ₦100,000 and Ekwueme gave a donation of ₦50,000. Present at this meeting with Omoboriowo were Adebisi Ogedengbe and Jolowo.

A sum of ₦600,000 was also released to the Ondo State NPN for the purchase of vehicles for constituencies. But the 'Situation Office' was always in debt because it was buying things on credit. Some of Omoboriowo's friends, too, donated money for the campaign, including one of those still in the UPN. On the whole, because of the feud with the old NPN, the Omoboriowo electoral machine was forced to run on low fuel.

Despite these discouraging developments, Omoboriowo was determined to do his best. He borrowed money from his friends to sustain the campaign and was putting all his irons in the fire. The contingent of anti-riot policemen guarding him were well fed and, apart from the official allowances, they were also being reimbursed by Omoboriowo himself. Moreover, the candidate was now more and more dependent on Olabayo, the spiritualist. He was fasting almost every day on the instruction of Olabayo for 'protection'. 'That was why I was lean', said Omoboriowo.

Sometime in June 1983, listeners to the newly opened Federal Radio Corporation of Nigeria, FRCN, station in Akure were surprised to hear the national anthem played in the afternoon. Later, Omoboriowo was introduced by the presenter, saying that the NPN gubernatorial candidate was to address the people of the state. It was unusual for someone who was not a head of state or a governor to have his address preceded by the playing of the national anthem. But that time was an era of strange happenings.

Omoboriowo's speech was violent and full of threats.

> About a week ago, the state chairman of UPN, Chief M.A. Ajasin, went on the air (OSBC) and made a distorted and biased account of recent happenings in Ondo State in order to cover up the criminal acts of the UPN and save their faces', he began. 'It is necessary to put the records straight so that the generality of our people may be aware of the series of atrocities committed by the UPN thugs and members against peaceful and law abiding members of the National Party of Nigeria in Ondo State.

He listed 20 instances of 'harassments, intimidation and violence' perpetrated against his supporters since the days of the UPN primaries. One of the allegations concerned the death of Mrs Janet Adeotoye and her husband who were 'brutally massacred in a questionable manner along Kaduna/Abuja road'.

The speech was concluded on a note of defiance. Said Omoboriowo: 'We hereby appeal to the President, Alhaji Shehu Shagari and the conscience of the public to arrest the wave of injustice going on against NPN members in Ondo State. The NPN leaders in Ondo State are being harassed because the party has taken over Ondo State. The Police and the Ministry of Justice have now conspired to harass and destabilise the NPN in Ondo State. The position should be controlled now because when the suppression of justice bursts out, nobody will be able to arrest the situation. We of the NPN are no cowards but we think more of the peace of the state. Our patience is being exhausted and time is running out'.

At the 'Situation Office', the mood was ebullient. There, Omoboriowo was addressed as 'the governor'. It was a taboo to refer to him as the gubernatorial candidate among this group of dream merchants. This confidence was exemplified by the content of a secret paper sent to the national secretariat of the NPN by the 'Situation Office' on the *Urgent and critical needs to deliver Ondo State to the NPN.-* 'At the moment, we are very certain that we will deliver Ondo State to the NPN, come August 1983,' declared the paper. 'The above statement is based on the following analysis of field support which is so empirical that anybody can be there to verify:

'The fact that the incumbent governor has offended and antagonised all Ekiti communities coupled with the fact that the Ekitis are determined to produce the next governor of the state makes it certain that we will deliver at least 30 of the 33 constituencies in Ekiti land.'

It was also predicted that the NPN would win in 16 of the 33 non-Ekiti constituencies. These are constituencies in Ilaje-Ese-Odo, Ikale, Ifesowapo, Idanre/Ifedore, Akure, Owo and Akoko South. Such ebullient spirit was not restricted to the yuppies in the 'Situation Office' alone. Chief R.A. Akinyemi, former chairman of the state NPN, said that with the coming of Omoboriowo into the NPN, the party could win the gubernatorial election. 'It is imperative that the NPN, as a party, must win the five elections in Ondo State with a comfortable majority this year by the grace of God or Allah,' wrote Akinyemi in his secret memorandum for winning the five elections in Ondo State by NPN in 1983. 'The party should not be gunning for 25% in Ondo State which will favour the president in respect of geographical spread. The party must have the inflexible determination to install an NPN Government in Ondo State in the overall interest of the party and our supporters. The issue of the party winning 25% of the total votes cast is already a *fait accompli* (Shagari won 4% in Ondo State in 1979). It is therefore my candid opinion that Chief Omoboriowo must not be disgraced.'

The ruling UPN knew this was mere empty boast. It was true that the NPN had made serious inroads into the traditional fortress of the UPN and the party now had a credible presence. But it did not pose apparently a serious threat to deprive the UPN of power. First, the UPN campaign machinery was colossal, and it had effectively sold the portrait of Omoboriowo to the electorate as an ambitious Absalom whose only god was power. Second, the party was appealing to the communal sentiments of the Yoruba people. This too, was quite effective, for the Yoruba were not about to disgrace Awolowo, the greatest hero of the nation since Oduduwa, in the greatest battle of his epochal career. Therefore, when Ekwueme led NPN chieftains to campaign in Ondo State June 1983, his reception was less than enthusiastic.

Senior citizens and community leaders in Ondo State were worried about the violent pattern of the campaign. On July 1, 1983 a peace meeting was held at the palace of Oba Adelegan Adesida, the Deji of Akure. It was brokered by Major-General (rtd) Robert Adeyinka Adebayo, former military governor of the defunct Western State and a leading member of the NPN. Gathered in the Afunbiowo Hall in the palace was the cream of Ondo State politics including leaders of the six registered political parties. Also in attendance were leading religious leaders, *obas* and Emmanuel Allagh, the commissioner of police.

General Adebayo was uniquely qualified to broker such a meeting. Though a member of the NPN, he was respected throughout the state as a man of integrity and fairness. As former governor of the West, he was regarded as a leading statesman whose paternal stature was not diminished by his involvement in partisan politics. He was a leading actor during the first decade of military rule in Nigeria. He was the first Nigerian chief of army staff; and in this position, he was an intimate witness of the gory saga of the turbulent sixties. He was abroad during the time of the second coup when his friend, General Ironsi was assassinated. He was governor of Western State from 1966 until 1971 when he was made commandant of the Nigerian Defence Academy, NDA until he retired in 1975. A man who mixed freely, Adebayo had a wide circle of friends and he was able to straddle the political divide.

Speaking to the 100 leaders present, General Adebayo said it was a pity that politicians were forgetting the lessons of history so quickly. 'You remember what happened to us Yorubas before 1967?' he asked rhetorically. 'You can hardly see two Yoruba leaders sit side by side to discuss a common issue. Now, the drum of chaos is beating louder than it was in 1965, especially in Ondo State.' Speaking in similar vein, Emmanuel Gbonigi, the Anglican bishop of Akure warned: 'The leader who does evil should beware! He should remember what happened to those who did evils in the past.'

The political leaders were allowed to state their cases. Dr. Falaye Aina, who was now Ajasin's running mate, defended the UPN, blaming the Omoboriowo group in the NPN for the crisis in the state. He said before the Omoboriowo group moved to the NPN, both members of the NPN and the UPN were living peacefully in the state. 'It was a family quarrel we had in the bedroom', Falaye said, 'when they got to the streets, they turned it into a war of guns, clubs and daggers'. But Prince Banji Adewole, Omoboriowo's running mate and a member of the old NPN, replied Aina's allegations, saying that the NPN was dedicated to peace. 'The NPN is not a party of violence,' said Adewole. 'I am not competent to say whether the decampers are those causing trouble. However, they are quite capable of defending themselves of the charges.'

It was a fruitless meeting despite the efforts of people like Adebayo, Adesida and Oba Adetula Adeleye, the Elekole of Ikole-Ekiti. Allagh, the police boss, said an earlier meeting in his office between leaders of the UPN and the NPN had been fruitless and he blamed the two parties for the tension in Ondo State. The meeting resolved that a council be set up to work for peace in the state. Political parties were also enjoined to eschew violence, abusive slogans and the use of thugs. A communique was duly issued at the end of the meeting but nothing was ever heard of the peace council again. So much for General Adebayo's trouble.

As the August 6 presidential election drew nearer, the campaign in Ondo State reached fever pitch. More anti-riot policemen were drafted to the state and the wailing of sirens could be heard on Akure streets daily. Party muscle-men drove recklessly on the roads, terrorising citizens and brandishing dangerous weapons. The battle too continued on the airwaves and on the pages of newspapers. The theme of Omoboriowo's campaign was that Ondo State could not afford to be in the opposition. 'As of this election, the 1983 registered voters from the 10 Northern States are about 35 million', stated one of the propaganda write-ups of the NPN. 'Yorubas and Bendel voters are about 15 million. Eastern voters which are made up of Ibos (Igbos) and minorities (who vote predominantly NPN) are 14 million. It is therefore evident that without a single vote from Yorubas or Ibos, President Shagari will win resoundingly. Any vote for Awo or the UPN is wasted; it is a vote for the opposition and confrontation. For the interest of our state, the future of our children and the stability of this nation, we must end this political stigma.'

On Monday, August 2, Omoboriowo made a broadcast on FRCN Akure which revealed his ebullient self-confidence.

> 'I have no iota of doubt that the present happenings in our state are an act of God designed to bring about a change for the better in the deplorable living conditions of our people,' he began. 'The poverty of Ondo State can be blamed on successive administrations starting from the time when Chief Awolowo was the premier of the old Western Region. My mission as NPN flagbearer for Ondo State is to redeem

this state from political, economic and social stagnation brought about by the deceit-oriented administration of Chief Adekunle Ajasin. The issue at stake is whether or not Governor Ajasin should continue to regard this state and all its resources as his personal property. Fellow citizens of Ondo State, my goal therefore is to lead a progress-oriented, dynamic, responsive, honest and open administration in Ondo State from October. Vote for me - Akin Omoboriowo, as governor of Ondo State, for progress, a new social, economic and political order. Reject the present sluggish administration. Vote NPN all the way. One Nation! One Destiny!! One God!!!'

By the time Omoboriowo was making this broadcast, the NPN had done its homework well. It had perfected plans to manipulate the election and ensure for itself 'victory'. The planning for this took months and the tireless efforts of top party officials in collaboration with FEDECO chieftains, the police and the men of the National Security Organisation, NSO.

Strangely, history was about to tread on an already beaten path. During the controversial 1965 Western regional election that set the West aflame, supporters of Akintola and his NNDP were known to have operated from the polling booths, to ensure victory for the unpopular government. Women, pregnant with ballot papers, dutifully 'delivered' into Akintola's ballot boxes, ensuring that he won a legal 'victory'. In 1983, the rigging plan followed similar pattern, though now more sophisticated.

In Ondo State, the man at the centre of action was Chief Adeniyi, the FEDECO administrative secretary. Adeniyi, a retired school principal, was a member of Akintola's NNDP in the sixties. A cool and calculating man, Adeniyi nonetheless regarded Omoboriowo's fight as his own. A few weeks to the election, when the final list of electoral officials was compiled, Adeniyi made sure it was dominated by NPN partisans, most of them nominated by the 'Situation Office'. Among those who were given letters as Assistant Returning Officers, ARO, were two of Omoboriowo's personal aides. Chief Adeniyi also ensured that the 'Situation Office' was fed with day-to-day information about FEDECO activities.

The NPN men were not leaving everything in Adeniyi's lap. A task force was set up on the election comprising twelve members, all decampers from the UPN. The task force included two former commissioners and four legislators. In its meeting of Friday July 22, 1983, attended by seven of its members, important decisions were taken on the elections. At the end of the meeting the following resolutions were taken:

1. The task force resolved that the assistant chief electoral officers (there were 17, one to each local government area) must be policed effectively on our own. Rapport must be established with them and their political credentials must be checked. The most problematic for the force is Chief J.A. Afolayan of the Ifesowapo local government.

2. It must be made clear that no electoral officer must come back without electoral victory. The electoral officers should not allow passive influence or mediator of any kind in the discharge of their duties in ensuring victory for NPN. In almost all the constituencies, except where we are very strong, no electoral officer shall release more than a booklet of ballot papers at a time for the presiding officers. The meeting also resolved that we would brief the electoral officers and they in turn would brief the presiding officers.

3. Decidedly, some areas would be starved of ballot papers so that the maximum votes cast in such areas would not exceed between 100 to 200. Much we realise, however depends on the quality of leadership in the areas concerned. If any leader is pushful and trustworthy enough to get extra papers for the NPN into the boxes, such leaders would be encouraged on merit.

4. The last issue examined by the force was the intelligence report reaching members on what the UPN's plans are for the elections. (a) They are preparing to cause chaos in all the areas we are strong. (b) They are recruiting agents for other dormant

*parties in the state. The meeting resolved to effect appropriate
counter action to neutralise them.*

In an earlier meeting on Sunday July 17, attended by nine
members, the task force also discussed ways and means of getting easy
victory for the NPN in Ondo State. It was agreed that effective rigging
had to take place at the polling booths. One of the members suggested
that this 'would involve wilful non-payment of attention by the police,
the collusion of presiding officers, returning officers and the electoral
officers'. Members also agreed that 'six local government areas in which
we are strong must be identified and pockets of resistance there be
subjected to high dose of terror, so that opponents there do not score
above 25%. Another deterrent approach is starving our weak spots of
ballot papers. Rapports have to be established with the police and all
(party) agents at the polling booths'.

The UPN camp, was aware that the NPN was planning something
big, but how big was not clear. It was generally acknowledged that the
NPN was set to dramatically better its dismal performance in 1979
when it scored only four per cent in Ondo State. The main drawback
the NPN had was that its pockets of strength were restricted to small
and medium size towns. The four urban centres of Akure, Ado-Ekiti,
Owo and Ondo were apparently controlled by UPN. The UPN was
therefore confident of victory. Few of the party members believed that
the NPN would win more than 20 per cent of the votes.

On Sunday, August 1, 1983, five days to the presidential election,
the OSTV did a special documentary on the electoral fortunes and
battles of Chief Awolowo. It was an emotional piece, showing the old
man from the days of the Action Group to his later political exploits.
The film footage was backgrounded with rousing music from the
turbulent sixties calling the Yoruba to battle against Akintola and his
NPC backers. Awo was portrayed as the triumphant avatar who was
destined to rescue his people from irascible philistines. In the documentary,
Awo was boastful and self-assured. Replying charges that his leadership
had set the Yoruba backward, he declared: 'I do not recognise two

classes of Nigerian citizens. All Nigerians are first class citizens of their fatherland. I make bold to say that I am proud of my service as premier of the former Western Region. People of that area today enjoy the highest standard of living in the country. This is because I started a revolution in education and social services which no rascal can reverse.'

The documentary was concluded with a poignant parable. Awo told a story about a distant land where the king wanted to make his-son-in-law the prime-minister. The people, however preferred another candidate. Elections were conducted and the king's son-in-law was declared the winner. 'Did you vote for him?' Everyone was asking his neighbour and that one would reply 'no, I did not vote for him'. Concluded Awo: 'The people were then asking: who voted for him? They realised they had been fooled and robbed. They then marched to the palace and chased away the king and his son-in-law.'

15

The People's Vote

Three days to the presidential election of August 6, 1983, the telephone rang in the office of Dr. Olatunji Oyejola, 44. Oyejola, a Moscow-trained agriculturalist, was the project manager for the Cocoa Development Unit, Akure, a state government parastatal. The caller identified himself as Chief Adeniyi, the FEDECO administrative secretary for Ondo State. 'Please come right away,' Chief Adeniyi was saying. 'You have been appointed the State's Presidential Deputy Chief Returning Officer.'

The FEDECO office in Akure was situated in the heart of Isikan market along Oba Adesida Road. It shares border with the Deji of Akure's palace. The place was heavily guarded by armed anti-riot policemen who scared away people even from the sidewalks in front of the FEDECO office. The one-storey building, made of clay bricks and painted in fading yellow, was the party office of the defunct Action Group in the sixties. Now it housed the referees of the new dispensation.

Oyejola was promptly admitted into Adeniyi's office for his name had been given in advance to the fierce looking men at the gate. Earlier in the year, Oyejola had put forward his name as an electoral official, but when the selection was made, his name was not on the list. Those chosen were later trained at Oyemekun Grammar School, Akure. Oyejola thought that was the end of the matter until that afternoon call from Adeniyi. The FEDECO scribe apologised for the delay. He informed Dr. Oyejola that other Deputy Returning Officers had gone to Lagos. He then gave Oyejola some handouts which included the Electoral Act, guidelines to returning officers and immediately sent him to meet the Executive Secretary of FEDECO in Lagos.

The following day, Friday, August 5, Oyejola drove to the Onikan headquarters of FEDECO in Lagos. He was busy reading the handouts from FEDECO during the 350 kilometres journey from Akure. The executive secretary was surprised that Oyejola was coming so late, but appeared relieved when he learnt that Oyeloja was already familiar with the electoral guidelines. The interview was brief, lasting barely 20 minutes. 'He said I should be fair and firm to all sides,' Oyejola recalled later. Before leaving Lagos, Oyejola called on his elder brother, Dr. Bayo Oyejola, a top civil servant, who was worried that his brother should take on such a delicate job.

Early on election day, Saturday, August 6, 1983, Oyejola was at the Akure FEDECO office, armed with an electronic calculator. Chief Adeniyi told him the job would not start until later in the day. A room was prepared for the Deputy Returning Officer with a long table and several chairs. He was also given four officers to help him. The agents, two for each party, were also present. Oyejola spoke to the politicians: 'You should remember you are citizens of this state and this country and you should respect the rules. We are going to do everything in the open.'

The politicians stared at one another suspiciously. Representing the UPN were Wumi Adegbonmire and Alex Adedipe; while on the NPN side were Ayodele Morakinyo, a lawyer and decamper-member of the House of Assembly and Dr. Olowoporoku. Both sides knew that even if angels were to conduct the elections, they would still be alert and suspicious. Earlier June 30, Chief O.I. Afe, the resident Electoral Commissioner for Ondo State, had spoken to some political leaders about preparation for the election. Chief Afe succeeded Colonel Ayo-Ariyo who was transferred to Bendel State, where Afe hitherto presided as electoral commissioner.

'Lack of information about what we are doing leads to a lot of suspicions,' Afe told the politicians. 'In the presence of ignorance, anything could happen. I want to assure you that electoral officers were selected because of their unblemished record. We have all taken oaths of allegiance to serve the country. We in FEDECO are determined to carry out a free and fair election.'

Afe was confident that the elections would go smoothly if only the politicians would obey the rule of the game. The preparation indeed seemed fool-proof. There were 7,275 polling centres in Ondo States, 3,000 were newly constructed polling booths while the rest were public buildings, mostly schools. Unlike in the past, there would now be only one ballot box while voters were to indicate their preferences on the ballot paper where spaces for the six political parties were provided. Unlike in the past too, counting would now be at the polling centres and results declared openly after being signed by the presiding officers, the security agents, and the party agents. In case of late voting, the federal government ordered for lanterns worth N14.5 million. Chief Afe was especially proud of the novelty of counting at the polling booths. 'The mechanics would make rigging impossible,' he said. 'Unless you are a magician.'

Now as Oyejola sat with the party agents in the FEDECO office, it was time to find out whether FEDECO's magic would work. The election was mostly peaceful except for few pockets of violence. Late in the afternoon, the results started trickling in. Oyejola was recording these on a big board where the party agents could easily see. As the Assistant Returning Officers, ARO, were coming in with their results sheets under police escorts, party agents were busy handing over results from the constituencies to their agents at the collating room.

There were no problems with the first three results. Then the ARO from Ekiti West Constituency IV came in with his result and there was trouble. Adedipe, the UPN agent, protested loudly alleging that the result of his party had been given to the NPN. According to the ARO result, while the NPN scored about 60,000 votes, the UPN had only 10,000. Olowoporoku countered Adedipe's protest saying the ARO results was on the proper FEDECO form duly signed by all the party agents including UPN's which made the result authentic. The ARO also stood his ground. To resolve the stalemate, Oyejola asked the ARO to bring the returns from all the pooling centres in Ekiti West. The result was then duly tabulated, polling booth by polling booth. In the end, it was conclusive that the ARO had given UPN result to the NPN, but the general tally was correct. He apologised profusely and was allowed to go.

From then on, the pattern was predictable. The ARO would come in with a result, the UPN would protest while the NPN would counter that Oyejola had no right to question what had been duly filled and signed on the prescribed FEDECO form. Oyejola would then insist and count from the polling booths result and only to confirm that the ARO had 'mistakenly' given the UPN result to the NPN. At a stage, Oyejola ordered the arrest of one of the ARO's but later allowed him to be freed reasoning that his arrest might send panic to other lesser FEDECO officials on the field.

Real controversy was to come with the result from Ifesowapo local government. The pattern was the same, but the protesting UPN agents had a weak case. Their own copy of the result duly signed by the ARO and the other party agents was entered on an ordinary piece of paper torn from an exercise book. Oyejola refused to accept the UPN result preferring the result of the ARO duly entered on authorised FEDECO form. There was a shouting match, but Oyejoja stood his ground, saying that there were enough FEDECO forms to go round. He said the UPN result lacked authority and authenticity. The UPN agents accused him of adhering to the literal wording of the Electoral Act, and accused him of robbing the party through officiousness. For a change the NPN agents were praising Oyeloja for firmness, while the UPN's were raining abuses on him.

The Ifesowapo victory was little consolation to the NPN men who could read the handwriting on the wall. At the end of the collation of results, Sunday August 7, it was clear that Awolowo was maintaining his dominance of Ondo State politics. He had polled 1,412,539 votes or 77.26% of the total votes. Shagari, however made impressive gains from his 1979 rating of 4%. This time around, he polled 366,217 votes representing 20.03 per cent. The NPN men knew this improvement was not commendable, considering the constitutional requirement that stipulated 25% of total votes to indicate that a candidate had a foothold in a state. Olowoporoku and Morakinyo were not in a jubilant mood.

Another person who was not happy about the result was Adeniyi. He called Oyejola and asked sadly: 'Other states are returning NPN. What are we going to do about this result?' Oyejola replied that if that was the way Ondo State people voted, there was no alternative than to relay the result to Lagos. Adeniyi agreed and the result was duly transmitted to Lagos.

It was indeed a landslide victory for President Shagari. Despite the six-cornered battle, he had routed his foes and humbled them on the field of battle. He polled 12,047,684 votes and scored more than 25 per cent in 16 of the 19 states of the federation. Awolowo, his closest rival polled 7,885,434 votes and scored 25% or more in only seven states of the federation. Dr. Azikiwe came third with 3,534,633 votes and 25% score in only four states. The PRP had 1,037,481, GNPP 640,128 and the newly registered NAP 308,842. Both the GNPP presidential candidate, Ibrahim Waziri, and NAP's Olatunji Braithwaite did not score 25 per cent in any state, while the PRP scored more than 25 per cent in only Kano State with 36.63%.

However, despite Shagari's landslide victory, the Ondo State NPN knew the president had been re-elected without their help. At 7 .p.m. Sunday August 7, when Oyejola had tallied all the results, Olowoporoku and Morakinyo joined an NPN leaders meeting taking place at Omoboriowo's house about half a kilometre from the Situation Office at Ijapo Estate. The meeting was a heated one. Both Morakinyo and Olowoporoku wanted Omoboriowo to head straight to Lagos that night and protest to FEDECO about Oyejola's intransigence. Though he had a complement of 25 police bodyguards, Omoboriowo preferred to delay till dawn.

The following day, Monday August 8, Omoboriowo wrote a petition to Chief Adeniyi, protesting the conduct of the presidential election in Ondo State. 'Throughout the voting, unknown to us, the

UPN, the ruling party in Ondo State employed massive terrorisation, kidnapping, brazen tempering with electoral personnel and processes to rig the elections,' he wrote. 'It is more regrettable when it is discovered that these illegal activities of the UPN received the co-operation of certain characters within the Nigeria Police and the Nigeria Security Organisation, in Ondo State. The list of election malpractices is endless.' He urged the commission to cancel the result of 14 constituencies, nine of them from Ekiti. He followed this up with a similar petition to Ovie-Whiskey, complaining specifically about the activities of Dr. Oyejola. Said he: 'Constituencies wherein the Return Sheets of the Assistant Returning Officers which form *prima-facie* pieces of evidence were fraudulently and maliciously ALTERED by allowing inferior, extraneous and illegal pieces of paper as sufficient evidence to rebut the validity of the AROs Return Sheets. These were perpetrated by the Deputy Chief Returning Officer, the one and only Dr. Oyejola'.

Wednesday, August 10, Omoboriowo was in Lagos to see Adewusi, the Inspector General of Police, IG, and present his petition to FEDECO. He also left a note for Umaru Dikko at his 16, Alexander Avenue, Ikoyi residence. 'You will no doubt be disturbed by the massive manipulation made on our election result by the UPN and certain characters in FEDECO, Akure, in the last few days', he wrote. 'The election was not an election at all. I feel highly outraged, cheated and insulted by the manipulations but wish to assure you by the grace of God that the position will be reversed on Saturday at the gubernatorial level. There is no doubt that a good number of elders in the state have some soft spot for Awolowo as a Yoruba leader, but the dare-devil and fascist method of the UPN last week did not allow a fair election and fair recording of election results.'

Omoboriowo came to Lagos with a delegation comprising Olowoporoku, Morakinyo, Falodun and Ogunyimika. They insisted that Oyejola must not be allowed to conduct the gubernatorial election. At their meeting with top FEDECO officials, it was finally agreed that Oyejola would be changed and a new man would be sent to relieve him from Lagos.

Oyejola was not aware of the fire ranging close to him. On Monday, August 8, a day after he had sent the presidential election result to Lagos, he was in his sitting room with his family when the familiar face of Segun Adegoke, the UPN publicity secretary, filled the television screen. Adegoke was complaining bitterly that Shagari would not have won up to 20% but for the 'manipulations' of Dr Oyejola and other top FEDECO officials. He mentioned the specific example of Ifesowapo local government, where he said it was impossible for the NPN to defeat UPN. By the way he was speaking, it was clear that the UPN had not anticipated that Shagari could poll up to 20 per cent of the votes in Ondo State. Oyejola was however deeply hurt by Adegoke's outburst and he decided to resign the FEDECO job there and then. By the time he called at FEDECO office the following day, Adeniyi had already received the go-ahead from Ovie-Whiskey to relieve Oyejola of his job. Oyejola was accordingly informed, and he too told the FEDECO scribe that he would no longer be able to continue. It was not to be the end of the matter as Oyejola was later to find out.

With the exit of Oyejola, the NPN and Chief Adeniyi now believed that there was a chance for an NPN victory the next Saturday. With the visit to Lagos of the NPN delegation, there was the chance now that the police would also be cooperative. During the presidential election, the NPN had complained that some police officers were 'blatantly hostile' to the party. After his meeting with Adewusi, Omoboriowo wrote a formal protest to Emmanuel Allagh, the police commissioner, dated Friday, August 12, the eve of the gubernatorial election. He stated inter alia:

> Throughout yesterday, the UPN Gubernatorial Candidate, Chief M.A. Ajasin, interrupted programmes on the OSBC to allege among other things that my party — the NPN — has in preparation for tomorrow's election produced new voters' register containing the names of our supporters alone. Incredible!
>
> That ballot boxes and ballot papers were being kept by our party and that actual stuffing of the ballot papers into the boxes were being done in my house at Ijero, one Mr. Oludaye's house at Afo Akoko,

Chief Awe's house at Ogbagi-Akoko, Mr. Olu Olofin's house at Igede and Lawrence Agunbiade's house at Oda Road, Akure. I want these irresponsible allegations investigated promptly.

3. That UPN supporters should come out on Saturday to 'harass', 'intimidate' and 'attack' my supporters throughout the state with intent to scare them from voting.

All these allegations carried on OSBC by Chief Ajasin are false, highly inciting and a calculated attempt to generate a break-down of law and order in the state tomorrow.

We are no cowards. We are prepared to take the challenge of Chief Ajasin, if his intention is to cause chaos and disorder.

As a custodian of law and order in this state, I strongly appeal to you to:

a: Call the bluff of OSBC. We should not sit down here to see a state radio desecrating the office of the President of Nigeria.

b: Please endeavour to tell the people of the state to steer clear of violence in any form. In as much as we would not take it low with the UPN in whatever way they behave tomorrow. It might interest you that Governor Bola Ige of Oyo State made similar inciting announcements on "Radio O-Y-O and the State Television in Ibadan the day before yesterday, but your counterpart in Oyo, Alhaji Umaru Omolowo, in less than an hour of the commencement, told the people of the state on radio and television that the police and the army are equal to the task of maintaining law and order.

A stitch in time saves nine'.

Copies of the letter were sent to Shagari and Adewusi. At this time, Allagh was not the most popular man in NPN circles. Though he was from Benue, an NPN state, the Omoboriowo group did not completely trust him. He was frequently accused behind his back, of harbouring pro-Awo sentiments. He was often compared to Omolowo, the Ebira man from NPN-controlled Kwara State, who was enthusiastically pro-NPN. Even if he wished, Allagh was in a weak position to shore up the Ondo State NPN. Most of his officers were from the LOOBO states, a quarter of them from Bendel alone. While they might be regarded as loyal officers of the federation, the NPN suspected their sentiment for President Shagari and the NPN.

The discovery that the AROs were altering results obtained from the polling booths put the Ondo State UPN on red alert. Segun Adegoke, who was now the commissioner in charge of information and local governments, summoned the local government secretaries to Akure. The secretaries, though civil servants, were regarded as loyal Awoist. They were direct appointees of the governor. During the gubernatorial election, they would co-ordinate with the Deputy Returning Officer at each of the 17 local government areas. Moreover, they were to liaise with the Divisional Police Officers, DPOs, to ensure the safety of electoral materials.

Adegoke's brief to them was precise. They were to obtain their own copies of the result declared at the local government headquarters. This must be signed by the DRO, the DPO, the local government secretary, and the party agents. They must ensure that the result tallied with the returns from the state's constituency headquarters and the polling booths. They should also ensure that the results were entered on the official FEDECO form. The UPN was not willing to allow a repeat performance of the Ifesowapo incident. Moreover, the party was determined to reduce the margin of NPN victory during the gubernatorial election. The local government scribes understood their assignments and they decided to act accordingly.

But the UPN ace-card was its human resources. Unlike its rival, the NPN, it had among its ranks, the best and brightest of the educated elite that Ondo State could boast of. Every polling booth, constituency and local government centre, was manned by dedicated UPN agents who were mostly university graduates. This corps of men would be difficult to intimidate, corrupt or deceive.

On Thursday, August 11, A.S. Iriah, the Chief Federal Electoral Officer sent a message, tagged 'most immediate, very urgent', to all state chief federal electoral officers, complaining about the report of shortage of electoral materials during the presidential election. Said he: 'Complaints have also been received that in some polling stations, presiding officers were alleged to have complained of shortage of supply of Form EC.8A - Statement of The Result of Poll. Records to state branch offices indicate that sufficient number of copies of Form EC.8A were distributed to and signed for in all the branch offices. It is therefore a matter of surprise to learn of shortage of these forms. Administrative Secretaries ought to realise that the issue of Form EC.8A to party agents is a statutory requirement. In future, administrative secretaries should produce locally any forms which are in short supply in order to avoid similar complaints, provided that the number to be printed is limited to the actual needs for the Elections.'

Basking in the distant glow of Shagari's victory, the Ondo State NPN prepared for the crucial gubernatorial election. Speaking a few days to the election, Chief Omoboriowo said while it was possible for Ondo State people to vote for Chief Awolowo, they would definitely reject Chief Ajasin. 'Saturday's battle is not a battle between NPN and UPN as such, it is a battle between Chief Akin Omoboriowo and Chief Adekunle Ajasin,' said Omoboriowo.[95] He alleged that the presidential election was rigged by the UPN, warning: 'But next Saturday, it is going to be a total war against the UPN. We shall prevent them from rigging this time, even if by force.'[96]

Omoboriowo's paper, *The Premier*, in its edition of Friday, August 12, predictably carried a story on its back page that in a private opinion poll, majority of Ondo State citizens supported Omoboriowo for governor. In an editorial in the same edition, the newspaper urged Ondo State citizens to abandon the UPN boat now that Awo had lost the presidency. '*The Premier* believes that a state like Ondo State where the UPN leaders and supporters have shown so much confrontation and bellicosity to the central administration should, as from this moment, change for the better,' the paper wrote. 'We believe too that there is no better time for such a change than now. Now that Chief Awolowo has been defeated at the polls, we feel it would be foolhardy for UPN supporters in the state to continue to live with Governor Ajasin in the same world of confrontation. The reality of contemporary Nigerian politics is that whichever state or party decides to loath or be recalcitrant to the central administration, stands to lose and the loss is colossal and absolute.'[97]

Reaction to Shagari's victory was mixed. Partymen, perhaps not really expecting the margin of the victory, were restrained. Gone were the victory rallies of 1979. Apart from a small rally in Sokoto, the rest of the nation was calm. Abiola said Nigerians were not happy at Shagari's re-election. 'What the NPN has achieved is not a victory but a conquest,' the Concord publisher said. One man who was fully elated about the victory was Umaru Dikko, Shagari's point-man and most powerful minister. Dikko said with Shagari's victory, the bandwagon effect would create a clean sweep of the gubernatorial and other elections. He said if Nigerians witnessed landslide in 1983, they should expect 'moonslide' in 1987.

It was numb silence from the opposition camp. Waziri and Braithwaite cried wolf, but both Zik and Awo were initially taciturn. Awo had said if he should lose the election, he would not contest the verdict in court. A few days after the presidential election, Awo issued a statement urging his supporters not to abandon the battle. 'I urge you to turn out in larger numbers than you did last Saturday to vote for the governorship candidates of the UPN', he declared. 'You must uphold your right as sacred and inalienable, and treat your duty as inescapable'.[98] Commenting on the massive irregularities that attended the presidential election, he added: 'He who steals another man's property stands to lose it, even if he fails to surrender it to the rightful owner.'[99]

16

Days Of The Magic Men

The day started early for the governorship election on Saturday, August 13. In Ondo town, it started shortly after mid-night. Both the UPN and NPN were suspicious of each other as expected. Unlike in 1979 when Ondo local government was a walk-over for the UPN, the party leaders knew that the opposition now had a presence that can be felt. Moreover, Omoboriowo's running mate, Prince Adewole, was an indigene of Ondo town. Therefore, neither camp was taking anything for granted. A day to the election, rumour had swept the UPN circles that the federal government had ordered the massive arrest of UPN leaders and that one Daddah, the deputy boss of the Nigerian Security Organisation, NSO, Ondo State command, was in Ondo town to effect the arrests. The rumour was given more credence when it was reported that Daddah led a contingent of detectives to the home of Chief Segun Adegoke to arrest him. However, he was absent at the time.

What fuelled suspicion was the rumour that the NPN was using the police to facilitate the rigging of the gubernatorial elections. It was alleged that some top NPN leaders in Ondo State already had ballot boxes in their homes where illegal votings were already taking place, a charge that Chief Omoboriowo vehemently denied in a letter to the commissioner of police. But in Ondo town the rumour was persistent. A police source told the UPN leadership in the town that the NPN

223

leaders would be at the Ondo town central police station, to witness the collection of ballot boxes at 4.a.m., two hours earlier than the stipulated time. Moreover, it was only FEDECO officials who could collect electoral materials including ballot boxes. Because of this information, the UPN leaders decided to get to the police station early. When they got there at 3. a.m., August 13, they met the NPN leaders there.

Events went smoothly at the police station and after the distribution of electoral materials, some of the party leaders lingered on at the place. At about 10.a.m, after voting had been going on smoothly for more than two hours, Seto Akinkugbe, a leader of the old NPN, came to the police station to complain. He met Chief Adegoke and freely shared his kolanut with him. They were old friends despite the political divide. Akinkugbe later drove away in his Peugeot 504 saloon car, with a police constable. About 10 minutes after Akinkugbe left, people came wailing into the police station, that Akinkugbe had been attacked at Oke-Lisa part of the town. He was suspected by some people to be carrying ballot boxes in his car. Akinkugbe was attacked, tortured and a long six-inch nail was driven into his skull. The murderers of Akinkugbe, who was an NPN candidate for the legislative assembly election, escaped before policemen arrived at the scene of the crime.

That day, it was as if Ogun, the patron deity of Ondo town and Yoruba god of war, was abroad in his incendiary presence. The disturbance in Ondo town was far reaching. Two other NPN leaders, Chief Olu Oladapo and Boke Sogun, were killed. Several houses were burnt, including the NPN secretariat at Barrack Road. Starlite Hotel, owned by one of the local NPN chieftains, was torched by people who alleged that illegal voting was going on in the building.

The violence in Ondo town was a chilling presage of the carnage that was to come later. At Igbara-Oke, voting went on peacefully in the early hours of the morning until about 11. a.m, when trouble broke out. Eye-witnesses alleged that some people attempted to snatch ballot boxes from some of the polling centres, but were forcibly prevented. One of the alleged culprits was captured and was only saved from painful death by the quick intervention of the police. In Ilawe-Ekiti, voting was relatively peaceful. The only incident was the attack on Mr. Akomolafe, erstwhile political leader of the community, who was beaten into a state of coma and was to spend more than two weeks in the hospital. At Ijero-Ekiti, hometown of Chief Omoboriowo, voting went on without incident. By noon, voting was already completed and the NPN cleared the polls. UPN did not score a single vote. In Akure, though it was not without incidents, voting was mostly peaceful. One of the incidents was the attack on a reporter for Omoboriowo's *Premier* newspaper. Unknown assailants attacked him with a dagger, as he was on the queue to cast his vote.

But August 13, 1983 was an eerie warning to the people of Ondo State and the nation. In the state capital of Akure and the outlying countryside, the danger in the air could be felt like an electric current. As if the forces of history wanted the people to learn a lesson, a macabre co-incident occurred that day. As the Starlite Hotel went up in flames and Boke Sogun was in the throes of death, a correspondent of the OSTV came into Ondo town to cover the process of voting. Therefore, some of the gory scenes were filmed live and shown later on OSTV until the state government ordered the station to discontinue it. Seventy-two hours later, Ondo State was to become a burning pyre, consuming the Second Republic. The warning of August 13 was not heeded.

But events went too smoothly in many constituencies throughout the country for many people to feel the terrible omen in the air. Nowhere was more typical of this seeming calmness than Ondo State, where, but for the carnage in Ondo town and the other pockets of disturbances, events went on peacefully.

Francis Oluwemimo Ogundayomi, a teacher, was the Assistant Returning Officer, ARO, for Ifesowapo Constituency I. At the close of polling on August 13, he was the key player at Gboluji Grammar School, Ile-Oluji, where the presiding officers at the constituency polling stations, met him to submit their results. The school hall was crowded with politicians, party agents, security agents and a contingent of policemen led by a deputy superintendent. After adding up the figures from the polling booths, he entered the collated result on forms

EC8A and form EC4OJ, signed them and stamped them. The party agents present also countersigned. Ogundayomi then gave copies to the party agents and the police DSP. It was a landslide victory for Chief Ajasin, the UPN candidate who received 50,598 votes to Omoboriowo's 1,725 votes. At the end of counting, Ogundayomi was escorted by policemen to Ore, the local government headquarters to submit his constituency result to Ransome Akinola Aruleba, the Deputy Returning Officer, DRO, for Ifesowapo local government.

James Fola Adenodi, a produce superintendent, was the ARO for Ifesowapo Constituency II, Okeigbo. By 7 p.m. all the results from the 71 polling stations in the constituency had been brought to the collation centre, Okeigbo, by the presiding officers. Adenodi, after adding the results and ensuring that there were no objections from the party agents present, signed copies for the party agents. The copies were also endorsed by the agents. An assistant Superintendent of Police, who led the police team to the collating centre was also given a copy. It was again Ajasin who carried the day with 26,631 votes to Omoboriowo's 885. Under police escort, Adenodi took the result to Aruleba at Ore.

James Adepoju Akinro, an accounting officer with the Federal government-owned Nigerian National Petroleum Corporation NNPC, Lagos, was the ARO for Ifesowapo Constituency III, Ore. His experience was similar to those of the other AROs in the two constituencies. Voting was low in the constituency, but Ajasin still carried the day with 28,786 votes to Omoboriowo's 1,115 votes.

For Felix Olumuyide Giwa, the secretary to Ifesowapo local government, the gubernatorial election day was especially a busy one. The three AROs who presided over the election were appointed that morning from the reserved list, when the three originally billed to serve failed to show up. Chief Adeniyi, the Ondo State FEDECO boss had given powers to local government secretaries to appoint electoral officers if those earlier appointed failed to show up or were found unsuitable. The local government secretaries were also to act as over-all co-ordinator for FEDECO in their zones. Giwa, therefore, appointed three new AROs from the reserved list: Ogundayomi, Adenodi and Akinro.

Luckily however, the DRO, Ransome Aruleba, showed up. Aruleba was a teacher at Community High School, Orisunmbare, also in the same local government council. At about 9.p.m. the results were in from the three constituencies. Chief Ajasin polled a total of 106,015 votes to Omoboriowo's 3,725 votes. Aruleba prepared the final results, endorsed by the party agents, and he gave copies to the police, NSO, Giwa and the agents. Aruleba was to claim later that he did not receive results from Ifesowapo Constituency III, alleging that Omoboriowo actually carried the day in the constituency. Aruleba's result: Omoboriowo, 46,678 votes to Ajasin's 8,209 votes.

At Idanre Ifedore local government, election went smoothly. At constituency I collation centre, local court room, Idanre, the adding was done with minimum fuss. Chief Ajasin polled 13,298 votes to Omoboriowo's 2,127 votes. At constituency II at the Youth Centre, Idanre, the UPN agent was Jileye Akinduro, a lawyer who ensured that the counting procedure was followed to the letter. The ARO duly gave copies of the result to party agents, police and NSO representatives. Chief Ajasin scored 9,528 votes to Omoboriowo's 1,820. At constituency III Ilara-Mokin, the UPN candidate also carried the day with 40,364 votes to Omoboriowo's 1,241 votes. Tobi Ademujimi Olofinmakinwa, a civil servant with the Ondo State Cocoa Development Unit, Akure, was the ARO for Idanre-Ifedore constituency IV at Ijare. The collation centre was at Youth Centre, Ijare. Here, Omoboriowo polled only 530 votes compared to Ajasin's 22,730 votes. Olofinmakinwa, after giving copies of the result to party agents, the police and NSO representative, drove to Owena, the local government headquarters, to submit his result to the DRO.

Emmanuel Blessing Kayode, a member of the House of Representatives, was the UPN counting agent at Owena. By 9.p.m. the results from all the four constituencies in the local government were in. Kayode and the other party agents were present at the Divisional Police Officer, DPO's office which served as the collation centre for the local government, when the AROs brought in their results. All the four AROs submitted their results to Babatunde Akindoju, a staff of the

Nigerian Airport Authority, who served as the DRO. But Akindoju complained that he did not have the prescribed FEDECO form to enter the results. After a mild argument, the DPO suggested a solution. He ordered his typist to prepare a form, type out the results which were then endorsed by Akinkoju, signed by the party agents and sealed with the FEDECO stamp. Kayode was in an expansive mood for his candidate, Chief Ajasin had won a landslide victory. He scored 85,920 votes or 91.98 per cent while Omoboriowo scored 5,718 or 6.12 per cent of the total votes. But Akindoju was to claim later that Omoboriowo carried the day in Idanre-Ifedore local government with 112,048 votes to Ajasin's 17,492.

By 6.p.m, on election day, the town hall, which was the counting centre for Ekiti-North Constituency I, Ikole-Ekiti, was already full. The UPN agent in the hall was Tunji Adeyemi, a businessman. Here, the governor scored 31,253 votes to Chief Omoboriowo's 6,390 votes. The results in the other three constituencies of the Ekiti-North followed similar pattern. In Constituency II, Odo Aiyedun, Ajasin scored 30,220 votes to 14,705 of the challenger. At Constituency III collation centre, Obalatan Comprehensive High School, Ilupeju, the UPN was represented by Emmanuel Dele Adu, a chartered accountant and the NPN by Chief Olu Fajemibola, a community leader. In this constituency, Ajasin scored 34,721 votes to Omoboriowo's 10,375 votes. The collation centre for Ekiti-North Constituency IV was Anglican Secondary School, Oye Ekiti. Here also, the result went to Ajasin who polled 24,190 votes to Omoboriowo's 1,907 votes.

Early on election day, Ayinde Samuel, a Deputy Superintendent of Police, DSP, who was the DPO for Ekiti-North local government, received a visitor in his Ikole office. The visitor, Wale Akinsete, introduced himself as the DRO and Samuel duly made his office available for him for the collation of the results. The results came in late from the constituencies and the last one was received early on Sunday morning, August 14. Akinsete complained that he had no official form for the collation of the result. Samuel suggested that plain sheet be used and the party agents agreed. Akinsete therefore entered the results on a plain sheet, signed it, and it was countersigned by the party agents, Samuel and the NSO man present. Following earlier instructions, Samuel sent the result by radio to the police command headquarters, Akure. Ajasin scored 120,384 votes or 74.60 percent while Omoboriowo scored 33,377 votes or 20.68 percent of the total votes cast. FEDECO and Samuel Adesina, former deputy speaker of the Ondo State House of Assembly, who was Omoboriowo's agent for Ekiti-North, were to claim later that the result was different. Adesina who was also present during the collation at the DPO's office, Ikole, claimed that Omoboriowo scored 146,174 to Ajasin's 26,150 votes.

Events followed similar pattern in Ekiti West local government area. This was the home local government of Bola Akingbade, the deposed speaker of the state assembly. Some of the towns in Ekiti-West are Aramoko, (the headquarters), Okemesi, Efon-Alaaye, Iddo-Ajinnare and Ikogosi. Political consciousness was quite high in Ekiti West and some of its sons and daughters had played prominent roles in politics since the colonial days. Chief H.O. Davies, one of the most prominent leaders of the nationalist struggle and a stalwart of the legendary Zik, had his roots in Efon-Alaaye. Chief Oduola Osuntokun from Okemesi was one of the first ministers to serve in the cabinet of Chief Awolowo in the defunct Western Region.

On election day, Cornelius Omoyele, an accountant, represented the UPN at the counting centre for Ekiti-West Constituency I, Aramoko. The ARO, Mr. I.O. Osanyintuyi, said he had no appropriate forms for the collation of results after the presiding officers had handed him the results from the polling centres. At last, following the insistence of the UPN agent, forms were obtained at the police station, Aramoko. Osanyintuyi then recorded the results on the prescribed form. Ajasin scored 11,160 while Omoboriowo scored 2,627 votes. At Constituency II, Efon-Alaaye, where Osanyingbemi Ayodele was the ARO, collation of results went without incident. Chief Ajasin received a total of 42,381 votes to Omoboriowo's 3,825.

Early on election day, one Richard Bamidele introduced himself to the police at Efon-Alaaye, saying that he was the returning officer for

Constituency III. He claimed he was an officer of the Federal Housing Authority, FHA, Akure. (It was only after the election that it became known that 'Bamidele' was actually Mr. Ogun from Ilawe-Ekiti. Ogun was discharged from the Nigerian Army and had no steady means of income). 'Bamidele' showed the police his identity card from FEDECO and he was later escorted to the collating centre at Christ Apostolic Church Grammar School, Efon-Alaaye. By 9.p.m. all the results were in from the various polling centres and were added up by Bamidele. Chief Ajasin scored 36,208 votes to Omoboriowo's 5,155. Contrary to the electoral act, Bamidele insisted that party agents had no right to get copies of the results and that they were not required to sign it. The situation was degenerating into a shouting match with the NPN agent backing Bamidele. In the end, Bamidele was escorted by the now angry crowd to the police station where he was compelled to issue copies of the result to the party agents. But he did not allow them to sign the copies.

Collation went smoothly in constituency IV and V. Akingbade represented the UPN at the collation centre for constituency IV, at Ikogosi/Erinjiyan Grammar School. The ARO, Julius Ajayi, signed and stamped copies of the result which were also endorsed by the party agents, and he gave copies to the agents. Ajasin polled 17,550 votes to Omoboriowo's 2,918 votes. Voting was concluded early at Constituency V, Okemesi-Ekiti. The ARO, J.O. Bamiteko, pitched his tent at the Town Hall where the collation took place. The UPN agent was Osuolale Oyeniyan, a lecturer at the College of Education, Ikere-Ekiti, and one of the intellectual powerhouse of the party. Representing the NPN was Ajiboye Dada, a Lagos businessman. At the end of the counting, the UPN polled 34,826 votes to NPN 3,573 votes. After the result sheets were duly prepared by Bamiteko and endorsed by the party agents, copies were distributed and the ARO, followed by the agents, headed for the local government headquarters, Aramoko.

It was indeed a hectic day for Olufemi Olajide Ogunjobi, the secretary of Ekiti-West local government. Earlier in the day, he had welcomed James Dada, a well-known teacher and the vice-principal of African Comprehensive High School, Ikere-Ekiti, one of the best run secondary schools in Ondo State. Dada told Ogunjobi that he was the DRO. By 11.p.m. the results were in from the five constituencies and were handed over to Dada who set up shop at the Divisional Police Headquarters, Aramoko. It was a landslide victory again for Governor Ajasin who scored 142,130 votes to Omoboriowo's 18,098 confirming his political hold on Ekiti-West. Dada was to claim later that Omoboriowo scored 159,074 votes to Ajasin's 21,652 votes. Dada duly prepared copies of the result which were endorsed by Akingbade for the UPN and other party agents. Copies were given to the agents, representatives of the NSO, the DPO, and Ogunjobi, the council secretary. When everything was concluded, Dada in a convoy of vehicles led by police siren, drove to Akure to submit results at the FEDECO office. At the same time, Akingbade and his men, making sure that Dada safely arrived at FEDECO headquarters, detoured to the Governor's lodge where a committee was working round the clock monitoring the election.

Election went on peacefully in the six constituencies of the Ikale local government. The collating centre for Ikale Constituency 1A was Comprehensive High School, Ode-Irele. The ARO, one S. Akinduro, gave copies of the result to party agents at the end of collation. Chief Ajasin polled 23,591 votes to Omoboriowo's 1,777 votes. Stephen Demehin, a teachet, was the ARO for Ikale Constituency 1B. The collation centre was Jowiri Grammar School, Ajagba. Here too, Ajasin defeated his challenger by 20,175 votes to 1,965 votes. Mrs Ileola Ogunbameru, a teacher, was the ARO, for Constituency II. The collation centre was at the Court Hall, Okitipupa. Here, Ajasin scored 20,865 to 5,076 votes for Chief Omoboriowo. The ARO for Constituency III was F.A. Ibitoye and the collation took place at Divisional Teachers Training College, Ode-Aye. Here Ajasin scored 14,448 to 3,637 votes for Omoboriowo. For constituency IV, the collation centre was the Police Station, Ilutitun-Osoro, where one Mesika presided as the ARO. Here Ajasin scored 15,118 votes to Omoboriowo's 6,779 votes. Ikale Constituency V was at Igbotako where R.O. Adeowinle was the ARO. Here again, Chief Ajasin scored 15,303 votes to the challenger's 7,036 votes.

The DRO for the Ikale local government was Nelley Naiyeola Faborode, an officer with the Federal Housing Authority, Akure. He pitched his tent at the DPO's office, Okitipupa, the headquarters of the local government, where the six ARO's met him to submit their results. At the end of collation, Faborode gave copies of the result to the party agents, including Kayode Iwakun of the UPN, the DPO, NSO agent, and the secretary of Ikale local government. Here, Ajasin polled a total of 109,500 votes or 77.6 percent while Omoboriowo polled 26,270 votes or 18.61 per cent. Faborode was then escorted by six policemen to Akure FEDECO office to submit the result. But what he submitted in Akure was different. Faborode now claimed that Omoboriowo scored 183,811 votes to Ajasin's 11,695 votes.

In Ekiti East local government, it was a close race between Ajasin and Omoboriowo. In Constituency I, Omoboriowo had a clear lead with 30,000 votes to Ajasin's 13,925 votes. In Constituency II, the ARO was Sam Fadahunsi and collation was at Saint Mary's Primary School, Ode-Ekiti. At the end of collation, Fadahunsi gave copies of the result to Akinola Ayodele, a mechanical engineer and retired major who was UPN agent, and other party representatives. The tally: Ajasin, 29,281 and Omoboriowo 3,839 votes. Ajasin also carried the day at the collation centre for Constituency III, Technical College, Iluomoba. He scored 11,525 votes to Omoboriowo's 4,178. The ARO was one Akeju while Christopher Morakinyo was the UPN agent. The collation centre for the local government was Omuo High School, Omuo-Ekiti, the headquarters of the local government. For the whole local government, Ajasin scored 54,731 votes or 55.73 per cent while Omoboriowo scored 38,945 votes or 39.65 per cent of the total votes. FEDECO was to claim later that Omoboriowo scored 72,479 votes to Ajasin's 28,613.

It was also a close race in Ekiti South local government. The tension was high in Ikere-Ekiti where the UPN and NPN were present in almost equal strength. Reverend Akintayo Adeniyi, a teacher, was the Assistant Chief Electoral Officer for the local government. At the end of polls, Adeniyi moved to the DPO's office, Ikere, for the collation of results from the five constituencies. Soon, party agents from Constituencies I and III came to complain to him, Bunmi Akinniyi, and the DRO. They were complaining that the ARO's refused to give the party agents copies of the results as it was done during the presidential election. Akinniyi said the ARO's were right, but the agents and Adeniyi said they should be given copies of the results. At last Akinniyi and the two AROs relented and they duly issued copies of the results to the party agents. At the end of the day, Ajasin led in four of the five constituencies in the local government. In Constituency I, Ajasin polled 4,622 votes to Omoboriowo's 1,889. In Constituency III, Ajasin scored 10,201 to Omoboriowo's 4,614. In Constituency V, Ajasin scored 30,689 votes to Omoboriowo's 7,408. But Omoboriowo made up for this with a landslide at Ilawe, Ekiti south Constituency IV. Here, Omoboriowo polled 44,672 votes to Ajasin's 5,260. On the whole, Ajasin scored 59,516 votes or 44.93 per cent while Omoboriowo scored 63,990 votes or 48.31 per cent. But Akinniyi was to claim later that Omoboriowo polled 155,247 votes to Ajasin's 16,443.

In many parts of the country, nothing seemed to have gone amiss. But like what happened in Ondo town, the god of power was already receiving its sacrifice of blood in other parts of the country. About 10 persons were killed in Oyo State alone on the day of the gubernatorial election, most of them in Ibadan. In Lodge and Imalefalafia streets of Oke-Ado, Ibadan, two men accused of attempting to snatch ballot boxes from polling booths were burnt by an irate mob. Four men alleged to be NPN thugs attempting to snatch ballot boxes were also lynched at Odo Ona area. Three men were killed along Odutola road, accused of transporting fake ballot boxes. Another NPN leader was killed in Molete. Apart from Ibadan, vehicles, houses and other properties were also destroyed in several other parts of Oyo State. In Ilesa, one of the largest towns in the state, at least eight houses belonging to known NPN leaders were burnt over unsubstantiated allegations that illegal voting were going on in those houses.

There were also disturbances in Lagos, Anambra, Ogun, Bendel and some other parts of the country. It was as if the politicians were bent on repeating the sorry saga of the First Republic. Correctly reading the omen, Tunde Obadina, a Nigerian journalist warned earlier: 'We might as well compose the epitaph for the Second Republic now: born of hope, died of hopelessness.'[100]

By the night of August 13, 1983, the undertakers of the Second Republic were already at work throughout the federation. At the Ondo State FEDECO office, the man at the centre of action was a top federal civil servant who was destined to play a pivotal role in the tragedy that was soon to engulf Ondo State. Joseph Adedapo Alibaloye was a deputy secretary in the Federal Ministry of Mines and Power. Dark, thick-set and rotund, Alibaloye gave the impression of someone permanently on edge. He is an indigene of Ondo State, from Ire-Ekiti. He replaced Dr. Oyejola as the electoral officer for Ondo State.

Alibaloye set up shop in the same room where a few days earlier, Oyejola held court. Representatives of the parties were present, notably Olowoporoku and Morakinyo for the NPN and Professor Akintoye and Alex Adedipe for the UPN. Unlike the vigil during the presidential election, the party stalwarts were soon to know that they were in for a long stay. By the early morning of Sunday August 14, Deputy Returning Officers (DRO) had started coming in with results from the local government areas.

As the DROs were reporting one by one, accompanied by armed police escorts, it was clear that something was amiss. Unlike what happened during the presidential election, the NPN candidate, Chief Omoboriowo was now having a field day. It was clear that what was happening was an upset and a landslide for the NPN. As was expected, the UPN agents protested, but Alibaloye ignored them, saying what the DROs brought were the 'authentic results'. When the UPN agents showed him the results from the constituency levels, Alibaloye was not interested. 'They are not entered on the prescribed form,' he dismissed the results. The NPN agents on the other hands were in a jubilant mood.

The UPN leadership was totally unprepared for the upset. They had reckoned that with block voting, Omoboriowo might capture Ijero and Ilawe and to some extent Oka-Akoko. But what they were facing now was an NPN blitzkrieg. They had expected that Omoboriowo might improve on Shagari's electoral fortune and, maybe, score as much as 25 per cent of the votes. By the night of Sunday August 14, most of the results from the constituencies were in and Omoboriowo had apparently walked away with the victory prize.

Alarmed, UPN election agents trooped to the Government House to complain to Chief Ajasin that Alibaloye would not even consider their petitions. Present in the Government House were a few of Ajasin's top advisers, but most of the big wigs were still in their local government areas to monitor the election.

As was done during the presidential poll, a small committee was monitoring the election results at the Government House. The compilation was made mainly from authenticated returns from the polling booths submitted by party agents who had accompanied the DROs to FEDECO office. By Sunday night, all local government secretaries were also requested to come to Akure with their own copies of the results since they all served as co-ordinators during the election. At the time, two academicians, Dr. Olu Agunloye and Dr. Olugbemi Akinkanye were present at the Government House. Dr. Akinkanye, who just returned from the United States, came in with a portable computer which was used to calculate the results, polling booth by polling booth. It was clear from Akinkanye's calculation that Ajasin had won by a comfortable majority, but now the table was about to be turned at the FEDECO office.

It was not clear why the result of the gubernatorial election was not released that Sunday, August 14 when most Ondo State citizens expected it. By Monday morning, August 15, rumour had spread round Akure that Omoboriowo was to be declared governor-elect. There were general commotions at Erekesan market near the FEDECO office. That morning, market women staged a peaceful demonstration in front of the office asking that the result be released and pledging their support for Chief Ajasin and the UPN. When Chief Omoboriowo called briefly at the office he was booed. Later Chief Ajasin came to FEDECO office where he met with Chief Afe, the resident electoral commissioner, complaining about the delay in the release of the results and arguing that by the returns from UPN agents, he should be declared the winner. Afe asked him to sip the water of patience, promising that justice would be done.

That afternoon, Chief Ajasin made a broadcast on the government radio and television stations. He announced that he had already won the election and challenged FEDECO to release the result. According to him, the following were the results:

GNPP, 10,334 votes or 0.49 per cent

NAP 12,743 votes or 0.6 percent

NPN, 418,889 votes or 19.84 per cent

NPP, 17,723 votes or 0.84 per cent

PRP, 6,689 votes or 0.31

UPN, 1,633,692 votes or 77.39 per cent

Chief Ajasin said despite this, FEDECO had refused to announce the result. 'You can see from these figures that I have won a clear victory over the other candidates,' he declared.[101]

That night, Professor Akintoye and Adedipe were pressing Alibaloye to reconsider his verdict and check the results with returns from the polling booths and the constituency levels. But Alibaloye insisted that he would only take results 'on the prescribed forms.' By 2 a.m., Tuesday, August 16, it was clear that Alibaloye was bent on declaring Omoboriowo as governor-elect and Adedipe and Akintoye tearfully left FEDECO office.

Events moved rapidly from that 2.a.m. Chief Omoboriowo and his supporters were in a festive mood. There was celebration throughout the night. He recorded his victory speech which was given to Radio Nigeria, Akure. Security reports had indicated that there might be trouble if Omoboriowo was declared governor-elect, but the police and the NSO believed it was containable. Also Adewusi, the IG, had ordered that rioters and other trouble makers be shot at sight. Akure was swarming with armed anti-riot policemen. Indicative of the tension, was Omoboriowo's residence which was like a fortress. But nobody was sure of what might happen and the air was pregnant with foreboding:

In the midst of that reverie, a police officer came for Chief Omoboriowo. The governor-elect was wanted at the Command Headquarters, Oyemekun Road, where Allagh, the commissioner was waiting. Omoboriowo met Allagh, fully dressed, pacing his office worriedly. Their discussion was unfriendly. The commissioner told Omoboriowo that he was bringing him to the headquarters for safety, under instructions from Lagos. Later Omoboriowo was kept in another room with two fierce-looking armed mobile policemen guarding the door. The governor-elect was understandably uneasy and scared. Often, it would appear as if he was hearing the sound of guns being cocked and he feared he was about to be assassinated. The commissioner remained incommunicado. Omoboriowo was later allowed to go when two of his supporters came for him around 6 a.m. They assured the C.P that the governor-elect was safe in the well-guarded precinct of his Ijapo residence.

Throughout that morning, security agents moved fast to ensure the safety of selected public officers and politicians. At the unholy hours between 1 a.m. and 4 a.m., senior civil servants, officials of FEDECO, Radio Nigeria and other federal parastatals as well as some top members of the NPN were roused from sleep and taken to safety at the barracks of the 19th Mechanised Battalion, Akure. The commander, Lt.-Col Emmanuel Bala-Gbogbo, assured them of their safety. Some top NPN big wigs too were given armed police guards in their homes. Many of them already had orderlies. But by this time, Fate had already marked its victims and by dawn, it would claim its gory harvest.

17

The Return Match

Chief Segun Adegoke, the Ondo State commissioner for information, was declared wanted by the police shortly after the August 16 and 17 riots in the state. Many UPN leaders were arrested but many more, like Nimbe Farunkanmi, a senatorial candidate and one of the UPN leaders in Akure, Alex Adedipe, former majority leader of the House of Assembly, and Banji Kuroloja, the publicity officer of the party, escaped arrest. Everyone knew where Adegoke, and many of the other wanted men were hiding, including the police. Most of them were guests of the state governor. In the sprawling Government House, Alagbaka Estate, Adegoke was staying in one of the guest chalets. To truly hide himself, he stayed in-doors throughout the day and come out only in the night. Adegoke and the fugitives believed they were saved temporarily from the unfriendly arms of the police.

Adegoke woke up as usual in his chalet in the morning of Thursday September 29, 1983. That day he had a visitor, Dr Olugbemi Akinkanye, who was his classmate at Ondo Boys High School. Akinkanye was now a lecturer at the University of Ibadan. Unknown to Adegoke and his guest and any of the fugitives, there were many other unwanted callers in the periphery. At dawn that morning, scores of armed anti-riot policemen had taken positions in the bush and the Government House was now completely surrounded.

At 7 a.m. Adegoke stepped out to see his caller at the corridor. It was then hell broke loose. Convinced they had secured every outlet, the police roared into the compound in several lorries. As they were jumping down and racing to secure every one of the buildings in the large compound, Adegoke was petrified for a second. It was then Akinkanye opened the booth of his Peugeot 504 saloon car and beckoned to him to get in. Adegoke obeyed. Akinkanye was able to fool the policemen that he was an early caller to see Governor Ajasin. With his cargo, he sped to Ilesha road and after driving some kilometres, pulled to the kerb and allowed Adegoke to come out and join him in the car. By this time, the commissioner was almost dead from suffocation.

That night, Adegoke slept at the University of Ibadan Guest House and from there moved to Abeokuta where he was a guest of Governor Olabisi Onabanjo for several weeks.

The storming of the Government House was a shock to Governor Ajasin who believed that a governor's residence was immune to police action without a search warrant. But there were other surprises waiting in store for him. The following day, Friday, September 30, Ahmed Sheidu, the new acting commissioner of police, phoned the governor, seeking urgent audience. Ajasin agreed. When he came, Sheidu brought bad news. He told the governor that since his petition was still being contested at the Appeal Court (the election tribunal in Akure by this time had overturned Omoboriowo's victory and declared Ajasin duly elected), he had clear instructions from Lagos to prevent him from presiding over the October 1, twenty-third independence anniversary. He explained that the federal government believed that he might be sworn-in for a second term when his victory was still being disputed. The following day therefore, Ajasin duly stayed home. School children, workers and others who had gathered at the stadium for the customary march past, dispersed in disappointment.

In apparent preparation for the rescheduled elections and to forestall violence, the federal authorities moved in policemen in full force. It was a determined show of power to the people of Ondo State. Therefore,

Allagh stepped aside for Sheidu as state's police boss and Victor Pam, assistant inspector general of police, was in charge from force headquarters. Police armoured vehicles daily paraded the streets of Akure and policemen in battle-ready gears swarmed all over the state.

Unlike in the urban centres, however, it was in the smaller towns that the full impact of the policemen was felt. When a band of anti-riot policemen roared into Okemesi, Ekiti West local government area and met the central market in session they threw tear gas into the crowd and the market dispersed at mid-day. When they got to Efon-Alaaye, 20 kilometres from Okemesi, they met an empty town. The people had heard that the anti-riot policemen were on the way and they ran into the surrounding hills. The policemen fired into the empty houses and many of those houses are still bearing pock marks of that unholy day. Not every town was as lucky as Okemesi and Efon-Alaaye to escape with minor scars of the police pacification efforts.

On Tuesday, September 20, Oke-Igbo a hitherto sleepy community and hometown of the famous Yoruba novelist, Daniel Fagunwa, felt the full fury of that uncertain era. An aide of Chief Omoboriowo, an indigene of the town, had come to town that day with some armed policemen to effect the arrest of some suspects whom he alleged spearheaded the burning of his house during the August 16 riot. Apparently, the new policemen did not inform the police station in the town of their coming. They started picking people on the streets into their landrover. Those arrested were then taken to the police station, Oke-Igbo. The invading policemen had come with some persons whom the people suspected were NPN thugs. When it was learnt that the arrested men were at the station, a mob soon surrounded the place, vowing that the suspects would not be taken out of the town. The mob set up barricades of burning tyres and other materials.

Some policemen, apparently in the attempt to scare away the mob, made up mostly of relatives of the arrested men and sympathisers of the UPN, were firing into the air. But instead, the mob became more incensed. One of the policemen, alarmed that the mob might storm the small police station, ran out with his Mark 4 in his hand. He was pursued by the now violent mob. His attempt to defend himself failed; despite his gun he was captured by the mob. The mob then attempted to take the station by storm. Panic set in and in the ensuring melee, one of the captured policemen was killed. One of the men alleged to be a thug of the NPN who brought the policemen to Oke-Igbo was also captured by the mob and thrown into the police landrover. Both the man and the vehicle were then set on fire. The arrested suspects were then forcibly freed, but the resident cops of Oke-Igbo were spared. After this horrible incident, the residents of the town were gripped with fear. They knew there must be an aftermath.

The aftermath indeed came like a deadly cyclone. A few hours after the incident, armed mobile policemen roared into the town. On seeing them and knowing their mission many people fled. But some people believing that only the guilty had reasons to fear, stayed. The invading policemen then started picking people on the streets and ordering them into their lorry. Two members of the Celestial Church of Christ, a man and a woman in their white flowing gowns, were picked up. An old man, who was a day guard at the town's water works was also picked up. Then the policemen drove out of town. As they did so, gunshot rang out. The two men and the woman picked up by the police were shot and their bodies thrown out of the lorry. As the policemen got close to the town gate, they came in view of a funeral party. The dead was lying in state. They fired more shots into the crowd. On the whole, about 10 people were killed that infamous day at Oke-Igbo.

Apart from those who faced the aimless fury of the anti-riot policemen, hundreds of people were also arrested. One of those arrested was Chief Fasoranti, the commissioner for finance. While other UPN leaders fled, Fasoranti stayed in his home on Ado-Ekiti road, Akure. On Monday, September 12, he was arrested and driven to the headquarters of the Nigerian Security Organisation, NSO. He was thrown into the cell of common criminals. In order to make him 'confess to the crime of murder', he was tied to the ceiling of the cell. His torturers debated whether they should fire tear gas into the place or not, but at last, he was spared that ordeal. When his wife attempted to find out why Fasoranti was arrested, she was driven away by NSO operatives.

The following morning, Fasoranti, then 56, in handcuffs, was charged for murder before an Akure chief magistrate. His co-accused were Ajayi Ologbonsaiye, 36, and William Okoro, 70. It was alleged that the three accused persons 'and others at large, on the 16th August, 1983, at 11, Methodist Church Street, Akure, killed one Olaiya Fagbamigbe'. They were also accused of arson for allegedly burning the home of Fagbamigbe valued at ₦1.46 million.

As the arrests and detentions of UPN leaders and suspects were going on, the struggle between the party and the ruling NPN was continuing in other spheres. One significant aspect was the law court. Ajasin carried his petition to the electoral tribunal to challenge the victory of Omoboriowo. Representing the governor were an array of lawyers led by Godwin Olusegun Kolawole Ajayi, a Senior Advocate of Nigeria, SAN. Omoboriowo originally was billed to be represented by Chief Rotimi Williams, SAN, first attorney-general of the defunct Western Region, and first among the nation's legal giants. However, it was Mr. Duro Ajayi, a Lagos lawyer, who led the defence team for Omoboriowo, FEDECO, Chief Adeniyi and Alibaloye.

Unlike the approach of other lawyers handling similar cases before election tribunals throughout the country then, Ajayi's approach was that FEDECO officials simply did not count the votes scored by the candidates correctly. Chief Ajayi called 40 witnesses who helped him prove his case from constituency and local government levels. Building the pyramid of his case, he concluded that having lost in all those constituencies, there was no way Omoboriowo could have emerged governor-elect. Duro Ajayi, sensing where the argument was leading, attempted to stop the train early, but with considerable failure.

Duro Ajayi rested his case on two platforms. First that the documents and result sheets tendered by the plaintiff's witnesses were not from 'proper custody' and were also not recorded on 'the prescribed form'. This argument was rejected and the results tendered by the witnesses, mostly UPN polling agents, constituency returning officers and local government secretaries, were accepted. Two witnesses who must have helped the tribunal in making up its mind were Adeniyi and Alibaloye.

In his evidence before the tribunal, Chief Adeniyi, FEDECO's chief administrative secretary for Ondo State, said though enough materials were supplied for the gubernatorial elections, results written and countersigned by FEDECO agents and party agents were also valid even when not written on 'the prescribed form'. However, under cross-examination by Chief G.O.K. Ajayi, Alibaloye insisted that results not written on the 'prescribed form' were automatically invalid. Said Alibaloye: 'Even if the A.R.O's and the D.R.O's added up the figures correctly, I will still reject the results if they are not on the prescribed forms... The party agents were showing a lot of papers which were not relevant because they were not on the prescribed forms. If the figures produced by agents conflict with the figures before me signed by the A.R.O's, I will reject the former.'

Question: 'If there was a shortage of the prescribed forms for returns in a constituency or local government, what would you expect the A.R.O or D.R.O. to do?'

Alibaloye: 'There is an assistant chief electoral officer in charge of every local government and an assistant electoral officer in charge of every constituency. I expect the A.R.O. to report to the A.E.O. and also the D.R.O. should contact the A.C.E.O. who would communicate to me. If they contact me and they have agreed to use another form I would accept.'

On Tuesday, September 10, the tribunal, after hearing evidences from 40 witnesses for Ajasin and 18 for Omoboriowo, delivered its judgment. The high court venue was expectedly tense. Armed policemen searched every person entering the court room. Akure too was like a ghost city as everyone stayed indoors, unsure of what the judgment and the reaction to it would be. Both Ajasin and Omoboriowo were absent. Chief G.O.K. Ajayi was also absent. Justice Olakunle Orojo read the 63-minute unanimous judgment. Orojo said from the evidence before the tribunal, Ajasin won the governorship election.

'We therefore hold that the total votes received by the Petitioner in the gubernatorial election for Ondo State held on 13th August 1983 is 1,563,327 and that the total votes received by the 1st Respondent is

703,592,' declared Orojo. 'We also find and hold that the petitioner obtained 25% or more votes cast in 16 of the 17 local governments of Ondo State, while the 1st Respondent received 25% or more of the votes cast in 7 of the 17 local governments of the State.' (see appendix).

Their lordships also awarded a ₦1,000 cost against Chief Omoboriowo and ₦2,000 cost against Chief Adeniyi, the administrative secretary of FEDECO.

As news of the judgment reached the town and it was confirmed on Ondo Radio, people trooped from the safety of their homes and Akure was agog in celebration. The centre of it all was the Governor's lodge at Alagbaka. It was free drinking and merry-making for the partymen and their sympathisers. Some people in the town however overdid it. When some of the revellers were returning home in the dead of the night, they were accosted by armed anti-riot policemen. The cops ordered them to lie prostrate face-down, both men and women, and they were not released until about 6.a.m.

On Tuesday, September 27, the Appeal Court, sitting in Benin, capital of Bendel State, rejected the appeal of Omoboriowo. At this stage, the former governor elect was now being represented by Dr. Mudiaga Odje, SAN, who based his argument on the technicalities of the law. Two of the Appeal Court judges, Justice Othman Mohammed and Justice Nnameka Agu, upheld the argument of Omoboriowo's counsel that the NPN chieftain was duly elected. However, five judges upheld that Ajasin's victory was well-deserved. The judges were Honourable Omo-Eboh, Sunday Efe, Adenekan Ademola, Rowland Okagbue and Barclay Pepple.

Having lost at the Appeal Court, Chief Omoboriowo took his case to the highest court in the land, the Supreme Court. Many people perceived the Supreme Court presided over by Chief Justice Atanda Fatai-Williams as the bastion of conservatism. It was perceived as a place filled with judges who were NPN sympathisers. Moreover, politicians and their sympathisers were putting pressures on Fatai-Williams and other judges of the Supreme Court about election petitions. On Tuesday October 4, Fatai-williams issued an unprecedented public statement asking such people to leave him and his judges alone. He threatened that if they did not desist, he would invite the police 'to deal with those who are seeking to pervert the course of justice in the country'.

Fatai-Williams' statement was full of helpless anger. 'In the last few days, all sorts of persons, some eminent, others not so eminent, from a particular state in the country, have been trying to dictate to me as to who and who should sit on the appeal against the decisions of the election petition tribunals which are before this court', stated Fatai-Williams. 'I have informed these misguided persons, in clear terms, that this is my prerogative, and that under no circumstances will I change the panel as it is presently constituted. Those who know me know that when I say this, I mean every word of it. I have complete and unalloyed confidence in the integrity and dedication of the justices of the Supreme Court. We have shown Nigeria over and over again that the court is totally committed to the pursuit of justice to all manner of people, without fear or favour, affection or ill-will'.

On Saturday, October 15, the Supreme Court, sitting in Lagos, finally dismissed Omoboriowo's appeal. The court was filled to the brim, mostly with people from Ondo State. There had been rumours that some people were planning to burn (or bomb) the magnificent Supreme Court if Omoboriowo's appeal was upheld. It was therefore a great relief when the victory of Ajasin was confirmed. The only dissenting vote out of the seven judges was that of Justice Ayo Irikefe. Those in favour of Ajasin were Justices George Sowemimo, Mohammed Bello, Andrew Obaseki, Kayode Eso, Augustine Nnamani and Mohammed Lawal Uwais.

A day before the Supreme Court's judgment, Omoboriowo met with President Shagari. The president had been able to confirm that his man was losing at the Supreme Court. It was not the happiest meeting between the two men. Shagari offered the former governor-elect the option of ministerial appointment but Omoboriowo graciously declined. During Shagari's first term, two men, Chief Claudius Agboola Bamigboye and Chief Adebisi Ogedengbe from Ondo State served in the federal cabinet of President Shagari. Omoboriowo said he would prefer that Olowoporoku be made a minister. Shagari expressed reservation about Olowoporoku's personal appearance and his rather rustic sartorial taste. But in the end, he gave his words that Olowoporoku, who within 24 months turned his Ilawe-Ekiti hometown into an impregnable NPN stronghold, would become a minister. The impression he gave then was that at least one out of the two old ministers from Ondo State would be retained. In the end, while Shagari appointed three ministers from some states like Sokoto and Bendel, he picked only Olowoporoku from Ondo State. Both Ogedengbe and Bamigboye were dropped. Shagari's reaction was seen as a punishment for Ondo for giving the NPN bandwagon and landslide theory a bad name.

Expectedly, both Omoboriowo and Ajasin and their supporters saw the outcome of the legal battle in different lights. Said Omoboriowo: 'There was a judgement which robbed me of victory. I was convinced I won as announced by FEDECO. My opponent hijacked my victory. But I remain undaunted by the outcome of it all.' Said an ecstatic Ajasin, however: 'What FEDECO had taken away from the people, the court has given back to the people.'

The riots had led to the suspension of elections in Ondo State. To conduct the remaining elections, FEDECO had to start almost from scratch. Most of the polling booths, the FEDECO headquarters and many of its vehicles were destroyed during the riot. All polling booths, except five, were destroyed in Akure. Many of the staff too, including the resident electoral commissioner, Chief Afe, fled. After things had cooled down a little, the commission fixed new dates for the remaining elections in consultations with security agencies and Governor Ajasin. The elections to the Senate would now be held Wednesday, September 21, State House of Assembly, Friday September 23, and the Federal House of Representatives, Sunday, September 25. The man to preside over this new series of elections was a veteran of the terrain, Colonel Ayo Ariyo.

Ariyo was as subtle as a tank. A stubborn soldier, he was a brigade commander during the civil war when he served with the famed Third

Marine Commando division. His promotion was stalled for many years for alleged insubordination and he retired as a lieutenant-colonel early in 1975. As a FEDECO commissioner, he was accused of bias in favour of the UPN, perhaps because he was once appointed a board chairman by Governor Ajasin. Before he moved over to Akure again, he had presided over elections in Bendel State where UPN Governor Ambrose Alli was defeated by his NPN challenger, Samuel Ogbemudia. Like Ariyo, Ogbemudia was also a civil war hero and he rose to the rank of brigadier before he was dismissed from the army in 1975 by General Murtala Mohammed administration for alleged corruption. Ogbemudia was governor of Bendel State from 1967 until 1975. He left a track record of achievements, turning Bendel (then Mid-West) into a pacesetter among the then 12 states of the federation especially in sports. But his second coming was controversial and his 1983 electoral victory was regarded as one of those dubious laurels won by the NPN.

With the destruction of the old FEDECO office, Ariyo pitched his tent in some of the houses in the federal government housing estate (Shagari Village). He said he was not eager to take on the Ondo State elections. 'I was prevailed upon to accept this assignment,' he said. 'I have completed my own portion in Bendel, but this is my state. If I cannot do it, who else would accept to come here? I consider it a great risk not only to my person, but also to my family, risk to everything I have laboured for and above all, a risk to the good name and reputation which I had built over the years.' Ariyo said he regarded the new assignment as another draft into the war front.

A war front it was indeed. Ariyo was provided with an helicopter to help him monitor the elections. It was mostly peaceful, with the UPN sweeping the polls. But it was also marked by intimidation of political opponents. A case in point was Ijero, Chief Omoboriowo's hometown and an impregnable fort of the NPN. There, the NPN candidate for the House of Assembly election scored 30,405 votes, NAP and NPP scored four and five votes respectively. The UPN, PRP and GNPP all scored zero in Ijero Constituency I. A similar scenario was also played out in Ilawe-Ekiti.

Seven of the 66 seats of the State House of Assembly were won by the NPN, a considerable improvement to its early position when it had only one member. The party was to make a surprise again when Mr. Lawrence Agunbiade, millionaire businessman and former chairman of Wema Bank, emerged winner in the Ondo State Central Senatorial District. He polled 191,968 votes (50.1% of total votes) to defeat his UPN opponent, Mr. Bamidele Olumilua, a retired diplomat and businessman. Olumilua said, however, that he was robbed and he took his case to the election tribunal. The petition was still being held when the military struck again December 31, 1983.

Olumilua had reasons for believing that he was robbed. According to the Electoral Act, the result of the senatorial contest was to be declared at the senatorial headquarters. In the case of Ekiti Central Senatorial District, the headquarters was Ado-Ekiti. Thirteen state constituencies made up the district. After the election on Friday, September 13, politicians, party agents, FEDECO officials and others gathered at the Ado-Ekiti Town Hall for the result. By Sunday, September 15, 9 a.m. 12 results of the 13 constituencies were in. The only result being awaited was that of Ode-Ekiti, in Ekiti East.

The tally of results already in showed a close contest between the two rivals. In Agunbiade's hometown of Ise-Ekiti, the NPN candidate scored 26,000 votes to Olumilua's zero vote. In Iyin-Ekiti, hometown of General Adebayo, another NPN chieftain, Agunbiade polled 33,000 votes to Olumilua's only four. However, Olumilua was able to make up for these massive setback by his showings in other areas, especially in Ado-Ekiti and Ikere-Ekiti, his hometown. He scored more than 50,000 votes in Ado-Ekiti and was already leading with more than 20,000 votes when the 12th result was recorded. Olumilua was now confident of victory knowing that Ode, hometown of Professor Aluko and a UPN stronghold, was the only result being awaited. He was to wait in vain in Ado-Ekiti.

On Monday, September 16, Olumilua and his agent, Olusola Akintayo, heard reports that the senatorial result had been declared by FEDECO in Akure. According to FEDECO, Olumilua polled only 2,000 votes to Agunbiade's 26,000 in Ode-Ekiti. The UPN candidate alleged that he was robbed, saying that the result was swapped and that he was the one who polled 26,000 in Ode. He alleged that the presence of Uba Ahmed, the NPN National secretary in Akure during the election and after, had something to do with his misfortune. Ahmed, in the company of other NPN leaders, including the NPN chairman for Oyo State, Olaniyan Alawode, came to Akure during the senatorial poll of Friday September 23. That afternoon, at about 12.30, they held a meeting with Ariyo. They later called on Ariyo again at 5.p.m. at the FEDECO commissioner's chalet at Owena Motel. When Olumilua challenged Ariyo about the result, the latter said he had no evidence that the UPN candidate won the election. He dared him to go to court if he believed he won. Olumilua went to court.

In the aftermath of the second round of elections in Ondo State, the problems for the two parties were different. For Ajasin and the UPN, it was how to manage victory; for Omoboriowo and the NPN, it was managing defeat. Only 13 of the old members were re-elected into the new House of Assembly as most of them had cast their lot with Omoboriowo during the controversial UPN primaries of 1982. When the new assembly met Thursday October 19, it elected Chief Akin Olafunmiloye (UPN Ifesowapo Constituency 3), as speaker. Olafunmiloye, a teacher, was one of the old faces. Chief Olorunfemi Adu (Ekiti Central 5) was elected deputy speaker. Other leaders of the House were Ayodele Oni (Majority Leader) E.K. Olanipekun (Deputy Majority Leader), Olusola Atiroko (Chief Whip), Oladipo Akinde (Deputy Chief Whip), Dr. J.A. Adeyinka (Secretary to Parliamentary Council). The only woman member of the House, Mrs Beatrice Adeleye (Ekiti North 2), was elected Assistant Whip 1, and Francis Omogbemiro was elected Assistant Whip 2, S.U. Yayu (NPN Ilaje Ese-Odo) was elected minority leader while S. Akinola (NPN Ekiti South 3), was elected assistant minority leader.

Two days before the election of the new Speaker, Governor Ajasin was sworn-in for a second term. The ceremony, performed by Justice Olakunle Orojo, took place at the Government House lawn with delegates from the other UPN states present. Also sworn-in was 'the deputy governor, Dr. Falaye Aina. Ajasin was a triumphant man, but the ceremony was solemn with little of the extravagant festivities that accompany such occasions in Nigeria. The governor warned civil servants to stay loyal or stay out of government employment. Reflecting on the last governorship election and the outcome, Ajasin said: 'One episode is that truth and justice, however much suppressed, shall always triumph in the end.'

Managing defeat in the NPN camp was a much tougher task. There was a general scramble among the NPN men for federal government board and diplomatic appointments. Several lists were prepared with names of top NPN leaders, like Major-General Olu Bajowa and General Adebayo featuring prominently. Some of them even wrote to the president offering their services for board chairmanship, considering the sacrifices they made during the last elections. Several millions of naira that were sent to the state as initial relief fund were allegedly divided among the warring bigwigs, while victims, like the family of the late Chief Fagbamigbe, were left high and dry.

All these brought into the fore the schism between the old NPN members and the new converts led by Omoboriowo. The old NPN believed that having lost the election, Chief Omoboriowo had lost the moral right to lead the party. After the election, many party members accused the Ojomo-led state executive of showing ineptitude. Therefore, the National Executive Council of the NPN decided to dissolve the executive of the party for Ondo State and appointed a caretaker committee in its place. The new committee was headed by Chief Omoboriowo. This kindled the ire of the old partymen.

Chief Nathaniel Adamolekun, a renowned administrator, former registrar of the University of Ibadan and former chairman of the state's public service commission, addressed a press conference on the matter in Akure Monday November 21, 1983. He accused the Omoboriowo group of taking the NPN for a ride, saying that they had breached every convention of the party. He said the appointment of Omoboriowo as chairman of the caretaker committee and of Olowoporoku as minister, both from the decamper's camp and from Ekiti contradicted 'the federal character principle' of the party. He argued that leadership of the party should be vested in those who knew and respected the constitution and practices of the NPN.

Adamolekun also accused Omoboriowo of mindless ambition, saying that he had brought tragedy to members of the old NPN. 'It is now known in fact that it was in order to destroy the decampers that hell was let loose on the 16th of August,' said Adamolekun. 'Unfortunately, the brunt of the killings and arson fell mostly upon the old NPN. The Omoboriowo group had premonitions based on their conduct at the election and escaped clean clear'. He said Omoboriowo wanted to lead at all cost and promised that the old NPN members, in defiance of the national executive, would set up its own caretaker committee. Said he of Omoboriowo: 'If Chief Ajasin calls him to take over, I have not seen an evidence that he would not agree to go back to the UPN.'

18

The Twilight

Almost everyone knew something would happen after the turbulent 1983 elections. Elections had always been the big test of democracy in Nigeria. During the 1964 federal elections, the United Progressive Grand Alliance, UPGA, had boycotted the poll in most parts of the country, but at the end of the day the Nigerian National Alliance was declared victorious and Prime Minister Balewa returned to power. It was the beginning of the end. Now, many Nigerians felt history was about to repeat itself.

One class of Nigerians that was happy about the turn of events was a clique of conspirators in the army. The ring leaders of this clique were three ambitious young soldiers who had participated in all successful coups in Nigerian history except that of January 15, 1966. They were Mohammadu Buhari, Muhammed Bako, and Ibrahim Babangida. All three were brigadiers though Buhari and Babangida were to be promoted major-general later, holding crucial commands in the army. One of them, Buhari, was a close confidant of President Shagari who made him the GOC of the Third Division in Jos, Plateau State.

Most of these conspirators were loyalists of Major-General Yar'Adua who had looked forward to his being appointed minister of defence in Shagari's government. They also backed Adamu Ciroma for the presidency in preference to the dour Shehu Shagari. Like the president, they had prayed for an NPN victory in the 1983 elections, though for different ends. They had reckoned that Shagari would be an easier opponent to handle than Chief Awolowo, his rival. They believed that Awolowo, with his fanatical support at the grassroots, would create a messy target for a military coup. They also calculated that Awolowo, with his vast network of supporters within the armed forces, would unearth the plot and would have dealt with the conspirators with ruthless finality. Therefore, when Shagari was re-elected for a second term, the plotters were jubilant.

There were many plots against the regime during the second republic, but many of them were amateurish and doomed to failure. Alhaji Bukar Mandara, a Maiduguri-based businessman was even arrested by security agents for wanting to finance a coup to topple Shagari. The soldiers he was to use were never identified. Shagari's tactics of dealing with such matters were to finger the affected soldiers and retire them quietly from the army. But when it came to the conspiracy of the big boys, he was in a dilemma. Most of the members of the Buhari-led clique were known NPN sympathisers and had won their commands on that score. Shortly after the presidential elections, security reports reached Shagari of unauthorised movements of troops under Buhari command. He summoned the GOC to Lagos and confronted him with the allegation that he was plotting a coup. Buhari promptly saluted and denied flatly that he was conspiring to overthrow the commander-in-chief.

To further appease the restless soldiers, Shagari approved the promotion of many officers. Seven of them were promoted from brigadier to the rank of major-generals. The new generals were Muhammadu Buhari, Ibrahim Babangida, Mamman Jiya Vatsa, Anthony Hananiya, Alfred Aduloju, Mohammed Jega, and Zamani Lekwot. Apart from the army, similar appeasements were made to the navy and the airforce. At the same time, the mobile unit of the police was being armed and turned into a special force that Shagari perceived wrongly, could help thwart a coup. So much was his belief in Sunday Adewusi, the IG.

The controversial victory also won Shagari and his NPN members more enemies from the public. Security men were afraid that the president and his henchmen could become targets of crackpots and lone assassins. Early in 1983, in anticipation of this, a special bullet-proof landrover was bought from Britain for the president at a cost of sixty thousand pounds. After the elections, Shagari never appeared in public without his bullet-proof vest. Other NPN top notchers, ministers, and assemblymen, governors, chairmen and other leaders were given bullet-proof vests. Chief Omoboriowo's own was taken away by NSO men who searched his house after the coup.

Reactions of the generality of Nigerians were that of perplexity, confusion and fear. 'If you are victorious in any human endeavour, you jubilate,' said Abiola while commenting on Shagari's second coming. 'I have not seen the NPN jubilating. On the contrary, I see people in a mourning mood. This only happens when you have just experienced a conquest, not a victory.' Abiola's hyperbole was appropriate, though not entirely accurate. There were pockets of jubilation in Sokoto, Bauchi and some other places, but the impression you got was that the NPN people were scared of the magnitude of their victory.

The opposition parties believed that the NPN engineered its massive victory in order to impose a one-party state on the nation. Dikko, in the aftermath of the elections had boasted that though it had been a landslide in 1983, by '87, Nigerians would witness a 'moonslide'. Akinloye, too, in a moment of expansive heartiness, had said that in a few years time, only two parties would survive, the NPN and the military. Even in that moment of heady victory, the wily Akinloye still recognised that the army was waiting in the wings.

If this was the NPN plan, the opposition was not prepared to wither away. Said Babatope of the UPN: 'Within the next one month, Nigerians will witness the mad rush to the NPN by men of AGIP (Any Government in Power). By then, the dreams of the NPN for a one-party state for Nigeria would have been realised... We of the UPN will however continue to resist fascism of whatever guise.' Babatope was speaking at a press conference in Lagos, Friday, September 2. The following day, Saturday, September 3, 1983, *The Guardian,* in an editorial, warned that a one-party state would constitute danger even for the NPN. Stated *The Guardian:* 'The NPN, should it be tempted to err, may want to be reminded of the old saying about riding on the back of a tiger. Getting on may be easy, even tempting, but you never get off.'

By far, the bitterest attack on the NPN came from Dr. Azikiwe who addressed a press conference in Lagos on Thursday, August 24, in Lagos. The following is an excerpt from Zik's statement:

I am 78 years nine months one week today, and I thought that I should write and congratulate certain politicians on their inglorious and futile attempts to destroy the soidisant 'Zik myth'.

In spite of the *New Nigerian,* the NTA, the FRCN, etc, whose propensity for calumniating my reputation blatantly, has become pathological and incessant, and whose penchant for sycophancy in order to entrench unpopular governments, is now an open secret, my head is bloody but unbowed. They should take note of the handwriting on the wall of history, that so long as there breathe Nigerian citizens of conscience and integrity, who are neither godless nor inhuman, so long would stratagems to impose unpopular political leaders on the silent majority of Nigerians fail woefully, because the latter is becoming enlightened, articulate and resentful of calculated acts of injustice against the body politic.

Despite the blizzards of inspired onslaughts on my person by evilly-disposed politicians or mercenary hirelings or literary hacks, I shall continue to remain calm, cool, collected and unruffled. Of course, occasionally, I shall be compelled to return fire for fire in the best traditions of the profession (not the occupation) of journalism.

If Alhaji Shehu Shagari and his cohorts have any qualms of conscience, it should have dawned on them that the last presidential election was unfairly manoeuvred to enable an unpopular but powerful political party exercise power, at the expense of the silent majority of the electorate of Nigeria. As a patriot who struggled alongside other compatriots to make Nigeria free, I see my country on the brink of dictatorship because of the arrogance of power exhibited by the party in power throughout.

I am supremely confident that Almighty God will frustrate their knavery and ultimately expose their machinations and consign them to the garbage heap of forgotten tyrants. History will continue to vindicate the just and God shall punish the wicked.

Finally, may I now recount the disputations of those who are using the print and electronic media to make a mockery of old age. Here I kneel and pray to Almighty God, the Creator of the universe, my maker, who knows why I was created and what is my destiny, to demonstrate to infidels and miscreants that they will not live to be old. And I trust that they will die unwept and unsung, like a flower that is plucked in its bloom, as an example of the vanity of human wishes and the futility of insulting old age.

Verily, it is un-African and inhuman to make mockery of old age, because Africans and all human beings pray to God to prolong their life span. Nevertheless, those Nigerian politicians who indulge in this abomination shall not live to be old. Unlike the hope of Prophet Joel (2:29), these beasts of creation shall not prophesy; and see visions; but the old men and women shall dream dreams which shall come to pass and redeem their children from generation to generations yet unborn.

Edward Fitzgerald, the Poet, wrote in *Oma Khayydym* (1.51): 'the Moving Finger writes; and having writ, moves on: nor all thy piety nor wit shall lure it back to cancel half a line. Nor all thy tears wash out a word of it.'

So let it be, my God, Creator, and the Governor of the Universe, Amen, Amin, Ise, Ashe.

Zik, throughout his five decades of public career, had never given vent to such anger. The flourish and the rhetorics were his, but the venom was tragically new and unexpected. The NPN was not going to allow Zik's challenge to go like that. The man who picked up the gauntlet was Chuba Okadigbo, a maverick but brilliant intellectual. Okadigbo, a special adviser to Shagari, was one of the young carpet-baggers from Igbo heartland who were ready to prove that they were holier than the pope in order to retain their privileged position in the corridors of power. Okadigbo carried out his assignment with expected alacrity. He dismissed Zik's protest as 'the irresponsible rantings of an ant'. He said the statement was 'nihilistic' and 'an exercise in religion and poetry rather than politics and government'. He then warned the old man and Waziri of the GNPP, who had also criticised the result of the elections, that the NPN had many more arrows in its quiver. 'Zik and Waziri should guard their tongues,' Okadigbo warned. 'The more they talk, the more they remind us that they are no longer qualified for registration. We will take that more seriously later.' It was not an empty boast since Ovie-Whiskey's FEDECO, which was charged with the registration of parties was now almost totally under the influence of the NPN government.

In a lengthy address to the UPN congress held in Abeokuta, Ogun State capital, Thursday, December 15, Chief Awolowo laid out his case against the NPN. He said his party won in 13 states: Bauchi, Bendel, Borno, Cross River, Gongola, Lagos, Kaduna, Kwara, Ogun, Ondo, Oyo, Rivers and Sokoto. But by the results of the 1983 elections released by FEDECO, the NPN now controlled 12 of the 19 states of the federation: Anambra (formerly NPP), Bauchi, Bendel, (hitherto UPN), Benue, Borno (formerly GNPP), Cross River, Gongola (hitherto GNPP), Kaduna (ex-PRP), Niger, Oyo, (ex-UPN), Rivers and Sokoto. The NPN lost the state of Kwara to the UPN. The GNPP lost its old two states to the NPN.

In examining the ramifications of this victory, Chief Awolowo warned that the NPN would self-destruct by its own greed. Said the UPN leader: 'We have been robbed of victory by force of brigandage and arms, and by calculated subtlety. Nonetheless, our honour and integrity, as individuals and as a party remain safe and unimpaired by the barbarity and despoliation of the NPN, the police and the FEDECO. I feel sad for the dismal, almost hopeless plight of millions of our people who through no fault of theirs, had and still now have, imposed upon them a federal government they never voted for and which undisguisedly, they still do not want.' He continued: 'The goal of dialectic process is perfection: It aims at the perfect attainment of all the virtues embodied in it. Whether we like it or not, all human beings are inescapably involved in the binary compounds of thesis and antithesis of the dialectical procession. In other words, all of us in the UPN and those of them in the NPN and other parties are already in the thesis-antithesis war. When the war is over, only the best of us will be accommodated in the synthesis, with the best in the antithesis in complete dominance.

After a deep and prolonged cogitation, I do not hesitate to aver, in all sincerity and solemnity, that the NPN, together with its political regime and all that it stands for, symbolises the thesis, and that the UPN together with all those who are conscientiously and honestly opposed to the NPN, symbolises the antithesis. The war between the two is already being waged with vehemence and inflexible resolve. Sooner or later, I believe much sooner than later - the figurative 'explosion' will occur in which the forces of the thesis and the antithesis, in their original forms, will disappear. Then the synthesis will appear which will embody the best in the NPN (thesis) and the best in the UPN (antithesis). But the dominant feature of the synthesis will be the best in the UPN.

Let no one be deceived by the heavy and impregnable armour with which he is clad; let no one be deluded by the fabulous wealth with which he can bribe and buy his opponents; let no one put his faith in these mundane devices acquired for the protection of evil. The dialectics explosion is sure to occur. When and how are beyond human ken and prediction.'

The dialectics that Chief Awolowo was talking about were already present in the UPN. After the 1983 elections, some of the partymen vented their frustrations on the party officials at the national headquarters. The two men who were so targeted were Ajuluchukwu and Babatope. Ajuluchukwu, the director of research and publicity, was facing opposition from top members of the party, including Awolowo, over his handling of some party matters, especially his unauthorised pronouncements on the relationship between NPP and UPN. Babatope was facing problems over the handlings of the same elections, though from a different direction.

Many top party men were already uneasy with Babatope's growing profile. There were speculations within the top leadership that Chief Awolowo was grooming Babatope to take over the leadership of the party. It was said that the patriarch was passing over the governors and other veterans of the old AG days to pick Babatope as his successor. Babatope was not the first person to be the target of this kind of speculations. Omoboriowo was once a target of such conjectures, in his hey days as a confidant of Chief Awolowo, when he was the first among equals within the league of UPN deputy governors. As it did for Omoboriowo, this also recruited enemies for the mercurial Babatope. For Babatope to be targeted in this manner was like a kiss of death. Chief Awolowo praised the two men profusely and the congress then accepted Ajuluchukwu's resignation while Babatope was granted leave of absence to study law in the United Kingdom.

By December 1983, the rot was everywhere and there was no solution in sight. The military was politicised and there were talks of radical soldiers taking over. The universities, the civil service and every sector of society was affected. Worst hit was the judiciary which, in its adjudication of the 1983 election petitions, showed that it was no longer the last bastion of justice. A case in point was what happened in Oyo State.

The governorship election in Oyo was a straight fight between Ige and Omololu Olunloyo of the NPN. Among the Yoruba states of the West, the NPN had a foothold in Oyo especially in Ogbomosho, Ibadan and Modakeke. But it was not strong enough to win the election in a straight fight. The election was marred by unbelievable irregularities and there were violence in Ibadan, Osogbo, Ilesa and Iwo during the voting. When the result came, Modakeke, a settlement in Ile-Ife peopled mainly by those of Oyo descent, entered into the lore of Nigerian politics. Modakeke gave more votes to the NPN than the entire population of Ile-Ife. This was later regarded as valid by the judicial tribunal sitting in Ibadan. Moreover, because of violence during the polling, election results in Ibadan, Ilesa and Ile-Ife were cancelled and Olunloyo was declared governor by default.

The Abeokuta congress of the UPN was used as a podium to address many other national issues. The host governor, Bisi Onabanjo, in his address, called for the re-arrangement of the federal structure. He proposed a confederal arrangement. He said every nationality within the Nigerian state should have the right to self-determination while the central government should be concerned mainly with those issues like common currencies and defence that may be agreed upon by the component nations. There were many people in the audience who believed that even if the confederal arrangement may be far-fetched, the issue of the federation still needed to be fully addressed. Many were of the opinion that the Hausa-Fulani elite, who had been ruling the country since independence, were treating the rest of the country like conquered territories.

There was no doubt that tension was mounting in the air, especially in the wake of the triumphant and arrogant vauntings of the all-conquering NPN lords. Many of the newspapers were openly calling for the military to take over. The *Nigerian Tribune* started publishing on its front page the statement of American President John F. Kennedy: 'Those who make peaceful change impossible make violent change inevitable.'

These last days of the Second Republic were played out in a surreal fashion. The UPN in Ondo State felt especially triumphant since it was the only state in the federation where a purported victory of the NPN was reversed. In the House of Assembly, therefore, this fact was never allowed to escape the minority NPN. It was a sobering fact that Ondo State had paid a heavy price for this victory.

During one of its sittings in November 1983, a member of the UPN brought an allegation that the NPN was planning violence for the forthcoming 1984 local government elections. E.K. Olanipekun of the UPN alleged that the NPN held a secret meeting for this purpose at Ilupeju-Ekiti, November 4. It was alleged that a retired army officer was in charge of the operation. It was further alleged that the NPN was planning violence so that the federal government could declare a state of emergency in Ondo State.

The debate on the issue was heated. NPN members in the House denied the allegation. Even some of the UPN members were sceptical about the story. Kayode Iwakun, (Ikale III) cautioned that the House should not discuss rumour.

'They say they would carry boxes, they carried it,' said J.A. Ijabiyi, (Akoko North III). 'They would not find us unprepared or inadequate. If they carry out their plans, they would be completely wiped out from this state.'

Added another UPN member, Fatoyinbo of Akure: 'They told us

they were going to steal our votes and they did it.'

Deji Fowowe (NPN Ekiti South West II), denied that the NPN was planning anything violent, least of all, a guerrilla warfare. 'There is nothing like that,' said Fowowe. 'We are ready to cooperate with you. I want to enjoy life. Treat us as gentlemen. Even if it comes to face-to-face blow, we know you will finish us,' retorted Dele Awopeju of the UPN: 'If you bring us guerrilla warfare, we shall reply you with elephant warfare!' he concluded.

The count down had begun for the final demise of the Second Republic.

19

The Longest Night

December 30, 1983 was not the best day for President Shehu Shagari. That morning, he held a meeting with his security advisers about the report of an impending coup. Present were Umaru Dikko, Sunday Adewusi and Shehu Galadanci, the National Security Adviser and a few other trusted aides. Some of the men present wanted tough action to be taken, but the president was indecisive. The plotters were known and they were men whose career Shagari had promoted since his days in the cabinet of Prime Minister Tafawa Balewa. Now, he reasoned, these group of officers wanted to repay him with ingratitude.

In the fortress-like State House (former Dodan Barracks), Shagari felt insecure. The previous day, he had received reports from the National Security Organisation, NSO, that a group of officers, among whom were Babangida and Buhari, had decided to overthrow the government. Those involved were mostly those the NPN regime had patronised with choice appointments. All of them, because of this, were virtually millionaires in uniform. They had direct access to the commander-in-chief and were regarded by their colleagues as part and parcel of Shagari's government.

Shagari also knew these were tough men who were not afraid of shedding blood. Afterall, most of them played prominent roles in the July 1966 coup, the bloodiest in Nigerian history, that brought Gowon to power. Shagari also knew, however, that these men, like himself, were dedicated to the preservation of Hausa-Fulani hegemony. He believed it might be ill-advised to move too rashly against them. What if a more radical group, totally unknown and unfriendly to Hausa-Fulani cause, should seize power? It was then decided they move cautiously against the conspirators.

At that time, Shagari was one of the unhappiest presidents in the world. He was troubled by the violence that greeted his second coming. Also, he knew that the unofficial winner of the 1983 elections was Chief Awolowo and this fact, which was also known to the conspirators, weakened him morally and eroded his resolve. Everything was going bad for him. The economy was now in terrible strait. Only on Thursday, December 29, Alhaji Abubakar Alhaji, an indigene of Sokoto like the president and permanent secretary for finance, had informed Shagari that there was only half-a-million naira left in the national treasury. The president was now more taciturn and morose and he took solace mainly in his Benson and Hedges cigarette.

Shagari had also been disturbed by public attitude to his 'victory'. Tunji Braithwaite, the leader of the Nigeria Advance Party, NAP, described Shagari's victory as an 'electoral coup'. Like the *Nigerian Tribune,* the Kano State owned *Triumph* newspaper was virtually calling for army intervention. Said the paper in an editorial: 'Shagari and the NPN must be reminded, in the event they forgot, of the consequences of the rigged elections of 1964. Nigerians do not want a repeat of what happened then, but if that is precisely what the NPN is driving us towards, by any means we are ready.' General Obasanjo also criticised the regime as unserious and profligate. In an interview with Dele Giwa, editor of the *Sunday Concord,* he said Shagari's government was extravagant, when it expected the rest of the country to endure some austere times. Shagari had just appointed a jumbo cabinet of 42 members including seven special advisers. All these criticism were wearing down the president.

After recording the speech he intended to broadcast to the nation on January 1, 1984, he worshipped at the mosque close to his office. He later flew to Abuja. It was a melancholy president that went to Akinola Aguda House that night. A security cordon was thrown round the new city. But the president was not impressed. He could trust no one. A phone call came from Britain to confirm to him that the conspirators were moving in that night. That evening, the president was informed by a young army officer about the impending coup. The soldier had been led to the president's office after he insisted that his message was for the president's ear alone. The president thanked him for the message. He was as instructable as ever. He waited and did nothing.

Shagari was still awake when the coup plotters struck at 2 a.m. at Akinola Aguda House. He was in the living room watching a documentary film on the Arab-Israeli war of 1973. He then fled with some of his aides, as the ring of fire closed in. He later took refuge on a farm in Nassarawa, Plateau State. When he was able to confirm the following day that the coup had actually been executed by the Buhari gang, he was relieved. At least he knew he would be in relatively friendly hands. He gave himself up and was flown to Lagos. Twenty-four hours earlier, he was the commander-in-chief; now he was a prisoner.

Governor Jakande of Lagos State was one of the few politicians who got to know about the coup before the rest of Nigerians at dawn of December 31, 1983. As governor of Lagos, this outstanding journalist and former editor-in-chief of the *Nigerian Tribune,* worked at a frenetic pace. He had won the second term with a landslide victory over his opponents of the other five parties. A workaholic and strict disciplinarian, he was severe and serious. Though he did not possess the cosmic halo of Awo, he had shown himself a tested public administrator like his political mentor. He threw himself into the execution of the UPN programmes with feverish ardour and within four years, had changed the face of Lagos. He abolished the shift system of education (under which students went to school in shifts because of the shortage of classrooms and schools), and built utilitarian school blocks to the annoyance of members of the upper and upper middle class. He opened the doors of hitherto elite schools like Igbobi College to the children of the poor and made educational and health services free in the state.

While the coup plotters were securing their grip on power, Jakande was busy at his desk on a long term plan for Lagos State till the year 2000 AD. It was something close to his heart. Not only would the Metroline Project have been functioning for many years, Lagos would then be a truly modern city. To ensure this, he had been following strict financial discipline. For ten years before he was elected in 1979, Lagos State was having budget deficits each year of between ₦3 million and ₦114 million. Not only was he able to balance the budget within his first 12 months in power, the budget surplus for 1983 was ₦255 million. The credit balance as at December 1983 was ₦264 million. Jakande therefore had reasons to be optimistic for the year 2000 AD. His mind was still on this when one of his aides came in, that an army officer wanted to see him. The young officer was shown in and he appeared surprised to find the governor at his working desk. The governor was immediately arrested. It was 3 a.m.

Unlike Jakande, most of the other top politicians and other public office holders got to know that they had lost their jobs only in the morning when Radio Nigeria, Lagos, opened with martial music. By this time, the president was already safely in custody of the conspirators. At 7 a.m, the unfamiliar voice of Brigadier Sani Abacha, commander 9th Mechanised Brigade, Ikeja, came on air to announce the death of the Second Republic. The short speech was a masterpiece adorning treason in patriotic garments:

> Fellow country men and women, I, Brigadier Sani Abacha of the Nigerian Army, address you this morning on behalf of the Nigerian armed forces. You are all living witnesses to the grave economic predicament and uncertainty which an inept and corrupt leadership has imposed on our beloved nation for the past four years. I am referring to the harsh intolerable condition under which we are now living. Our economy has been hopelessly mismanaged. We have become a debtor and beggar nation. There is inadequacy of food at reasonable prices for

our people who are now fed up with endless announcements of importation of foodstuff. Health services are in shambles as our hospitals are reduced to mere consulting clinics without drugs, water and equipment. Our educational system is deteriorating at an alarming rate, unemployment figures including the graduates have reached embarrassing and unacceptable proportion. In states, workers are being owed salary arrears of eight to twelve months and in others there are cries of salary cuts, yet our leaders revel in squandermania. Corruption and indiscipline, continue to proliferate public appointments in complete disregard of our stark economic realities. After due consultation over these deplorable conditions, I and my colleagues in the Armed Forces have, in the discharge of our national role as promoters and protectors of our national interest, decided to effect a change in the leadership of the government of the Federal Republic of Nigeria and form a Federal Military Government.

This task has just been completed. The Federal Military Government hereby decrees the suspension of the provision of the Constitution of the Federal Republic of Nigeria 1979 relating to all elective and appointive offices and representative institutions, including the office of the president, state governors, federal and state executive councils, special assistants, the establishment of the national assembly, and houses of assemblies including the formation of political parties. Accordingly, Alhaji Shehu Usman Aliyu Shagari ceases forthwith to be the President and Commander-in-Chief of the Armed Forces of Nigeria. All the incumbents of the above named offices shall, if they have not already done so, vacate the properties in their possession and report to the nearest police station in their constituencies within seven days.

The Clerk of the National Assembly, the President of the Senate, and Speaker of the House of Representatives shall, within two weeks, render account of all properties of the National Assembly. All political parties are banned. The bank account of FEDECO and all the political parties are frozen with immediate effect. All foreigners living in any part of the country are assured of their safety and will be adequately protected. Henceforth, workers not on essential duties are advised to keep off the street. All categories of workers on essential duties will however, report to their place of work immediately. With effect from today (31/12/83), a dusk-to-dawn curfew is imposed from 7 p.m. till 6 am. each day until further notice. All airways flights have been suspended forthwith and all airports and seaports and border posts closed. External communication has been cut. Customs and Excise,

Immigration and the Police should maintain vigilance and ensure water-tight security at the borders and their area administrators and commanders will have themselves to blame if any of the wanted people escape.

Fellow country men and women, the change in government is bloodless and painstaking operation. We don't want any one to lose his or her life and you are warned in your own interest to be law-abiding and to give the Federal Military Government maximum cooperation. Anyone caught disturbing public order will be summarily dealt with. For the avoidance of doubt, you are forewarned that we shall not hesitate to declare marshal law in any area or state of the federation in which disturbances occur.

Fellow country men and comrades at arms, I will like to assure you that the Armed Forces of Nigeria is ready to lay down its life for our dear nation, but not for the present irresponsible leadership of the past civilian administration.

You are to await further announcements. Good morning!

This was the speech that announced to the nation that the Second Republic had become history. The coup met most of the politicians in a state of unpreparedness. Though rumours of a coup had been in the air for sometime, most of them were not expecting anything to happen that festive period of New Year's Eve. Chief Akinloye, the chairman of the NPN was in his house in Ibadan, preparing to play host to a new year party. He had imported special champagne, brewed and labelled in his honour (Akinloye Champagne). Everything was set, the cows to be slaughtered and the food for the festivities. When he heard the announcement, the wily politician made his calculations. With the help of some members of the armed forces, he escaped through the border to Benin Republic and later surfaced in Great Britain.

Some other politicians too were also able to escape that morning. Umaru Dikko, the powerful minister of transport, was able to escape with the help of some soldiers; Joseph Wayas, the president of the Senate, Ali Makele, the minister of steel development, were all able to escape. Contrary to expectations, the conspirators did not call at the homes of these top members of the government.

In Akure, like many other towns in the UPN-controlled states, a farcical drama was taking place. On hearing the news of the coup, people trooped out celebrating. Some were shouting from their cars, Awoo! Many of them simply believed that the coup plotters had taken over power to hand over the reins of government to Chief Awolowo.

'They are giving the government to Papa,' many of them were saying. 'Happy New Year! Happy new government!!'

One of those who knew this could not be so was Dr. Aina, the newly-elected deputy governor of Ondo State. That morning, a thanksgiving service was to be held in his honour at Otun Ekiti, his home town. When the news came on the air waves, the drivers, the honour guards, the policemen and the numerous government vehicles that went with him to Otun simply melted away. The military magic wand had stripped him of all the paraphernalia of power. The service was held nonetheless. After the service, some of the policemen, knowing that they now had a new master, arrested the deputy governor.

A similar drama was taking place in Ijero-Ekiti, home town of Chief Omoboriowo. A thanksgiving service was to be held for him that Saturday at the Catholic church for surviving the violence of the 1983 elections. He heard the coup announcement before heading for church in the morning. Twenty-four hours earlier, the Ajero (traditional ruler) of Ijero had honoured Dr. Olowoporoku, a minister in the Shagari government, with a chieftaincy title. Olowoporoku was to hold a party at Ilawe that Saturday too. By the time Omoboriowo returned from service, the two policemen at the gate of his country home had disappeared.

Governor Ajasin did not get to know about the coup until some few minutes after Abacha's announcement started. An aide came to tell him and he was able to confirm it by turning on the radio. He then packed a few things in a hand bag and left the Government House in his private car. For the first time in four years, there were no sirens and no fawning escorts. He came back briefly later in the afternoon before finally retiring to his country home in Owo. The following day, Sunday, January 1, 1984, he wrote a letter to Ahmed Sheidu, the commissioner of police, asking for permission to pack his private property from the Government House. On Monday, January 2, he reported in Akure as directed by the new ruling junta. His meeting with Sheidu was short, courteous, formal and distant. Chief Ajasin, like all the other politicians who had given themselves up, was asked to fill a form detailing his position in the *ancien regime*. Sheidu then told him that he was to proceed to the Government House and stay there until otherwise directed. He was now under arrest.

On Monday, January 2, entering the Government House now, Ajasin was no longer the governor, but a prisoner of the state. His wife, Babafunke, followed him and so did his two daughters. Many of his former aides too, hearing that the boss was back at Government House, trooped there to keep him company. Many of them could not believe that the old order had changed. Some few hours later, policemen came and drove the politicians away, leaving Ajasin, his wife and daughters and Alex Adedipe. Later, upon pleadings by the ex-governor, they allowed one of his daughters, who was then nursing a baby, and Adedipe to leave. Chief Ajasin, his wife and Mrs. Waleola Okunrinboye, the other daughter, were compelled to stay. In the middle of the night, the former governor was roused from his fitful sleep by soldiers who said their boss would like to meet him. Ajasin, his wife and daughter, were then taken in an army landrover into one of the government's guest chalets.

Chief Ajasin and his wife and daughter, Mrs. Okunrinboye, were in this captivity for almost one week. For 24 hours everyday the chalet was surrounded by fierce-looking armed soldiers. About 6 a.m. one morning, soldiers led by a young officer drove in. Chief Ajasin was told that the new military governor, Commodore Michael Bamidele Otiko was now ready to meet him. He had not had his breakfast. He came out as he was directed. He was searched thoroughly and was then asked to sit in the compartment behind the driver in the landrover. The vehicle then drove on in a circuitous route through the city until they got to the army barracks in Akure. The door was opened and Chief Omoboriowo, bible in hand, took his seat. Chief Adebisi Ogedengbe, former Shagari's minister, also entered the landrover. Dr. Olowoporoku was made to seat on the floor of the vehicle at the back, in the midst of armed soldiers. Common adversity had now brought Ajasin and his erstwhile deputy together after more than 12 months of separation.

Chief Omoboriowo's journey to detention was equally as dramatic. As directed by the coup plotters, he had surrendered himself to the police on Monday, January 2. He was allowed to go. He later went to Ibadan where he was arrested by soldiers. *The Punch* had carried an erroneous story that Chief Omoboriowo had been declared wanted. After he was interviewed briefly by military police at the second division headquarters, Ibadan, he was led under armed escorts to Akure and handed over to the Commissioner of Police. He was then allowed to go into temporary freedom.

January 7, 1984, his home in Ijero was invaded by a combined team of soldiers, policemen and operatives of the Nigerian Security Organisation, NSO (now State Security Service, SSS), led by an assistant commissioner of police. It was 3 a.m. and the former deputy governor was told that he had to come to Akure immediately. He sat at the back of the landrover which was driven recklessly from town. Agitated about the fate of her husband, his wife, Ebun, followed in her Peugeot 505. The convoy headed for Ilawe where Olowoporoku was picked up. Ebun was forced to go back by the soldiers. They now headed for Akure. At the army barracks where he was taken, Omoboriowo then met other detainees. It was from here that he was picked up with Ajasin and the others.

Their destination was Ibadan where they later met Bola Ige and his successor as governor of Oyo State, Olunloyo. They were taken to the Police Command headquarters at Eleyele where they met Sunday Afolabi, former Shagari's minister; Janet Akinrinade and Olunloyo's deputy, Olatunji Mohammed. The men of yesterday, which also included former governor of Kwara State, Adamu Atta, were then driven in a big bus to Bonny Camp army barracks. Bonny Camp simply played host to the who-was-who in the Second Republic. All the governors, their deputies, ministers, important contractors and advisers were all there.

Only very few of them were able to leave Bonny Camp for freedom, like Dr. Olunloyo and Chief Christian Onoh, former governor of

Anambra State. They left the relative comfort of Bonny Camp for the various prisons in the country, notably Ikoyi and Kirikiri prisons in Lagos and Agodi prison in Ibadan. Some of them were taken to Ita-Oko detention camp, a mosquito-infested island in the middle of the Atlantic. The new regime of Major-General Mohammadu Buhari set up military tribunals presided over by military men which handed over heavy sentences (sometimes up to 250 years) to politicians said to be guilty of corruption.

Not just the governors or the ministers knew who was now in charge, all cadre of politicians knew who had won the war. In Akure, all former commissioners and other top party men were arrested. They were asked to sit in the sun from morning till evening when they were dumped in a single room. The only lady-commissioner, Mrs. Osomo, was among them. Most of them, including Omoboriowo, were to stay in detention throughout the entire reign of Buhari. A Roman conqueror could not have performed better.

One man who knew the impact of the new regime was Chief Awolowo. Four days before the coup, he had asked Nigerians to fast and pray for three days so that there could be positive change in the country. Twenty-four hours after the fast ended, Buhari was foisted on the nation. Most politicians, including Chief Awolowo and Dr. Azikiwe, had their passports seized and they were forbidden from travelling abroad even for medical treatment. Chief Awolowo was especially involved in a running battle with the regime which accused his governors of corruption. His house in Apapa was broken into by soldiers said to be searching for incriminating evidence. It was a sad time for Awo who was now presiding, like a king in exile, over the remnant of his party.

The politicians nicknamed Agodi Prison, the tomb of the living-dead. The soul of the people, their freedom and liberty were also in captivity. After four years of heady experiment in democracy, darkness had fallen again. Democracy had entered its long night. It would take a long time for the dawn to come again.

Epilogue

W hy did the Second Republic collapse? I am sure history will come up with many explanations. I believe the Second Republic was a victim of the ingrained contradictions in the Nigerian federation. Others may point to the nature of the civilian steersmanship, especially the colourless, dour and spineless leadership under Shehu Shagari and his crowd of buccaneers. But it would be unfair to blame the calamity of the second coming of the military entirely on this class of elites.

Nigerians are used to being governed by leaders who came to power through unorthodox, and, indeed, criminal means. This had to do with the nation's historical experience as a colonial outpost of the British. To the British overlords who got Nigeria as part of their booty during the Berlin Conference of 1884/85, their government could hardly be said to have any moral foundation. The British derived their legitimacy from the real superiority of their fire-power and their willingness to use it. Since the amalgamation of Northern and Southern protectorates of Nigeria in 1914 by Lord Frederick Lugard, only two rulers of Nigeria, the late Prime Minister Tafawa Balewa and President Shehu Shagari, had any measure of direct mandate from the people. The military, who had dominated Nigerian politics since 1966, are direct descendants of the colonial overlords, not only because they got their mandate directly from their fire-power, but because the Nigerian military was a colonial creation like the Nigerian state. Indeed, its precursor were the band of mercenaries used by ravaging empire builders like Lugard and Thomas

Goldie that subdued independent states in this part of Africa and placed the territories under the Union Jack.

Since crimes have been rewarded with power in the past, the belief is reinforced that they would continue to be so rewarded. Therefore, coup de'tat and rigging of elections are considered worthy avenues to power. This is more so since both crimes are rarely punished and it is even rarer for the criminals to be identified. Despite its calling itself the corrective regime, the military has often steered clear of identifying election riggers. The General Aguiyi-Ironsi regime made some attempts in 1966 to unravel the debacle of the 1965 Western Regional election. General Ibrahim Babangida, who seized power from Major-General Buhari in August 1985, even made a bolder attempt when he appointed a judicial commission to probe the disastrous 1983 elections. The commission was presided over by Justice Bolarinwa Babalakin, a highly respected judge of the Federal Appeal Court (he was later promoted to the Supreme Court). The Babalakin panel blamed very few people specifically, and those it did were the unknown quantity in Nigerian politics, or those who were safely dead. It did not recommend anyone for criminal prosecution.

Election riggers and their co-travellers are spared often because they share the same interest with those who take over through criminal coup de'tats. Both coup and rigging are important weapons in the arsenal of the ruling Hausa-Fulani oligarchy. Coup plotters and riggers are not considered as criminals, but as courageous frontier men who were prepared to take risk for the common good. Such men are amply rewarded. Coup plotters and election manipulators who were not Hausa-Fulani were also often rewarded like valued collaborators or paid off handsomely like worthy mercenaries.

It would be wrong to conclude that this is the conscious policy of the Hausa-Fulani elites, but they are the principal beneficiaries of the aberrations of the Nigerian state. Indeed, many members of this elite group are truly uncomfortable with this phenomenon. The rest of the country perceived them as conquerors to be appeased or resisted or barely tolerated. The military wing of this oligarchy had attempted to address this phenomenon, but since the problem was wrongly diagnosed, the treatment has been off the mark.

The military has created more states in order to address the problem of nationalities in Nigeria. Some have interpreted this too as a solution to the problem of Hausa-Fulani hegemony. But the solution has created more problems of balkanization and increased frustration within the polity. Nigeria has become a state of constant tension. In order to de-emphasize the issue of ethnicity and statism, the military has outlawed the use of coats of arms by the states. It compulsorily acquired states' institutions like universities, television and radio stations, and outlawed powerful cultural and ethnic organisations.

But despite the pretence that Nigeria is one, 'no North, no South', members of the military themselves feel this tension in the federation. In 1975, Akin Aduwo, who later rose to the position of Admiral and Chief of Naval Staff, objected to the forcible take-over of the Western State government-owned University of Ife. As punishment, Aduwo was unceremoniously removed as military governor of Western State by the then head of state, General Murtala Ramat Muhammed. Also in 1978, Chief Ayo Ogunlade, then federal commissioner (minister) for information was removed from office when he clashed with entrenched Northern interest over his implementation of the federal government policy of bringing the old regional radio and television stations under federal control. The prize at stake was Radio-Television Kaduna, RTK (now Radio Nigeria Kaduna), which Ogunlade wanted to reduce from short-wave broadcasting to the less powerful medium wave. In addition, like the old Western Nigeria Broadcasting Corporation and the Eastern Nigeria Broadcasting Service, RTK, was also unilaterally acquired by the federal government. Ogunlade was to learn that the federal government may be paying the bill, but it has little or no control of the RTK. To appease Northern interest, he was fired by General Olusegun Obasanjo, then head of state.

The charade of Nigerianness was not restricted to the electronic media alone (*New Nigerian* Newspapers and *Daily Times* were also forcibly acquired by the federal government to portray national identity), but was also evident in other federalized institutions. The federal government acquired regional universities like University of Nigeria, Nsukka, Ahmadu Bello University, Zaria, and Obafemi Awolowo University (former University of Ife), Ile-Ife. They have retained their old hues despite acquiring common foster parents.

Nowhere is the contradiction more glaring than in the military. Normally the army is supposed to be meant for the ablest and the willing. Now, to maintain national unity or at least, existence, recruitment into the military is done according to quota system. Every state of the federation, from the most populous to the least, is expected to give equal number of recruits to the military every year. The same quota system formula, to a varying degree, is used in recruitment into the civil service, the department of customs and excise and federal government-owned parastatals like the Nigeria National Petroleum Corporation, NNPC. It is only in the field of sports, like football, that Nigerians would allow merit and competence to dominate. I suspect this is so because the country simply cannot compete well internationally if its sports ambassador are chosen on the basis of their pedigrees instead of their skills and competence.

How well we have failed in this obtuse art of unity is borne out in certain hilarious and sometimes tragic realities. In obedience to the quota system formula, it is not unusual for children who scored 70% to be rejected in favour of those who scored 20% in the universities' entrance examination, so that the quota law can be obeyed. In the police, it is not uncommon for a superintendent of police from the old Bendel State to have a Northern classmate who had already become a commissioner of police. The same anomaly is true of the army.

Only few men have been able to soar above the barrier of the quota system. It is indeed rare to find people like Chief Olu Falae who became a federal permanent secretary at 39, despite the limitation of his state of origin, a rare tribute to his intelligence and diligence. In 1983, the late Major-General Mamman Jiya Vatsa was able to break through the barrier because of his closeness to President Shagari. He had protested to the president when he was not included in the list of officers to be made major-generals because some people argued that another Niger State man, Ibrahim Babangida, had already filled the state's slot. Vasta had his way. Many more people, not having the same crucial political connections, are left to suffer in career wilderness.

Nigerians have paid dearly for the federation. More than one million lives were lost in the civil war. There had been other regional upheavals which, though were not as cataclysmic, are nonetheless equally significant. There were the Western regional uprisings of the sixties, the Tiv revolt of the same period and the rebellion of Ijaws led by the late Isaac Adaka Boro. As recently as 1990, a group of army officers led by Major Gideon Orka, professing common interest between the South and the Middle-Belt, staged a coup against the regime of General Ibrahim Babangida. Orka promised to excise six Northern states out of the federation.

The nationality issue is at the centre of the modern state system. Nigeria is no exception. I believe that the nationality issue is at the core of the problems of the federation and the survival of democracy. This is one issue that Nigerians have to address boldly if the federation is to survive or if democracy is to take root. All over the world, this is being done in states that have multi-nationalities. The old Soviet Union collapsed not so much because of the wrongness of communism, but because under the authoritarian state structure of the Soviet system, the nationality issue was not properly addressed. Multi-national states like India, Ethiopia, old Yugoslavia and Czechoslovakia are facing ferments and upheavals because of this nationality issue. The lid can only be maintained on such disruptive upheavals by imaginative understanding of the problem, or by brutal repression, like in Iraq, or manipulation, cajolery and deceit. But we know the ice cap cannot stay on the volcano forever.

Nigeria is a deformed federation. The component nationalities have few logical basis for relating to one another. There are not many Nigerians, including Hausa-Fulani, who do not feel uneasy about the nature of the federation. A federation is supposed to be a state where the component nationalities have a measure of control over their destinies.

Component units are supposed to be autonomous and economically viable units. They are supposed to have linguistic affinity and cultural cohesion. But since the coming of the military in 1966, they have transformed the federation into one of very strong centre and very weak states. Now the federal government has become a monster terrorizing the states.

Now we have a federation of 30 states, created with hardly any discernible logic. The Yoruba people have control over six states: Oyo, Ogun, Osun, Ondo, Lagos, and Kwara, the Igbo four states: Abia, Enugu, Anambra and Imo; the Hausa-Fulani six states: Katsina, Kebbi, Kano, Jigawa, Sokoto and Bauchi. The Kanuri of the North-East and related nationalities have control over two states of Borno and Yobe. The minorities of the Middle-Belt have control over seven states: Niger, Kogi, Plateau, Benue, Taraba, Adamawa and Kaduna. The minorities of the West control Edo and Delta states. The minorities of the East control Rivers, Akwa Ibom and Cross River states.

I believe there is no reason why the Hausa-Fulani, the Yoruba and the Igbo should have more than one state each in the federation. The weakening of the nationalities and the component states of the federation has led to the decimation of the big nationalities. The smaller ones are even worse off, suffering from collective crisis of identity. All these have exacerbated tension in the federation, making the fight for the control of the centre the equivalent of war. The situation is not helped by the attitude of the Hausa-Fulani oligarchy, whether as the elite of the NPN or as members of the kitchen cabinet of Mohammadu Buhari, Ibrahim Babangida or Sani Abacha who treat the rest of the country like conquered territories.

The status-quo is not in the interest of all Nigerians. It has hindered competitive development. Everyone is interested in keeping his neighbour down, and there is qualitative decline in every section of the Nigerian state. Worse still, everyone looks at the federal government as a no-man's land. If a man steals money from the federal purse, he would be welcomed by his own people as a hero who had succeeded in getting for them their own part of the national cake. The reaction would be different if he is from Kano State and he steals Kano State's money. He would rightly be identified as a thief.

The solution would be to redefine the federation. Everyone should be master of his own home and the rightful owner of the resources herein. I would recommend that Nigeria should be restructured into seven states only, with each of the following occupying one state each: Hausa-Fulani, Yoruba, Igbo, Kanuri and their related ethnic groups, the minorities of the Middle-Belt, minorities of the East and minorities of the West. All these should be autonomous territories having control over everything except those affairs like defence, external relations, and fiscal policies which should be vested in the federal government. The federal government should control only those items agreed upon for the good of the commonwealth.

If this is done, Nigeria would be a model for the rest of Africa. Tyrants are able to survive and flower in Africa because they are seen by their ethnic groups as ethnic champions whose downfall would be tantamount to the downfall of the ethnic group. More often than not, such people can only be brought down at a terrible cost. Witness the career of men like Mobutu Sese Seko, Marcia Nguema, Samuel Doe, Idi Amin Dada, and Gnassingbe Eyadema.

It is easy to see that nations containing one dominant nationality are often more successful than multi-national states. Compare Israel, Singapore, South Korea, Hong Kong, Taiwan with the likes of the old Soviet Union, India and Nigeria. After centuries of wars, upheavals and social ferment, including the two world wars, Europe had discovered that the nation-state is the primary basis for sustainable development. Now we have France for the French ethnic group, England for Englishmen, Germany for Germans.

But Europe has also shown us that Nigeria must be preserved at all cost. Having to a large extent settled the problem of everyone being a master of his home, Western Europe has shown the world the benefit of a large market open to all without discrimination. The formation of the Common Market is a reaction to the need for the large market. A common market guarantees common prosperity. Nigeria also has the large market that only a viable and stable political structure can fully maximise.

Addressing the nationality issue would only go one step forward in ensuring the survival of democracy and the polity. Solving the nationality problem, as could be seen in Somalia, Vietnam and Cambodia, does not guarantee democracy, freedom and progress or economic prosperity. The second pillar is the building of a strong civil society, to fight those evils which the modern state system is capable of. Bodies like the Civil Liberties Organisation and other human rights groups in Nigeria have shown that the future is bright in this direction.

But the immediate test of democracy in Nigeria is transition. Would a democratically elected government be able to preside over a peaceful, free and fair election? When a democratic regime succeeds in supervising the organisation of an election that may lead to its own exit from power, then democracy has taken roots. The Balewa regime failed in this test and so did the Shagari regime.

It is when a democratically elected government succeeds in addressing these two questions of nationalities and democratic elections that democracy and freedom can survive and thrive in Nigeria. It is then that Nigerians would be spared the replay of the 1983 nightmare. This is when Nigerians would be freed from the ravages of military rule and the cankerworm of hegemonic ambition. The federation cannot be in good health if some people feel they are first-class citizens and some others second- and, indeed, third-class citizens.

Lagos, June 12, 1992.

Appendix

In the High Court Of Justice
Ondo State Of Nigeria
In the Akure Judicial Division
Holding At Akure

Before their Lordships:

1. Dr. J. Ola Orojo - Chief Judge
2. Hon. Justice E.A. Ojuolape - Judge
3. Hon. Justice S.A. Afonja - Judge
4. Hon. Justice S.A. Akintan - Judge
5. Hon. Justice A.O. Ogunleye - Judge

This Saturday, the 10th Day of September, 1983

In the Matter of the Gubernatorial Election under the Electoral Act 1982 For Ondo State held On the 13th Day of August, 1983

Suit No. AK/EP.1/83

Between:

Chief Michael Adekunle Ajasin   Petitioner/Applicant

and

1. Chief Akin Omoboriowo   )
2. The Chief Federal Electoral   )   Respondents
    Officer for Ondo State,   )
    Chief J.A. Adeniyi   )

Parties present:

Mr. J.O. Akinbamidele for Mr. G.O.K. Ajayi S.A.N. for petitioner. (with him Mr. O. Afuye, Mr. Bisi Akinbola, Mr. Smart Omodunbi, Mrs. O.O. Anifowose, Mr. Dele Awopeju, Mr. A.A. Adeniyi and Mr. Niran Disu). Mr. Duro Ajayi for Chief F.R.A. Williams for 1st respondent, Mr. Duro Ajayi for second respondent (with him are Mr. I. Filani and G. Adurota).

Judgment

This is a petition brought by the petitioner Chief Michael Adekunle Ajasin following the gubernatorial elections of 13th August, 1983 praying the court to determine that the 1st respondent Chief Akin Omoboriowo was not duly elected or returned, and that the petitioner was duly elected and ought to have been returned.

The pleadings show that both the petitioner and the 1st respondent were candidates in the election. The 2nd respondent is the Chief Federal Electoral Officer for Ondo State.

The grounds for the petition are contained in paragraphs 3, 4, 25 and 27 of the amended petition which are as follows:

"3. Chief Akin Omoboriowo was at the time of the election, not duly elected by a majority of lawful votes at the election."

"4. Chief Michael Adekunle Ajasin received a total of 1,652,795 of the votes cast in all the 17 local government areas of Ondo State and received 25 per cent or more in more than two thirds of all the Local Government Areas in the state, whilst Chief Akin Omoboriowo received a total of 421,401 votes."

"25. The petitioner further avers that the final figures for the election were declared arbitrarily in favour of the Ist respondent, Chief Akin Omoboriowo, in utter disregard of the figures properly declared and verified at the polling stations and collating centres."

"27. The 2nd respondent has wrongfully declared the 1st respondent, Chief Akin Omoboriowo, to be duly elected and wrongly declared him to have received 1,288,981 votes and at the same time wrongly declared the petitioner, Chief Michael Adekunle Ajasin to have received 1,015,385 votes."

In paragraph 7 of the amended petition the petitioner avers that the results of the election as announced by the 2nd respondent were falsified in various constituencies and local government areas in Ondo State, and in paragraphs 8 to 24, he gives particulars of the votes received by the parties in respect of each local government area and also of the alleged falsification. In their amended reply the 1st and 2nd Respondents admitted paragraph 2 of the petition and denied all other paragraphs. They also pleaded, inter alia, that the 1st respondent was duly elected and returned having satisfied the provisions of section 164 (7) (a) and (b) of the constitution (paragraph 5), that the petitioner has failed to satisfy that provision (paragraph 6), that the 1st respondent received 1,288,981 votes whilst the petitioner received 1,015,385 votes (paragraph 13) and that the figures quoted in paragraphs 4, 9(ii), 20(ii) and 21(ii) of the petition are fictitious and not figures officially submitted by the Federal Electoral Commission accredited officers and officials (paragraph 14).

On the pleadings, it is clear that there is no dispute as to the election and the number of votes received by the petitioner and the 1st respondent in respect of six of the 17 local government areas, namely: Akoko North, Akure, Ekiti Central, Ilaje/Eseodo, Ondo and Owo. It was agreed at the trial that it was not necessary to produce evidence in respect of the figures for these local government areas. Just before the time of petitioner's case, he filed an amended rejoinder in which he conceded the figures pleaded by the 1st and 2nd respondents in respect of Akoko South local government, Ero local government, Ekiti South West local government and Ijero local government. Thus, issues were joined in respect of the remaining seven local governments only.

In his amended petition, the petitioner avers in various paragraphs that he will rely on the relevant statement of result of poll form EC8A, the schedule of total valid votes form EC40J and the Declaration of Result of Poll Form EC8 and Form EC8B. The 1st and 2nd Respondents also in their amended reply pleaded that they will rely on the forms

EC8A containing the particulars of the votes received by each of the candidates and the percentages as well as the total votes cast in the election prepared and signed by the Returning Officer (para. 11) and also on the declaration of result of poll gubernatorial elections form EC8B containing the detailed results of the election in each of the 66 constituencies prepared and signed by the returning officer (para. 12). They also pleaded various electoral forms in paragraph 14(b).

The petitioner did not give evidence but called 40 witnesses in support of his case.

The 1st respondent also did not give evidence, but called 18 witnesses in support of his own case whilst the 2nd respondent gave evidence and called no witness.

At this stage, we think it will be useful to clear a few general matters so as to better appreciate the evidence and avoid unnecessary repetition.

First is the procedure from the close of poll, to the declaration of results as emerged from the evidence. The evidence of the petitioner's witnesses is to the effect that after the close of polls, the presiding officer at each polling station would count the votes polled by each candidate in the presence of the political party counting agents in accordance with section 62 of the Electoral Act of 1982. He would enter the number of votes scored by each candidate in a form provided for this purpose and sign it. The candidates or polling agents present would sign to testify to the correctness of the figures and would be given copies.

Thereafter, the results are taken to the collation centre for the constituency. Here, the result brought by presiding officers are submitted to the Assistant Returning Officer (hereinafter called A.R.O) who, in the presence of party counting agents present, would enter them into a large sheet prepared for that purpose, called Form EC8B. He would add up the figures for each candidate in the presence of the agents, and enter the result, that is, the total number of votes scored by each candidate, on to another form, namely, Form EC40J, headed schedule of total valid votes, or sometimes Form EC8A which is the 'statement of results' or both. Where there are no printed forms available, he would type out the results or otherwise improvise a form for the result. The ARO would read out the results to the hearing of the agents and others present. He would sign and stamp it, and the agents would then sign the result as correct. He then gives a copy to the agents of each political party, and to the police and any representative of the N.S.O. present.

The next stage is the collation at the Local Government level. The ARO from all the constituencies in the Local Government would submit the collated results in their large sheet Form EC8B and also the summary contained in Form EC8A above to the Deputy Returning Officer (hereinafter referred to as D.R.O.) at the Local Government collation centre. He adds up the scores of each candidate in all the constituencies of the Local Government and enters the respective totals in a Form which he stamps and signs and makes other copies of the result. Some used form EC8A, and where none is available, they type out the results. These are countersigned by the party agents, and a copy is given to the agents of each political party and to the police and N.S.O. members present.

The respondents, however, sought to show that the A.R.O's were not expected to issue any form to party agents and in the case of the D.R.O. they were to submit form EC8 and Form EC8B together with the A.R.O's form EC8B to the state returning officer.

Secondly, the pleadings and the evidence show that the main issue between the parties is to ascertain the correct and authentic figures of votes scored by each of the candidates of the political parties, especially the petitioner and the 1st respondent. The issue before the court therefore, is to decide which of the conflicting documents and figures are correct and genuine on the face of the evidence produced before it. Ideally, the procedure to prove the total number of votes scored by the candidates is:

(a)   to prove the votes received at each polling station by each candidate and then add them all up for each Constituency and then for each Local Government; this is the foundation for any calculation;

(b)   failing (a) above, to prove the entry of the figures received by each candidate at the polling station in some form and their total for each constituency;

(c)   to prove that the addition of all the votes cast for each candidate in all the constituencies in each local government is correct.

It is not practicable, in the circumstances, to produce the record of the results from each of the polling stations in every Local Government where issues are joined. In order therefore to ascertain what figures, are proved or established, the court will have to bear in mind the need to relate figures submitted, to the very foundation of the figures and in deciding on what is the true or acceptable figures in the light of the evidence adduced, the court will, as an accepted principle in civil proceedings, decide on the balance of probabilities.

Thirdly, and arising from the evidence is the acceptability of the forms. It has been the case of the respondents not only on the pleadings, but also on the evidence and in the submission of counsel that the forms and exhibits relied on by the petitioners were not those acceptable to FEDECO and should be ignored and so the figures in them rejected. In particular Mr. Alibaloye, the state chief returning officer who testified as the 18th witness for the 1st respondent, left the court in no doubt that he rejected certain results submitted to him on the simple ground that they were not on the prescribed form. He was emphatic that form EC40J had no bearing on the election, and so, results entered on them were unacceptable. A *fortiori,* results on ordinary sheets even though duly signed, and however genuine the figures in them might be, would not be acceptable. We are grateful to the 2nd respondent the chief federal electoral officer, Chief Adeniyi, who in his evidence threw valuable light on how form EC40J came into circulation. It was an alternative form devised by FEDECO, in case first counting was to take place at the counting centre, and not polling station because for some time, it was not certain what would be the fate of the proposed amendments to the Electoral Act 1982, as regards the counting of votes. In that event, both Form EC8A and Form EC40J were supplied and distributed to FEDECO officials in the field, and so both became handy for use for recording the votes scored. It is abundantly clear that most A.R.O believed that Form EC40J was the form for them to use for the summary of votes recorded in the large sheet Form EC8B.

We take the view that this is not the type of exercise where one can insist on a mere formal technicality to hinder the investigation. The matter in issue before us is the number of votes received by the petitioner and 1st respondent respectively. To resolve the issue, what we have to do is to ask how many votes were cast for each and in arriving at the truth, any evidence that will support any contention should be given due consideration. If the record of the votes scored is duly authenticated, it should not matter whether it was set on a specially printed paper or not. We are of the view that it does not matter for the purpose of these proceedings, and at arriving at the truth whether the results collated by A.R.O's were written on a prescribed form or not. In fairness to R.W. 18, we would observe that his powers were limited, and he did not have the judicial power which we have, as a court to investigate and adjudicate. We will therefore consider all the exhibits admitted in this trial on their probative value with little, if any regard, to their form.

Fourthly, Mr. Duro Ajayi, learned counsel for the 1st and 2nd respondents submitted first, that FEDECO should have been joined and secondly that as the 2nd respondent was not the state returning officer, the allegations against him are not proved and he should be dismissed from the petition. On the first point, the short answer is that this is a case where there are statutory respondents and FEDECO is not one of them, and with regard to the other point, the Chief federal electoral officer being a statutory party, it makes no difference whether any allegations are made against him or not. (See section. 121(2) of the Electoral Act 1982).

Having dealt with the above general preliminary matters and before considering the evidence led in respect of areas in dispute, it is appropriate to set out the position of the parties, as a result of the admissions and concessions made as stated earlier. In respect of the ten local government areas where there is now no dispute, i.e. Akoko North, Akoko South, Akure, Ekiti Central, Ekiti South West, Ero, Ijero, Ilaje/ Ese-Odo, Ondo and Owo, the total votes received by the parties according to the pleadings are as follows:

Petitioner   =   885,134 votes
1st respondent =   413,469 votes

The petitioner received 25 per cent or more of the votes in 9 of the 10 local governments and the 1st respondent received 25 per cent or more of the votes in 5 of the local governments.

With the above background, we will now proceed to consider the evidence led in respect of the local governments in which the figure of votes are disputed. These are Ekiti East, Ekiti North, Ekiti South, Ekiti West, Idanre/Ifedore, Ifesowapo and Ikale, but before dealing with specific local governments, we would like to state the general principles for assessing evidence and which we have followed.

In **A.R. Mogaji & Ors. V.R. Odofin & Ors.** (1978) 4S.C. 91 at p. 93, the procedure which a judge should follow in assessing evidence in a civil proceeding was set out by the Supreme Court, *inter alia,* as follows:

> ...the totality of evidence should be considered in order to determine which has weight and which has no weight at all. Therefore, in deciding whether a certain set of facts given in evidence by one party in a civil case, before a court, in which both parties appear is preferable to another set of facts given in evidence by the other party, the trial judge, after a summary of all the facts must put the two sets of facts in an imaginary scale, weigh one against the other, then decide upon the preponderance of credible evidence which weighs more, accept it in preference to the other...

In concluding, the Supreme Court said, *inter alia,* 'In short, before a judge before whom evidence is adduced by the parties before him in a **civil case** comes to a decision as to which evidence he believes or accepts, and which evidence he rejects, he should first of all put the totality of the testimony adduced by both parties on that imaginary scale; he will put the evidence adduced by the plaintiff on one side of the scale and that of the defendant on the other side and weigh them together. He will then see which is heavier, not by the number of witnesses called by each party, but by the quality or the probative value of the testimony of those witnesses. This is what is meant when it is said that a civil case is decided on the balance of probabilities. Therefore in determining which is heavier, the judge will naturally have regard to the following:-

(a) Whether the evidence is admissible;
(b) Whether it is relevant;
(c) Whether it is credible;
(d) Whether it is conclusive and
(e) Whether it is more probable than that given by the other party...'

These principles have been repeatedly confirmed by the Supreme Court. See, E.G. **Woluchem V. Gudi** (1981) 5 S.C. 291 at pages 306-310 per Nnamani J.S.C. **Magnus Eweka V. Bello,** Suit No. 90/1979 of 30/1/81 per Kayode Eso J.S.C.

We wish to say that in assessing the evidence given in these proceedings we shall adhere very carefully and strictly to the above principles.

We will now proceed to consider the evidence led in respect of each local government where the figures are in dispute.

Ifesowapo Local Government
Five witnesses testified for the petitioner. For Constituency 1, P.W.3, the A.R.O. and P.W.5 produced exhibits PET. 6 and PET.9 which were form EC40J and PET. 9A which is Form EC8A. All were prepared and signed by the A.R.O. and endorsed by two party agents.

For constituency II, P.W.1, the U.P.N. party agent produced Exhibit PET. 1, which is form EC40J and PET. 2 which is a typed out form. Both were signed and stamped by the A.R.O. who, as P.W.2 acknowledged them as what he signed and issued. They were endorsed by agents of U.P.N. and G.N.P.P. and PET.1 was endorsed by an A.S.P.

For constituency III, P.W.4 and P.W.5 produced exhibits PET.7

and PET.10 i.e. form EC40J and exhibits PET.8 and 10A, which are the same. They were all prepared and signed by the A.R.O. who as P.W.21 acknowledged his signature. They were also countersigned by the party agents and the police. For the total number of votes in the local government, P.W.1 produced exhibit PET. 3 which showed the total votes received by each party in the local government.

For the 1st respondent, P.W. 13, 14, 15 and 16 testified. Mr. Aruleba the D.R.O. who was R.W.13 produced exhibit RE.18 as showing the total votes received by each party in the local government. He said that the A.R.O. in constituency III did not show up. P.W.14 who was N.P.N. agent in constituency III said that there was no collation. We later had the evidence of 2nd respondent who gave instruction to the coordinator and later the D.R.O to appoint A.R.O. if the one appointed still did not show up.

We have considered the evidence produced for the petitioner and that for the 1st respondent and we have no difficulty in preferring, by far, the evidence of the petitioner's witnesses in respect of the votes in this local government. Not only has the petitioner produced documentary evidence all along the line from the receipt of the results from the presiding officers, but some of the witnesses for the 1st respondent, especially R.W.13, R.W.15 and R.W.16 did not impress us as witnesses of truth. Accordingly, we accept the evidence of the witnesses for the petitioner and hold on the evidence before us that the votes received by the petitioner and the 1st respondent at the election as per exhibits PET.1 to PET.3. PET.5, PET.7 to PET.10A which we accept are as follows:

Constituency I: petitioner, 50,598;   1st respondent, 1725
Constituency II: petitioner, 26,631;   1st respondent, 885
Constituency III: petitioner, <u>28,786,</u>   1st respondent, <u>1,115</u>
                              <u>106,015</u>   <u>3,725</u>

The Petitioner therefore received a total of 106,015 votes i.e. 95.07 per cent of the total votes while the 1st Respondent received a total of 3,725 votes, i.e. 3.34 per cent.

Idanre/Ifedore Local Government

For the petitioner, P.W.II, an N.P.P. agent in Constituency I, produced exhibit PET. 15 compiled in his presence and signed by him as the result of the collated results from the polling stations. P.W. 12, a U.P.N. agent confirmed the evidence of P.W.II in respect of exhibit PET 15. On Constituency II, P.W.10, a U.P.N. agent testified and produced exhibit PET.14 which is signed by the A.R.O. and compiled from results submitted by presiding officers.

On Constituency III, P.W.9 gave evidence and produced exhibit PET. 13 which is Form EC40J prepared by the A.R.O. duly signed by him and party agents.

On Constituency IV, P.W.7 the U.P.N. agent produced exhibit PET. 12 which is Form EC40J duly stamped and signed. It was acknowledged by the A.R.O., P.W.8 who made it.

With reference to final collation at the local government centre, P.W.6 produced exhibit PET.11 which is the result for the local government, the signature was confirmed by P.W.8, the A.R.O. for constituency IV who was present when it was made.

For the 1st Respondent, R.W.9, the D.R.O. testified that he collated the results from the Constituencies and produced Exhibit RE.12 as the copy of the result. At the back were what he said were signatures of the A.R.O's. He denied writing or signing Exhibit PET.11. He said that he signed a document EC8B for P.W.6 but this was not produced. On constituency IV results, he said he acted as A.R.O. for the constituency. R.W. 10, an N.P.N. agent at the local government collation centre, produced Exhibit RE.12A which is similar to RE.12.

There is evidence from the petitioner's witness of how the figures for each constituency were obtained and collated. There is therefore a continuous chain of events leading to the final figures. On the other hand, the witnesses for the 1st respondent have shown no basis for their final figures. Even the signatures at the back of exhibit RE.12 purporting to be those of A.R.O.'s were not acknowledged apart from that of the D.R.O./A.R.O.

In these circumstances, we prefer and accept the evidence of the witnesses for the petitioner and hold that on the evidence before us the votes received by the petitioner and the 1st respondent in Idanre/Ifedore local government at the elections as per exhibits PET.11 to PET.15 and which we accept are as follows:

Constituency	Petitioner	1st Respondent
I	13,298	2,127
II	9,528	1,820
III	40,364	1,241
IV	22,730	530
	85,920	5,718

The petitioner, therefore, received a total of 85,920 votes i.e. 91.98 per cent, and the 1st Respondent 5,718 i.e. 6.12 per cent.

Ekiti North Local Government
Five witnesses testified for the petitioner. P.W.30, a U.P.N agent for Constituency I produced the result exhibit PET. 32 which was signed by him, the agent of NAP and the A.R.O. and compiled from results brought by presiding officers. For constituency II, P.W.31 a U.P.N agent produced exhibit PET.33 signed by the A.R.O. and the agents of U.P.N., G.N.P.P. and N.A.P. For constituency III, P.W.32 a U.P.N. agent produced Exhibit PET 34 signed by the A.R.O. and the UPN and NPN agents. For constituency IV a UPN agent P.W.33 produced exhibit PET.35 signed by the A.R.O. and endorsed by the agents of G.N.P.P., U.P.N. and N.P.N. For the local government result, P.W.29 produced exhibit PET.31 which was prepared and signed in his presence by the D.R.O. This was confirmed by P.W.34 the D.P.O. for Ikole at that time.

The two witnesses for the 1st Respondent R.W.4 and R.W.5 were N.P.N. party agents at the local government collation centre at Ikole. R.W.4 testified that the figures brought to the D.R.O. were collated in his presence and he produced Exhibit RE.6 which he said were signed at the back by the A.R.O's. At the back are figures listed for the constituencies but there is no evidence how those figures were obtained. He admitted that he knew nothing of the figures until exhibit RE.6 was issued. His evidence was confirmed by R.W.5 who also identified exhibit RE.6 as the form prepared by the D.R.O.

All that R.W.6 did was to show that the D.R.O. prepared RE.6. There was no evidence of the figures the D.R.O. was adding or collating. Neither the D.R.O. nor any A.R.O. testified for 1st respondent. From the above, we have no difficulty in accepting the evidence of the petitioner's witnesses which are quite cogent and consistent and related directly to the results obtained from the polling station. We reject the evidence of the 1st respondent's witnesses wherever it conflicts with that of the petitioner's witnesses and we hold that on the evidence before us, the votes received by the petitioner and the 1st respondent in Ekiti North local government at the elections as PET Exhibits per.31 to PET.35 and which we accept are as follows:

Constituency	Petitioner	1st Respondent
I	31,253	6,390
II	30,220	14,705
III	34,721	10,375
IV	24,190	1,901
	120,384	33,377

The petitioner, therefore received a total of 120,384 votes i.e. 74.60 per cent, and the 1st respondent 33,377 i.e. 20.68 per cent.

We wish to observe that we noted the error on exhibit PET.31 in respect of constituency II where the figure 30,720 was entered in instead of 30,220 since the figure on exhibit PET.33, the primary document, is 30,220. We believe that the error is clerical especially as paragraph 13(ii) of the amended petition contained the correct figures.

Ekiti West Local Government

On constituency I, P.W.24, a U.P.N. party agent produced exhibit PET.27, i.e. Form EC40J, which was signed by the A.R.O. and the

NPP and UPN agents. For constituency II, P.W.25, a UPN counting agent produced Exhibit PET.28 signed by the A.R.O., and countersigned by the witness. For constituency III, a GNPP party agent produced exhibit PET.29 which was signed by the A.R.O. and the UPN agent. For constituency IV, a UPN counting agent produced Exhibit PET.26, signed by the A.R.O. For constituency V, P.W.27, a UPN agent produced exhibit PET.30 signed by the A.R.O. and countersigned by the agents of UPN and NPN.

With regard to the total votes for the local government, P.W.22, the FEDECO coordinator, for the local government produced exhibit PET.25, signed by the D.R.O. and countersigned by the agents of the UPN.

On the other hand, the D.R.O., R.W.1, testified for the 1st respondent. He received results from A.R.O's and collated them in Form EC8B but did not produce a copy in court. He produced exhibit RE.3 which he prepared for the local government. At the back is a list of the break down of the results for the constituency signed by him. R.W.2 was the A.R.O. for constituency III. He said that he entered the results from polling stations in a Form EC8B in the presence of the party men and the police present there. He said that he submitted this to the D.R.O. but he did not give any copies to the agents. R.W.3 was an NPN agent at the local government collation centre. He confirmed that he saw exhibit RE.3 but denied that PET.25 showed the correct figures.

We observe that the exhibit PET.25 was countersigned by agents of parties but there was no endorsement of exhibit RE.3 and we are left only with a document signed by the D.R.O. and not countersigned by anyone. He denied his signature and our impression of him is that he is not a truthful witness.

Comparing the evidence of the two sets of witnesses, we are of the view that the evidence of the petitioner's witnesses is more probable, especially in view of the fact that the separate results for each constituency was produced before the court. We accept their evidence and reject those of the 1st respondent's witnesses, wherever they conflict with those of the witnesses for the petitioner. We therefore hold that the total number of votes received by the petitioner and the first respondent in each of the five constituencies as contained in Exhibits PET.25, 26, 27, 28, 29 and 30 which we accept are as follows:-

Constituency	Petitioner	1st Respondent
1.	11,160	2,627
2.	42,381	3,825
3.	36,208	5,155
4.	17,555	2,918
5.	34,826	3,573
Total	142,130	18,098

The petitioner therefore received a total of 142,130 votes i.e. 88.78 per cent and the 1st respondent 18,098 i.e. 11.17 per cent of the total votes.

Ikale Local Government
Eight witnesses testified for the Petitioner in respect of this local government Area. For constituency IA, P.W.15, a U.P.N. counting agent produced Exhibit PET.18 which is the result of the collation at the constituency level, signed by the A.R.O. and countersigned by the agents of N.P.N., N.A.P., and U.P.N. The document was also signed by the D.R.O.

For Constituency IB, P.W. 16, who was the A.R.O. for the Constituency produced Exhibit PET.19 which contains the result of the collation at the Constituency level and signed by himself and countersigned by the D.R.O. (R.W.17).

For constituency II. P.W. 17 who was the A.R.O. for that constituency produced exhibits PET. 20 and PET 20A signed by him. The two documents contain the collated result for the constituency signed by him. Exhibit PET. 20A was counter-signed by the D.R.O. while exhibit PET. 20 was counter-singed by the agents of U.P.N.

and N.A.P.

For constituency III, P.W.13, a U.P.N. counting agent produced exhibits PET.16 and PET.17 exhibit PET. 16 is the collated result for that constituency signed by A.R.O. and counter-signed by the agents of N.A.P., G.N.P.P., P.R.P., N.P.N., and two U.P.N agents, i.e. the witness and P.W.19. This witness also produced exhibit PET. 17 which is the collated results for the whole local government area signed by the D.R.O. in the presence of the witness and the P.W. 14 who was the FEDECO coordinator for the said local government.

It was also counter-signed by the agents of the G.N.P.P., N.A.P, U.P.N., and N.P.P.

For constituency IV, P.W. 18 who was the U.P.N. counting agent for that constituency, produced exhibit PET.22 which is the collated result for that constituency, signed by the A.R.O. in the presence of the D.P.O. and counter-signed by the D.R.O., and the agents of NAP, NPN, PRP, and UPN.

For constituency V, P.W. 20, a U.P.N. counting agent produced exhibits PET.23 and PET. 23A which are the collated results for that constituency, signed by the A.R.O. in the presence of the D.P.O. Exhibit PET.23A was counter-signed by the agents of GNPP, NAP, NPN, and PRP.

For the 1st respondent the R.W. 17, who was the D.R.O. for that Local Government produced exhibit RE.23, which he claimed was signed by him. This document was not signed by any party agent. He denied the signatures credited to him on exhibits PET.17, PET.18, PET.20A, PET 22 and PET.23.

For the evidence above, we have also come to the conclusion that the petitioner's witnesses have itemised the sources of their figures right from the constituency level to the local government level, whereas the first respondent's witness has failed to satisfy us on the genuineness of sources of the figures contained in exhibit RE.23. We therefore prefer the evidence adduced by the petitioner's witnesses to that of the 1st respondent's witness, who has not impressed us as a truthful witness.

We therefore accept the evidence of the witnesses for the petitioner

and hold that the correct collated figures for Ikale local government are
as follows:-

Constituency	Petitioner	1st Respondent
1A	23,591	1,777
1B	20,175	1,965
2	20,865	5.076
3	14,448	3,637
4	15,118	6,779
5	15,303	7,036
TOTAL	109,500	26,270

The Petitioner, therefore, received a total of 109,500 votes i.e.
77.60 per cent and the 1st Respondent 26.270 i.e. 18.61 per cent of the
total votes cast in the local government.

Ekiti East Local Government:
There are three constituencies in this local government area. The
petitioner adduced no evidence in respect of constituency I.

For constituency II, a UPN party agent produced exhibit PET.40
which is the collated result in respect of that constituency signed by the
A.R.O.

For constituency III, P.W.39, a UPN party agent produced exhibit
PET.41 which is the collated result for that constituency signed by the
A.R.O. Both P.W.30 and P.W.39 testified to the effect that a copy
each of exhibits PET.40 and PET.41 was given to the D.P.O. and each
of the party agents present.

For the first respondent, R.W.6, who was the D.R.O. produced
exhibits RE.8 which he said was the collated results for the three
constituencies in the local government. The exhibit (RE.8) contains
total votes for the Local Government.

The witness denied that the A.R.O.s signed exhibits PET.40 and
PET.41 in his presence. He could not produce before us the forms signed
by the A.R.O.s and submitted to him from which he produced exhibit
RE.8.

R.W.7 was an NPN agent at constituency I and also at the local government collation centre. He said he was present when the A.R.O.s collated the figures at the constituency level, but he too failed to produce the A.R.O.s' report. He however, produced exhibit RE.9 which is similar to exhibit RE.8 and which he alleged was given to him.

R.W.8 was the A.R.O. for constituency II. He said he prepared Form EC8B which he took to the D.R.O. This document was not tendered before us.

We are also satisfied that there is no credibility in the evidence adduced by the witnesses for the 1st respondent, and we therefore, reject their evidence.

We accept the evidence of witnesses for the petitioner, and accept the figures established by the petitioner in respect of constituencies II and III.

As regards constituency I, we hold that the petitioner has failed to prove that no election was held in this constituency and has also failed to prove that the result declared by the State Returning Officer (R.W.18) in Exhibit RE.24B in respect of that Constituency is incorrect.

We therefore accept the figures declared by the State Returning Officer (RE.18) in Exhibit Re.24B as the correct result for that Constituency.

The correct results for this Local Government which we accept are as follows:-

Constituency	Petitioner	1st Respondent
1	13,925	30,928
2	29,281	3,839
3	11,525	4,178
TOTAL	54,731	38,945

The petitioner therefore received a total of 54,731 votes i.e. 55.73 per cent and the 1st respondent, 38,945 votes, i.e. 39.65 per cent of the total votes cast.

Ekiti South Local Government

For the petitioner, P.W.35 an assistant chief electoral officer for the local government testified about the difficulty which the agents had in obtaining copies of results from A.R.O. He produced exhibits PET.36 and PET.37, which were for constituencies I and III. exhibit PET 37 was signed by the U.P.N. agent. P.W.36 a U.P.N. agent in Ekiti South constituency II produced exhibit PET. 30 signed by NPN., N.P.P and U.P.N. agents. P.W. 37 an agent of the U.P.N. produced exhibit PET.39 in respect of constituency V. There was no evidence in respect of constituency IV.

On the part of the 1st respondent. R.W. 11 who was D.R.O. he gave evidence and produced exhibit RE.15 which he signed. At the back of the exhibit is a breakdown of the figures into constituencies and endorsed by the A.R.O.'s Another witness was R.W.12, an N.P.N. agent at the Local Government collating centre. He produced exhibit RE.15A which is similar to exhibit RE.15. There was no evidence at all from any A.R.O. or about what took place at any of the Constituency collation centres.

We accept the evidence of the petitioner's witness as against those of the 1st respondent in respect of constituencies 1, II, III and V as showing the correct figures for each of these constituencies. As there is no evidence in respect of constituency IV, there is a presumption of regularity in favour of the figures for that constituency in exhibit RE.24B. We therefore find and hold that the votes received by the Petitioner and the 1st respondent in respect of the local government are as follows:

Constituency	Petitioner	1st Respondent
I	4,622	1,889
II	8,744	5,407
III	10,201	4,614
IV	5,260	44,672
	30,689	7,408
TOTAL	59,516	63,990

We therefore find and hold that the petitioner received 59.516 votes i.e. 44.93 per cent and the 1st respondent 63,990 i.e. 48.31 per cent of all votes cast in the local government.

From the foregoing, the total number of votes received by the petitioner and the 1st respondent in respect of the disputed local governments according to our findings based on the evidence are as follows:

Local Government	Petitioner	1st Respondent
Ekiti East	54,731	38,945
Ekiti South	120,384	33,377
Ekiti North	59,516	63,990
Ekiti West	142,130	18,098
Idanre/Ifedore	85,920	5,718
Ifesowapo	106,015	3,725
Ikale	109,500	26,270
Total	678,196	190,123

When these figures are added to the total figures admitted or conceded on the pleadings, then the total number of votes received by the Petitioner is 1,563,327 and by the 1st Respondent 703,592. We therefore hold that the total votes received by the Petitioner in the Gubernatorial election for Ondo State held on 13th August 1983 is 1,563,327 and that the total votes received by the 1st Respondent is 703,592.

We also find and hold that the Petitioner obtained 25% or more of the votes cast in 16 of the 17 local governments of Ondo State, while the 1st Respondent received 25% or more of the votes cast in 7 of the 17 local governments of the State.

Accordingly by virtue of the provisions of section 164(7) of the Constitution of the Federal Republic of Nigeria 1979, we hold that the Petitioner, Chief M.A. Ajasin was duly elected and ought to have been returned. This Petition succeeds and it is hereby declared that the 1st Respondent, Chief Akin Omoboriowo was not duly elected or returned, and that the petitioner, Chief M.A. Ajasin was duly elected and ought to have been returned and this determination shall be certified to the Federal Electoral Commission in accordance with section 149 of the Electoral Act 1982.

(SGD.) DR. J.OLA OROJO, CHIEF JUDGE

(SGD.) HON. JUSTICE E.A. OJUOLAPE, JUDGE

(SGD.) HON. JUSTICE S. A. AFONJA, JUDGE

(SGD.) HON. JUSTICE S.A. AKINTAN, JUDGE

(SGD) HON. JUSTICE A.O. OGUNLEYE, JUDGE

References

1. Weekend Concord, Saturday, April 8, 1989, page 9
2. National Concord, August 23, 1983
3. Daily Sketch, August 20, 1983, front page
4. The Guardian, August 27, 1983, page 5
5. ibid
6. Akintola in an interview, Drum magazine, May 1965.
7. Okolie, Chris, *Newbreed* magazine, End March, 1978, page 8
8. Author's write-up in *Newswatch* magazine special publication, October 1985, page 47.
9. *New Nigerian*, October 23, 1978, front page.
10. *New Nigerian*, editorial October 24, 1978
11. *Newbreed*, End-March, 1978, page 8
12. *Daily Times*, November 1, 1978
13. *Daily Times*, November 15, 1978, front page
14. *West Africa*, December 11, 1978, page 2473
15. *Daily Times*, November 1, 1978, page 11
16. *Nigerian Tribune*, November 8, 1978
17. *Nigerian Tribune*, December 13, 1978
18. Oluleye, Major-General James, *Military Leadership in Nigeria, 1966-1979*, University Press Limited, Ibadan, 1985, page 199.
19. ibid. page 206
20. *West Africa*, editorial, August 20, 1979, page 1491
21. Ake, Professor Claude, *The State of the Nation*, keynote address to the Political Science Association of Nigeria, 1982. Quoted in

Falola, Toyin, et al, *The Rise and Fall of Nigeria's Second Republic*, 1979-84, Zed Books Ltd., London, page 70

22.   Fatayi-Williams, Mr. Justice Atanda, *Faces, Cases and Places*, Butterworths, 1983, page 77

23.   Quoted in *Sunday Tribune*, November 4, 1979, page 4

24.   Fatai-Williams, op.cit. page 167

25.   Fatai-Williams, op. cit. page 169

26.   *Daily Sketch*, October 5, 1979, page 13

27.   *Daily Times*, October 4, 1979, front page

28.   *Daily Times*, October 8, 1979.

29.   *National Concord*, June 9, 1981, front page

30.   Oparadike, Innocent, *National Concord*, July 9, 1982, page 3

31.   *National Concord*, December 11, 1981, front page.

32.   *National Concord*, October 4, 1982, front page.

33.   S.T. Labode, *Party Power: The Experience of an Accountant*, Gbemi Sodipe Press Limited, Abeokuta, Nigeria, 1988, page 81.

34.   ibid., page 81

35.   Babatope, Ebenezer, *Awo and Nigeria, (setting the records straight)*, Ebino Topsy Publishers, Ikeja, Lagos, 1984, page 40.

36.   S.T. Labode, *Party Power;* op. cit, page 88.

37.   ibid. page 93.

38.   *Ondo UPN Governorship Crisis - The Election Robbery of 1982;* a pamphlet of the Omoboriowo Group published by Balloon Publicity, Ijapo Estate, Akure, Nigeria.

39.   *Sunday Concord*, January 3, 1982, front page.

40.   *The Akin Omoboriowo Story (Portrait of a Fake Awoist);* a pamphlet published by the UPN National Secretariat, Lagos, page 13.

41.   ibid. page 14.

42.   *Ondo UPN Governorship Crisis — The Election Robbery of 1982;* op. cit. page 38.

43.   *National Concord*, Wednesday, November 17, 1982, page 18

44.   *Ondo State Governorship Crisis;* op. cit. Page 5.

45.   *Daily Times*, November 27, 1982, back page.

46.   *Daily Times*, Tuesday, November 23, 1982, back page.

47. *The Punch,* Thursday, December 2, 1982, front page.
48. *Daily Times* (back page) and *The Punch* (front page), November 16, 1982.
49. *The Punch,* December 8, 1982, front page.
50. *The Punch,* Wednesday, December 1, 1982, front page.
51. Daily Sketch, Thursday, December 9, 1982, front page
52. *The Akin Omoboriowo Story,* a pamphlet, op. cit. Page 22.
53. ibid. page 27.
54. *The Punch,* June 8, 1983.
55. *National Concord,* May 18, 1983.
56. *Ondo UPN Governorship Crisis, The Election Robbery of 1982;* op. cit. Page 45.
57. *The Punch,* February 25, 1983, page 5.
58. *Dismissed from the UPN, Why We then Opted for the NPN,* a pamphlet by the Omoboriowo group, 1983, page 11.
59. *National Concord,* Friday, January 14, 1983, page 12.
60. *National Concord,* Saturday, January 15, 1983, front page.
61. *Tribune,* January 15, 1983, front page.
62. *The Guardian,* August 22, 1989, centre-page.
63. *The Sunday Tribune,* June 1, 1979, centre-page.
64. *West Africa,* August 27, 1979, page 1533.
65. *West Africa,* October 8, 1979 page 1833.
66. *Newswatch,* February 3, 1986, page 48.
67. *Newswatch,* May 20, 1985, page 18.
68. *The Nigerian Tribune,* July 3, 1981, page 9.
69. *Nigerian Tribune,* July 6, 1981, page 3.
70. *Newswatch,* May 20, 1985, page 18.
71. *Sunday Concord,* December 13, 1981.
72. *Sunday Concord,* March 7, 1982, front page.
73. *Daily Sketch,* Friday, December 3, 1982, front page.
74. *Daily Times,* December 20, 1982, back page.
75. *Daily Times,* December 21, 1982, front page
76. *National Concord,* June 8, 1983.
77. *National Concord,* Thursday, May 26, 1983, front page.

79. *Daily Times,* Monday, March 21, 1983, front page.
80. ibid.
81. *Nigerian Herald,* March 5, 1983.
82. *National Concord,* Tuesday, July 19, 1983, page 4.
83. *National Concord,* Friday, January 14, 1983, page 4.
84. *Babatope, Ebenezer, Not His Will: The Awolowo-Obasanjo Wager,* Jodah Publications, Benin-City, 1990, page 126.
85. ibid. page 123.
86. *The Punch,* Wednesday, April 27, 1983, front page.
87. *The Punch,* Thursday, April 28, 1983, front page.
88. *The Guardian,* July 11, 1983, front page.
89. *Nigerian Tribune,* April 8, 1983, page 2.
90. *National Concord,* May 14, 1983, back page.
91. *National Concord,* April 13, 1983, front page.
92. ibid.
93. *National Concord,* April 20, 1983, page 13.
94. *National Concord,* April 13, 1983, front page.
95. *The Premier,* Friday, August 12, 1983, front page.
96. ibid.
97. ibid.
98. *The Punch,* Thursday, August 11, 1983, front page.
99. ibid.
100. Obadina, Tunde, *National Concord,* Saturday, May 21, 1983, page 3.
101. *Daily Sketch,* August 16, 1983, page 1.

Index